"[A] literary spellbinder as intricately plotted and seductively readable as A. S. Byatt's *Possession* . . . [*The World Before Her*] rings with the truth of profound emotion and transcendent passion."

—Megan Marshall, author of *The Peabody Sisters*

"[Weisgall's] writing is tender, drowning you in its drunken energy."

—*St. Petersburg Times*

"Weisgall's well-researched historical fiction is dense, romantic, and provocative."

—*Publishers Weekly*

"*The World Before Her* presents a difficult doubling act, which Weisgall performs with grace and delicacy."

—*Boston Globe*

"The real reason to read Weisgall's novel is not for its various culminations, but for the richness of the fabric—as heavy, baroque, and well-constructed as an old tapestry—that goes into it."

—*Buffalo News*

"A compelling novel of introspection . . . enhanced by vivid attention to the artistic and literary detail in both the historical and contemporary settings."

—*Booklist*, starred review

"Weisgall is a master of sky, water, air, of landscapes and languishments; of the clashing coinages of art and money. This is a novel to relish both for its audacious history-wide lens and for its enchanting jeweler's loupe."

—Cynthia Ozick, author of *Heir to the Glimmering World*

"A riveting and psychologically profound examination of the institution of marriage and the dilemmas of romantic love."

—Jill Ker Conway, author of *The Road from Coorain*

"In a novel as smooth and alluring as a gondola ride, Deborah Weisgall glides us through the canal of time on the Venetian holidays of two unlikely couples. Despite the century that separates these pairs, yearning and misguided love repeat themselves, and we as readers long for their fulfillment and happiness."

—Susan Vreeland, author of *Girl in Hyacinth Blue*

The World Before Her

BOOKS BY DEBORAH WEISGALL

A Joyful Noise

Still Point

The World Before Her

The World Before Her

Deborah Weisgall

MARINER BOOKS
HOUGHTON MIFFLIN COMPANY
BOSTON   NEW YORK

First Mariner Books edition 2009
Copyright © 2008 by Deborah Weisgall

For information about permission to reproduce
selections from this book, write to Permissions,
Houghton Mifflin Harcourt
Publishing Company, 6277 Sea Harbor Drive,
Orlando, Florida 32887-6777.

www.hmhbooks.com

Library of Congress Cataloging-in-Publication Data
Weisgall, Deborah.
The world before her / Deborah Weisgall.
p. cm.
ISBN-13: 978-0-618-74657-6
ISBN-10: 0-618-74657-9
1. Eliot, George, 1819–1880 — Fiction. 2. Women sculptors
— Fiction. 3. Venice (Italy) — Fiction. 4. Married
people — Fiction. 5. Domestic fiction. I. Title.
PS3573.E39796W67 2008
813'.54 — dc22   2008004734
ISBN: 978-0-547-23796-1 (PBK)

Book design by Melissa Lotfy

Printed in the United States of America

DOC 10 9 8 7 6 5 4 3 2 1

For my mother, Nathalie Weisgall

The World Before Her

Chapter 1

Venice, 10 June 1880

THE LADY WORE a sober dress of gray silk that shimmered like the sea on an overcast day. It was the silk that first caught James McNeill Whistler's eye, the rich ripples of light and darkness, but the lady held his attention. She was slender and small in stature, and Whistler was drawn to her straight, easy posture, her eager gait. He could not see her face, but he guessed that she was not young and not old either — thirty-five, perhaps.

From the cut of her dress and her confident progress through the flocks of pigeons and people milling about the Piazza San Marco, she was an Englishwoman. A tall man accompanied her, and they proceeded with an assurance that humans and birds alike would yield the path. The couple had entered the square from the direction of the Hôtel de l'Europe, where the English preferred to stay. Who had recently arrived? In Venice, news carried quickly, like sound over water. Maud would know.

He decided that the lady was one of those gentlewomen who moved inside a carapace of their homeland and on foreign soil disdained everything not English. Just now, she would be complaining to her companion about their accommodations in Venice's best hotel — and if Whistler were to encounter her at a dinner, she would complain to him as well, after she recalled vaguely that he was involved in some distasteful scandal having to do with the eminent critic John Ruskin, whom of course she worshiped. Although she would gaze diligently upon Venice's treasures, its squalor was what she would remember; she could understand that better than its beauty. Beauty lay beyond borders of feeling she would not permit herself to cross. Hanging in her country house would be portraits of her dogs.

Nonetheless, her bearing intrigued Whistler. He sat at a table at the Café Florian in a state of heightened receptivity — alert to the action of light, dazzled from his morning's expedition, his senses prickling with beauty. He had not yet absorbed what he had seen, had not yet organized its illusory perspective of sea and city and mountaintops. Now, with a kind of visual elation, he saw everything with preternatural clarity; he felt as if he could see emotion.

He had risen at six, fighting his desire to sleep off the excesses of the night before; his gondolier, Cavaldoro, had ferried him into the lagoon past the Giudecca to see the snowcapped crags of the Dolomites rising behind Venice like a painted scrim, glittering and hallucinatory in the golden eastern light. Maud had protested when he kicked off the sheet. "You paint fog," she remonstrated. "You paint fog better than anybody, you say so yourself. Stay with me — you came home so late." Pink and yielding she smiled and showed large pearly teeth.

"You can't paint fog unless you know what it hides," he had answered, and slithered out from under her. Was he doing so only to demonstrate the limits of his mistress's hold on him? No — the sight of the mountains did exalt him, released him for a moment from ambition and doubt. But amidst the crowded sense of urgent amusement in the piazza, his oppression returned.

He opened his sketchbook and drew the Englishwoman's figure, the graceful line of her back and waist, her opulent skirt — he smudged the pencil with his thumb to catch its subdued glimmer — her parasol's dark ruffled cloud. The lady held the man's arm and walked slightly behind, yet she seemed to be leading him. They could be husband and wife — but they clung closely, and there was something tentative about their closeness, as if it were new. The man's coat of fine, light wool drooped from his shoulders; either it was badly tailored or its wearer had diminished in size. Perhaps the man was not well. Whistler recalled his own illness last winter, the disheartening looseness of his own clothes. It could be that the man was recovering, and this journey was part of his cure. It could be that the woman loved him.

Undaunted by importuning birds and beggars, oblivious to the clamoring guides for hire and the photographers, with their tripods and cameras, the couple approached the Basilica of San Marco. It was shrouded in scaffolding; the mosaics over the doorways were being restored, badly. The air was still crisp and green with spring. Slender Venetian girls pretended to modesty as they tugged their black shawls tight across their breasts and sashayed in little chirping clusters through the extravagant light and space of the piazza. Their mothers, thickened and slow, kept to the shadows. In hot robes, priests weary from the weight of piety trudged across the gray paving stones.

The musicians of Florian's orchestra had taken their places and begun their Strauss, and from across the piazza the rival orchestra at Quadri played its different waltz. Whistler relished the cacophony, foreign music for foreigners: another veil Venice wore to keep her secrets. She was a great courtesan, reflecting her visitors back to themselves while remaining herself a mystery.

At the scaffolding the English lady gestured with her parasol as if it were a frilled spear. She would be parroting Mr. John Ruskin's prescriptions, perpetrating Ass Ruskin's reverence for each and every blasted medieval stone, complaining again and with righteous anger about the scaffolding that obscured the façade. The city of Venice had decided on the restorations, a pity, but the plan had one great virtue: it had driven Ruskin mad with impotent rage. He had organized an international protest — these treasures belonged to the world, not only to Venice — which ensured that the city's government paid no attention to his objections. Workmen were replacing those hallowed crumbling tesserae with their coarse and hideous version of the past.

So Ruskin had set plodding Mr. John Wharlton Bunney to paint the building in exhaustive detail, preserving a record of each sacred shard. Bunney had been at it three years already — wasting his life.

Every afternoon, weather permitting, he set up his easel among the pigeons and hoisted his umbrella against the birds' efforts to improve his work. Bunney needed noon for his task; oblique dawn or sunset obscured particularities. He would be horrified to see what a heresy Whistler had committed — painting the basilica at night, scattering specifics like so many fireworks, subjecting the church to his will and reducing it from stones to light, from monument to shape and mood, changing it from a shrine to the past into a portent of the future, including the scaffolding in his picture.

Whistler caught a glimmer of red in the man's hand — the ubiquitous Baedeker, telling them what to see on which day, as if they could not trust their own eyes. San Marco was always the first stop. Only monuments for them; he was sure they would worship at only bona fide, guidebook-certified Sights. They would disdain the small streets he had been drawing — no Art there, no famous façades, only cats and girls and brick — a living Venice as beautiful as their dead one.

He shook his head at his own vehemence, but he was betting his life on the Venice he saw. He was forty-five, feeling the shortness of time — and of money. He fished coins from his pocket, counted them, and decided he had better wait to have breakfast. Maud Franklin was meeting him soon; he would treat her to a coffee here at Florian's, a public coffee, to atone for leaving her alone so often while he went out in the evening.

The English pair seemed to have changed their minds. The lady reopened her parasol, they conferred under its shade, then turned and crossed toward the arcade, skirting Florian's tables and chairs. The woman moved with an elastic, energetic gait, almost a lope, as if she were suppressing the urge to run. She let go of her companion's arm, and he lagged behind, apparently unwilling to compromise his dignity, or perhaps too exhausted to keep up with her. Had she fled from her dog-loving husband and escaped with this man to raptures in Venice?

She reached the loggia, just past the last rank of Florian's tables, and then abruptly she stopped, furled her parasol, and bent over, studying the pavement, searching for something, proceeding at a shuffle as if she had lost a jewel or a keepsake. But she did not seem distressed, and she was oblivious to the puzzled glances of passersby. Whistler closed his sketchbook, got up from his table, and sauntered under the loggia, pretending to examine an abysmal copy of a Titian Madonna in a shop window.

Suddenly the lady stood straight. "Oh, Johnnie!" she exclaimed. "Johnnie! Here, I found one! Look here! Hurry!" She laughed. "Not that it will run away!" English, of course. She spoke as if they were alone, sure that nobody could understand what she was saying — if she had noticed Whistler at all, she would assume him to be a picturesque native, with his shabby clothes and disheveled hair. It was his intention, wherever he traveled, to become invisible, to observe without being seen.

But she had a beautiful voice. It astonished him: rich, low, and youthful, resonant as singing. There was something strenuous about it as well, a timbre faintly discordant, as if the lilt cost her an effort. He could imagine her face: thin, petulant lips, upturned little nose, pale complexion webbed with fine lines, holding a memory of that ephemeral English luminescence, and incongruous dark eyes, large, black eyes and arched eyebrows to match the musical, melancholy richness of her voice.

She pointed with her parasol to a spot in the gallery's pavement — rectangular slabs of Veronese stone: orange marble mottled with white and ochre like a paint-spattered floor. "Johnnie! A snail!"

Whistler was astonished; one did not seek out snails in Venice.

The man she called Johnnie reached her and peered at the ground. "My dear *Beatrice*," he said, "I see nothing."

His voice was thin, enervated. Whistler groaned. My *Beatrice* — four syllables; the man's Italian pronunciation was execrable. Despite the lady's fascination with gastropods, those two could have had RUSKIN branded on their foreheads. Beatrice, the girl Dante loved from afar, how medieval; certainly a man would not address his wife like that — she would laugh at him.

She was saying, "Just here. Do you see — a spiral, a whorl, like a nautilus?"

"A natural pattern in the rock."

"No. A snail." She touched the curves with the toe of her boot. "You see? The spiral, each rib delineated? An enormous, petrified

5

snail — its shell has turned to stone. A ghost in stone. You can see the chambers. This marble was once sand, the sea floor; we are stepping on the depths of an ancient ocean."

"So you will be my fish as well as my angel — my guide under the sea as well as through the heavens?"

"For that you'll want Monsieur Verne, I'm afraid." The lady laughed again. Her enthusiastic lecture was not at all in keeping with the peevish gentlewoman Whistler had assumed her to be. "No," she continued, "this ocean has dried up and been buried, then quarried from the earth. Here, this snail — like the fossils in the chalk cliffs — is evidence of that; it is evidence of time — of thousands, millions of years. George found the snails in these paving stones fifteen years ago, when we first came to Venice. We hunted them everywhere — we even found one on the front of a church." Her voice had changed and grown softer. She paused. Her head was lowered, possibly from sadness. Was she a widow? She was not wearing mourning. He yearned to see her face; her nose would be stronger than he had first imagined, long and narrow, her lips fuller, her complexion olive, exotic. "We made them our secret." Her voice had regained — almost — its animation.

The man took her arm again, possessing her. "And now, my dearest, they will be ours. But you will have to teach me. I am not very good at that sort of thing. For me it must be far more obvious, not all swirled together like pudding."

Again that lovely laugh, pliable and generous. "Well, then, I will." She started off, intent on the hunt. The gentleman trailed behind her, letting her tug at his arm. He turned his head, and as he glanced at the reproductions of devotional paintings in the shop window Whistler finally saw his face. A square jaw, finely arched brows, full lips, a straight nose: a handsome, serious man, solid and established, a man of consequence. But the mouth was melancholy, the pale cheeks were thin and the bones too prominent. Sick circles shadowed his deep-set eyes. He seemed distracted, almost blind, as if he needed a guide, not through heaven or hell, but here on earth. He looked as though he could barely see where he was walking, much less pick out ancient snails lurking in the pavement.

"I want one more," she said without looking up. "Only one more

6

snail." She stopped abruptly. "You're not tired, are you? I seem to be indefatigable." She laughed.

"Yes," he said. "You are."

"Am I already too much?"

"No, no," he assured her, but his voice was subdued. He would, Whistler supposed, be considering his future trailing after a lady naturalist.

"Then what shall we do? What is your pleasure? You've seen the snails — let's see San Marco, before it closes. And we are here." She stepped out from under the shade of the loggia, opened her parasol, and started in the direction of the basilica. Something in her bearing had changed — her gait had slowed, or her assurance had diminished; something rendered her vulnerable. Whistler had followed them for hardly ten paces when they were set upon by one of the photographers who stalked the square like bandits, prepared to waylay any foreigner who ventured within range.

Whistler recognized the man; Leporello he called himself because he boasted that he kept a list of all the illicit goings-on in Venice. Regardless of the season he wore a grimy, threadbare overcoat as voluminous as the cloth that covered his head while he aimed his camera. The photographer accosted them — did he know who they were? "Mister? Madam? *Inglese?*"

Of course they were English, and the English couple of course would ignore him. To Whistler's surprise the woman stopped and addressed the photographer: "*Buon giorno.*" And to the gentleman she said, "Johnnie, wouldn't it be nice to have a photograph of you here — I have no pictures of you at all."

"You don't need one, my dearest, because I will always be with you. Please, no," he protested, in that querulous tone. "Cameras make me nervous — as if that eye sees all my secrets."

"What secrets would you have?" she teased.

While she was speaking, the photographer had closed in. Spreading his arms as if about to launch into an aria, he gestured toward the grand architecture surrounding them. "What is your pleasure? The Palace of the Doges? The Campanile? The basilica?"

"*Il palazzo dei Dogi,*" the lady answered. Her accent was really quite good. She stepped aside, out of the scene. The gentleman tried to escape, but Leporello had maneuvered between him and the lady. The gentleman was trapped. Whistler was amused, if a little sorry for the Englishman, as the photographer did a little dance that blocked retreat.

"*Prego!*" the gentleman admonished. "*Prego!*"

The photographer reached into his overcoat's sagging pocket and pulled out a handful of crumbs, which he tossed onto the ground at the gentleman's feet. Whistler had witnessed this often; Leporello seemed convinced that pigeons, descending from the heavens like a flock of filthy angels, would ensure a large tip.

Suddenly the gentleman was engulfed in flapping wings. "Oh!" he exclaimed. He flung out his hands, defending himself against the swirling birds. Alarmed, the lady whirled around, and at last Whistler saw her. He stared, astonished. Her face was large and bony: a long jaw, a high-bridged, exuberant, and lumpy nose, slack lips. In dismaying contrast to her graceful figure and supple voice, the lady was — she was ugly; there was no other word for it. Moreover, she was far from young; she was decades past thirty-five. Whistler gazed at her, startled and fascinated, and as he watched, her face changed. When she realized that her companion was beating back an onslaught of pigeons more interested in pecking at the food at his feet than at him, a mischievous smile started around her mouth and her eyes. Her eyes, large and luminous, the palest blue-gray, were beautiful, their expression tender and humorous, open to the world. Whistler felt a shiver of recognition.

But seeing the man's distress, the lady composed herself, rid her face of mirth, advanced toward the pigeons, and kicked efficiently, causing them to scatter. "Oh, Johnnie, they're as tame as hens," she scolded, taking his arm. "You must deal with them firmly."

The gentleman shuddered, now more humiliated than frightened. "They seemed to come from nowhere."

"*Mi dispiace!*" Trying to salvage the situation, the photographer bent in a low, extravagant bow. Then he lifted his eyes and scrutinized the couple. "Ah," he said, nodding, understanding everything. "*Per favore, signora, mi scusi di nuovo. La prego di perdonarmi per avere turbato suo figlio.*"

"What was he saying?" the gentleman demanded.

"He was begging forgiveness for having upset you."

"What else did he say?"

"Nothing else."

"What did he call me? *Figlio*. Son. I understand something, you know." He blushed deep red.

The lady cringed — the blow was to his pride, not to hers — but put her hand on his arm to quiet him. "I kept chickens when I was little, Johnnie; they can be quite terrifying." The quality of effort, of strenuousness, had returned. She looked up and caught Whistler staring. Her gray eyes narrowed in irritation.

Abashed, he turned away and was relieved to see that Maud Franklin was sitting at a table at Florian's. She must have arrived while he was absorbed with the English couple. Maud had draped a black shawl across her shoulders; she had mastered the Venetian art of hugging the shawl close to the swell of her breast, and with her red curls and pale skin she could have been a Venetian girl. She had arranged herself in a graceful contrapposto for his pleasure. Faithful Maud. There was no solution; if he married her, their situation would worsen. Nobody would receive either of them. They might carry it off in America, where birth mattered less, but he could not retreat to America and go home a failure. Maud could have refused to follow him to Venice; it had been her idea to leave their infant daughter with a foster family. "I am not a nurse," she had maintained, but she had nursed Whistler through the freezing winter when he was too sick to work.

He was working now, producing pastels and etchings like a man possessed, abandoning her all day long. He tiptoed up behind Maud and clapped his hands over her eyes. "*Chi sono?*" he asked in his thickest Italian accent.

"Jim. Who else?" Maud pried his fingers away, and turned her long, graceful neck, and smiled up at him.

"You weren't even surprised," he complained.

"I might have been if this were the first time."

Whistler signaled to a waiter.

"How was your snow? Was it everything you hoped? Well, it must have been — it's made you extravagant. What are we having?"

"Only a coffee. I wish you had come with me."

9

"Next time."

"It doesn't happen so often that you can see them."

Maud smiled as if the thought of mountains was enough. "You're quite windblown — you look positively galvanized!" She attempted to smooth the streak of white hair that sprang like a bolt of lightning from his forehead.

Whistler twisted, out of her reach. "Maud — tell me — you'll know, I'm sure — I saw two people." He described the couple, the woman with the beautiful voice, the gaunt man. "They're still here, walking under the loggia, across the piazza." It would be impossible to find them in the crowd.

But Maud nodded and delicately sipped her coffee. "Why, that would be Mr. and Mrs. John Cross." Maud heard secrets before their owners realized they were keeping them. "They have just arrived; this is their wedding trip."

"Ah," Whistler nodded. "She could be his mother. No matter — I would like to know Mrs. Cross."

"You know of her already, I am sure." Maud smiled, enjoying her advantage. "She was Marian Evans before she married." She smiled again. "A novelist."

"A novelist? I don't read lady novelists." He frowned. "I've never heard of her."

"Yes, you have," Maud teased. "And you've read her books. Everybody has."

"Tell me, Maud."

"She writes under a nom de plume."

"I have no idea." He grasped her wrist. "Maud, tell me!"

"You can't make me!"

"I'm sorry." He let his hand linger on the soft skin of the inside of her arm, and Maud relented. "She is George Eliot!"

Of course. He had seen that face in engravings, that famous ugliness; an image could not convey how her light eyes and musical voice mitigated her unfortunate bones.

Maud shrugged. "When George Lewes died, everybody said that they had had the most perfect marriage." She lowered her eyes and said quietly, "No children, though. She was too clever for that. And he already had three — at least."

Whistler tried to imagine the baby Maud had a year ago — his child too — what that infant would look like now; he tried to conjure emotions warmer than wonder and annoyance.

Maud went on, her voice playful, her expression guarded. She was, he saw, fearful of displeasing him. She leaned toward him, her back straight, her neck white and soft, her shawl tight. "I wonder how Mr. Cross manages."

"Maud, you're wicked. Perhaps he doesn't have to — manage."

"Everybody's talking about them. But everybody's always talked about her." Maud laughed thinly. "It makes no difference, though — she's gotten her way."

Whistler heard the quavering edge of jealousy. He took her hand; it was not a lady's hand: her peasant palm broad, her tapered fingers still rough from winter. He remembered that George Eliot had lived for years with a man who was not her husband. But she was a personage, a great writer; she had exempted herself — she could do as she wished. Poor Maud — all she could hope for was that he would immortalize her in his paintings. So far that had not happened, and he doubted if that kind of fame — notoriety, really — would earn her invitations to dinner, let alone proposals of marriage. He and Maud never talked about love or discussed permanence; he suspected that he did love her, but his affection was stunted by its inappropriateness. He ran his spoon around the inside of the cup, scraping off the clinging milk foam.

Maud leaned back in her chair and swung her foot in time to the music. "Do you know where they are going tomorrow?"

"How could I know that?"

"They are going to take tea with your friends Mr. and Mrs. Bunney."

He raised one admonishing eyebrow. "You know very well they are not my friends."

JOHN CROSS clenched his fists. "That blasted photographer!" His voice was pinched with distress.

She laid a reassuring hand on his forearm. "Don't be angry for me, Johnnie. He was only doing what he imagined would please us. Most people want pigeons in their photograph; he couldn't know that you didn't. He meant to be kind — and he tried to apologize. At any rate, I am not so thin-skinned as that." She gazed at him in the expectant way he found discomfiting and added, "It was an honest mistake that he made."

"I don't understand why people can't mind their own business."

"Do you want to go to the hotel? I'll do what you want."

"I need a moment. I just need to catch my breath." He studied her, alert to the shade of impatience in her voice. "Then you are not unhappy?"

"Of course not. And you should be pleased that you look so young and handsome."

"You are an angel, a saint."

"I don't know about that. You need not flatter me in return." But she smiled again, and he was relieved. It daunted him, sometimes, to realize that this great soul had been entrusted to his care, that he was responsible for her happiness — she was, really, a saint. His mother had worshiped Marian, whose books had given so much to the world and who had been such a generous friend.

She headed back to the shade of the loggia. "We might want to go to the Accademia. It's quieter there." She stopped abruptly, avoiding a flock of nuns. Moving toward prayer or toward acts of charity, starched wimples sharp as beaks, they swept with holy determination along the pavement, threatening to engulf Johnnie and Marian in their dove-gray habits. Johnnie shuddered.

"What is it?" his wife asked.

"Oh, nothing, nothing — it's only the nuns," he said, with a self-deprecating smile. "They remind me of — of pigeons. But Marian, I'm not sure I'm up to great art quite yet. After all, it's only our first day."

"Yes, that's true. Then what shall we do?"

He detected her frustration. "Well, actually, I've made an appointment."

"But whom do we know here — besides the Bunneys?"

"You'll see." John Cross led his wife around the perimeter of the piazza, urging her forward when she slowed to tease out a snail from a pattern in the mottled marble. "Dearest, come along. The pavement won't shut for lunch." But he stopped to buy her violets from a girl selling flowers.

Marian smiled. "You spoil me."

"I hope I do," he answered. "It's my intention." He peered into the windows of a shop offering silks and velvets and announced, "We must order you a gown." Next door, a shop displayed glass from Murano. "And what about a chandelier in the entrance hall at Cheyne Walk? To remind us of Venice."

Marian laughed. "Johnnie, I believe you would buy the entire city. If you must possess that chandelier, then we will have to telegraph to be sure that there is a place for it in the plans. I worry that changes will delay progress."

"It's our house, and we can do with it what we like. Besides, they have all summer to accomplish their work." It was endearing to Johnnie how much she thought was impossible, how little she desired. He led her along the gallery beneath the Venetian library and stopped at a small display window where an intricate necklace in the Etruscan manner, beaded gold set with pearls and diamonds, was arranged on a velvet cushion. "What do you think?" he asked.

"An extravagant ornament," Marian answered. "Quite luxurious, reclining there on its pillow."

"I mean, do you fancy it?"

Marian hesitated. "It's very beautiful."

"I absolutely agree." He rang the doorbell.

"Won't we be late for your mysterious appointment?" she asked.

"This is my appointment."

"With a jeweler? Why, Johnnie? To buy trinkets for your sisters?"

He smiled indulgently; she never thought of herself.

"And then we can find masks and puppets for the grandchildren. Perhaps I'll find something for Charles's Gertrude here. I have no jewels from Charles's father to give her, except for this." She touched the cameo at her neck.

"You are the one who needs something else," he said impatiently. "You wear that all the time."

"Of course I do. George gave it to me —"

But he was her husband now; Johnnie felt a pinch of annoyance. She should wear a gift from him.

She went on. "And you gave your mother one like it. You remember — you admired this cameo one evening, and the next day you bought her one. A lovely one, a locket. You have such good taste,

Johnnie. I suppose, though, that I cannot believe in ornaments — for myself."

"Are they so dangerous? Are they like idols one is forbidden to believe in?"

"Certainly not, but jewels are for beautiful women, not —"

"My dear, I find you lovely," he protested. It would not do to tell her that he cared not at all what she looked like. It was her spirit that ravished him.

"Johnnie, I am speaking the truth. And, more than that — they imply possession."

"But you are mine, are you not? You wear my ring."

She looked down at her left hand, where the new wedding band gleamed, brilliant and unscratched.

"Well, Mrs. Cross," Johnnie teased. "What do you say to that?"

"It still surprises me," she answered. "It's like a magic charm, changing everything." After a moment, she added with her unsettling smile, "And anyway, Johnnie, it is my ring now."

To his alarm she raised her hand as if she might caress his cheek there on the street. But she drew back as a tall boy with olive skin and dark eyes opened the door. Lean and pliant, the boy bowed, ushering them up a flight of stone stairs, along a gallery, and into a small room with a leather-topped table occupying the center. The walls were upholstered in dark green leather: an ostentatious opulence. A small bronze statue stood on the table: a naked youth with one arm upraised, his lithe body caught on the verge of manhood. Johnnie looked away; in the presence of a woman, nudity, even in miniature, even in bronze, made him uneasy.

"How beautiful he is!" Marian exclaimed.

Before Johnnie could answer, a thin man with a sharp, prominent nose and dark lips that stretched over long teeth entered the room. "Good day," he said in English. "Please, may I help you? I am Giuseppe de Levis. And you are Mr. Cross?"

"I am, and this is my wife."

"But how did you know?" Marian asked in surprise.

De Levis bowed. "Mr. Bunney sent word that you might be paying a visit. I am honored."

"Johnnie, you consulted Mr. Bunney? When?"

"Oh, a note on the back of my card—I'll show him what we've accomplished when we take tea with him and Mrs. Bunney."

"How clever you are, Johnnie; but what will we have accomplished?"

"I should like to see the necklace in the window downstairs."

The proprietor beckoned to the boy, who was surely his son, and handed him a little key. The boy slipped from the room. The jeweler turned to Marian. "Signora Eliot, if I may say so, I have read your books—in English—and I have especially admired *Daniel Deronda*. Most extraordinary; a wonderful book for my people. Jews are not often heroes."

John Cross had anticipated a transaction, not an intimate encounter. The jeweler was too forward. Moreover, Johnnie agreed with those critics who observed that the Jewish element in *Daniel Deronda* had weakened the book. Certainly it made Johnnie uncomfortable, though he had liked the character Deronda well enough at the start of the story, when Deronda was a young man of obscure origins. His sympathy had practically evaporated when Deronda, having discovered that he was a Jew, chose to embrace his race. Johnnie had thought it unnecessary—unrealistic, even. Not that he would ever discuss this with his wife—when the book was first published, he had asked the question in a general way, and Marian had dismissed it with a remark about obscure histories. Later, George had warned him off; George had always shielded her from adverse criticism, even well-meaning questions from her closest friends.

She was a paradox. Her actions—and some of her ideas—were so *radical*, while she was by nature deeply conservative. He understood what marrying him had meant to her: the profound comfort it had afforded her soul, putting to rest a guilt, a lingering pain of transgression that even a quarter of a century of happiness with George Lewes could not lift from her conscience. She was independent of mind, but she needed to be cared for. To make her an honest woman had been the happiest moment of Johnnie's life. He supposed he must protect her now, not only from criticism but from praise.

He watched Marian collect herself; she became grave and reserved. This was how he had supposed she would be as his wife, self-possessed and prudent. It seemed, though, that this was her public demeanor. During the past five weeks she had gathered a dangerous energy. He had imagined her ardor would be spiritual, quiet, a concentrated stillness, but instead she had displayed a physical eagerness and appetite that troubled him and left him confused and even frightened. She was, as she said, indefatigable. But it was more than that, and it was causing him terrible anxiety. He had lost weight; he craved respite.

"Thank you for your kindness, signore." Marian smiled her gentle, distant smile, serene as carved marble, the smile Johnnie adored. She went on. "But I must tell you that Signora Eliot exists only in my books. I am Signora Cross."

"Of course. I apologize, and I hope that I can accommodate your wishes." The jeweler's English was almost perfect, the vowels a shade too rich, the consonants a touch too precise: English words set to Italian music.

"My husband's wishes." Marian smiled graciously at Johnnie.

The boy returned and presented the necklace on its pillow to the jeweler, who held it out to John Cross. Johnnie lifted it; the pearls and stones hung in a gorgeous cascade. "It is finely done. Very fine." He spoke with the authority of a man accustomed to luxury and experienced in the business of its acquisition. He held it up so that the diamonds glittered. "What do you think, my dear?"

"I can see it around the neck of a Roman lady — Terentia, perhaps."

"Cicero's wife was a formidable woman," said the jeweler. "Too much in love with her own power. A dishonest woman —"

Johnnie was perplexed by his wife's quick, hungry smile as she answered. "Or she was prudent, while her husband was profligate."

"He was a public man, a politician."

It seemed to Johnnie that they had forgotten the necklace. "Will you try —" he began, but Marian was already speaking.

"Her fortune made his career possible. And then he divorced her. I cannot forgive him, but she did, evidently. Did you know that she lived to be a hundred and three? I'm not sure I would wish for that. Oh, this necklace — it requires at least a countess, which I certainly am not."

16

"I never much cared for Cicero in school," Johnnie interrupted. "I couldn't sort out his grammar. But the Americans — I have spent some time in America . . ." He paused. Against his better judgment, he was engaging this Jewish jeweler in conversation.

"And?" encouraged Marian.

"Oh, it's nothing."

"Tell us, please."

"Well, the Americans quite like him, you know, because they have their republic. They take him as their civic model, quote him everywhere —"

"And only sixteen years after his death, Rome had an emperor," Marian interrupted. "I'm sorry, my dear — go on."

"Yes, well, I don't really have anything else to say. It never occurred to me that Cicero had a wife. I thought he spent all his time orating. Now, Mrs. Cross, although you are not Mrs. Cicero —"

"Mr. Cross, you are good for me!" His wife laughed, and he could not be sure that she wasn't teasing him. He approached her with the necklace. He would have liked to drape her in pearls as some statues of saints were adorned; he would have liked to give her rings for every finger.

She stepped back. "You intend to put this on my neck?"

"I insist."

"Does not Deronda return an Etruscan necklace to Gwendolyn?" asked the jeweler.

"Why, yes, of course!" Marian exclaimed. "How well you know the book, signore. But I didn't imagine that trinket to be anywhere near as fine as this. If it had been, I certainly would have let her keep it and pawn something else."

"To my mind," said Johnnie, "this necklace comes closer to the one Grandcourt gave to Gwendolyn."

"Grandcourt forced her to wear those jewels," countered de Levis. "The diamonds were heavy shackles, *brutti* — ugly. Brutal, like Grandcourt."

"But Gwendolyn finished him off," Johnnie retorted; this jeweler assumed that his knowledge of Marian's work gave him the right to intimacy with its author.

"Listen to you," said Marian. "Discussing my books as if I weren't here! And Johnnie, it is not at all clear what happened between Gwendolyn and Grandcourt in that little boat. She might have been unable to save him from drowning."

"Of course, my dear, you should know. Now stay still, please, just for a moment!"

But Marian shifted her head as Johnnie tried to drape the necklace around her throat, and one of its fine links snagged on the catch of her cameo. "Oh!" she exclaimed, as if she were hooked, a hapless fish.

Signor de Levis hurried toward her with a silver looking-glass, and she tried and failed to untangle the chain. "Johnnie, please — you must help me." The jeweler stepped away, and Johnnie gingerly extricated the necklace.

"There," he said. "It was nothing. My dear, you must unpin the cameo."

"But this necklace does not suit me."

"I thought you said that it was very beautiful."

"It is. Not for me, though, not for me."

He felt her sliding away from him, slipping through the net of his adoration. But he heard the agitation in her voice; she was not dissembling. He was too slow to catch her shifting moods. "I'm so sorry — I shouldn't have forced my desire on you." He took her hand. "You will forgive me?"

"Of course, Johnnie; really, there's nothing to forgive. You are so very generous. But I worry that we are wasting Signor de Levis's time. He has no souvenirs, only precious ornaments."

De Levis protested. "Please, signora, stay as long as you like. I do not care if you buy anything at all. Your admiration is enough."

"Marian, we must have something; I insist. Something smaller — a brooch, I think." He smiled at his wife. "Something with emeralds, perhaps" — he glanced at de Levis — "emeralds, as in *Middlemarch*."

"Emeralds," mused the jeweler. "Dorothea chooses emeralds, does she not?"

"For their spiritual beauty," Johnnie said, and smiled.

But Marian exclaimed, exasperated, "Well! You would think that I wrote about nothing but jewels!" She tried to smile and mitigate her outburst. "And I am not my characters," she added rather too sharply, with a glance in Johnnie's direction.

"Emeralds," he repeated. He wanted them for her; she could not resist emeralds.

"I will show you what I have." Signor de Levis opened a cabinet concealed behind a leather panel and withdrew a tray partitioned into compartments, containing an array of brooches. He placed the tray on the table and once again whispered to the boy, who left the room. Johnnie wished that the jeweler were as unobtrusive as his shadowy son.

"Johnnie, you must choose." Marian smiled. "I cannot be trusted." She had regained her composure, and her voice was once more modulated and calm.

"What appeals to me won't necessarily please you," he said.

She pointed to a circular brooch in the form of a golden lattice. "Didn't your mother have one very much like that?"

"Why, yes. My father gave it to her—come to think of it, he bought it in Venice—possibly even here."

"It had to have been here," said de Levis. "This is a piece that my grandfather devised and that we still make; it was based on a pattern that his father, my great-grandfather, invented."

"Your family have been jewelers for a long time."

"Goldsmiths and jewelers since we came to Venice from Augsburg."

John Cross lifted the brooch from its tray. "Mother wore it always —even at the end. I used to pin it to her collar; she told me that it reminded her of her eternal reward—she knew she would meet Father again." He returned the brooch to the tray, and his hand lingered on the jewel. He straightened his shoulders, bracing himself. When the sadness passed he said briskly, "Perhaps you would like to try it on?"

She hesitated, then shook her head and started to speak, but stopped herself as de Levis's son came back with a small leather case.

"If I might," the jeweler said, taking the box from his son. He opened it and placed it on the table beside the tray. Inside lay a brooch: arabesques of gold surrounding an emerald. The arabesques were the coils of a serpent lacing itself through the boughs of a tree blooming with pearl buds. The emerald, a deep, clear green that condensed light to a liquid intensity, hung like a fruit.

"This is exquisite," said Marian. Johnnie resolved to have the brooch. It would be expensive, far more than he had intended to spend. But he could afford it; perhaps the jeweler's admiration for his wife would lower the price.

De Levis removed the brooch from its case and held it up to one of the high windows. "This is a very fine emerald, one of the finest my family has possessed. This is a piece to which I am quite attached. Indeed, I thought never to sell it."

"Perhaps you should not have shown it to us," John Cross said.

"I could not resist," de Levis parried. "I made it for my own pleasure, modeled on a brooch in a portrait by Titian."

"Which one?" Marian asked eagerly. "Where may I see it?"

"Alas, signora, it is in the collection of a family, the lady's descendants. She was of my race. I had an ancestor—I bear his name—I would like to think that ancestor made the jewel in the portrait."

"Did your ancestor make that marvelous statue?"

"He did."

"It is Apollo, is it not?"

"Or David," said de Levis. "The hand is empty. He could be holding the head of Goliath or a knife to flay Marsyas; he could be either, or both."

"I imagine that as a Jew your ancestor de Levis cultivated ambiguity."

Johnnie was relieved to detect a note of censure in his wife's comment, but the jeweler nodded as if she had articulated a truth.

She added, "You might be reluctant to part with the brooch."

De Levis inclined his head. "There is a time for everything."

"Who was the lady whose portrait Titian painted?"

"She was a brilliant lady, a musician and a poetess, renowned throughout Venice, and she was also very beautiful." He handed Marian the brooch, and she held it in her palm and traced the sinuous loops of the serpent's body with her finger. "Then the lady was a courtesan?" As she turned the brooch to the light, the green flared and deepened. "You have even worked the snake's scales," she said.

"What does it matter who she was?" Johnnie blurted. He took the brooch from Marian and scrutinized it. "Isn't the flaw in this emerald a bit obvious?"

"This occlusion is as small as one can hope to find in a stone of this size," explained de Levis. "And it is off to one side and so does not affect its ability to collect light. The signore is, of course, aware that it is the nature of every emerald to exhibit some irregularity. It is like a human being in that regard. We love it all the more for its fragility and its flaws."

"But my wife is flawless." Johnnie smiled at Marian. The jeweler was right; this was an exceptionally beautiful emerald. It was not overly large, but its color was mesmerizing, and he had to admit that the setting was as fine as the stone. He wanted this for her; this was not a jewel a son would buy for his mother. "Try it, please, my dear," he asked.

She removed the cameo from her blouse. Johnnie threaded the pin of the brooch through the lace of her collar and centered the ornament over the hollow of her throat. It settled, perfectly balanced, against the knobs of collarbone. He stepped back. "There," he announced with satisfaction.

She took up the looking glass again, and Johnnie saw her frown at her reflection.

"Its effect is wonderful," he reassured her. "The emerald lends your eyes a green cast, and it gives your complexion a tinge of gold. Turn your head toward the light and look in the mirror." Her expression eased; the jewel did infuse her face with grace. "Well, Mrs. Cross, what do you think?"

He saw in her reflection surprise and pleasure.

"If Signor de Levis would let it go —" she said.

"Of course he will," said Johnnie. "It is yours. My wedding present to you."

"I will walk around with my hands at my throat."

"You will get used to it, my dear." He touched his lips gently to her forehead. "And now I must have a word with Signor de Levis."

The jeweler gazed at the brooch, then smiled at Marian. "I am happy this is going to you, signora. Would you like to wear it now?"

"Certainly." Johnnie spoke for her.

"In that case, let me put your cameo away." He carefully tucked the carved brooch into the leather case and presented it to Marian. "Value is not always measured in terms of price," he said.

The boy reappeared and led Marian back along the corridor to another small, sumptuous room. Its leather walls were hung with mirrors and painted views of Venice; two large windows, with a little writing desk between them, overlooked the Piazza San Marco. The windows were open, and their gauze curtains fluttered in the breeze. A cacophony of waltzes ascended from the cafés, mixed with the humming of the crowd and the percussive flapping of the wings of pigeons.

Marian drew aside the curtains and looked down at the scene as if she were watching a pantomime. Gently she put the little casket holding the cameo George had given her on the desk.

SOMETHING OLD: on the morning of her wedding, Marian held the cameo up to her collar. Even today? Not to wear it on her wedding day would be dishonest. And George would have wanted her to take this step, she was convinced, or she would not be doing it. She steadied herself against a small swell of uncertainty and pinned the ornament on.

She inhaled to feel against her ribs the perfect fit of the gray silk costume. Johnnie had chosen it — gray tinged with blue to match her eyes. Its cut showed off her narrow waist, and she was pleased and abashed that from behind she appeared so youthful. No ghosts of beauty haunted her, and at sixty, she was not so changed as other women. She brushed out her hair, the auburn stranded with gray but still lustrous. With the back of her hand she stroked the pillow, George's pillow, which she had not been able to remove from beside hers. She laid her head on his pillow to conjure one last time his sweet proximity.

IN THE LITTLE sitting room overlooking the piazza, Marian felt vaguely discontented, and she was suddenly tired. Last night she had not slept well; it might have been the bed. She touched the jewel casket. Another small betrayal — but she must stop thinking like that. It was a laying to rest.

"Had I been a theologian," George had once said to her as they rested in their big, comfortable bed, "I would be far more concerned with heaven's furnishings than with its hierarchies of angels." He rolled onto his side, facing her, his light brown hair curling exuberantly after sleep. "What do you think? Do newly arrived souls join the ranks immediately upon admission — a quick hello to family and friends and off to be fitted for a robe and a halo? Or does desire survive death? If it were up to me, heaven would be full of beds."

"This bed is heaven enough for me," she had answered. "Which is good, since I doubt that you and I would be sent to heaven — if there were one. Anyway, I don't think I'd want to go to a place, or whatever heaven is — a state, a condition — from which all earthly desire has been refined. And I hope you wouldn't, either."

She believed in no afterlife and found no comfort in the anticipation of a celestial reunion. The new brooch lay heavily against her throat; in even the most distant of her reflections repeated in the mirrors she could make out the snake's undulating gold. She could not escape her image, and it was strange to see herself so adorned, strange and thrilling. To possess something so voluptuous made her almost ashamed, as if she had been seduced. Maybe in marriage there could be no seduction; maybe her luck with George had derived from the precariousness of their situation.

She and George would have discussed the price of the brooch and decided that it was too dear. They would have laughed at the extravagance. She and Johnnie did not laugh like that — from shared folly or even from shared discovery. Their laughter was carefully constructed, achieved. She should not compare.

Anyway, money was Johnnie's business, the material world his arena: buying and selling, gauging the reliability of investments. He had attended meticulously to every detail of the arrangements for their honeymoon and fretted that due to him some connection might be missed, some indispensable piece of baggage mislaid. They had been reading Dante together, but Dante did not supply the words for *timetable, first-class compartment,* or *porter.*

Dante had brought them together; they had to spend their honeymoon in Italy. Reading Dante: what began as mutual consolation — for the death of George Lewes, for the death of Johnnie's mother, within a week of each other — had flowered into love.

GEORGE HAD DIED in November, the darkest part of the year. For almost two months afterward, she could bear to see nobody but his eldest son, Charles; the first visitor she permitted was Johnnie Cross. She had to attend to her finances; that had been her excuse to herself. On that January day, just a year and a half ago, he had brought from his mother's conservatory a gardenia on the verge of bloom. "Put it in a window," he commanded, "and remember that the leaves must be sprinkled every morning." Marian obeyed, and within a week the gardenia's perfume filled the parlor.

Since the beginning of their friendship, Johnnie had been in the habit of bringing her flowers, and she was touched by his considerate frivolities. Johnnie had managed their investments; she called him Nephew and he called her Aunt. He saw to all the terrible mundanities of death: the will, the disposition of property. The legal process only exacerbated her grief. As capable as Johnnie was, he could not spare her indignity, and he and Charles had to accompany her to probate court and act as witnesses when she took—too late—the name Lewes, not as George's wife, but as inheritor of his estate.

Throughout the spring and summer Johnnie visited almost daily. They spoke of the dead and noted the first crocuses, the blooming shrubs, the leaves on the elms unfurling pale and translucent. In the early dusk of a late September day she opened her piano for the first time in almost a year. The lid creaked. She ran through one scale, then another, but stopped when she spied Johnnie leaning against the parlor door. "I thought you had gone," she said.

"I heard you and came back."

"You don't want to listen; I'm out of practice."

"You will remember. Sing something, Aunt. Sing me a song. It's been a long time since I've heard you sing."

She shook her head. "I'll sound like an old screeching owl."

"I remember a nightingale. Please."

She found a volume of songs in a stack beside the piano, and when she placed it on the music rack and began turning pages, it opened by itself to "Wanderers Nachtlied." "Goethe. You know how George loved Goethe."

"I must read the biography—I wish I had time to read more."

"Never mind, dear boy. You are active, not contemplative. But listen. Schubert's setting is the one George preferred, though Liszt played his version for us when we knew him in Weimar. Schubert's is simpler. I like it better, too."

"Should I light a lamp?" Johnnie asked.

"No, no. I want the darkness."

She played. The low opening chords shimmered from major to minor and back, and she sounded out the first measure or two of melody. Then she sat, head bowed, hands resting on the keys. She began the introduction once again, and her alto floated in the dim room, soft, disembodied, distant: "*Über allen Gipfeln ist Ruh . . .*"

The last chords whispered, an altered echo of the vocal line.

"What do the words mean?" Johnnie asked.

"'Peace is over all the peaks, in all the treetops you barely feel the wind's breath. The little birds stay silent in the forest. Only wait, soon you, too, will rest.' Listen to how Schubert repeats — 'wait, wait, only wait,' and then that rising phrase, that held note — *balde* — 'soon.'"

She repeated the song.

"It is very beautiful when you sing," he said softly.

"A poem about what is not. Not a breath of wind, not a sound. It makes death beautiful; it makes you yearn for death."

She closed the keyboard and leaned her forehead against her hands. Johnnie crossed the room and gently and deliberately placed his palms on her shoulders. "Marian." He whispered her name. "Marian, you will have peace. In your life. If I can help it, you will." His hands radiated comfort. She stayed still so that he would not be frightened off.

HE HAD BEEN wounded in his pride by that thoughtless photographer. It must be that he was exhausted; Venice was their first rest in five weeks. Before the wedding he had bought their new house in Cheyne Walk, organized the plans for its repairs and decoration, seen to Marian's complicated affairs, and all of this in addition to attending to his own business in the City. It was too much for him. She feared that *she* was too much for him.

Had he not foreseen that some people might mistake him for her son? He was twenty years younger than she was. When she had pressed him to consider the difference in their ages — pressed him none too hard — he had shrugged it off, and she had been satisfied.

She was accustomed, though hardly inured, to irregularity. Before she and George had eloped to Germany, he had wondered if their connection might better be kept secret.

"It is not in my nature — or in yours — to hide. Would you rather we skulked around and pretended that there was nothing between us, would you prefer to set me up in lodgings like a tawdry *petite amie?*"

"It would not be like that, Polly."

"Yes, it would. Everybody would know, and talk, and laugh at us."

"They laugh at me already — for acknowledging each infant my wife and Thornton Hunt bring into the world. But what would I do instead? The situation of their parents is not their fault, poor little souls." Angry sadness had spread across his face, a stain on his naturally sweet expression.

Marian had rushed to reassure him. "No, no — I don't blame you — I admire you — I love you for it — I argued with Spencer about it."

"Yes, he told me."

"He did — and what else did he say?" She could not hide her anxiety.

But George shrugged. "Nothing — just that you understand me. This was last summer, after he visited you at Broadstairs."

"That's all he said?"

"Yes. No — he might have said that you quite liked me. Why?"

She smiled with relief; Spencer had said nothing about what had passed between them. Men talked, but perhaps not Spencer. "For no reason. Gossip — how things change in the telling. I told him I thought you were kind."

"That's not how people usually describe me."

"Then they don't know you. You have been kind to your wife — and kind to your friend."

"His father helped me — without his interest my life would have gone nowhere. The least I could do is help his children. But because I have done so, we cannot marry."

"We cannot live apart," she said. "And I will not hide."

She had called herself by his name — Marian Evans Lewes — and she had called George her husband, and the world — her friends, at least, all except for her brother Isaac — came, finally, to honor their union.

Yet her marriage to Johnnie had caused as much talk as had her elopement with George. If she had married an eminent physician, a widower close to her own age, or if she had married Herbert Spencer — and the idea made her smile, with the small twinge of affection and antagonism that still accompanied any thought of him — people would have smirked and said, "Two dried-up old husks. They deserve each other." All her life she had been the subject of speculation. It was as if gossip reflected her own discomfort, as if she prowled the perimeter of society's safe pasture and was noticed and judged.

This marriage would — it must — succeed. Beginnings were difficult. But she and Johnnie could not live isolated in the country or locked behind the doors of their house in Cheyne Walk. They would have to begin; Mr. and Mrs. Bunney were expecting them tomorrow. They would have to venture into the world. It would require will, courage, effort; she had experience of that. Better to act, and then confront the world with the irrevocable. The world would give way.

None of her friends had known of her intention to marry; she and Johnnie had told only Johnnie's sisters and Charles, George's eldest son. She instructed the family solicitor to inform her brother Isaac; she wrote to her friends telling them her momentous news:

By the time you receive this I shall have been married to Mr. J. W. Cross, who you know is a friend of years, a friend much loved and trusted by Mr. Lewes, and who now that I am alone sees his happiness in the dedication of his life to me. This change in my position will make no change in the ultimate disposition of my property. Mr. Cross has a sufficient fortune of his own.

She touched the brooch. The golden snake was cool and the minute scales delicately rough under her finger. Was this compensation? A flash of annoyance replaced distress. No. Johnnie had examined the jewel with a connoisseur's pleasure, with loving attention; he had wanted *that*. But how did he love *her*? He had caressed her when he pinned the brooch to her collar. What did that mean? She did not know; she was waiting; she did not know what else to do.

A maid appeared with tea, which she placed on the desk. Marian dropped the case holding her cameo into her pocketbook, and with her cup stood at the window. The photographer was posing a family — they looked to be American — before the doors of San Marco. The two children were laughing at the pigeons perched on their heads, and it seemed that their mother was scolding them because presently their expressions became grave. It would be difficult to remain serious beneath a pigeon.

Then, in front of Florian's, she saw the man who had been staring at her when the photographer made his unfortunate pronouncement; she remembered the electric white streak of hair at his forehead. Now on his arm he had a striking, tall young woman with fine features and lustrous red hair. The man's shirt seemed ready to fly loose from his trousers.

The girl clung to him—Marian recognized in that gesture her own determined intimacy with George in Weimar—as they started across the crowded square. Abruptly they stopped. Marian thought she saw the man smile. He led his companion back toward the galleria. For a moment Marian lost them, but she spotted them in the shadow of the arches. Here the man stopped again, as if he were looking for something, searching the ground.

Then he pointed and the woman stared. The man inscribed an arc on the marble with the toe of his boot. Marian was appalled—and delighted. So he had been eavesdropping, intruding! It was outrageous, insufferable, rude beyond imagining—and wonderful. She nearly laughed out loud. She must tell Johnnie—no, he would not find it amusing. The man fished in the pocket of his coat and dropped to his knees, and with a stick of charcoal seemed to be tracing on the marble the spiral shell of the ancient stone snail.

AFTER A QUARTER of an hour Giuseppe de Levis ushered Johnnie into the little chamber. Johnnie was smiling; he moved with new spirit, and Marian was reminded of the way he used to stride into the Priory. Radiating enthusiasm and good cheer, he would report on the success of investments, comparing manufacturing concerns with transportation companies, reciting percentages of return over time with the concentration of a scientist describing the order of the natural world or a scholar unraveling the twisted threads of historical evidence. Johnnie had introduced her and George to the realm of abstract finance, and his enthusiasm had energized them both. Marian's own experience lay in a bygone economy, in the yield of the land, the straightforward ledgers of agriculture. Johnnie had brought the future with him, the heady arcana of exchanges, where it was possible to profit from American railroads or Australian mines. She had loved his competence. Now she saw again in his face evidence of that assurance. Negotiations must have gone well, but she was sure he would not tell. In this new economy wives and numbers did not mix, and now she was a wife.

"Signora Cross, I am sorry that we have kept you waiting," said de Levis. His voice was subdued.

"But I am happy. Tea, San Marco," Marian responded. "Who could want more?" She touched the brooch. "And I do have more — I have this beautiful jewel."

"It is beautiful, one of the best I have ever made." De Levis inclined his head. "Now that it is no longer mine, I hope you will forgive me for saying so." He paused, but before Marian could answer, he continued. "There is a favor I would ask of you."

Johnnie lost some buoyancy. But Marian liked Signor de Levis. She had enjoyed his speculation about the character of Cicero's wife, though Johnnie had minded, a little. He should not; he knew she had not married him for his learning. De Levis also loved his métier, not only the inherent luxury of the materials, but their potential for transformation. Gold into a snake, an emerald into a glowing fruit. Marian said, "I will grant it — if I can."

"I assure you, it will be easy." He glanced at the door. The request, it seemed, would arrive imminently, and she was content to linger in the jeweler's exquisite little chamber.

Johnnie cleared his throat. "Marian, we must be going, don't you think? We will be late."

"Late for what, my dear? Everything is closing, the churches, the galleries, even your chandelier shop; it is almost one. We have nowhere to go." She had meant to placate him, but her words had the opposite effect. She had failed to understand that he was in a hurry to savor his victory. Rebuked, he stood at the window looking out, feet apart, his hands tightly clasped behind him.

There was a quick knock. "*Permesso?*" The jeweler's son, flushed from running, handed his father a book. It was her *Daniel Deronda*, the first edition, in English. "Signora, would you be so kind as to inscribe this book?"

She blushed with the old satisfaction of seeing her work appreciated. At the same time she felt a new, disturbing distance from the book. Since George's death the idea of writing had filled her with lassitude and dismay. "Why, of course I will." She opened the scuffed front cover, loosely hinged from having been read and reread. "To Signor de Levis? I'm so sorry, but I have forgotten your given name."

"Not for me, for my son, Daniele, Daniele de Levis. He has read the book, and it has given him a gift. You have shown him a modern Maccabee. The dream of a homeland." De Levis lowered his voice. "You have also given him another way of understanding himself — you, a stranger, find nobility in a Jew. You must know how one begins to believe untruths if one hears them often enough."

"Indeed, signore, I know that. And I know that it is seductive to attribute sins and shortcomings to those who are unfamiliar to us. Now, Master Daniele" — she addressed the jeweler's son — "what shall I say?" She took up a pen from the writing desk, and without waiting for a reply, she began to write. "There," she said, giving the book to the boy.

"What has the signora written?" asked his father. Daniele looked doubtfully at the jeweler. "Go on, read it. You speak English. Don't be shy!"

The boy's gaze, bashful and proud, flickered in Marian's direction. He took a breath. "It says: 'To a real Daniel, who can grow up to become a hero to his people. Mary Ann Cross — George Eliot.' *Grazie, signora, molte grazie.*"

"Quite appropriate, my dear." Johnnie smiled. "I do think, though, that we must take our leave."

"May I offer you my gondola?" asked Giuseppe de Levis.

"That won't be necessary," Johnnie answered. "We've engaged one beginning tomorrow."

"For this afternoon."

"We're staying close by. We have no need."

"Of course." The jeweler smiled at Johnnie, but he addressed Marian. "You might perhaps enjoy a short *giro*, an excursion. My gondolier knows the most beautiful places in Venice, secret places, gardens, little *campi* that are not described in your guidebook." He indicated the Baedeker that Johnnie carried. "It might be, signora, something that would give you pleasure."

"We are going to the Lido." Johnnie addressed his wife.

"We will still have our afternoon at the Lido." Marian turned to de Levis. "Yes," she said, "it would give me pleasure. But we are already in your debt." She touched the brooch with the tips of her fingers.

"I am not speaking of debt, signora, but of goodwill."

MARIAN LEANED back against the gondola's cushions with Johnnie beside her. The boat was splendid, its gleaming black lacquer ornamented with carved and gilded arabesques, its pillows covered in cut velvet. She ran her hand over the fabric's silky nap and smiled as the gondolier propelled them along a narrow canal. "It's as if we've settled into Cleopatra's barge."

"Well, I'll say that it certainly is more than a little—oriental," Johnnie answered.

"Johnnie, what are you saying?"

He looked at her innocently, deflecting her indignation.

Her voice wavered. "I have upset you."

"It's not you." He turned so that he leaned on his side beside her. His eyes shone, his cheeks were flushed, he appeared fierce and protective. "It's that I see what you have to endure—you, the public you—with the most, the most—unlikely people. I wanted to sweep you out of there, but I felt I could not, without your permission. Yet you seemed perfectly oblivious to the fact that they were forcing themselves on you; you seemed even happy."

"I seemed so because I was." She spoke coolly. "And, tell me, what was unlikely about those people? Was it that they were Jews?"

Johnnie winced. "It was that they took advantage of a commercial transaction and exploited *your* goodwill, your generosity—"

"I did not know that you felt this way." She hesitated. "About Jews."

"I was talking about de Levis," he countered. "Not about Jews."

She had not heard this warning in his voice before. "Johnnie, they were exploiting nothing." She kept her eyes on the brackish canal, the ripples in the water fracturing sunlight. "All I did was write my name in a book for a boy. Signor de Levis out of gratitude has lent us his gondola, has given us this jewel—"

"Not given."

"I am guessing that you made out very well."

Johnnie nodded, acknowledging his success. "That emerald is very fine."

"It would not be so beautiful without the mounting, which is of his own design, a reconstruction of a Renaissance ornament. I'm sure he never thought to sell it, certainly not to anybody who happened into his shop. You changed his mind."

"That was your doing."

She heard a trace of resentment. She smiled at her husband to appease him and touched the knot of muscle at the angle of his jaw; she felt him stifle an impulse to flinch. "What is it, really, Johnnie? Are you unhappy about sharing me? Is that the truth?"

He shook his head, relenting. "Oh, my dear, that must be what it is. I have had you to myself all these months. If we were not married"—and he smiled at her, his guileless, boyish grin—"if we were not married, we would be spending our time alone with each other. I was not prepared for how public marriage is." He took her hand, which she had rested on his knee, and pressed it into the cushion. "We were so happy," he said softly.

The boat drifted through the maze of canals. As they passed fine palaces, the gondolier murmured their names; a reticent guide, modulating his voice to the heat of the day. They glimpsed courtyards through gateways, and their boatman slowed so that they could see bright orange and red nasturtiums cascading from a balcony and a child playing below them, a cat stretched in the sun on the hot stones at the curb of the canal. A girl, her dark hair loose and her feet propped on a footstool, bent over lace bobbins, but her hands were idle. Who lived in those palaces? Who was that child—was he the illegitimate son of an American manufacturer of railroad cars? And the girl? Marian felt neglected filaments of imagination aligning into patterns.

"That girl making lace seemed distracted," she mused. "I wonder why—does she wish she were somewhere else? Has she been deserted by her lover? Our gondolier? He is handsome, don't you think?"

"I can't see him."

She glanced behind her and saw the gondolier's gaze flicker away from Johnnie toward her. She smiled, and the gondolier lowered his eyes. "It happens all the time, you know—the gondoliers amuse themselves with Americans and Englishwomen. Tell me, Johnnie, what do you think?"

"I haven't looked."

"I meant the girl. What do you think about the girl making lace?"

He sighed. "I didn't even notice her. Speculations are your province. I wouldn't have the slightest idea—if I'd seen her I would have thought she had indigestion." He shrugged. "Where do you think we are?" he asked.

"I don't know, but it doesn't much matter."

"As long as I am with you," he murmured drowsily.

"Did you sleep well last night? Was your bed comfortable?"

"It was hard," he said.

"You should ask for a softer mattress."

He closed his eyes and Marian watched him, his beautiful face finally in repose.

People had described George as ugly; in that regard he and Marian were considered well matched. He was wiry and nervous, slight of build, his complexion scarred from smallpox; his light brown hair coiled in curls. A mimic, he would have caught the heavy shuffle of the photographer with his pockets full of bread crumbs. The man with the lightning bolt in his hair would have intrigued him. George would have noticed him far earlier than she had; he would have managed to find out who he was. Everything amused George. He undressed her seriousness—he had said that to her once. Only in private, however; in company they were reserved and decorous, exemplars of respectability. Unmarried, they had achieved an ideal of marriage.

She had been thirty-five when they met and despairing of love. She could not imagine the circumstances under which she and George would have found themselves at that expensive jeweler's. A pity—he would have liked Signor de Levis; probably he would have asked to visit the workshop. They would have ended by meeting the family, opening a drab door into enclosed opulence, encountering learned daughters. Enough. George had thought the world of Johnnie, had delighted in his combination of social reserve—innocence, almost—and financial sophistication.

33

Johnnie's olive skin had a dense, resilient texture, but it had grown sallow during the last frenetic month. He was beginning to show the first small signs of age: rays of wrinkles at the corners of his eyes, the crease of a smile after the smile had relaxed. She loved those marks; they brought him closer to her and made her less shy of his physical perfection. And marriage, indeed, was public. It had been a complicated progression, from friendship to courtship to marriage. They were moving cautiously.

The canals were quiet, the little streets and squares almost deserted; the gondolier rowed languorously, rocking them into reverie. In the silence of midday, he began speaking:

> *Nel mezzo del cammin di nostra vita*
> *mi ritrovai per una selva oscura*
> *ché la diritta via era smarrita.*

"Johnnie!" Marian whispered. "Listen —"

"What is it?"

"Dante. The first lines. Where we began —"

"Yes, I read somewhere that they do that, the gondoliers. They say it's quite romantic." He turned his head to face her and rested his cheek on the soft velvet. His eyelashes were as long and thick as a boy's. He smiled. "And it is, don't you think, like music, a little?" He opened his eyes and tilted his head back. The gondolier was watching and smiled, stretching his lips tight across his large white teeth. Johnnie looked away abruptly, as if he had seen something disconcerting.

Marian listened to the gondolier chant the poetry in his sibilant Venetian dialect. His speech cut through the lapping waves, and she imagined she could hear George's voice mimicking the guttural sounds. He would have teased her over her rapture. George was too much in her thoughts this afternoon.

In the narrow canal, sunshine laid a mesh of silvery glaze on the water, and, like a trick of theatrical lighting, it gleamed on the white marble arc of a bridge while the pavement on either side remained shadowed. The bridge crossed the canal in a pyramid of broad, shallow steps; the Hapsburg functionaries had somehow overlooked this one when they ordered the installation of railings.

A man stood beside the bottom step at the edge of the embankment, peering into the canal; he could have been searching for an aquatic creature, a sea worm or snail, a species that would thrive in the fetid water. Marian could barely make him out, but she could see enough — his slight frame, his fly-away curly hair, his deep concentration. "Oh!" She choked and half rose. The gondolier shouted as he balanced the rocking boat, and Johnnie reached for her arm and pulled her back onto the cushions.

"Marian! What is it? What have you seen?"

"*Va tutto bene?*" the gondolier called.

"*Si, si, mi scusi!*" Marian managed to apologize. She lay back in the boat, her eyes squeezed shut.

As the gondolier slowed the boat, Johnnie bent over her. He stroked her hand. "Marian. What happened? Tell me — tell me! Do you want to stop? Is the boat making you sick?"

"No, no. Nothing like that. Tell him, Johnnie, tell him, please, to go on." She opened her eyes and stared at the man at the bridge. He was, she saw, fifteen years younger than George would have been, an ordinary seedy little man idly observing a piece of floating rubbish — which was, she now realized, the bloated carcass of a rat. She shuddered and cried out again. The man looked up and laughed.

"Marian! What did you see? You must tell me," Johnnie commanded.

"The rat," she whispered. "Horrible!"

"Close your eyes, then, don't look; we'll soon be past it."

She shook her head. "It's only a rat. I've seen dead rats before."

"You thought you saw George, didn't you?" Johnnie gazed at her, his eyes bright with sympathy. "From a distance that man looked like him. Of course the resemblance didn't hold up. What a nasty grin."

"Resemblance?" She refused to concur; she was terrified. She would not acknowledge what she had seen — no, *not* seen. If she had seen him, her mind was tricking her into seeing not the world as it was, but the world according to her desire. A trick of light, an illusion, a deception: that was understandable. But the specificity of the illusion dismayed her. It wore his coat — she would have recognized the feel of the wool under her fingers. And it cast a shadow; its familiar, angular shape made her frantic with longing and with fear for the solidity of her own mind.

Johnnie, with a dreadful instinct for kindness, said, "Love doesn't die with death."

"That is simply pain."

"But death is a mystery."

"In life there are mysteries enough." He had meant to comfort her; she had to appear to be comforted. She nodded. Johnnie had not laughed at her revelation of snails; she should, she supposed, remain open-minded on the question of spirits. Evidence had limitations, even this evidence of her mental instability. Certainly the leap of faith was real enough, if its landing place was not; her impulse to deny death had been an aberration, a mystery.

For a quarter of an hour, they sat in silence. They had floated into the center of Venice, the innermost chambers of its nautilus; buildings five and six stories high crowded together and blocked the sun from the narrow canals.

"We must be in the ghetto," she said and tried for levity. "I wonder where our Charon is taking us. Past what other ghosts?"

"It's certainly dark as hell in here," Johnnie answered. "And not very interesting."

The gondolier swung the boat around a sharp corner into a little *rio,* its narrow passage opening into glittering sunlight; they had arrived at the Grand Canal. "Oh!" she exclaimed. "How beautiful!"

Her husband smiled, once again in a place he recognized.

Desiring peace, she reached for his hand. "Oh, Johnnie, forgive me," she said.

"There's nothing to forgive." She saw from his satisfied smile that he believed she had offered a confession. He lifted her hand and softly kissed her fingers with his dry lips.

SHORT, RAPID, dark waves slapped at the Lido beach, their movement unfettered and violent after the contained calm of the lagoon. Marian and Johnnie sat on the terrace of the hotel where they had dined; the sea breeze teased her bonnet.

"Do you think it's the afternoon light," Marian asked, "that darkens the sea? Or is it something in the water itself?"

Johnnie laughed. "I have absolutely no idea. Are you cold? Is the wind giving you a chill?"

"Oh, no. I love the wind. But I would like to move into the sun."

"I'll fix your chair."

She rose and took a step toward the edge of the terrace. "Perhaps we should go on to Greece. I've never been there."

"It will be far too hot for you, my dear."

"Yes. Odysseus sailed from Ithaca, at the southern tip of the Adriatic. So this is the northern edge of his wine-dark sea. There must be something in the water, the minerals that have leached into it."

Johnnie, angling the chair into the sun, did not answer; he must not have heard her over the scraping of its legs. No matter.

"You know, I think I'd like to swim," he said, settling her in.

She shivered. "The water's too cold; it's too early in the season. You'll catch a chill."

"But the air is warm. A swim might be just what I need."

"There's nobody in the water."

He laughed. "I'll go and test the temperature. Would you like to come with me — or have I made you too comfortable?"

She sighed. "I am quite happy here. And my finery" — she touched the brooch — "is not quite the thing for a stroll on the beach. Go." She patted her little pocketbook. "I have my books and my letters. But Johnnie — don't swim. I don't want to lose you."

He took her hand and kissed it and started off toward the sand. She watched him, his long stride, his easy posture, the back of his neck pale and tender below his close-cropped dark hair; he had grown so slender that from behind he could have passed for a boy. She had not seen him from such a distance for several weeks. She sighed. Mrs. John Walter Cross. The sun was making her drowsy. She reached into her bag and pulled out a little book, another gift from Johnnie. The day before their wedding he had presented it to her, its blank pages elegantly bound in a leather spine and its boards covered with marbled paper. On the spine were printed in gold her new initials: MAC. "For your notes," he had said, "your notes for your next book."

She had laughed lightly and dismissively and thanked him; how could he know that she made her notes in plain cardboard books?

A beautiful thing like this was too precious for raw thought. And how could he assume that there would be a next book? She closed her eyes. Blank, dead calm. This growing sense of detachment and numbness: was this a different kind of happiness?

Or was imagination turning traitor? When she thought—when she sifted through the intricacies of a story or laced together the strands of an idea—there was a buzzing at the base of her skull, a rushing energy, a flood of information and sensation. It was also a kind of precariousness, fraught with doubt and anxiety, a terrifying feat, like crossing a narrow bridge over a gorge. I cannot, she had believed. "Try," George had said when she told him she wanted to write a story. "You will know if you have something."

"You will tell me, too?"

"Of course I will."

"The truth?"

"Always."

She could not have written alone—could never have fashioned her characters, never decided their fates, never risked publishing her stories—without George. If she could not legally bear his last name, on the title page of her books she was George.

He cherished—as if it were a child—her ambition. *Ambition:* she did not like the word; it was inadequate. That necessity, that passionate curiosity, that hunger for love and knowledge, that ambition had cost her dearly. It had lured her from her childhood faith, from her father's God; it had driven her from home. But her imagination still lived in her childhood countryside, the slow rivers and slower customs, the flowering meadows and the encroaching mills, the implacable steeples and gentle hills. Its boundaries, the stubborn and heartbreaking integrity of her father and brother, boundaries she had long ago transgressed, still defined her mental landscape. She had written of them with an exile's yearning.

The waves, splashing and sucking, crashing in relentless and undifferentiated noise, agitated her. She thought to get up and follow Johnnie along the beach, but she felt heavy and lethargic, bound, inert. Opening the little book, she took out a letter she had stowed inside the front cover. It had been written promptly, as she had imagined it would be, and she had received it in Milan. She unfolded it and reread it:

I have much pleasure in availing myself of the present opportunity to break the long silence which has existed between us, by offering our united and sincere congratulations to you and Mr. Cross ... Believe me

Your affectionate brother,
Isaac P. Evans

Long silence: more than twenty years. *Between us:* it had been all his doing. But she had as much as dared him to renounce her. She could go home now — if she wished. How much time had been lost and how much affection — time and love beyond recovery. Isaac was a grandfather now; did his grandsons resemble him; did they linger outside until it was too dark to see; were they graceful and lanky; did their little sisters adore them and follow them everywhere, as she had followed Isaac? Isaac would speak to her now that she was Mrs. John W. Cross — now that, finally, she had achieved her proper happy ending.

She took a pencil from her case. She would describe the scene: the terrace, the beach, the afternoon shadows darkening the golden sand, the figure of her husband at the edge of the sea. Where would that lead? She would mark up this book. She wrote her name. *Mrs. John W. Cross. Mary Ann Cross.* The waves, the sky, the shadows, her husband — words, facts, sufficient unto themselves. She filled a page with *Mrs. John W. Cross, Mary Ann Cross.* Mary Ann: the name she was baptized with. The letters of her name, capitals and lowercase, curled and rose and fell in graphite waves across the page.

Chapter 2

Venice, June 10, 1980

I AM HAPPY. If you say you are, it's true — an act of will. *I* am *hap*py. Caroline Spingold walked the streets of Venice, walking out anger. She shouldn't be angry; she had no right. Even the paving stones, small blocks of basalt, a dark mosaic underfoot, recalled a time when she had been glad. *I* am *hap*py. The words marched through her mind.

It was the other way around; she was marching to the words. *I* am *hap*py. Trochees. She stepped to trochees, to poetic feet. And suddenly a memory of happiness, vivid and physical, assailed her. It was solid and shining, a beautiful thing she had once possessed. Though she wanted it desperately, she could not pick it up and carry it across time into the present.

The memory brought tears to her eyes. Happy tears — or tears of loss. She wasn't thinking clearly. It was five in the morning New York time. She should have listened to Malcolm and slept and waited to show him what she remembered of Venice — would he be disappointed? But she had been angry at him for bringing her back here. And now she had come upon a memory fueled by touch and smell and sight: the elusive safety of her father's love. She reproved herself; she did not need that treacherous happiness. Malcolm gave her everything she desired.

Caroline Spingold: thirty-three years old, possessed already of a frivolous new dress after less than two hours in Venice; for a decade married to a man who wanted only to take care of her. But this distant, familiar, and disturbing lightness, this exuberance bubbling in her throat and fizzing in her arms and legs, felt nothing like the permanence and comfort she identified as happiness with Malcolm.

I am *hap*py. The words teased her with a lilt, a skip, a little polka, and she kicked at the clumsy shopping bag that didn't know how to dance. She walked, not quite aimlessly, to where the tight street widened into an airy oval, a little *campo* and Santa Maria dei Miracoli. The diminutive Renaissance church moored to the embankment of a small canal: a domed marble box, its walls adorned with colored marble as if it were a beautiful object for God to play with. Its improbability made her laugh out loud.

Caroline had not seen the church since she was eleven years old, when she had lived nearby with her parents in a rented apartment during the last season of their married life. That summer for two months she had passed it every day.

Fetid water, engine oil, overripe vegetables, olive oil heating in kitchens where wives and maids prepared lunch, centuries of urine — all this condensed into a sweet odor of habitation, deeply ripe, not a smell that everybody could love. Malcolm, for instance, would hate it. He did not much like water, either: it had been easy to avoid Venice.

She had not been back for — she had to calculate; marriage had made her lose track of time — twenty-two years, close to a quarter of a century. The number sobered her. That was — that had been — one of the beauties of marriage to Malcolm; time ran in circles, in seasons. The gap in their ages — he was twenty years older than she — need not matter. Nothing had to change. It had, though; they had. They had shifted, a fault had opened between them.

In this piazza even the *gelateria* on the corner had not changed. She remembered the pungent yellow Italian vanilla on her tongue, how at first she had recoiled from its richness, overwhelming after the pallid American flavor, and had then surrendered to it. Her father had laughed and said, "Caro, do you know what you do?" He put his arm around her shoulder and pulled her against him. *Caro* — it meant "dear" in Italian, the masculine form of the adjective, but he relished the pun. "You begin by hating what you end up loving the most."

"I thought it was the other way around," her mother had said. Her father had frowned — startled, as if her mother's remark had revealed in some careless and terrible way what Margaret had pretended not to know. Caroline, frightened, had turned to her mother, and Margaret had smiled; it had been an innocent observation. All that summer her mother had smiled, her expression fixed and bright as marble, for her daughter's sake happy in Venice.

Caroline circled the little church, the work of Pietro Lombardo and his sons Tullio and Antonio; now that she could parse the proportions of its decoration, its vocabulary of arches and pilasters, and now that she understood the effort of chiseling stone, the building was even more marvelous than she remembered. She was glad that she was alone. If Malcolm were with her, he would take precedence; if he were here she could not be — what? — herself? She banished that suspicion, and she spun in a little waltz step.

When she married him, Malcolm ran a small investment firm. He traded in currencies and commodities, he hedged; it was not what you traded, he believed, but how you interpreted the movements of the market. His clients gave him free rein, although he made no promises. "You have to be willing to lose," he told them. "That's the only way to win. Money — the market for money — is chaotic. What I do is quantify chaos."

In the beginning Caroline had marveled at how he pared philosophical, political, economic, even emotional complexities to short sentences.

"I want you," he had said to her then. "I want you in my pocket."

MALCOLM FINISHED his *Wall Street Journal*, tossed it onto the floor, and said, "It's going to be ten years. Our anniversary. I want you to go away with me."

It was a Thursday morning in May; they were sitting at breakfast at their house in the country. Caroline had been looking up raptors in *The Field Guide to the Birds*, studying wing structure and the proportions of wing to body. Malcolm had flown in from Hong Kong late; she had been awakened by the shift of the mattress as he climbed into bed and had asked him why he had not spent the night in the apartment in the city. "I wanted to be with you," he had answered.

He had been traveling relentlessly. Three, maybe four years ago he had removed himself from the day-to-day investment decisions of Spingold Equities, delegating that work to teams of business school graduates, while he began publishing a newsletter, *The Web*, a subscription to which cost tens of thousands of dollars. In it he announced that he was expanding his monetary formulas to predict the future and identify trends, to quantify the changing world. At first it did well. There were many people who counted on Malcolm Spingold to spill secrets and reveal strategies, but he did not always deliver. If Malcolm had an instinct for the next thing, he also had a predilection for predicting disaster. To Caroline, the newsletter seemed untrustworthy, alternating between insight and grandiosity, but what did she really know about his business?

Nonetheless, she had been distressed — for Malcolm at first, then by him. When the publication continued to lose money, Malcolm assumed the market was not ready; it was not his fault. He reminded Caroline of her father, railing against the disappearance of poetry, and her sympathy mingled with pity, an unsettling variant of love. But Malcolm was neither an idealist nor a poet. He understood the world.

Then six months ago he went back to Spingold Equities. The American economy, with interest rates at almost 20 percent and the market stagnant, was close to imploding. The potential for catastrophe consumed him; almost weekly he flew to London or the Far East, giving trading instructions verbally, leaving no traces, no phone calls or faxes, no telexes.

"You're exaggerating," Caroline ventured, before he'd left on this trip to Hong Kong.

"It's what I do," he answered, stowing a clean shirt and a change of underwear into his briefcase. He traveled light. "I imagine the worst case and work backward."

New leaves, lizard green, filtered sunlight, and in the distance, at the bottom of the long lawn, the Hudson River glistened silver. "Come with me," he repeated.

"I have to have everything at the foundry by August," she said.

"It used to be that you went with me everywhere."

43

Caught by the tenderness in his voice, and by an old sense of shared adventure, she closed the book. Malcolm covered her wrist with his wide hand. His fingers were blunt, his nails square; his hands were reassuring. His forearms were already tan. At about the time he started his newsletter, he had acquired a bulldozer and spent afternoons cutting brush and excavating an ever-expanding pond, where Caroline swam and he did not. At home on machines, he maneuvered his behemoth smoothly, as if it were a toy.

"Where would you want to go?"

"I want to surprise you."

"Can't we put it off? My show opens in September."

"Postpone your show. Deirdre's your friend."

She freed her hand; he was not smiling. "She's also my dealer. It's been scheduled for two years. You know that."

"You have plenty of time. We'll go in June, in three weeks. We stay a week. That's nothing."

She did not answer; every conversation was fragile. To hide her anger, she picked up the binoculars she kept near the window. It was the time of the spring migration: warblers and ducks, grosbeaks and coloratura orioles. Adjusting the focus so that the river's glitter sharpened into waves and the window's mullions dissolved into fuzzy bars, she tracked across the lawn to the lilacs — lilacs like clouds, white and lavender, cumulus and thunderhead.

When he first bought the bulldozer, Malcolm had decided to backfill a cellar hole in the brush past the edge of the lawn. The hole was bordered by thick-stemmed, blowsy lilacs.

"Leave it," Caroline begged.

"It's a nuisance, it's dangerous," he said.

"It's history." She had been unable to stop herself from bursting into tears. Malcolm settled on clearing undergrowth, leaving the cellar hole in place, and the lilacs had thickened and flourished.

"See anything?" he asked.

"Nothing," she said dismissively.

Malcolm stood up. "What were you looking for?" There was a suggestive edge to his voice that she did not trust.

"Birds. Deer. What else would be out there? Pirates sailing up the Hudson?"

Malcolm shrugged. "I wouldn't know." He was tall and muscled and his black hair was turning gray; he had the ability to stay very still. Like a hawk, he was sudden and sleek, lethal. This morning the skin around his eyes was dark from fatigue. The furrow between his eyebrows had deepened, and she feared that he was losing resilience, showing weakness. He started to leave the room.

"Why were you asking?"

He did not answer. His tolerance for discord was greater than hers.

"Malcolm, tell me — I thought you hated surprises."

He turned and she saw an echoing shadow of apprehension in his amber eyes. "I'm not the one being surprised."

"How will I pack?"

"If you need something, you can buy it — you would anyway."

TEN YEARS. For Malcolm, a decade was not much time. Men of his generation had been married for a quarter of a century; those embarked on a second marriage, like his Swiss banker friend Artur Heismann, had already produced a second batch of children. In the beginning Malcolm talked about a baby, but Caroline put him off. Their marriage had been enough.

After they married, she took a leave of absence from her graduate work at the Museum School, forfeiting her scholarship, and the leave became permanent. She went everywhere with Malcolm, to London, to Denver, to Kansas City; she learned to wait while he conducted business. She shopped, visited museums to look at Renaissance bronzes, cowboy bronzes, statues modeled in clay by nineteenth-century American ladies and carved in marble by Italian artisans — she saw whatever was available. She made conversation at lunch with colleagues' wives assigned to entertain her. For Malcolm she mastered French cooking and learned to run an apartment in Manhattan and the house on the Hudson. She adapted the structured costume of an affluent wife of Malcolm's generation into the slightly rebellious informality appropriate to a young woman of her own and refused to join the boards of the charities she made Malcolm contribute to.

At first, marriage had supplanted ambition. She had fashioned herself into Malcolm's wife, but nothing she did was essential. She feared becoming frivolous, that her sculpture — little silver figures like Renaissance baubles — would become a way to fill time, an indulgence; she feared that she herself was becoming an object. For five years she worked every day; she drove to Boston for advice from Sam Gruson, her old teacher. The problem was how to make the figures more than ornaments — how to make them dangerous.

Just before Malcolm began his newsletter, Deirdre Morris, who had been Caroline's roommate at the Museum School, opened a gallery downtown. "You don't have to take me on because we're friends," Caroline had said when Deirdre asked if she would show with her. After school they had not seen each other for several years until they met at a dinner party given by one of Malcolm's fund managers. Deirdre's husband, Geoff, had made partner at his law firm, their child was entering nursery school, and they had moved from their one-bedroom apartment on East Ninety-fifth Street to a loft downtown: while Caroline remained suspended Deirdre was catching up.

"I'm not running a charity," she answered.

BEFORE THEY were married, Caroline had presented Malcolm with a spinning wheel, three inches high. She had cast it in silver and chased it until it was as beautiful as she knew how to make it: an offering of her best self. Still, she worried that he would be insulted by the reference to the hook-nosed dwarf in the fairy tale.

He studied the little sculpture dispassionately, as if it were a financial instrument: the meticulously turned spindle modeled into the shape of a woman's head, the gold filament strung between the spindle and the wheel, whose spokes were twigs.

She asked, "I worried that you wouldn't like it — do you? Do you like it?"

"Rumplestiltskin. I love it. You guessed my secret."

"Like the miller's daughter guesses Rumplestiltskin's name."

"And goes free. I know. Mrs. Spingold." As he spoke, he watched her.

She flinched, and he noticed. "Is this a test?" she asked.

"In a way. Do you want to go free?"

His question distressed her, as if he had guessed her own secret — a need to save herself, to relinquish uncertainty, a fear of taking

46

her chances — which she was afraid to divulge. He had also been testing her acquiescence.

She answered with her own question: "Do you want to be free of me?"

He laughed. "Caroline, you are my freedom. And my secret is that I do worry — I worry that I do spin straw into gold. And that someday I'll lose the knack. Would you mind?"

She heard the small tremor of uncertainty. "Of course you won't," she said.

He said, "I don't know what to give you in return."

"You gave me the silver — and everything. And I didn't make this for you to get something back."

"Women don't give me gifts."

She laughed at him, at his mistrust and at his loneliness.

"What's so funny?" he asked.

"You," she answered, risking the truth, testing how far she could go with him. "How suspicious you are. You're afraid to say thank you — afraid it might cost you something. It doesn't have to work that way."

He glanced at her sharply and touched the tiny head at the top of the spindle. "You love making these little statues, don't you?"

"It's what I've always wanted to do."

"And what else do you love?"

She laughed, making him want her.

MALCOLM WAS afraid of flying. He contained his fear by concentrating it into the first few minutes after takeoff, when the most dangerous crashes occurred. He finished off his preflight glass of champagne, clenched his eyes shut, and gripped Caroline's hand. The NO SMOKING sign blinked off, then the FASTEN SEATBELT sign. He smiled and stretched and turned to Caroline and kissed her cheek. "I love you," he said, wistfully.

"Mmmm," she murmured.

"What are you thinking?" he asked.

"Nothing." She had been thinking about the spinning wheel, an alloy of innocence and cunning, wondering what had happened to it. She blinked away tears, but he had seen them.

"What's happened?"

47

She watched the lights on Long Island and the Connecticut coast brighten in the blue dusk. In the upstairs cabin of these 747's she felt superior and precarious, like a nineteenth-century Englishwoman riding high above the world in a howdah atop an exotic elephant. "What do you mean? We're fine. The plane's fine."

"To us?"

She shivered, guilty, unable to talk about drift and collision — about what was happening between them. She leaned her head against his shoulder, counterfeiting peace.

"Tell me."

She sat up. "Tell me where we're going."

"Venice."

She swallowed. "No," she wailed.

He tried to put his arm around her, but she shrugged him off.

"Why Venice?" she demanded. "Just tell me why."

"Shh. You're talking very loud. You were unhappy there, and I want to show you that you don't have to be."

"I wasn't unhappy. It was the opposite." She closed her eyes against him.

"That was when your father left."

"It was before he left. I had no idea he would leave." She started to get up.

"Where are you going?"

"Outside to play."

"Please, Caroline, do this for me." He gripped her wrist. "Maybe I made a mistake, a big fucking mistake. If you want, we can turn around, take the day flight. I'll do that. I'll do anything you want." He cradled his forehead in his palms. "Just tell me what you want."

"Why Venice? What's the real reason?"

"A project — I haven't told you about it — a wild idea."

"So you're not going for me."

"Everything's for you."

"Not this project."

"You love Venice, and it's dying."

"It's been dying for hundreds of years."

"I have an idea to bring it back."

"You and everybody else."

"Not the art, the economy."

"There's no economy to save."

"That's my point. If something doesn't change, Venice is going to turn into a waterlogged theme park. I'm talking about raising money, starting a fund, getting information, understanding what could revive the city — film, communications — new industries. An international fund to support these businesses, to turn Venice into a place with a future, not just a past."

"Why? Why do you care?"

"I have no idea how much more time I have. To live."

"What are you talking about? You're healthy."

"You never know. My father was healthy, too, until the day he dropped dead. He was forty-nine."

"I know. And your EKG tapes could wrap around the world."

"I figure I'm three years into borrowed time."

"I still don't get it. Why not save Providence? Providence really needs help, too, and you come from there."

He was, she knew, capable of concocting this plan for her — if there was a potential for profit. Everything turned on money.

"It's a way to hold on to our assets."

"Aren't we okay?"

He shrugged and blinked. He had rolled his shirtsleeves up to his elbows. Caroline tried to imagine him at her age. She had married him when he was forty-three; she had missed his youth. Was his jaw fuller now? Had his skin been prone to pimples? His narrow amber eyes less hooded and secretive? His forearms plump and not ropey, the veins cushioned in flesh? Had he ever laughed himself sick?

These thoughts flickered like bats in a twilight almost too dark to penetrate; she had grown used to them: disloyal details subverting the happy plot. Malcolm's older brother had been killed in Guam. He talked with bitterness about his dead father. Caroline's father was dead, too; his death, however, had absolved him of the harm he had done.

But Malcolm's wounds had congealed into character and hardened him, and over the last few years Caroline had watched him grow brittle. He entrusted his tender side to her, and she dreaded distressing him, pushing him to breaking.

"Want a Valium?" he asked.

"No. I need to think." She reached into her satchel for her sketch-book.

He swallowed a pill and retreated behind his eye mask. Caroline ate a bite of microwaved beef and turned the headphones up loud, blocking out the engine noise with Handel. How does a body fall into water? She drew a pinwheel of arms and legs. What are the physics of falling? In those seconds of weightlessness is there a revelation past terror?

"I have to make these figures big," she told Deirdre Morris. "And I want them cast in bronze. They're going to be rough, not like what I usually do."

"Like what you used to do?"

"You remember? They didn't work then."

"Go for it," Deirdre had said. "See how it turns out. People want big. They want to be startled. But make some small ones, too, to pay the rent."

"They'll be flying. Falling."

"Falling?" Deirdre had asked. "You've heard?"

"I read — in the paper."

"Are you all right?"

"No, I'm not — but what can I do about it? I want them mounted to a wall."

HEATHROW WAS empty, save for the passengers and a listless Indian janitor in a blue smock shuffling between the rows of seats at the gate. A cheerful electronic bell chimed, heralding a new batch of cities clicking into view on the monitor: Prague, Budapest, Warsaw, the dark cities her father's family had fled.

"Well?" Malcolm asked, putting down his briefcase. His cashmere blazer caressed him, and his shirt seemed as fresh as when he had put it on in New York.

"What about Leningrad? We can watch the sun never set. Or Nairobi? Lions and tigers and giraffes."

He did not smile. "I don't like communism and I don't like wild animals. Our bags are checked through to Venice. Ricky is meeting us. If you want to turn around I have to make some calls."

At the gate she said, "You knew I'd come with you."

"Hoped. Wanted." He pressed her head against his neck. "I couldn't do this without you," he whispered. She leaned into him, remembering how pliant she had been, how desirous of being needed.

Malcolm had made his first money in junk, scrap metal. He had inherited the bankrupt business from his father: wrecked cars, corroded water tanks, tired steel trusses, tangles of rusted wire — metal that could be bought and sold. His mother had contested the will, but Malcolm sued her and won and resurrected the business on the side while he worked at his first jobs in brokerage houses. Although they never spoke again, he had sent his mother a percentage of the profits until she died. It was the only thing his old man ever did for him, Malcolm said — die, so he could take over the junkyard. Girders supported Malcolm's intellect; he knew the composition of metals and had an instinct for what could be salvaged and sold.

AT THE VENICE airport a man from the hotel ushered Caroline and Malcolm to the launch. As they followed him out of the terminal, a gypsy girl, face streaked with dirt and a child in her arms, sidled up to them and held out her hand. Caroline pulled out a thousand-lira note from the bills Malcolm had given her at the *cambio*.

"What did you do that for?"

"My mother used to give them a hundred lira. I'm adjusting for inflation."

The man stowed their luggage in the launch. "Welcome to Venezia. This is your first visit?"

Caroline smiled. "*Ho passato due mesi qui quando ero una bambina.*"

"What did you say?" Malcolm asked.

She had spoken without thinking, and she laughed. "Did you hear that? The words just came out in Italian."

"What did you say?" he repeated.

"Oh, nothing — just that I spent two months here when I was a kid."

"Could you tell him I'm late?"

In a north wind, the hotel launch powered through choppy open water before it cut its engines to enter the city, the theatrical labyrinth of canals. Caroline stood in the stern, awash in memory. When she and her parents arrived in Venice, they had crowded into the rear of the *vaporetto*. Byron and Goethe and Browning and Rilke: her father spoke the names of the northern poets who found in Venice a musical reverberation and amplification of emotion. Her mother counted their luggage. How eagerly that summer Caroline had absorbed her father's brave and magical faith in art, incorporating those qualities into her own being so that he would recognize her.

Her chest tingled painfully as if her heart had fallen asleep and sensation was now returning. She gazed at the marvels concocted on foundations of silt and pilings, the array of palazzos lining the canal: Byzantine limestone lace, the austere proportions of the early Renaissance, Baroque extremes of shadow and light. An architectural beauty pageant. Malcolm would appreciate that; she should tell him.

"Malcolm." Caroline stepped into the hatchway to the cabin. He was studying his datebook, making notations. "Malcolm, the Grand Canal."

He closed his book, tucked it into the inside pocket of his blazer, and glanced out the window. Through salt-spotted glass the palazzos seemed two-dimensional, cardboard façades propped on the embankments. He shook his head. "They're all for sale. This city isn't about art," he said. "It's about money. Do you know what this is? Those buildings are monuments to capitalism. To what money can buy."

He wasn't wrong; he was never wrong. But he was reductive. "That's not all it is," she countered. "Beauty, spirit, what you can't measure, what you can't see? It's like dark matter. Just the feeling of being here."

He grinned. "That's your department. That's why I need you." He held out his hand, and she went back to sit beside him.

"Wait for me," he said. "Sleep in the room for a couple of hours. My meeting won't go long."

"A meeting to announce that we're witnessing the end of capitalism?"

He laughed. "I've already told them that. We're deciding what to do about it. We're deciding how to structure the fund—the Venice fund. Wait for me; I want you to show me Venice."

"Look now, Malcolm. I want to show you this."

Malcolm closed his eyes, refusing.

SHE HAD NOT waited. But on the flight from London she had wondered — and she was sure that he had wondered, too — if this trip could restore them somehow to the luxurious expansiveness that had marked the first years of their marriage. It had been a shimmering exchange, involving the material and the spiritual, money and art. There had been a grace to it once; it had coarsened into argument.

Malcolm had spoiled her with earthly possessions, given her so much, so easily that the romance of acquisition had diminished to a satisfaction trimmed with misgivings. And she, in return, had believed in him unconditionally; she had indulged his ideas. When they married he had been resolutely pragmatic and measured every transaction. Where other wealthy men amused themselves with yachts and polo ponies and women, Malcolm published *The Web*. He was a man of large ambition, interested in influence. Caroline guessed once that he might run for political office, but he laughed. "What I do is tell politicians what to do. I don't want to have to listen to anybody who says he knows better than me."

His life — their life together — was predicated on his money. His: the money was all in his name. He had so much it was beyond counting, at least beyond her ability to count, or so she had believed. The possibility that she had been wrong made her slightly sick. He had mentioned risky investments. Currency markets were volatile; small companies with new technologies could easily fail. If Malcolm was in trouble, how could he afford to concoct this plan to revitalize Venice? Caroline's father had done something similar; he had arranged their hopeless Venetian summer as if nothing in their lives was ever going to change. But Malcolm was not her father; Malcolm calculated.

She crossed the piazza to the *gelateria*. In its glass refrigerator, ice cream was arrayed in aluminum troughs like paints in a watercolor set. What would she have? Red raspberry — *lamponi*, she remembered, yellow *limone*? *Nocciola* — hazelnut? *Arancione* the color of the setting sun? She asked for a cup of vanilla.

I am *hap*py. Trochees. This elation was a child's greedy emotion, beginning in her stomach like hunger. She ought to push it away; it had nothing to do with her now. She pressed against the church door and the bolt rattled. It was locked and barred from the inside. Closed, of course.

"SANTA MARIA Sempre Chiusa" was what her father called Santa Maria dei Miracoli. Saint Mary Always Closed. "The miracle will be if it's ever open when we want to go inside," he said.

In Venice, Samuel Edgar worked in the morning, writing or preparing a course on Romantic Europe. Caroline and her mother went to the Lido. After overcoming her disappointment at a beach solid with cabanas and umbrellas, Caroline splashed in the gray waves and constructed canals in the sand. Her mother, coated in baby oil, lay face down on a chaise longue, a book opened in the sand below her. "Honey, if I lie here long enough, I'm betting that my freckles will merge into a tan," she said. Her blond curls fell loose around her head for optimal bleaching; she had combed lemon juice through her hair before they left the apartment. She unhooked the top of her bathing suit and pulled her shoulder straps down to avoid lines.

Caroline's parents were beings whom she knew intimately and not at all: mysterious as gods eternally consumed by domestic struggle, an ebb and flow of pleasure and aggravation that Caroline could not fathom and her mother denied. Even after her father left, even after his death when Caroline was sixteen, her mother remained loyal to him, loyal — Caroline came to believe — to the idea of him, and to their failed romance.

Margaret Stone had come to New York from Virginia during the fall of 1945 to study ballet. That spring, she met Samuel Edgar, newly discharged from the army, a graduate student in Romance languages and literature. "By the time he figured out that I wasn't Jewish — that my name hadn't once been Stein, it was too late," she told Caroline, in her soft drawl.

"How long was that?"

"About an hour." Margaret paused for effect. "It was love at first sight. It really was. No matter what happened afterward — no matter what he did."

"Could you have danced on stage in front of an audience?" Caroline asked, again and again.

"Honey, it was just a silly thing, dancing, just something I could do, and some things were more important, like him — and you." Her tone was loving and accusing.

Margaret's neck was long and smooth, and the lines of muscle along her spine met in a furrow over her vertebrae. At the Lido men smiled at her.

"Caro, he's watching you," her mother said one day, tilting her head in the direction of a bronzed, stocky young man.

"Nobody's watching me," Caroline retorted.

"Yes, he is."

It was the tone of her mother's voice, the teasing that masked something else, which made Caroline angry. She shouted, "It's not me! He's been watching you! I saw him. Leave me alone!"

She hunkered down in the sand. She could hardly stand to look at herself, tall and thin but with hips and breasts beginning. That summer, she caught her father regarding her with an expression of dismay, and she was ashamed, as if she should be able to stop herself from growing.

Halfway through the morning Margaret closed her book and fastened the top of her bathing suit. "Am I burned?" she asked her daughter every day. "Am I getting tan?"

"No," Caroline answered. "Yes."

Margaret rolled onto her back, and a few minutes after noon she rose lazily and strolled to the shore. As the waves lapped at her toasted ankles, she shivered and let Caroline tug her into the water. Once wet, she dove, her body sleek as she slid into the slapping surf, and water beaded on her oiled freckled arms. Caroline swam beside her into the deep water, purple under the cumulus. They were like two dolphins, Margaret said, and they arched under and surfaced. Back in the shallows, Caroline clung to her mother and rode her back, resting her head against the wings of her shoulder blades; her skin still held the heat of the sun. Afterwards, salty and dazed from the sun, they headed home for lunch.

"Back already?" Caroline's father would ask when they opened the door.

In the afternoons, they all explored: they went to churches and saw Titians, to the Accademia, to the islands in the lagoon, Murano, Torcello, even Pellestrina. They stopped in San Marco to watch the clock strike the hour. In the evenings they attended recitals in palazzas, opera at La Fenice. Samuel listened rapturously, with an amateur's uncritical love.

The way home led past Santa Maria dei Miracoli, tinged gold in the sunset or glowing white under the moon late at night after *Rigoletto* or *Don Giovanni*.

"We have poetic feet," her father said. He and Caroline skipped in iambs and waltzed in dactyls.

"Can you imagine," he said with bitterness, "can you imagine living in a place and time where beauty was urgent? Where poetry was read and poets mattered?"

"Sam, don't. Isn't it enough that we're here?" Margaret chided. "Sam, be happy."

"Is that an order?" he asked, and Caroline saw her mother wince.

"I was only trying to make you realize what you do have."

"Don't you think I know?" he retorted.

In August, Margaret stayed home in the afternoons; over the summer, the sun seemed to have bleached vitality from her. "Go," she told her husband and daughter. "Go. I'm tired. You'll have more fun without me." When they came back at twilight, she would have arranged two stacks of paper, originals and carbons, on the ornate grand piano in the *salotto* of their small apartment: Samuel's lecture notes or drafts of poems. They found her asleep, one of her husband's books splayed on her chest.

CAROLINE AND her father stopped first at the American Express office near the Piazza San Marco, and often as not the clerk handed Samuel a thin blue airmail envelope. He smiled at it, but he never opened it.

"Who are they from?" Caroline asked.

"School," he answered.

"Why don't they come to the apartment?"

"Those secretaries." He shrugged. "Before I knew where we were going to live, I told them to send mail in care of American Express." He tucked the envelopes into his shirt pocket. "Now, where to today? What about San Zaccaria?"

In August, the city had emptied of Venetians, but tourists never strayed far from San Marco. Caroline and her father strolled along the Riva degli Schiavoni — her father explained that *schiavo* meant "slave" in Italian, but Schiavoni were Dalmatians.

"Dogs?"

"No. People. Spotted people."

"Daddy, you're lying."

"But, Caro, wouldn't it be nice? Dalmatia is the old name for the coast of Yugoslavia, just across the Adriatic. It used to belong to Venice, but it doesn't anymore. Nothing does."

The day was humid and overcast and the oily gray water of the lagoon lapped against the embankment. Inside the cool church, Samuel wandered from chapel to chapel; as he did not like to be seen consulting a guidebook, he read beforehand, then by memory tried to match artists with their works of art. Sometimes, before she began staying home, Margaret slipped the book into her purse. "You're such a tourist, Meg," her husband said when she pulled it out. Caroline preferred her father's information, a conglomerate of anecdote, invention, and fact. "This must be the Bellini," he said, as they passed a chapel. "*Sacra Conversazione.* That means 'holy talk.' But don't worry about what these paintings mean — or what they stand for. It's all Christian legends. Your mother can explain them to you."

"She converted, Daddy."

"But that doesn't mean she forgot."

Caroline followed him through a door in the nave to a small, unadorned chapel with two altars. A painting stood on each one. Altarpieces, Caroline knew that much, with saints and Jesus Christ, who was Jewish, and his mother, Mary. "Her blue dress, Caro. The paint was made from ground-up lapis lazuli. Wonderful words. A semiprecious stone, the most beautiful blue. And the green — that's malachite. The halos are real gold. They painted it on, gold and lapis lazuli and malachite."

Caroline was dazzled by the colors and by their origins, and enthralled and frightened, too, by the faces showing grand emotion: tenderness, grief, and awe.

"'Old civilizations put to the sword,'" said Samuel.

"What's that?" asked Caroline.

"It's a line from a poem called 'Lapis Lazuli.' You'll read it one day."

"You can read it to me."

He touched her shoulder — she had grown too tall for him to stroke her hair the way he used to — and she was afraid of the love and misery she saw in his face. It was the end of August; they had only two more weeks in Venice.

"I am going to make statues out of gold and silver," she said.

"I am sure you will," her father told her.

That afternoon, when they returned to the apartment, Caroline picked up the sheaf of poems her mother had typed and left on the piano. For weeks she had been typing revisions, and revisions of revisions. "Give them a rest, Sam," Margaret said. "They're fine the way they are."

He had rebuked her: "What do you know?" Black letters cut into the heavy paper, and fuzzy gray ones floated like ghosts on the tissue carbon. The words resisted Caroline's efforts to grasp them. *Bone dust, burned memory, ashes blown south* — they caused Caroline's stomach to contract with anxiety.

"What is that about?" she asked.

"Nothing," her father answered, and he took the paper away from her.

"Daddy!"

"Nothing," he repeated. "Nothing. I was trying to imagine nothing. A poem isn't about — it started with the ghetto here, nothing is left, no life, no memory. I don't know if I managed." He hung his head. "Don't be a poet, Caro, whatever you do. It's too much for the people around you to understand —"

"But I understand."

"No, you don't."

"Don't understand what?" Margaret had gotten out of bed and stood at the doorway to their living room.

"Nothing," Samuel answered. He shook his head, as if he were getting rid of a pesky mosquito. He laughed, attempting to modulate the mood. "Well, what should we do?" He held out his arms to Caroline, but she did not come to them. "Now, come on, Caroline Edgar-di! Dactyls. I'm going to change our name, so we can waltz to it. Samuel Edgardi. Caroline Edgardi." He glanced at his wife in the doorway. "Margaret Edgardi. Signora Edgardi, may I have this dance?" He crossed the room.

But Margaret said, "There's no music."

"You're the dancer, Meg. You should know you don't need music."

"Was the dancer." She stood straight, arms tight to her sides, feet turned out from habit.

Samuel frowned, turned from his wife, embraced his daughter, and swung her in a waltz. But she pulled herself from her father's arms and ran after her mother into the bedroom. Margaret lay on the bed. When her daughter came in, she sat up, and her hair shone gold in the light of the lamp. She smiled. "Come here, honey," she said. Caroline lay beside her and curled to fit into the curve of her mother's outstretched arm. Nothing was wrong; her panic subsided.

That innocent summer she had waltzed with her father here, too, beside the canal, after gelato. *One* two three, *one* two three. Dactyls.

SUDDENLY, from one of the buildings that walled the square, Caroline heard a piano. She recognized the music: Beethoven. After a few measures the sonata broke off in a discordant, frustrated run; somebody was practicing. Caroline turned on the hemisphere of marble paving at the entrance to the church, confronting a memory. Ludovico — his frayed cuffs, his strong white wrists laced with veins beside her thin brown ones: her piano teacher that summer. A piano as splendid as the one in their apartment demanded to be used, and Ludovico had been recommended by another American professor. "You play the right hand; I will play the bass," he said, in his musical voice. He helped her fingers shift through the chords of the barcarole; she smelled the starch of his shirt over a slight stinging odor of sweat and shivered with pleasure and confusion. At the end of the afternoon the room was almost dark.

"Caro!" Her father switched on the light. Ludovico sat up straight. The piano bench creaked.

"I'm learning Beethoven," she pleaded, found out.

"*Sua figlia sente la musica col cuore.*" In his distress Ludovico spoke Italian. He corrected himself: "She understands with her heart."

"You leave her heart alone," Samuel shouted.

In the piazza, the pianist began again, more slowly. Caroline wiped away tears with the back of her hand. It was jet lag, that was all. She looked at her watch; it was nearly one. Malcolm's meeting was certainly over. He cared a great deal about time. She directed the driver of a water taxi to the hotel. He gunned the engine and they veered around a carpenter's scow and turned right into the Rio del Paradiso.

Will Lucas stood at the iron balustrade of a bridge, the sun behind him; he leaned out over the water as if he expected her. Caroline gripped the roof of the cabin; if she didn't hold on, she might lift off and float, weightless, past him straight into paradise.

It had to be Will. The man was slender and not too tall; he had dark hair and stood with a lazy grace. And time ran backward and fairy tales came true. "Will!" she called, and waved her arm. "Will!" The desperate joy in her voice jolted her, as if the sound had come from another person's throat. The driver looked at her quizzically. He slowed the taxi as it approached the bridge.

The man she was hailing was not Will. Blood flooded her face in embarrassment and anger.

Will was dead. His car had spun out of control on the Mystic River Bridge in Boston. He had been thrown free and had fallen into the river. How? Did he plummet straight? Did he tumble? She had read the news in a small article at the beginning of May, just six weeks ago, a wire service filler. He had not been wearing a seat belt, police said. The guardrails were inadequate.

She had folded the paper — the front page that morning carried the news of the eruption of Mount St. Helens — and laid it on the breakfast table. Will would have relished that tectonic catastrophe. And the Mystic Bridge: it might not have been an accident. "Where does the Mystic River go?" he had once teased. "How can I find out?" Or maybe he was just driving across in an altered state — mystical mushrooms? — and misjudged a curve.

CAROLINE HAD confessed to Malcolm each name on her little list of conquests, paring herself back to innocence in a grand absolution. With each one Malcolm possessed her again, relishing vicariously the gleeful promiscuity of her generation; he saw her as a pioneer. She did not contradict him. He regretted, he said, missing out on this revolution. "That was how you felt," she said. "No strings."

"But the girls didn't agree, so I ended up married."

"With a baby."

"That one always got what she wanted." Malcolm shrugged. "Will, though — he lasted," Malcolm said.

"Not even a year." She sought to make Will sound inconsequential; she did not reveal herself completely to Malcolm; she kept Will back.

"What happened to him?"

"I don't know. He stopped drawing — he made beautiful drawings, but he said art didn't mean enough to him anymore. He was thinking about architecture; maybe he's an architect now, maybe even a geologist. He'd started to smoke a lot of dope. He said that it made him believe that sitting was a worthy thing."

"Did you?"

"Did I what?"

"Smoke pot?"

"Sure, everybody did. But I didn't do it a lot."

"Can you get some?"

"Probably."

"Poor kid. What did he mean about sitting?"

"He lost sight of ambition, maybe. I'm not sure."

"He sounds like he was nuts."

She shrugged. "Maybe. Possibly."

CAROLINE HAD met Will at the Isabella Stewart Gardner Museum, a Venetian palace translated to the sluggish Muddy River around the corner from the Museum School. It faced the street brown and windowless, a middle-class fortress against the industrial age.

She and Will met in the courtyard, at the stairs. Caroline and Deirdre were going up, Will Lucas and Stan Lerner were coming down. Deirdre introduced Will reluctantly.

"Looks like a funeral today, doesn't it?" Will nodded toward the pots of lilies banking the low walls.

"Or Easter," said Caroline.

"Same thing," said Will.

"Well, I think it looks like Eden."

"Maybe you're right." Will smiled at Caroline with reckless receptivity, a charged absence asking to be completed. "What are you doing here?"

"Going to look at the Cellini bronze," Caroline answered, "the bust. Not that you can see it, the way it's stuck so high on the wall."

Will nodded. He wore paint-splattered jeans low on his hips, and in the dim loggia, his deep blue eyes were changeable, like water. Caroline knew his reputation for damage. Deirdre started up the stairs.

"I'll come with you," Will said.

"What about your friend?"

"Stan's in love with his piano teacher. He's going to hear her rehearse — you know, lurk in the back."

The red silk brocade on the gallery's walls had faded to an autumnal rose. They gazed up at the bronze head. "Bindo Altoviti." Will read the label.

"You like it because it's the same kind of thing you do," said Deirdre to Caroline.

"I wish."

"Raphael painted his portrait," Will said, "when Bindo was a young man. The painting's in the National Gallery in Washington. He was beautiful when he was young. Bindo." Will grinned when he pronounced the name, tasting its sound.

"I never thought about him. Bindo." Caroline imitated Will's pronunciation.

"He was a rich banker. He gave artists work."

"Then thank you, Bindo." She studied the banker's lined and pensive face, his strong nose and sensual lips and luxurious beard. In middle age Will, though now beautiful and young, might look like this.

The sound of a piano rose through the courtyard. Deirdre had disappeared.

"She doesn't like you," Caroline said, smiling. "I tried to learn this sonata once, but I was too young."

She crossed the room to Titian's *Rape of Europa* and gazed at the lapis sea and the laughing cupids, the girl's tunic and cloak gusting off her flailing, parting legs in a red and orange pinwheel, the sunset clouds catching their colors from her drapery.

"Look at the mountains," Will said, "the Dolomites."

"The mountains?" She smiled. "This is not a painting of mountains."

"But they're there. I like geology."

"I see." She was not looking at mountains.

"Caroline," said Will.

"Caro," she said.

"Caro. The music. It's a barcarole," he said. "Water music. Perfect."

What do I do? Caroline thought. Dance? Cry? Laugh? Toss my clothes to the winds right here?

"The poor girl doesn't have a chance," she said.

"She climbed on the bull's back." Will smiled. "And she's holding his horn."

"Yes," Caroline said. "Yes, I do believe she is."

IN THE DAYS following Will's death, she had begun modeling a falling figure. "What is this?" Malcolm asked.

"Icarus." She lied. "Icarus. I took the legs from Brueghel's painting. You can see only his legs as he falls into the sea."

"I don't like it. Too depressing."

"Don't look at it then." A desire to accommodate Malcolm had gone dead.

"You saw that obituary in the *Times*?" he asked.

"Which one?"

"Your friend — William Lucas."

"There was an article."

"Too bad."

"Yes. It was an accident. It was terrible."

William Lucas. May 10, 1980. Survived by his parents Robert and Sandra Lucas, grandfather David Lucas, grandparents Irene and Martin Rosenbaum, brother Henry. Suddenly.

GILBERT PRYCE stood on the bridge daydreaming about falling — a drunken stumble, a well-timed shove, and into the canal: convenient for revenge. There had been no bridge railings until the nineteenth century. It was interesting, this shifting to the state of the responsibility for protection; it coincided with the diminishing belief that God, if there even was one, paid attention to human affairs. Interesting, but the truth was, Gilbert was at loose ends. Massimo Farsetti had canceled lunch — something had come up. With Massimo, it was always up.

"If you wouldn't wear those clothes . . ." Massimo had said.

"What's wrong with my clothes?"

"So American. You can't tell what's in there." Massimo tugged at the voluminous fabric in the legs of Gilbert's khakis. "You would meet women, too."

"What if I don't want to? I don't want to meet women. That's why I'm here — one of the reasons, anyway."

"If you're like that . . ." Massimo shrugged, eloquently, suggesting that he wouldn't judge.

"I am not like that. It's complicated."

Massimo shrugged again. "No, Gil" — he pronounced the name with a soft *g* — "really, it is simple."

The woman was waving at him. She was nobody he knew; unlikely people turned up in Venice, but equipped with his phone number, not his picture. She wore dazzling white — white pants and a white sweater that hung loosely on her tan shoulders. She looked immaculate, too clean to be outside, too perfect to be wildly waving at a stranger.

He gripped the Hapsburg railing; the strength of his response — attraction and aversion — unbalanced him. As her boat approached, he realized he was not who she thought he was, and he witnessed her disappointment and embarrassment. It was too late to look away. No matter: he would never see her again.

She had a narrow face, with a long nose and full lips, too strong for her pointed chin and sharp jaw. Her short dark hair gleamed like a raven's feathers. At first she had appeared to be in her twenties, but from the angles of her sharp bones Gilbert guessed that she was older.

The boat pulled up at a landing just past the bridge. As the woman disembarked, her shopping bag got tangled in her legs like a puppy. She laughed and paid, and when the driver opened his pocketbook to give her change, she refused, smiling. She looked from side to side, took a few steps, then stopped and looked again. Glancing at her watch, whose wide metal bracelet enclosed her wrist like a handcuff, she strode off in her high, thick-heeled sandals with elaborate straps — shoes like those of an eighteenth-century Venetian courtesan, exaggerated platforms that lifted a woman over the muck and flooding of the streets.

Gilbert sighed and kept walking. He walked every day to clear dust from his lungs and oppression from his mind after his work in the ghetto, whose tall houses tilted like tombstones in an ancient graveyard. Passing the iron sheaths, which once held hinges for heavy gates and now remained embedded like fossils in the stone wall, he felt as if he had been released from prison.

He had spent this morning in the Scuola Grande Tedesca, where a rabbi, Leon Modena, had presided in the seventeenth century; Gilbert was writing his biography. The rabbi had written an account of his life, a record of the Jewish community's precarious existence at the whim of Christian authority. Reconstructing Jewish Venice, Gilbert located obscure manuscripts in ecclesiastical libraries and tracked names in civic archives; that kind of legal research had not changed in centuries. He was indulging in a sabbatical from his firm, funded by a small grant and a legacy from his grandmother. What had begun as curiosity had become a calling; it had also provided an escape from disappointment in love. Massimo, if he knew, would laugh and shrug; Massimo scorned romantic obligation.

In the synagogue, with its cracked and dismal paneling, its dulled brass menorahs, Gilbert had, that morning, deciphered one of Rabbi Leon's sermons, dense with allusions to biblical verses and elaborate puns interlacing Hebrew and Italian. Now he walked off disappointment; he had been looking forward to describing its arcane brilliance to Farsetti.

He slowed down. The woman in white was ahead of him, walking fast, but she hesitated at a corner and entered an alley that doubled back on itself. Gilbert liked that little street, that *calle,* for its devious, wicked Venetian humor. The woman emerged, started off in one direction, then made an about-face, her lips compressed. She hiked her purse, a pale leather satchel soft as a pillow, onto her shoulder and turned into another obscure *calle,* by luck or instinct choosing a shortcut to the Piazza San Marco. His route, too: he had an appointment at the library later.

The noon sun erased shadows, and it grew hot, a bright, fresh June heat. Tomorrow, if the weather held, Gilbert decided to go out into the lagoon; the Dolomites would be visible. He would like to ask this woman to come with him, he thought, irrationally; he could say "This is your chance to see why there are mountains in the background of all those altarpieces. It happens only a couple of days a year." She might well think that an altarpiece was an article of clothing you tied behind your neck. He was lonelier than he wanted to admit.

When she reached the Orologio in the corner of the piazza a faint smile of success curled at the corner of her mouth. She darted through the strolling crowds. "*Scusi,*" she said. "*Permesso.*" Her voice was light; he had not expected her to speak Italian. She paused for a moment to glance into the vitrine of an antiquarian shop, where a small bronze figure was displayed. She raised her hand to block her reflection in the glass, and an enormous diamond flashed on her finger.

Gilbert laughed at himself. She belonged to somebody. If he saw her again, it would be by luck.

IT WAS JUST one o'clock; Caroline restrained herself from going in to inquire after the little statue. Instead, she went back to the Orologio, its cobalt face blue as heaven and ringed by the constellations of the astrological year. The two bronze Moors flanking the clock raised their mallets and struck their bells and the Magi made their mechanical procession. The girl she had been, and the young woman, crowded in on her: her childish delight, her young woman's rapture.

She was wrung out. Her feet were blistered. She shouldn't have left the taxi, but she had lost her bearings. It was jet lag; she wasn't herself. Or she was, as she had been.

Marriage had muted feelings; she had married Malcolm to limit their sway, to shore herself up. Will used to sing a song:

> *I leaned my back up against an oak*
> *Thinking he was a trusty tree,*
> *But first he bended, and then he broke;*
> *And so did my false love to me.*

But Malcolm was an I-beam. If there was no give, she had believed that he would not break; she had expected him to gird her against —life. She started across the piazza.

Pigeons and people swirled, clustering and separating. A child

66

flapped his arms and charged the birds. Caroline approved; she'd done that herself. She hated pigeons. During her Venetian summer, she had suffered direct hits twice here in San Marco. Her father laughed while her mother daubed at the slime with a napkin begged from Florian's. Margaret Edgar had been thirty-three, the age Caroline was now. She wore full skirts in bright colors, orange and red, and wide belts. When she walked with her dancer's turnout she commanded the stage of the piazza.

Now, from Quadri's and Florian's, competing orchestras dueled in amplified cacophony. Nothing had changed. As Caroline strode across the piazza, a squadron of pigeons took off, wings snapping, and flew low, burbling and cooing in their angry avian dialect. She ducked and veered away from their onslaught, caught her heel on a paving stone, and crashed into a tourist.

The girl fell heavily, with Caroline on top of her. The shopping bag skidded across the basalt pavement, a frill of yellow silk spilling from tissue paper. The girl screamed; the crowd shifted in the direction of the noise. "*Scusi, scusi! Mi dispiace! Le ho fatto male?*"

The girl lay still; she wore no makeup, her dark hair had been pulled into a careless ponytail, and her faded T-shirt read A WOMAN WITHOUT A MAN IS LIKE A FISH WITHOUT A BICYCLE. Cleaned up, she would be pretty; Caroline realized that she was speaking the wrong language. "Are you okay? I'm so sorry! Can you get up?"

"You broke my tailbone."

The girl's companion, a tall, freckled girl with a heavy red braid down her back, crouched beside her. "Perry! What did that crazy woman do to you?"

"Courtney — she speaks English, she's —"

"American," Caroline said. She laughed, from embarrassment and exhaustion and at the idea of sitting in San Marco in her white silk pants. She could not stop laughing, and the crowd, sensing a diminishing drama, dispersed.

Perry sat up. "What's so funny?"

"Me, mostly."

"It is pretty funny." Perry glanced at Caroline's hand and Malcolm's diamond. It was a recent acquisition, not precisely an anniversary present, more of an investment. Caroline had designed the lattice of platinum in which it was set to draw attention away from its daunting size. She stood, elegant and unsteady, retrieved her shopping bag, and tried to brush the dirt off her pants.

"It looks like pigeon shit," said Perry, as she hoisted her backpack.

"It wouldn't be the first time," Caroline said.

"Venice is full of them."

"They're mostly here, in San Marco. Like tourists."

Perry blushed. "Well, we just got here. Tell me something — you know the city?"

"I used to."

"By the way, I'm Perry, and this is Courtney."

"Yes, I heard. I'm Caroline. Caroline Spingold." She extended her hand and smiled to herself at the adolescent assumption that first names sufficed.

"Spingold?"

"Like Rumpelstiltskin."

"The Hôtel de l'Europe. We can't find it."

"It's on the Grand Canal near here. I'm going in that direction — come with me."

"Not the Europa," Perry said impatiently. "The Hôtel de l'Europe. They're not the same."

"Sorry." Caroline looked across the square. It was the light and water: light came from below, reflecting up from the water's surface onto parts of her heart she had kept hidden. She was losing her armor, her immunity, her sense of safety. Even these girls taunted her with their liberty.

Courtney pulled a book bound in worn red leather from her backpack. "I have this Baedeker — here; it says it's the grandest hotel in Venice." She handed the book to Caroline.

"But this was published in 1903."

"I know. It's a little new," Perry said. "George Eliot stayed there in 1880 when she came to Venice on her honeymoon. I'm writing my senior thesis on her. I'm calling it 'How George Eliot Betrayed Marian Evans.'"

"Marian Evans?"

"Her real name," offered Courtney.

"She infuriates me," said Perry. "Her heroines get married, at least some of them, the ones who don't die. They get boring, happy endings."

"What's wrong with a happy ending?" said Caroline. "It's better than throwing yourself under a train."

"Practically the same thing, if you ask me. Why do you always need a guy?"

Caroline figured she was twelve, maybe thirteen years older than these girls, though it felt more like a generation separated them. Perry's T-shirt could have belonged to an older sister or an aunt. It could even have belonged to Caroline, if she had not mistrusted collective movements. She could not attribute personal difficulties to societal injustice. Her weaknesses — her doubt, her need to not be alone — she saw as her own responsibility. She was not a generalization.

"Biology?" Caroline said. "Love?"

Perry looked disgusted.

But there was something endearing about these girls. They were confident and serious, and they expected approbation. "It's a terrific title," Caroline said. "I wish I could have helped you find your hotel."

She handed back the book and moved away slowly, reluctant to leave this soft heat for the air-conditioned hotel suite.

As she took a few steps, she looked back and saw the man who was not Will. Courtney was approaching him, Baedecker in hand. He looked straight at Caroline over the girl's shoulder. He did not resemble Will at all; he was taller, his hair was lighter, and his clothes were shapeless. She had dressed him with desire.

She had to hurry. Malcolm would be wondering where she was, and when he was upset he got angry. He might call the *carabinieri*. She wouldn't put it past him; he was good at anger, and he enjoyed a scene. She would have to pay for provoking him.

Chapter 3

Venice, 11 June 1880

MRS. JOHN WHARLTON BUNNEY dressed like a pigeon, although she probably believed herself a dove. Her gray weskit puffed over her bosom, and the tails of her gray jacket folded along her back like wings. She bobbed her sleek head over the plate she handed Marian. "I wish we could offer our distinguished visitors a more elaborate tea," she cooed, "but Mr. Bunney has dedicated his life to Art, and I must make do." She paused, considered this particular visitor, and added: "As you have devoted your life, Mrs. Cross — but the world has rewarded your efforts."

Marian bristled at the hint of censure in her hostess's remark, then rebuked herself for being too sensitive. "The world, Mrs. Bunney, offers many rewards," she responded. "Mr. Ruskin admires your husband. In England everyone is talking about his great endeavor, which would not be possible without your help."

"It is my lot in life, and I do my best." Mrs. Bunney preened while her round eyes appraised the brooch at Marian's neck as if it were a tasty breadcrumb. "What a lovely ornament. It is from de Levis? Do you know him? A cultured man, even if he is —"

Marian raised her hand to her neck and shielded the jewel. "Did you not send my husband to Signor de Levis?" Mrs. Bunney was

Commerce to her husband's Art; probably she would demand a commission from Signore de Levis. Despite Mrs. Bunney's protestations, the couple seemed prosperous enough. It was a marriage Marian felt she ought to admire, but a disturbing parallel suggested itself; was this how Mrs. Bunney understood Marian's marriage to Johnnie? A similar arrangement? Artist and acolyte — and did the reversed roles offend this relentless little woman?

Marian blushed with shyness. This was their first social invitation since their marriage. Mrs. Cross — she was indeed Mrs. Cross. Her initial elation over her condition had subsided, replaced by caution, an awareness that every action, every word, public and private, was noticed and measured.

She smiled until the corners of her mouth were stinging with effort. Marriage required watchfulness. She might have been a novelist, but now she was a wife. Husband: how permanent it sounded when she spoke it preceded by "my" and reinforced by public ceremony. Married: no longer sustained by an act of will, but legally bound.

Mr. Bunney, angular and sprightly, a sparrow beside his wife, was talking to Johnnie, who listened with his perennial curiosity. The small room was well proportioned and light; its windows opened onto a little canal, and delicate architectural studies hung on the walls — Mr. Bunney's work. One end of the room was concealed by a curtain. Marian caught Mr. Bunney glancing meaningfully at Johnnie's teacup and then at Mrs. Bunney. Johnnie had barely tasted his cake, and his cup remained half full; each day he seemed to eat less.

"May I offer you a little more?" asked Mrs. Bunney, not reaching for the pot.

Johnnie declined; this seemed to be the signal. Mr. Bunney cleared his throat and stood beside the curtain. His fringe of graying brown hair was just long enough to suggest an artist's disregard for convention. "You have, no doubt, seen how restoration is destroying San Marco; how the magnificent mosaics — ancient and worn — are being replaced by coarse replicas."

"We have not spent much time there since the first day," Johnnie said. "We have kept to a busy schedule visiting the pictures my wife loves — I follow her everywhere. But now that I think about it, the scaffolding does rather spoil the façade."

"It is a desecration," Mr. Bunney answered, with quiet vehemence. "Nothing less. The city is being stripped of its glory. If some American millionaire were to come along and offer to buy a mosaic from inside the basilica, I wouldn't be surprised if the Venetians chiseled it out of the ceiling for him. But there will be a record — a poor alternative to the original, yet a record, nonetheless."

As he spoke, Mr. Bunney pulled on a heavy cord, and the blue velvet curtains parted to reveal his masterpiece. The basilica of San Marco loomed as large as a stage set, and as flat. Each stone had been faithfully, painstakingly rendered, astonishingly free from any emotion besides the fever to record. Mrs. Bunney, standing on the other side of the proscenium, gazed worshipfully at her husband's work.

Marian caught her breath audibly, and Mrs. Bunney smiled her appreciation. But the tableau — the painting and the couple — aroused in Marian pity mixed with exasperation: pity for the man, for his devotion, and for his wife supporting him; pity not only for their wasted time but for the work's hopeless premise. What was gone was gone; no painting could preserve it. Yet the Bunneys ridiculously claimed for themselves a holy purpose, a righteous superiority, as if they were beleaguered missionaries.

She wished that the painting did not evoke such feelings; she could be misunderstanding it. Perhaps it was simply amusing in its accretion of chaotic detail. It might be a monument to misplaced objectivity, a heroic misuse of the methods of observation, and Marian supposed that it could be in its mistaken way quite wonderful. Then Mrs. Bunney could be the accomplice in an inadvertent comedy. To see it like that would be a kindness, but Marian was not sure that she wanted to be kind.

"Ah," she breathed. But breath was no longer enough; Mrs. Bunney waited on edge as if Marian had forgotten her lines.

"I am speechless," she managed to murmur. "He has left nothing out."

"There is nothing that gives me more pleasure," said Mr. Bunney, "than to know that you approve of my small efforts."

"Your great efforts," Johnnie amended.

Johnnie approached the painting and peered at the mosaic archways, then stepped back to take in the whole once again. "It's marvelous," he declared. "Far better than a photograph. I don't like photographs. It's the colors, don't you think, Marian? This painting is more real to me than the building itself. And I must say, this room is far more congenial than that dirty, crowded piazza."

"Thank you," Mr. Bunney said heartily. "Thank you, thank you!"

"Where will it go?"

"Mr. Ruskin has promised it a home in England where the public will be able to see it."

"It is an homage to the past, a gift to the future."

Mr. Bunney beamed.

Marian frowned, amazed and disturbed that her husband could sincerely like such mediocrity. She was disappointed morally, as if he had failed an important test. But it was only a silly picture, only a matter of taste; their opinions did not have to be congruent. She should not allow herself to remember that she and George would have laughed about it, and about the Bunneys.

"Oh, Mr. Cross, you are astute!" exclaimed Mrs. Bunney. "You notice the colors—he must get the colors right. He refuses to paint from memory—"

"Absolutely not," interjected Mr. Bunney. "That would defeat my purpose."

"He suffers so for his work," Mrs. Bunney went on. "Why, just the other day, the most terrible thing—"

"Please sit down," Mr. Bunney hastened to say, and walked his visitors back to the sitting room. "If you permit me, I'll show you my sketches, and views of other Venetian monuments. My dear, I'm sure our visitors don't want to hear anything terrible."

"But yes," urged Marian. "Yes, we do. Terrible things are always interesting, I find. Tell us, please."

Mrs. Bunney, vindicated, nestled into the sofa. "It was just at noon—Mr. Bunney prefers noon light for his work, you know—and he had set up his easel and his umbrella—there are so many pigeons—well, I suppose they are picturesque—"

"I think they are abominable," said Johnnie.

Mrs. Bunney nodded. "And he felt a little pat on his back—it was that charlatan who calls himself an artist—oh, he makes me shudder. Jimmy Whistler—he leaned over my husband's shoulder and complimented him on his work. 'Well,' I said to Mr. Bunney, 'you should have known right away that something was up.' But my husband is utterly unsuspecting—"

"I was deceived. But I thought that a fellow artist—a bad one, but a colleague, nonetheless—"

"Mr. Bunney—would you like to tell the story?" his wife asked severely.

"No, no, my dear—you have the knack."

Mrs. Bunney's bright eyes flickered toward Marian. "Well, then. Mr. Bunney noticed that passersby were looking at him strangely. They often admire his work, but not with quite that degree of—incredulity. When Mr. Bunney reached into his kit for a sharp pencil, he discovered that someone—had tucked money inside—"

"As if I were a beggar!" interposed Mr. Bunney.

"Well, who should come by but dear Mr. Boit—you know him, of course, Mrs. Cross? No? An American, but he lives on the Continent. And he's a fine watercolorist, for an amateur. 'Bunney,' he said, 'do you know what you have on your back?'"

Mrs. Bunney paused and opened her avid eyes as wide as they would go. "Should I tell Mr. and Mrs. Cross what happened next?" She cocked her head and went on. "Mr. Boit pulled a square of cardboard from Mr. Bunney's back. That Jimmy Whistler must have stuck it there, and on it he had written"—Mrs. Bunney gazed at her guests, her eyes narrowed and her jaw clenched—"I AM BLIND."

Marian could not help herself. She smiled.

"You are amused?" demanded Mrs. Bunney.

"At the blindness of those who take what they read for truth, despite the evidence." Marian shook her head censoriously, she hoped. Johnnie was gravely shaking his head too, so she had made the appropriate response. She asked, "Now tell me, is this the same Whistler who sued Mr. Ruskin for libel?"

Mr. Bunney nodded solemnly. "The very same. He lost everything, you know. He had to sell everything to pay the court costs for that ridiculous lawsuit. He deserved to pay—accusing Mr. Ruskin of calumny!"

"But Whistler won, did he not?" Marian asked.

Mr. Bunney smiled. "He won a farthing in damages."

"What did Ruskin write about Whistler's painting?" Johnnie asked. "It was clever."

"'Cockney impudence,'" Mrs. Bunney clucked with satisfaction. "Mr. Ruskin wrote, and I quote, 'I never expected to hear a coxcomb ask two hundred guineas for flinging a pot of paint in the public's face.' Two hundred guineas — can you imagine?"

Marian was sure that Mrs. Bunney had, indeed, imagined, and had also in her imagination spent those guineas. She had a genius for the inconsequential. To turn the conversation, Marian ventured, "If I have a violent reaction to a painting or a piece of music, I might question my ability to understand it."

Mr. Bunney pursed his lips and shut his eyes. "Not this, Mrs. Cross; you would be right to despise this. His work offends me; it is unfinished, it is careless. The subjects are banal, or inappropriate — he saw fit to paint a coal works by the Thames. Mrs. Cross, I assure you, everything he does is ugly."

"But I wonder if ugliness does not lie at the core of art. Think of it: a crucifixion is a terrible death, but contemplating it in a painting we find comfort and exaltation."

Mrs. Bunney raised her eyes to heaven; Mr. Bunney coughed.

Johnnie looked alarmed. "But it happened so long ago," he said, and everybody had to laugh.

It was an unaccustomed sensation, to be rescued from embarrassment. Marian felt a growing sympathy for this painter who could so offend the Bunneys. "Then, tell me, what is Mr. Whistler doing in Venice?"

"Oh, some society took pity on him and commissioned him to make some etchings," said Mr. Bunney. "He's trying to salvage his reputation —"

"Reputation? He dresses like a common workman — and with that appalling white streak in his hair —"

They were describing the man Marian had seen in the Piazza San Marco on their first day in Venice.

"He can't help his hair," interjected Mr. Bunney.

"Parading around with that immoral girl on his arm — that girl he hired as a model — an upholsterer's daughter. And worse — they have had a child." Mrs. Bunney twittered with indignation.

Marian bit her lip. Was Mrs. Bunney unaware of her connection with George Lewes, or had fame rendered it legitimate? Marian said, "The girl must be having a hard time of it. Is the child with them?"

"At least she had the sense to send the child off to be raised in a decent household."

"Ah," Marian said quietly, gazing implacably at Mrs. Bunney, who fluttered her skirts nervously, finding herself in the sights of a cat.

"Please, will you show us your sketches, Mr. Bunney?" Johnnie said, jumping up from the sofa. "We are eager for a look. Why spend time discussing an incompetent artist," he insisted, glaring at his wife, "when we can enjoy the work of an artist of the first rank?"

Mr. Bunney, apparently noticing nothing amiss, placed a portfolio on the tea table, and Johnnie leafed through the fastidious drawings. "Which shall we have, my dear, to remind us of Venice — and of our new friends?"

"I must tell you," Mr. Bunney cautioned, "that the watercolors cost more —"

"But they are far more evocative," Mrs. Bunney inserted. "Why, the colors —"

"Yes," said Johnnie, "the colors."

The colors were pallid and insipid, as if they had faded in the sun. Marian could not look at them. If Mr. Bunney chose to waste his time, that was his business, but she did not want him to waste hers. She longed to be outside, away from this close, humid, suffocating apartment. "I am so sorry, but it is getting late," she announced suddenly, and rose and walked toward the door. "We have already taken up too much of your afternoon. And I — I am feeling quite light-headed."

She could not soften the sharpness in her voice. She wished that her spirit were pliable and her desires mild, that marriage had instilled in her the wifely virtues — patience and tolerance, compliance.

Johnnie, his tired blue eyes rimmed with dark circles, frowned; she had gone too far. She was frustrating him in his choice of society and in his passion for possession; he wanted these drawings.

"Finally, I have tired out my indefatigable wife." Johnnie spoke with an edge of triumph as he turned to Marian. "Mr. and Mrs. Bunney have very kindly offered to take us tomorrow to places tourists don't usually visit. They will show us the real Venice."

"It will be a great pleasure to show *you* something — you have seen so much, you have lived such a large life, I am sure I cannot begin to imagine it. But we have discovered places that will delight even you." Mrs. Bunney cocked her clever head toward Marian.

"You have already shown me a great deal." Marian smiled blandly. She could not determine if Mrs. Bunney was goading her or offering an apology. She argued with herself: these people had offered friendship at a price she and Johnnie could easily afford. It could be that she was finding unintended meanings in Mrs. Bunney's conversation.

Mrs. Bunney carefully replaced her husband's sketches and began to fasten the portfolio's ribbons. "The Curtises are coming this evening," she said carelessly. "Do you know them? Oh, you should, they are Americans — but so cultured! So interested in Mr. Bunney's work. They have not yet seen these."

"In that case" — Johnnie went back, untied the portfolio, and lifted out two watercolors. "Mrs. Bunney, if you could hold these aside for us, I'd be most grateful."

"I promise you, Mr. Cross, nobody will see them before you make up your mind."

Outside, the weather had changed. The clarity of the past week had diminished and the air had grown oppressive. Coal smoke smothered the city, and the sun shone white and vague through haze.

"I do not like those sketches," Marian said.

Johnnie shook his head. "I thought they would please you. The Clock Tower and the Bridge of Sighs. Those two, especially. But you are tired; we have done enough for today. You will like them better tomorrow."

"I won't. I will never like them. They lack life."

"You are a hard judge, Marian," Johnnie said, "and you were hard on Mrs. Bunney."

"She was provoking me."

"She is in awe of you. I could see that — couldn't you?"

He was Commerce, she reminded herself, and in commerce one

judged people by what they did, not by what they meant. But she went on. "Mr. Bunney and his dedication to Art. Did you hear that? And she was not kind to Mr. Whistler and his poor girl. No, she was cruel — because it was easy to be so."

"Why should that matter to you, Mrs. Cross?" Johnnie took her arm possessively, as if by marrying her he had rescued her and made everything all right. He steered her toward their gondola. "And I do like those drawings. They have more life, I think, than the engravings you hang in your study — they are originals. Not that I know about such things —"

She withdrew her arm. Could it be that she was not made for marriage? If her life with George had excluded her from the world, it had also protected her. She had seen only those people whom she liked and admired and who liked and admired her in return. She had been liberated from social banality. Isolation had given her freedom — of thought, of imagination, of desire — and George's inability to marry her had weighted them equally one against the other.

"That is just my opinion, my dear, just my ignorant opinion." Johnnie spoke innocently, and she understood that he was choosing to ignore her fury. He had ideas about marriage, too.

"Buy them if you want, then. I didn't mean to stop you. I was not feeling well."

"I am so sorry; I had no idea." And suddenly Johnnie became attentive and concerned. He guided her into the shade, and she reproved herself: she was judging him harshly, holding him to impossible standards.

"But really, Johnnie, I do not think that Mrs. Bunney approves of lady novelists," she said, keeping her tone light, and thinking that, for the most part, neither did she.

"How can you say that? You have no proof of that. Marian, you're being so thin-skinned."

She was thin-skinned. But did he think that by marrying her he had removed the root cause of her sensitivity? As they waited for their gondolier to draw the boat to the embankment, she turned on him.

"I was too easy with Signor de Levis because he was a Jew and too hard with Mrs. Bunney because she is — what? A respectable lady? With a small mind and an ungenerous disposition? And am I supposed to tell smug, untalented Mr. Bunney that his views of Venice are equal to Canaletto's? Johnnie, you must give me lessons in how you would like me to behave."

"Marian, you tease me too hard, and you take things too hard. I don't know what else to say," Johnnie protested as he handed her into the gondola. "The Bunneys would be our friends." A barge laden with produce passed their gondola. Flies swarmed above the fruits and vegetables, and their ripe odor hung over the water. Johnnie covered his nose with his handkerchief. "Oh, how I hate that stink!"

"I rather like it. But then," Marian said, despising herself for being unable to forgive her husband's harmless, human inconsistencies, "I am capricious."

SHE HAD wanted to go alone to the Accademia to see the Bellinis, but she lacked the heart — and the courage — to tell him so. In the afternoon it had rained briefly, adding to the heaviness of the air. Humidity and smoke made the sunsets beautiful; pinks and yellows washed the sky, and thin bands of cloud on the western horizon gleamed like red and gold embroidery on brocade. Marian watched it unmoved; her growing detachment unnerved her.

She had shown Johnnie everything, she had led him from church to church; they had contemplated altarpieces and frescoes by Carpaccio, Tintoretto, Cima, Bellini. She had told him the stories of the saints — how odd that she, a nonbeliever, knew more about them than he did; she had discoursed on grace, composition, expression, harmony. She had preached like a jaded guide, pretending to enthusiasm. But the truth was, nothing touched her. Her transports were false.

Inside the Accademia it was stifling. At the entrance to the rooms where the Bellinis hung, Marian released Johnnie's arm. She gazed at the paintings, their brilliance muted under yellowed varnish, yet all the more vivid for what imagination — or faith — supplied.

"Marian." Johnnie, armed with Ruskin and Baedeker, beckoned her. But she did not want to lecture him now.

"Just a moment," she said. "Wait. Please."

She gazed at the bodies rendered in paint, the illusions of smooth skin and articulated muscles, lips smiling with pleasure, parted in passion, the embroidered silk and soft velvet that draped their shoulders. They were sublime, but today they could not affect her. All she felt was an encroaching, terrifying numbness.

It was what she had feared most after George had died, that her feelings would dry up and wither, that she would be left with a brittle carapace of intellect, without love.

"Marian," Johnnie insisted.

She stopped still, caught up short, as if by a leash.

"Marian, listen. This is what Ruskin says: 'Giovanni Bellini knows the earth well, paints it to the full — glittering robe and golden hair; to each he will give its luster and loveliness, and then, so far as with poor human lips he may declare it, far beyond all these, he proclaims that heaven is bright.'"

"There is no heaven," she said.

He stepped away from her. "Then you don't accept this?" He gestured at the holy figures surrounding them.

He knew what she believed. Did he think to domesticate that, too? She went on: "It is all here, all here on earth. Memory is as close as we can come to heaven." Before the sentence was out, she wished she had not spoken it. He would guess what she meant. But — and she did not know if this was better or worse — he might not mind.

He pinched his lips together, preparing to speak — to admonish or persuade, she supposed — and she cut him off. "Memory is what survives death. Now, please, Johnnie, leave me alone." She walked, scanning the walls, searching the paintings, craving to find in herself a trace of sympathy.

Fifteen years ago, when she saw them with George, these paintings had affected her like music. All her senses had been receptive; she had been in love, she had been open to the world. Love gave her clarity. It had been a kind of ecstasy.

She turned and gazed at Johnnie, with his sleek dark hair, his sharp and elegant jaw. Gaunt and unhappy, he diminished the paintings; he demanded her attention. He watched her pace, wondering, she guessed, where she was going and what she could be thinking now. She was wondering, too — at herself. For love — for him — she had entered a church to become his wife.

"NO," SHE HAD declared to her father forty years earlier. "I will not go to church with you." She shook, from fear and also from a physical joy, an exaltation, a release. Her legs were weak and she gripped the banister railing, but her voice was steely and loud. She confronted him on the stairs in the house in Coventry, close enough to him so that he could strike her if he chose — but he would never strike her.

Robert Evans clasped his prayerbook; wrapped in his cloak and muffler, he was prepared to go out into the bleak second morning of January 1842. "Are you ill?" he had asked, choosing not to understand.

"No. I am perfectly healthy." She struggled to modulate her voice. "But I cannot believe, so I cannot go to church."

"Mary Ann, please believe that you will come with me." His voice was deep and resonant; since before she could remember she had loved the reverberation of his baritone singing hymns beside her.

She lowered her head and remained where she was. Her father reached for her cloak on the peg beside her. "We cannot be late." He held the cloak out to her; she did not take it. The church bells were ringing.

"I cannot pretend that Jesus is the son of God."

Her father let her cloak fall to the floor. "This is your friends' doing! Those wicked people — that manufacturer of ribbons — that Charles Bray and his idle wife!"

"Charles Bray is not wicked! And Cara is not idle!" she answered vehemently. The Brays understood the changing world; they scrutinized evidence. They had recognized the qualities of Marian's mind, and they had encouraged her to rely upon that mind, to question, to consider. She could no longer simply accept, although, in truth, she never had; she was her father's daughter. Robert Evans was independent of mind and should know that she would accept nothing — not even for love — nothing that she did not believe. She stared her father down. "If they are wicked, then I am also."

Fear flared into anger; she could not stop shaking. But there was some truth in his accusation: she *was* wicked now — not because she rejected faith, but because it was cruel to make this declaration to him. Faith had sustained her father through the deaths of two wives; to faith he attributed his success as the steward of a great estate despite the encroachments of industry. She had not intended this scene; neither had she considered just how to inform her father of her decision — how to steer between obligation and conviction.

But this morning she could not go to church. She could not answer the summons of the bells and sit still for hours professing what
she could no longer believe. Not after a fortnight confined at home
with a friend, two somber weeks during which this old friend — yes,
she reminded herself, she had invited this woman — had entertained
her with tedious pious tracts, had refused to walk outside, had clung
to Marian like an incubus. Two weeks devoid of laughter. She had
not even had the heart to play the piano. She knew that the Brays
were jolly at Christmas; the two miles separating her house from
theirs seemed like a hundred.

She pushed a loose hairpin back into place. Charles Bray had held
her head in his fingers, delicately tracing the topography of her skull,
divining from its lobes and depressions the shape of her character.
Intellect, of course — Marian Evans's mind was a wonderful thing,
they all agreed — but also amativeness. She required affection; she
could not live without love.

Even if she had reservations about phrenology, that diagnosis was
accurate. And she was too observant not to have caught Cara's worried frown. For Marian love would not be easy, despite her intelligence, her sweet voice, and her auburn hair.

"Father — you must hear me out!"

"Mary Ann, you are a good, plain, honest girl, but those people
tease you with ideas, they call you by fancy names — Marian, Pollian.
I took this house to give you a place in the world. You are throwing
that place away."

"Father — show me proof that Jesus was divine — that he was
God made flesh!"

"Is faith not proof enough? Is the Bible not proof?"

"No. The Bible is fiction."

The bells clanged. All her life she had given her heart and her
spirit to worship. Each bell struck its own rhythm. They rang over-
lapping, then separate, then in unison: heavy, thrilling sounds.

"But I don't reject its teaching," she offered, as if that would appease him. "Or the idea of divinity — of a connective essence."

Her father grimaced. "Come with me."

"I cannot."

Robert Evans slammed the door shut. Marian watched him

through the window. He hurried, head bent and shoulders hunched. The sky was gray with scudding clouds. The bells ceased, and Marian, amazed and horrified at her victory, burst into tears. A sliver of light shot through a hole in the clouds, and she watched it glide over the hills. She put her hand in her pocket and drew out Cara's note from the evening before. *Come tomorrow morning, if you can. If only for an hour, please come. We long for you.*

The lines seemed to her a song. She glanced at her reflection in the windowpane. Marian, Marian, you have beautiful hair, Charles Bray had whispered while his hands caressed her skull. She lifted her cloak from the floor and flung it over her shoulders, grabbing at its buttons as she ran out into the brightening new year.

CHARLES BRAY was almost seventy now, and Marian rarely saw him and his wife anymore; Coventry was not convenient to London. Cara had sent a brief, pained note, as if she had not received Marian's letter announcing her marriage; knowing just the bare facts of that marriage, she wrote, she could only express her gladness that her friend had someone to cherish her.

Six weeks ago, on the sixth of May, Marian had walked, with her old elation and fevered expectation, toward Johnnie down the aisle of St. George's, Hanover Square.

CHARLES LEWES held her hand in the carriage for the short drive from the Priory to Hanover Square. The day was fine and warm; dollops of cumulus flecked the sky, and everywhere lilacs smelled of promise. She hesitated outside St. George's; she had not participated in a church service since her father died. "Charles, I need a moment."

He took both her hands and gazed at her in his attentive way, like his father. "He would have wanted this for you," Charles said.

As her eyes adjusted to the darkness of the church, she looked across the pews toward her tall bridegroom, who waited beneath the fine stained-glass windows of the apse. He stood solidly planted at the altar, feet apart like the athlete he was; gladness showed on his face. In the front row, his sisters and their husbands awaited her.

It was too late for uncertainty; it was as good as done. She took a deep breath and felt a strange and comforting thrill. It seemed to her that George was nudging her. "Polly," he whispered with his wry and tender smile. "Polly, what are you doing here? A church?" *But it is for love. I cannot live without it, and, this time, I'm getting married.* Her eyes filled with tears. She took Charles's arm again, and they walked down the aisle past the empty pews.

The priest murmured the words of the service and asked for objections. At that moment there were none, not even a skip of protest from her own heart.

AND NOW she must hold her peace. She continued to pace the perimeter of the Accademia gallery. The first time they had come here, she had held George's arm, and he had pressed his free hand over hers; she felt its heat through her glove. They stayed for an hour looking at the Bellinis hanging in crowded tiers; they soaked them up, ravished by their opulence, their color, their truthfulness.

There had been a young Madonna holding her sleeping son, his arms and legs akimbo. "Look how that baby is spilling over; he's getting too big for her lap," Marian said, smiling. Across the room, there was a pietà, one of Bellini's last paintings. Mary, her aging face lined with sorrow, sat on a rock, cradling her dead son, his limbs splayed across her knees. "He is lying in the same position as the sleeping child," George had whispered. "She remembers." They had felt the new mother's pride and foreboding, the bereaved mother's agony.

Mary mourned in a landscape of barren fields and felled and leafless trees, but a blooming garden — lush lilies and roses — surrounded her. "Mary's *hortus conclusus*," Marian said, and she had quoted the verse from the Song of Solomon that foretold the Immaculate Conception: "A garden enclosed is my sister, my bride."

George had laughed. "And only God has the key. Polly, my sister, my bride, why did the church fathers turn pleasure into a miracle?"

"Well, it is, don't you think?" She remembered thinking then how well she knew him, the pressure of his arm against hers, the height of his shoulder, the spicy smell of his skin, the wrinkles at the base of his ears, his inability to remain serious for long, even at the end.

Now, standing alone in front of that pietà, Marian recalled a different passage: "I opened to my beloved, but my beloved was gone; I sought him, but I could not find him; I called him but he gave me no answer." She closed her eyes and clasped her hands.

When she had blinked away her tears, she saw that Johnnie was still watching her as if she, not the paintings, were the mystery. He smiled at her, a restrained but hopeful expression; maybe he thought she had been praying. And she had been, in her way, she supposed: remembering, keeping George alive, and herself alive, too.

But it was wicked to leave Johnnie alone; without instruction he could not see. She led him to a painting that hung at eye level: three women and a baby. The Madonna and Child and Mary Magdalene and St. Catherine, a *sacra conversazione*. She had told George how that Madonna reminded her of her sister; she would tell Johnnie, to help herself, as well: to find a way to feel again.

"I grew up with country girls like this Madonna," she said to him. "Chrissey was pretty like that, solid and sturdy. Those girls made good mothers; they'd taken care of their younger brothers and sisters. Not like me. I went to help Chrissey look after her own children, but I don't think she trusted what I might say. I was a dangerous influence." She smiled.

"You would have been a wonderful mother," Johnnie said.

"How can you know that?" Her anger surprised her. "I would not be who I am now."

Johnnie flushed. They stood apart, staring at the painting, which was infused with the mystery of connection. Marian would not speak first.

Johnnie yielded. "What does Ruskin say about this? It's quite lovely. A *sacra conversazione*, right?"

"You have the pamphlet."

"I'll see if I can find it." He rifled through the pages. "I don't see it here, but he writes that all Bellini's paintings are exemplars of faith."

"I am not talking about faith."

"Do you think this foreshadows the Passion?"

"Oh, absolutely. They all do, I'm sure. That baby could have been Chrissey's — maybe it contracted typhus and died, like her Frances."

"But this is the Virgin Mary."

"This was a girl that Bellini painted. A living, breathing girl, once."

"Please don't argue with me! I cannot answer you."

Her husband clutched Ruskin's pamphlets as if they were religious tracts and his red Baedeker as if it were the Book of Common Prayer. "I don't mean to argue. I was trying to show how these paintings are about life. That is their subject — not divinity. Does that make them less sacred? I think not. Look at the Magdalene — at her sturdy hands. She was a country girl, too, and Bellini dressed her up; he even gave her — it was a prop from his studio, probably — a jewel." She touched the heavy brooch at her throat. "I wonder — did he use her? Probably he did. Did he want to see how remorse would change her face?"

"Marian — I can't bear this." Johnnie left the room. She hurried after him, past the grand altarpieces with their saints standing on the Venetian plain bounded by rocky crags — the Dolomites, invisible in modern fog. She found her husband in the corridor, which was lined with medieval triptychs. He had stopped before a Last Judgment whose gold background had oxidized and turned green.

His jaw was clenched, the tendons on the side of his neck were taut, but when he saw her he tried to smile. "I cannot see what you see, and even trying upsets me."

"I'm sorry," she murmured. "That was not my intention." She was close to tears again, ashamed of forcing ideas on him that were as radical as the renunciation with which she had tormented her father. Johnnie could take his place beside her father in that painted medieval heaven, at the right hand of God. Perhaps the gold of his heaven would be bright, not as tarnished as it seemed here.

She had not meant to frighten him. Johnnie could not follow her thoughts, but kindness mattered more than learning. He was trying to be kind, and he had given her a great gift. He had made her Mrs. Cross. But she was beginning to make out an image of herself reflected in his eyes, and she did not recognize it. Mary Ann Cross. A burden willingly assumed: she could not have named a character more aptly.

He rested his hand gently on her shoulder and quickly removed it. "You shall have peace," he had said, that first time he touched her. For peace, she would remain silent.

. . .

86

WHEN THEY LEFT the Accademia, haze obliterated the sun, and a sultry south wind roughened the Grand Canal. Johnnie had told their gondolier not to wait. He desperately needed to walk, to take some exercise, to quiet his unrest. He craved a swim: weightless, mindless, breathless thrashing through water. But his wife worried, and he did not wish to unsettle her, though she certainly unsettled him. She dazzled him; her lack of faith unnerved him — not so much that she did not believe, but that she did not honor the images of faith, that she insisted on interpreting them differently. He had been taught that the forms of religion demanded respect. She would argue that she did indeed respect them, that she was making them human, and he would not know how to reply. He could only attempt a no to her yes, or a yes to her no.

"It might rain," Marian said.

"I hope it does. I hope it clears the air. I can barely breathe."

Slowly they climbed the shallow steps of the wooden bridge over the canal; still short of breath, Johnnie held on to the railing. Halfway across Marian stopped, pretending to watch the parade of boats, but really, he knew, to give him a chance to recover. She was infallibly solicitous about his physical comfort, but she gave his mind and his spirit no ease.

"You're kind to me," he said. "Very kind. You must have been kind to your father, too."

She started and looked at him. When she spoke, her voice was low, as if she were talking to herself. He had to lean close to hear her over the clamor of the canal. "How odd that you should say that. I've been thinking about my father — remembering how cruel I was. I declared war on him. I set his kindness against his faith. It wasn't until much later that I understood how he was at war with himself — on my account."

"But you apologized. You went back to him, and you went to church."

"Otherwise I would have had no place to live. Oh, I could have become a governess, I suppose, or taught at a school for silly girls — but nobody would have had me because I would surely have told them that I did not believe. I was too stubborn — I counted too much on my father's kindness."

"You stayed with him — you cared for him until he died."

"Doing my duty — and pitying myself for my loneliness, when I had my father who loved me despite everything, and the Brays —"

"Ten years — you cared for your father for ten years. You were a good daughter, Marian."

"You would have liked my father," she mused. "And he would have liked you, though he might not have approved of your working in the City."

"Times have changed — it's hard to profit from the land." He answered with confidence; this was something he understood better than she did.

"I wonder how Isaac manages as well as he does."

"Perhaps we should ask him to visit. I should like to meet him."

She shook her head violently.

"Why not?" he asked. Marian had shown him Isaac's letter, and he had seen how it made her happy. "This is the time for a reconciliation."

"I will decide that."

He lowered his eyes. Suddenly, for no reason, just like that, she pushed him away. Two gondolas traveling together passed under the bridge. The gondoliers rowed in unison, stepping and leaning into their graceful, twisting stroke; he envied them the use of their bodies. A large party of English tourists occupied the boats; they were laughing and calling back and forth, trying to incite a race, urging their gondoliers — who either did not understand what their passengers were shouting or ignored them — to row faster. Johnnie yearned to be a part of that simple cheerfulness; he was sure that those gentlemen did not spend their evenings improving their Italian. One of the gondoliers looked up and caught his eye, appraising him. Disconcerted, Johnnie looked away. In the hazy light the canal had turned a milky turquoise, opaque and viscous, as if its water could bear weight.

"How astonishing —" Marian smiled with an expression he did not completely understand. Mixed with tenderness and gratitude — that sublime smile that softened her face — there was something else, obscure and dangerous. A look of incredulity, he would have said, and disappointment, confusion, and expectation: something he feared to recognize. He looked down into the gleaming, glassy water. His wife placed her hand, with its wedding ring, on his sleeve and said, "To think that finally I have embarked upon the life my father wished for me."

AT THE Hôtel de l'Europe the concierge handed Marian a small package bound with a cord.

"What could it be?" Marian wondered.

"Probably from the Bunneys—another of Ruskin's pamphlets; I was asking them for it the other day. Of course they remembered." Johnnie's forehead was damp from perspiration, and his cheeks were pale as they climbed the stairs to their apartment. Unlocking the door, he fumbled with the key. The rooms were dark; the three Gothic arched windows shuttered against the midday heat. Coronas of gray light spilled around the frames.

Marian untied the string and pulled out a rectangle of cardboard wrapped in tissue paper. She frowned and then she laughed. "Johnnie, look! A little drawing! It's quite wonderful."

"So it was from Mr. Bunney."

"No. From Mr. Whistler."

"Mr. Whistler? He doesn't even know you. And you certainly don't know him."

"It seems that he wants to thank me."

"For what?" Johnnie glanced at the drawing and tossed it onto a table. "He's drawn what looks like a female person searching for something. A lost earring? Terribly large for an earring. Hardly an artistic subject—and why would he send it to you?"

Marian retrieved the drawing. "Because I am that female person. Not a suitable subject, I agree. Johnnie, sit down; you don't look well."

He obeyed. "I cannot make myself clear to you." He sounded defeated. "The person is not you."

"She is. Maybe you can't see; there's not enough light." Marian unlatched the shutters. "Here, this is my gray dress—look how he made the folds of the silk, and the long jacket, my bonnet, and my nose protruding beyond the brim of my bonnet. It's hard to mistake my nose. And I'm not looking for an earring, I'm pointing at a snail, Johnnie, a prehistoric snail. He was watching us—following us. He gave me a fright when I saw him that afternoon. I thought

89

he was a pickpocket, one of those thieves who prey on tourists — but then I saw him later from Signor de Levis's window. He had his girl — Maud, wasn't that her name? — with him. On his card he has written that he thanks me for opening his eyes."

"He was spying on you — on us!"

"I suppose I should be offended." She put the drawing down again. "But it's wonderful, don't you think? I shall write to thank him — perhaps we can visit his studio. I would like that."

"Mr. Whistler has found out who you are. He wants something from you. He is disreputable."

"According to the Bunneys."

Johnnie sagged into the sofa and wrapped his arms close around his body.

She held the sketch up to the light. "This doesn't amuse you? You don't find it clever, and lovely? It seems quick, but he has got me. And the snail is quite elegant. It makes me laugh. He may be disreputable, but he is no charlatan. I disagree with Mr. Ruskin — and with Mr. Bunney."

"Marian, what do you want me to do?" Johnnie looked at her, stricken.

"Laugh, too, please."

"At what?"

"At this, even if Mr. Whistler is a reprobate. At me, for my enthusiasms. At pompous Mr. Bunney and his pigeon of a wife."

"He has not drawn me," said Johnnie. "It's as if I weren't there." Johnnie turned his head away from her and the windows. "The light hurts my eyes."

"I'm sorry," she said, and closed the shutters. A lock of his hair had fallen over his forehead, and she yearned to brush it back and smooth away his frown.

"I am spoiling Venice for you," he said.

"I'm ruining it for you, I imagine."

"No. I'm tired, that's all. I'm very tired."

"Shall we go home?" she asked. "Back to England?"

"People will say that we cut short our honeymoon. They are already talking about us."

"What does that matter?"

"They will be cruel to you."

90

"I have learned not to listen to gossip. If you're not well —"

"Oh, my dear." He leaned back and let his arms fall open, exhausted, like a weary child.

She moved to his side, wrapped her arms about his waist, and rested her head against his shoulder. For a moment he remained still; then he placed his hands lightly against her back. He was trembling. Had he feared approaching her? She had been reticent; mutual delicacy might have led them to a misapprehension. She sighed, and pressed against him. But he recoiled from her in an involuntary shudder. Startled, she loosened her embrace. His muscles remained contracted, his breathing shallow; his fingertips tapped her spine, rising and falling in an irregular rhythm. She realized that he did not know what to do with his hands.

Releasing him, she sat upright. He remained motionless, eyes shut; he could have been unconscious. She felt unable to move, either to escape from him or to confront him; she wanted to weep with outrage and humiliation and rejection: a bedrock emotion. She felt a small, sharp pain at her neck; when she touched it, a drop of blood spotted her finger. Her brooch had cut into the skin of her throat. She pulled her handkerchief from her sleeve and dabbed at the little wound.

"My dear, what did you do to yourself?" Johnnie had opened his eyes and spoke calmly, as if nothing had happened.

Hands shaking, she fumbled with the catch, unpinned the jewel from her collar, and placed it on the table beside the little sketch. She faced her husband. "Johnnie. What *have* I done?" She could not suppress her anger.

He raised his palm, as if asking for mercy. His eyes were lowered.

"Johnnie, look at me."

He shook his head, frightened and ashamed, as if she had found him out, guessed some secret: it was that he did not want her. Then why had he promised to cherish her? How could she have so tenaciously assumed that desire would emerge after the wedding? How had she leashed herself to this man who could not touch her?

She got to her feet unsteadily, crossed to the window, and opened the shutters and the door to the balcony. "Johnnie, look at me," she repeated.

He twisted his head and shielded his eyes with one hand while he pushed himself into an upright position. "Marian, I adore you. Forgive me."

She hated the expression in his eyes: abject, spiritless, evasive. "You will not be touched. You will not touch me."

"I worship you."

"I do not ask to be worshiped," she said.

He covered his face and whispered, "I love you as best I can. I did not think that you — I cannot — I cannot do more." He rose from the sofa, stumbled across the room to his bedroom, and slammed the door shut.

She paced the room. If she did not move, she feared she would collapse. It was the same thing; she was too much and not enough; she was both overwhelming and insufficient. She should go to him. He was exhausted and depressed. She should go to him. But the old despair restrained her, a reluctance as bitter as anger.

Time frayed. The weave of months and years wore thin and translucent; one moment overlapped another, past into present. Composure and serenity — her dense, fabricated surface — unraveled. Johnnie had believed that seamless surface; it had made her appear complete and satisfied, as if she did not experience desire. He had no idea how it had been fashioned, how she had lived. He had not guessed how disappointment and finally love, albeit illegitimate, had provided its warp and weft. The realization sickened her: he had gotten her wrong.

She picked up the little drawing. Whistler had caught something strenuous in her posture, an effort in her outstretched hand and straight back, guessed a quality in her he could not have known. Amativeness. He had drawn her reaching — for the fossil snail, for connection. Nearly forty years ago, Charles Bray had held her head in his hands: "She was not fitted to stand alone."

Age had not tempered her; wisdom had not made her resilient. She sighed, a long, low exhalation, a groan from her heart. Putting the drawing down, she walked out onto the balcony, into the heat of the afternoon, into an old despair.

IT HAD BEEN hot, too, at Broadstairs in the summer of 1852. The air sat still, saturated, heavy as water. Herbert Spencer's train had been due fifteen minutes earlier; given the heat, it could well be late. To quell anxiety, Marian concentrated on the mazurka. Take it slowly, she told herself; it should ripple in chromatic languor. Frédéric Chopin had died three years earlier, in George Sand's arms. Sand lived as she pleased; she dressed as a man, wrote passionate novels, took lovers and abandoned them. She, Marian Evans, at thirty-two had translated, anonymously, the three thick German volumes of Strauss's *Life of Jesus*, arguing that Christ was not divine, knowing while she worked — the labor had taken years — that nothing she did could ever change her father's mind. Now she edited, anonymously, the words of the eminent writers who contributed to Mr. John Chapman's *Westminster Review*, and Mr. Chapman garnered all the credit. As for suitors, lovers — Marian slammed her fingers onto the keys in an ugly chord. She was so abjectly grateful to Chapman that she ran his review for no money.

When she announced that she was taking a vacation at Broadstairs unchaperoned, only her brother Isaac had protested. Unlike George Sand, Marian had no title, no fortune, and she was dismally plain, too plain, Mr. Chapman told her, to expect that any affection she might feel would be reciprocated. And she could travel where she pleased; few would imagine that a man would desire to take advantage of her, much less court her. "Marian, you will understand — you understand everything," Chapman had lamely explained. "The point is beauty. Beauty is life's enduring mystery; it is love's catalyst. Without it, don't you see —" She had interrupted his lofty discourse with bitter tears.

But Herbert Spencer was coming to visit. They had passed most of the spring in each other's company, and by next month, when she was to stay with the Brays in Coventry, she thought she might be bringing happy news. She sounded the dissonance again and resolved it into a major chord, dispelling doubts, assuaging apprehension. The mazurka wanted to begin slowly, then gather momentum, then diminish. In the sweltering room, she bent over the keys and worked to keep her fingers loose, languid as the notes. Eyes half shut, she leaned into the music.

"Brava!" Herbert Spencer, cool and slender in white trousers, leaned against the parlor doorway. His curly hair was freshly brushed and sprang from his high, domed forehead; with his long, clean-shaven upper lip and the fluffy beard that fringed his chin, she thought, fondly, that he looked rather like a milkweed. She cut off her playing and clasped his cool, dry hand, exclaiming, "I feared that you might change your mind!"

Despite the heat they went out to walk along the cliffs. "I must show you!" she exclaimed. "I have found more evidence for your ideas on evolution." Marian led him down the switchback path to the shingle, smiling over her shoulder as he exclaimed at the intricate fans and spirals, the ribbed whorls of ancient sea creatures. Until the cliffs were in shadow, he dug fossils from the chalk with his pocketknife, and she wrapped them carefully in handkerchiefs she had brought for that purpose. "If you take any more," she laughed, "the cliffs will crumble."

They crossed the shingle to the water. The waves lapped in soft exhalations. Marian's hair was coming loose from its pins. It curled at her neck, shining red and gold in the lowering sun. "Herbert —"

"Marian, you look very well. The seaside suits you."

She stepped toward the small waves until their froth parted around the soles of her shoes while he watched from the margin of pebbles. "I am glad that you are here."

"Your company gives me pleasure, and profit." He patted his pockets stuffed with fossils and began walking along the shore.

She said, "And London is very hot, and empty."

"Not empty. Mr. Lewes sends his regards. I have seen a great deal of him since you've been away. He never stops at home, and I can understand why, with that household — five children and two not his. But George does not complain."

"Mr. Lewes is a kind man."

"Oh yes, and foolish, too. He doesn't care that people laugh at him. I have never met a man so unconcerned with the opinions of others."

"Then why is he foolish? Unworldly, maybe, with more sympathy for human nature than for human laws. An evolutionary advancement. I can understand that, can't you?"

Spencer laughed. "I? Oh, Marian, I lack your perceptiveness."

"Herbert." She turned and looked at him, her gray eyes the color of the sultry sea, her hair wild, her face flushed from the heat. "Herbert, did you come only because of the heat in London?"

"And to be with you. To look for fossils with you, to talk —"

"And nothing more?"

"I thought you understood me."

She picked up a smooth, flat pebble and threw it sidearm across the water. It skipped once and sank.

"Where did you learn that?" Spencer asked, surprised.

"From my brother."

Herbert found a stone, flipped it across the water, and observed its jumps. "Fifteen," he announced.

She picked up another stone and skipped it.

"Eight," he said.

"Eleven," she corrected him. "But, anyway, you win. The arc of each hop diminishes exponentially. Have you noticed?"

He was choosing a stone, and as he stooped to pick it up, she shifted her position so that her shadow fell across him. He stood up, his arm pulled back, preparing to throw.

"I am not beautiful enough to love—that's it, isn't it?" She spoke softly, hardly louder than the little waves. "I am Marian who understands, Marian who will keep your secrets, Marian who will advise you on matters of the heart and mind. Marian who can edit the passions of others, though she cannot expect to know what love is like. But I can guess." She held her arms tightly against her sides, her fists clenched. "It is like this—the two of us walking here, talking, skipping stones, with all the world before us and the prospect of filling together all the time of our lives." She kicked at a rock and winced. "Oh, why did you bother to come? You knew very well that I could not keep silent, and now I have offended you and you will never speak to me again."

She started to run away along the hard sand. He caught her and took her wrist firmly as if she were a child. "I am not offended, far from it. But Marian, I must not continue to see you if I cause you pain." His face was flushed; his coat, weighed down with fossils, was slipping from his shoulders.

"Do not. Please. That would hurt me more."

He released her hand. "What a beautiful color—your hair," he said wistfully, and contemplated the gray sea. They continued along the beach toward the promenade at Broadstairs. Ahead of them a governess snatched a child back from the harmless waves. Marian thought to wade into the deepening sea, letting the water soak her skirts and weigh her down, until Herbert rescued her—which he

95

had refused to do. Drowning was supposed to be painless, euphoric even, at the end.

She ached to speak, but insufficient phrases jammed in her throat. Herbert glanced at her and looked away. There was nothing to say; all their words, the exchange of ideas, observations, gossip, the gradual interconnections of spirit, had led to this silence.

They climbed the stairs to the wooden boardwalk. At the top, Herbert Spencer stopped. "I cannot expect you to believe me when I tell you this. But I would love you if I could."

"Is that comfort?" she asked, and she smiled, then bit her lip and shook her head. "You remind me — oh, never mind."

"What?"

"You sound like Rosalind dressed as a boy talking to poor Phoebe. 'I would love you if I could.'"

Herbert blushed. "No. It's not like that with me, Marian, you've got that wrong. If I could love anybody — man or woman — it would be you. I know what I am capable of, and I am not capable of love. I am shallow, like the sea at low tide — you could walk halfway to Holland and never get above your knees. Maybe, if you were as beautiful as Helen, then I could love you, but I don't think so. I don't have the knack. I think how easy it would be to ask you to be my wife —"

"And I would say yes."

Spencer shook his head. "Oh, I know. And it would be a betrayal. You would wither. You would grow to hate me. I sound fatuous, I sound as if I am trying to justify my bad behavior, but, Marian, believe me. What else does Rosalind say? 'I will marry you if ever I marry woman.' But I'll not be married."

"Never?"

"No." They had reached the stairs. Without speaking, they strode along the boardwalk. Spencer kept his hands clasped behind his back. The sea lapped into the hazy sky. There was no horizon.

At her door Spencer took his leave. "You must believe what I say, Marian."

She fixed him with her wounded gray eyes. He blinked, but she did not relent. "Herbert," she burst out before she could stop herself, "if you ever do marry, I will die."

. . .

ACROSS FROM the lagoon, the façade of the church of San Giorgio Maggiore floated like a marble cloud in the mist that obliterated the horizon. Marian went back inside and closed the shutters. The memory of that rejection—the memory of despair—revived, bitter and fresh. But Herbert Spencer had, in his way, made things right. In the midst of her desolation, she had also felt the glimmerings of power, the moral force of her ardor. He had been moved by her—not with pity, but with a kind of awe. He had acknowledged an aspect of her temperament that Johnnie had not suspected.

In the months after George's death, she had been ardent only in grief; during his lifetime, she and George had kept their passion private. The woman Johnnie loved was an elderly lady, mild and kind, a woman he could fuss over and coddle, not desire. He had wished to heal a broken spirit, and, promising to marry her, he had assumed he had done so. She should be satisfied with that and blame herself for the rest. She thought she heard Johnnie calling to her, but it was only muffled noise from outside—slapping waves; sputtering, thumping steam engines.

He had promised to devote his life to her, as if she were a sibyl and he guarded her shrine. Devotion: that was where their understanding diverged. It was as much her doing as his. He was beautiful; how could she imagine that he found her attractive? She had deceived herself first in pretending that devotion was what she required and again in expecting to transform him. Teaching him Dante, she had intended to expand not only his linguistic capacity, but also his capacity for—not simply for love, but for life. In her pride and blind need she had sought to make him into what he was not. She feared that she did not know what he was.

The humidity was stifling. The city—built on water, a sensuous, fanciful, rotting impossibility—mocked her dream of a wedding trip. Johnnie's kindness was founded on a misconception. He had understood her incompletely and would broach no amendment of that understanding.

San Giorgio Maggiore shone, a play of luminous marble—flesh and spirit. Once, with George, there had been no division. She had been lucky. She should go to Johnnie; he would be ashamed to come out of his room. Perhaps he had fallen asleep; she would not want to wake him, since he slept so little at night, but she could not bring herself to stand up. She reached for Johnnie's heavy brooch and started to pin it to her collar, then put it back on the table.

There was mending to do, a loose bonnet string, frayed lace at the collar of a blouse; Johnnie's brooch had torn the delicate threads. But the room was too dim. She lay back and closed her eyes, lacking the heart even to read.

SHOUTING INTRUDED into sleep — Isaac, graceful and feral, ran in front of her along the riverbank — and tore into her dream.

What was it? An argument among the gondoliers — this Italian exuberance was just the sort of thing that upset Johnnie. She sat up, smoothed her skirts, and waited for him to emerge, tired and fretful, from his room. She would humor him — they had to reach an accommodation. It was too late for anything else. They had to ignore what could not be, what he had not offered. She had not counted on his own strength of will. Was this what her marriage taught — how expectations of happiness deteriorated into the subtle, poisonous maneuvering of adversaries?

They had not eaten lunch, and she was hungry; as his appetite had diminished, hers had increased. Surely he could not remain in his room. Curiosity or annoyance would bring him out.

She would be gentle with him. She would send a note to the Bunneys, asking for an appointment the next morning to collect their watercolors. The noise was growing louder. The hotel staff should put a stop to it. But these were shouts of distress: splashing and the scrape of gondolas colliding. A gondolier would go to almost any length to preserve his hull's glossy lacquer.

"*Ha saltato! Ha saltato!*" He jumped.

She rushed to the window. As she flung open the shutters, there was a violent knocking at the door. "Signora! Signora!" The concierge stood in the doorway, beckoning to her. He panted: "*Mi dispiace, suo marito — il signore Cross — é caduto nel canale!*"

Cross: the concierge gave it two syllables, Crosse. She concentrated on translating. "I'm sorry, Mrs. Cross, your husband, he has fallen into the canal."

She gripped the door handle. "Is he dead?" she whispered. "*É morto?*"

"No, no."

She ran down the corridor, tripped at the top stair, and nearly fell. The concierge grasped her arm as he guided her through the lobby. People stared, and she lowered her head against their eyes. Outside on the landing the shouting continued, but its tone had changed. A group of gondoliers clustered on the dock. She could not see her husband.

"*Ti giuro! Lui, l'inglese, lui ha saltato, e quando ho provato ad aiutarlo, mi a detto, no! No! Lasciami! Lasciami!*" The gondoliers laughed, telling the story.

"Leave me alone!" He had protested against being saved.

"What have you done with him?" she demanded.

"*Ha saltato! L'ho visto!*" One of the gondoliers pointed to a window on the second floor: his room in their apartment. He had leapt over the low stone balustrade into the canal. But he could swim; he was an athlete; he could not have hoped to drown. She began to shake from relief and outrage. The concierge led her through the ring of handsome, laughing gondoliers. They leered — the woman, the cause of the incident. "*Prego*," she commanded. Her voice sounded deep and metallic, as if another person were speaking. The men retreated, muttering and smirking.

Johnnie lay face-down in a puddle on the wooden deck, coughing and retching, drenched and shivering. His hair stuck out in soggy points; his shoulder blades protruded under his shirt; the bones were sharp, the muscle wasted. The linen shirt, filthy, streaked brown and green, clung to his ribs. His coat lay at his feet, a heavy heap of sodden wool. He must have been wearing it when he jumped, but the gondoliers had pulled it off him. She knelt beside him and touched his shoulder. He shuddered and rolled onto his side, drawing his legs toward his chest. His face was white; his dilated pupils eclipsed his blue irises. He stank of the canal.

"Johnnie! Johnnie! Can you speak?" He moaned and gazed fearfully at her. A rope of spittle dangled from the corner of his mouth. She mopped it with her handkerchief. Her tone, to her ears devoid of sympathy, must have sounded to him reassuring; he tried to smile.

"Carry him upstairs, please," she ordered.

The concierge whispered, "The canal, these waters, they are not healthy. That is the danger. The gentleman must see a doctor, signora. Perhaps an English doctor? I will send for an excellent man."

She nodded. "Please." As the concierge began directing the servants, she stopped him. "No. An Italian doctor." Not a gossiping expatriate.

The concierge nodded. "Immediately, signora." He whispered to three boys in hotel livery. Two reached for John Cross's shoulders, the third hoisted his legs. Johnnie struggled. The boy hung on to his thrashing legs; the gondoliers snickered anew. "*Anguilla*," Marian heard them say. Eel.

"Put me down," Johnnie sputtered. "I am capable of walking." The boy let go of his feet. Johnnie staggered between the two others into the lobby and up the stairs, leaving a trail of dirty puddles. Behind their procession, two maids armed with mops and buckets restored serenity.

A SERVANT had bathed Johnnie, dressed him in a clean nightshirt, and laid him on his bed. The doctor gave him a dose of chloral. He must sleep. The doctor would return in the morning — sooner, if required. The danger was from cholera.

Marian watched from a chair beside the bed. "I've sent a telegram to your brother. Willie will come and help us home."

Johnnie nodded. In the dim room, she could see his eyes on her, the pupils once again dilated as the chloral took effect. She went on: "You must rest. The doctor said that you were quite weak."

"Marian, I'm sorry."

"Sleep. You need sleep."

"Sing to me."

She began to hum. "*Schlafe, schlafe.*" She sang the words: a song by Schubert, a lullaby. "Sleep, may all your wishes be fulfilled."

Although he did not understand German, he murmured, "Thank you." He closed his eyes and thinking him asleep, she stopped singing and sat staring. But, resisting unconsciousness, he opened his eyes; they confronted each other. She could muster no gentleness for him. He was her match. He nodded and shut his eyes once more. After a moment he whispered, "Marian, I did this for you. I tried — I wanted to set you free."

. . .

MARIAN HURRIED through the small streets behind the church of the Frari, two of John Wharlton Bunney's watercolors rolled and wrapped and tucked under her arm. It was Sunday morning; almost a week had passed since Johnnie had jumped. Willie Cross had left London within hours of receiving her telegram and had arrived in Venice. Like his brother, Willie relished organization. He had made arrangements for their departure, and they had settled on an explanation: exhaustion. Johnnie, who had developed no fever, could travel safely.

The Bunneys had heard the rumors, and Mrs. Bunney, all pecking concern, pressed for information. Marian scattered a few crumbs: Johnnie was doing well now. He had collapsed — it was terrible — he had lost consciousness from exhaustion brought on by the strain of work, marriage, moving house, and travel. He had hoped to see the Bunneys again; he considered them friends. Marian was going to surprise him with these watercolors, the ones he had chosen; they would cheer him immensely. Alas, she could not sit down; no, she required no refreshment — she must be off. She had imposed on them already, visiting so early on a Sunday morning. She gave them a cheque and escaped.

The sun glinted off water in bright, shifting geometries. She stopped and watched, astonished by small things, like Persephone released from the underworld, dazzled by light, noise, and smells — and by the shortness of time. A sparrow skittered toward a crust of bread, and she marveled at the speed of its legs, the intricate white tracery of its wings.

All week she had sat by Johnnie's bed; he had become distraught when she left his side. At first she had been alone with him, consumed with the anxiety of nursing. Cholera did not worry her — he had not swallowed water — as much as his mental state. Until Willie arrived she slept in a chair in Johnnie's room, windows sealed against noise, shutters closed against light. Emerging after hours by his side, she was surprised to find that night had fallen.

The side door to the Frari stood open; a leather curtain hid the interior. Marian heard music and stopped. A slow, archaic sound: boys took the treble parts, their voices rising without vibration over the bass. She pushed aside the curtain and stepped into cool, incense-laden air. The great church was hardly full, and the choir sang from their stalls on either side of the high altar, flanking Titian's *Assumption*. They — she and George — had loved that painting. The choir's lower voices, echoing against the limestone vaults, seemed to come from the painted crowd witnessing the Virgin's ascent, and the sopranos could have been the putti lifting Mary through the clouds. Her robes swirled about her in the holy commotion of flight. "Maria, Maria," the choir sang. The sacred madrigal, tender and austere, opened a glimmering of pain and joy.

The congregants glanced covertly in her direction. Many an Englishwoman crept into these churches and dipped her fingers in holy water for the frisson of the ritual. Marian understood the craving for relief: the abdication to mystery, the hope for memory — for desire — to be made flesh.

What if George were waiting in the heaven of his own design — waiting to show her to their bed draped with fresh linen? He would have arranged her ascent in a balloon; certainly he would have searched the celestial kennels and claimed their dog, Pug; he would have found for her a desk at which she could write stories without suffering depression and doubt.

She bowed her head and rose and left the church. She should not have subjected Johnnie to this city where she and George had been so intoxicated with its accretion of beautiful things. Or would that have only delayed the inevitable disappointment?

She crossed the Rialto Bridge and followed the Merceria into the Piazza San Marco; this Sunday morning it was as empty as a moor. Even the flocks of pigeons had not yet made their entrance but were perched on the capitals of pilasters and on sooty windowsills, awaiting their cue to swoop. She could not bear the expectancy of the piazza, its anticipatory vastness; she was trying to expect nothing, anticipate nothing.

She traversed the Piazzetta and paused near the embankment. A gondola approached from the Giudecca, cutting a wake of small ripples in the still water. Alone and with no place to go, Marian watched a circle of blue sky widen overhead.

JAMES WHISTLER had been painting fog, but the fog was burning off. He had decided to wait out the change in the weather at Florian's. It was impossible not to recognize the lady who was watching him disembark. Her face was sorrowful, her skin slack, her eyes downcast. She had drawings rolled under her arm — an effort of Mr. Bunney's, probably. Maud had told him that the Crosses had admired Mr. Bunney's little doodles. Well, Mrs. Cross had one of his own efforts, too. This was bad timing, better make the best of it. Shirt rumpled, coat unbuttoned, his hat in his hand, his streak of white hair springing from his scalp, he stood before her, unprepared, with no cloak of bravado.

Her face and neck reddened; she recognized him. By now, she had heard everything about him; but he, too, had heard everything about her.

He put his hat on his head, then doffed it and addressed her. "Mrs. Cross, I am James Whistler."

"Yes," she said. "Yes. I know who you are."

He waited, slightly longer than he should have, then replaced his hat. It was her prerogative to continue, but she remained silent. "Good day, then," he said, disappointed.

"Mr. Whistler." She spoke firmly. "I should like to thank you."

He turned back.

"I must thank you for the lovely drawing. That day seems so long ago. What a surprise to see you — I meant to write, but — "

He nodded, acknowledging that he knew. "The drawing was an attempt to thank you — for the snails."

"The snails. Yes. I used to — well, you know. You spied on us. Never mind. I liked the drawing enormously; it was so full of life. I can't imagine why you chose to draw me, but I'm glad to have it — it will be my memory of Venice. I would have liked to see more of your work."

"I don't have much to show — only pastels and sketches." He gestured toward the gondola. "I've been out this morning. But I hope you didn't misunderstand me. It's not the sort of thing I do — I don't present people with drawings. Usually they pay for them."

"Would you like me to pay? I will, gladly."

He erupted. "No, *no!* That is not what I meant. I had no idea who you were. I could not resist drawing you."

"You have strange taste, Mr. Whistler."

"Mrs. Cross, I was struck — "

103

"Not by my beauty."

"I was going to call it grace."

"I must say, you were kind. You softened my jaw and straightened my nose most becomingly. At least you didn't shorten it — that's how I recognized myself, by my nose."

She's sanctimonious, Maud had declared, she lives in sin and writes about virtue. Lived in sin, he had corrected, past tense. But this lovely voice, the ardor; he did not remember her novels for their righteousness. Whistler asked, "Your husband, Mrs. Cross. He's doing better?"

"Much better, thank you. He was suffering from exhaustion." She did not flinch; her voice retained its discipline. As if tired tourists pitched themselves into the Grand Canal every day. Whistler had laughed when Maud told him the story; now it seemed less funny. She went on: "The strain of traveling was too great — and with the heat, the lack of exercise. My husband needs exercise. You understand."

"No, I'm not sure I do," he said.

She frowned. He had lost her; Maud had guessed right. But suddenly she smiled, lifting layers of concealment. "Mr. Whistler, you live up to your reputation."

"How so?"

"You are disgraceful, disreputable —"

"So I shall take my leave."

To his surprise, she smiled. "No, please. I was afraid that I would not have a chance to thank you. My husband does not like Venice. I've tired him out." A flock of pigeons swooped toward a photographer setting up his camera.

"If Mr. Cross doesn't like Venice, Mr. Bunney hasn't been a good guide."

"Mr. Bunney has been charming."

"A parrot is charming. You are delighted because it can speak; you forget that it is only repeating what it has been taught."

She lowered her eyes. He had offended her. But she said, "Mrs. Bunney seemed to me like a pigeon. Greedy and swooping."

He laughed. "With that dreadful iridescence. Mrs. Cross, if I may say so, you are not living up to your reputation. Not at all."

"Mr. Bunney is an earnest and diligent man, Mr. Whistler. Is that what I should be telling you?" The brightening morning tinged her gray eyes blue. "As a guide, my husband prefers him to me — he would certainly prefer him to you. Really, I think that Mr. Cross would be happy to sit in Mr. Bunney's studio looking at his sketches and never go out."

"You cannot make a person see, Mrs. Cross. I have given up trying — I lost everything trying. Most people would prefer to be blind — they're afraid of what will happen when they open their eyes. It's their loss."

"It's mine, as well." Sadness dulled her eyes for an instant.

"But you'll be back in September, after the heat?"

She shook her head. "We go home to England tomorrow. This is my last . . ." She hesitated.

The sky was blue overhead, the mist dissolving. Whistler asked suddenly, "Well, then, Mrs. Cross, do you have an hour? There is something I would like to show you."

He was sure she would refuse. She considered — formulating, he was sure, a polite refusal. Finally, she nodded. "Your Venice? Your dank canals with washing strung across? I've heard about that, too."

"No," he said. "Something else." They waited while his gondolier rearranged the boxes of pastels and pencils, the tablets of paper, the folding easel. Whistler handed Marian into the boat. Settling her into the forward-facing seat, he placed himself opposite her. "Cavaldoro, take us into the lagoon, in the direction of San Giorgio."

The gondola rocked through the water and the rising mist. Sunday morning: the lagoon was empty of commerce. They floated for a while without speaking, shy in their proximity. Marian closed her eyes, and Whistler studied her face, her large bones and finely textured skin, the anxious set of her mouth. He would have liked to draw her again, but he did not dare. She opened her eyes. "Mr. Whistler, what is in your portfolios? Will you show me?"

"Most are studies for etchings. I'm going to exhibit them in London. There are pastels — but they are not like Mr. Bunney's work." He glanced at the rolled drawing on the seat beside her.

"There are no secrets in Venice, are there, Mr. Whistler? Show me, please, if it's not too precarious."

"Cavaldoro keeps this boat steady enough for me to draw." He untied the strings of a portfolio. A narrow spit of black land on a white page, a beggar woman and her child, the angle of a canal. "Ah, there is your famous washing," she said.

Whistler gently lifted a sheet of paper by the margins. "Mind, the chalk hasn't been fixed yet. You don't want it to smear."

Buildings lay like a whispered grid of black lines over swaths of color: sky and water. Gondolas delicate as threads spun against a golden wash of sunset.

Marian looked and said nothing. Whistler laid them back in his portfolio and tied the strings. "You don't like them."

"I don't have words for them. I find them mysterious, and I don't understand them. Insubstantial, incomplete, I thought at first, but I think I am wrong. You have drawn the air of Venice; you have drawn weightlessness. As if it's all light, and everything else is superimposed on the light. You have drawn the feeling of Venice — something I have not experienced this week." She bent her head. Whistler restrained himself from breaking her silence. "I'm grown too heavy. I wish . . ." She sighed. "Forgive me, Mr. Whistler, if I forget myself." Her face in its sorrow was as open and unguarded as a child's. Whistler would have taken her hand — it lay in her lap with its thin wedding ring. As if guessing his intention, she clenched it into a fist.

"Where are you taking me?"

"Just here. Look over your shoulder, now."

Above the city, the peaks of the Dolomites pierced the fog. She gazed at them for a long time and Whistler saw that there were tears in her eyes. He looked away to the mountains and studied the trailing ribbons of snow, gauged the angle of crags, left her to herself.

"Thank you," she said, finally, her voice as soft as the lapping water.

He shrugged. "In return for the snails."

She nodded. "I must be getting back."

Whistler signaled to the gondolier.

"I would stay here all day if I could."

"Yes," he said.

When they were approaching the embankment, she said, "You've shown me what Bellini saw."

"I wouldn't know. I stay away from churches."

"But surely you've been to the Accademia."

"No, not at all." He grinned. "I am not interested in the past."

The gondolier stirred the water and drew them to the dock.

"Mr. Whistler, if I were here for even one more day, I would take you with me to the Accademia."

"And I would go. With you." He jumped onto the deck and handed her out of the gondola. "I was going to Florian's before I met you. May I walk you to your hotel?"

She shook her head. "It's just over there. When you are in England, I hope you will call." She handed him her card.

"I should be honored. Don't forget this." He handed her Bunney's watercolors, and she tucked them under her arm with a shrug and a deprecatory smile. She regarded him soberly. "Mr. Whistler — that girl?"

He felt himself blush deep carmine.

"Be kind to her."

She started walking in the direction of the Hôtel de l'Europe.

After a few yards she stopped, as if she had forgotten something, then she turned toward him. Whistler had the sense that she knew he would be watching.

"I shall treasure this morning," she said. She stood for a moment facing in his direction. Whistler could not make out her expression; he was sure, though, that she was not looking at him but at the pink brick and the pale water, the orange marble and its stone snails.

Chapter 4

Venice, June 10, 1980

T HERE WERE NO KEYS in the box at the hotel, and the message Caroline had left had been picked up. In the elevator she leaned back against the mirrored panels and loosened her sandal straps.

Blisters were the cost of elegance. And this ache in her chest? She shut her eyes. Her reaction to the man on the bridge: it was no good attributing it to fatigue and fickle memory. This morning, memory had proved reliable; it had led her to obscure places where she feared getting lost, but she had found her way.

Ricky was standing in the hall. When he saw her, his handsome, Iberian features relaxed. "I was going out to look for you." Ricardo Coelho had a lilting way of speaking. Though he appeared to be in his midforties, Caroline assumed that he was at least a decade older; he had worked for Malcolm for twenty-five years. She wondered if he dyed his hair.

"I left a note for him at the desk."

Ricky shrugged; forgiveness was not his province.

Caroline tossed her shopping bag on the reproduction rococo sofa in the suite's sitting room and knocked on the closed bedroom door. When there was no answer, she opened it.

The curtains were shut and Malcolm had turned on the dim lamp on the night table. He was stretched on the bed with his eyes closed, wearing his suit pants, shirt, and loosened tie, his feet in their black lisle socks incongruously delicate. He was on the phone; hands folded over his stomach, he cradled the receiver between his head and the pillow. The flesh of his cheeks sagged. He looked like an effigy on a medieval tomb.

"Malcolm."

He opened his eyes, regarded her with vexation, and covered the mouthpiece with his palm. "I'll be on this for a while," he said, with no trace of emotion, and closed his eyes again.

She listened, used to guessing at the meaning of his one-sided conversations. As he talked money, his hermetic language yielding profit, it crossed her mind that he might be manufacturing this urgent phone call for her benefit. She left the room.

"He's fine," she announced. "He's on the phone, of course. It's cold in here. Do you mind if I open a window?"

Ricky had been arranging stacks of papers on the coffee table. He coughed, a dry hack, as if he could not dislodge something in his throat.

"Ricky — do you need a glass of water?"

He took a rasping breath. "Sorry. I think I caught a cold, probably on the plane coming over."

"This will be better for you." She unlatched the French doors that opened onto a small balcony overlooking a piazza. Malcolm, requiring quiet, had taken a suite in back, away from the Grand Canal. A draft of soft air fluttered the papers.

"He won't like that."

"Blame me. Ricky — what is this Venice fund about, really? I don't understand." Sometimes Ricky told her things, sometimes he couldn't. He shrugged and slid some papers into an accordion folder. "Who was at the meeting this morning?" she asked.

"The usual — the Swiss."

"So it wasn't about Venice."

"No, it was. What did you buy?" he asked, glancing at her shopping bag.

"A skirt and a tunic. Very Venetian."

"Can I see? And what's that on your pants?"

"I don't want to think about it. Look." She pulled the clothes from the bag and shook them free of tissue paper. The fabric's tiny, irregular pleats caused it to shimmer with all possible yellows. "It's Fortuny fabric. Mario Fortuny. My mother loved him." She held up the tunic. "Feel it." With his thick fingers Ricky gingerly stroked the silk.

"Malcolm will say it looks like curtain material. If you want to see the store, I'll go back with you." She stowed them in the bag.

"You can get something for your mother," Ricky said.

"And you can help me pick it out; she thinks you have good taste."

"I thought you'd fallen into a canal." Malcolm stood in the doorway.

Caroline faced him. "I used to be a lifeguard. You imagine things."

"I was worried."

"I left a message with the concierge."

Malcolm glared at Ricky. "Why didn't I see it?"

Ricky looked down, avoiding Malcolm's eyes.

"It's hot in here," Malcolm said.

"I was cold," said Caroline, her voice as flat as his.

Malcolm shut the French doors and said to Ricky, "That's it, then."

With a quick glance at Caroline, Ricky left the room.

Caroline took a breath. "Malcolm, you got my message."

"I wanted you to wait." He stood against the window so she could not read his expression, but the harshness in his voice had dissipated. "I'm sorry," he said, inviting her to ignore his apparent cruelty — his anger at her, his accusation of Ricky — and assuage the nugget of hurt and need at his core.

But she stayed with the surface. "Why blame Ricky?"

"It's his job. I wanted you here when I came back."

"Ricky couldn't have kept me."

Malcolm shrugged. Caroline's vehemence seemed to surprise him. "Why are you upset? Don't be." He gave her a minute. "Where did you go?"

"To where we used to live."

"And it seemed smaller. You were disappointed."

"No, Malcolm, it wasn't like that. Everything was exactly the way I remember it." The phone rang in the bedroom. "Better, even," she declared to his back, as he went to answer it.

• • •

"I CAN'T get to Boston today. Something's come up, a client's in town." Malcolm woke her, his voice brisk and slightly impatient at seven in the morning. In the beginning he had flown to Boston two or three times a week. A meeting, he would explain, calling sometimes a day ahead, sometimes the same morning, making it sound like a lucky accident, a chance to meet for lunch or dinner.

His tone became gentle. "But I want to see you; I miss you. Come to New York. Take a cab to the airport, and Ricky will find you at the shuttle. Stay overnight; I'll put you up." He hung up; it did not occur to her not to do as he instructed. She stayed in bed until Deirdre had left for class. It took her an hour to pack, laying things out and changing her mind; she was foggy with apprehension and excitement, and she did not leave a note saying where she was going.

Ricky wore a navy blue suit that fit his stocky frame perfectly; it verged on a uniform but seemed much finer. He picked her out of the parade of passengers and took her satchel from her. When he opened the back door of the Mercedes, she asked if she could sit up front, and he said, "Malcolm told me I'd like you."

Ricky handed her a stack of tapes. "These were what I could find." A few days earlier, Malcolm had asked her for a list of her favorite pieces of music. She and Ricky crossed the Triborough Bridge, Beethoven blaring from the speakers.

"You don't mind this music?" Caroline asked, and Ricky shook his head as he beat time on the steering wheel.

"Maybe I'll learn something."

She laughed.

"What's so funny?"

"Everything. The car, the music — you driving me — me, that this is happening to me, and I don't even know where I'm going."

Ricky pulled up at the corner of Fifth Avenue and Fifty-seventh Street. "Why here?" she asked.

He pointed to the entrance to Bergdorf Goodman. "Go to the fourth floor and ask for Amelia."

"For what?"

"She'll help you." When Caroline reached for her satchel, he said, "Leave it. You're staying at the Plaza, next door. Like Eloise."

The fourth floor of the department store had very few clothes on display; the big room was hushed and pearly gray, like the interior of the Mercedes. In her gray flannel skirt and red turtleneck, Caroline approached the battalion of black-clad saleswomen. "Amelia?" she said.

Small and plump and stuffed like a pincushion into her gabardine coat dress, Amelia zipped and buttoned Caroline into dresses with silk linings and suits with little chains sewn inside the hems of the jackets and price tags beyond imagining. "That's lovely, dearie. Dearie, this green may not be quite right for you. What about pink? No, not pink? I'll bring you the black in a smaller size. Yes, perfect — you could be a model."

"My nose is too big."

Amelia bustled in and out of the little room, rapping sharply on the door before opening it, while Caroline surrendered herself to transformation. "Mr. Spingold is here," Amelia announced, and escorted Caroline, wearing the sleek black dress, into a sitting area.

Malcolm smiled and kissed Caroline on the cheek. "Much better," he said. "What else is there?"

"Why are you doing this?" Caroline asked, knowing the answer.

"Because I can. Because I enjoy it. Because I like what these clothes do to you." Amused and beguiled, she tried on everything again for him, emerging from the fitting room like a doll with endless new outfits; he approved and rejected and waited while the seamstress shortened hems — "With legs like yours!" exclaimed Amelia — and took in seams.

Caroline wore the black dress, a stark and opulent costume, to the Oak Room. Dressed so richly, reflecting Malcolm's desire, she barely recognized herself in the lobby's mirrors. That he had plotted the day for her delight made it even sweeter.

"How did you find Ricky?" she asked while the waiter served coffee.

"He was a poor Cape Verdean kid hauling trash for a removal service in Providence, and he plowed head-on into my father's car. He was stoned" — Caroline was not sure if that meant, for a man of Malcolm's generation, drink or drugs — "and he wasn't going fast, and he was polite; he was raised with good manners. When Ricky figured out that my father hadn't been hurt, he got into the truck, backed it off the car's hood, and drove away. My father's car was totaled. He loved his El Dorado, so he sued the removal company — which was not such a great idea — and Ricky. He wanted the kid in jail. My father was not a nice man." Malcolm paused. "So I hired Ricky a lawyer. My father claimed every injury in the medical manual, but we had photographs of him walking on the golf course. The removal guys owed me one, and I got Ricky."

"What did your father do when he found out?"

"He didn't. He died first." Malcolm smiled. "Every year my London tailor makes Ricky a suit. I don't care what it is as long as it's blue."

What Caroline took from the story was benign: a rescue. She was aware, though, of something tainted in that elegant solution. Malcolm liked to win, but he also liked the power over Ricky that winning gave him. She dismissed her uneasiness; Malcolm was a good man.

After dinner, Malcolm took the elevator with Caroline to her room. She could not refuse him. If she did, it would be for life. But he asked for nothing and kissed her with dry lips — he had all the time in the world — and left her at the door. In the morning Ricky drove her to the airport. For Malcolm possession was an art, and Caroline was enthralled by his mastery.

CAROLINE STOOD on the little balcony. The piazza below was empty; the city at lunch under awnings or already resting behind shuttered windows. A memory of afternoons in Venice and the closed door to her parents' room: an exclusion; but by the end of the summer her father spent the hour reading on the sofa, and she had been glad of his presence.

"Caroline!" Malcolm called. He had taken off his tie.

"Do you want to go out?" she asked. "You wanted me to show you Venice. But Artur and Louis are here — the Rescue Venice team. Are we having lunch with them?"

"Come inside."

Malcolm did not like heights, and Caroline stayed where she was. The shift had been imperceptible, tiny faults opening, the expected abrasion in any marriage. The chug of engines and the slosh of waves

from the canal reached her faintly. From the room she heard the rus-
tle of tissue.

"What did you buy?"

She hurried inside and took the shopping bag out of Malcolm's
hands. "I paid for it myself."

He reached for her waist. "Caroline."

"What? What do you want?"

"You. I always want you." He embraced her.

Ten years earlier, *always* had seemed to her a beautiful word, a
spell suspending time. With a rush of something like despair she recalled how they used to promise each other their presence, always.
He went on: "I imagined you floating in some filthy canal—you'd
tripped and hit your head and fallen in, and nobody noticed."

"Nothing's going to happen to me."

He walked her toward the bedroom and pulled her down beside
him to sit on the edge of the bed. She got up and crossed to the window. "Malcolm, it's daytime now even in New York."

"I don't want day." He pulled back the spread and held out his
hand.

"Don't you want Venice?"

Malcolm's amber eyes gauged her reluctance. "Come here," he
said. She sat beside him. His hands began their slow progress, pushing her sweater off her shoulders and tracing the ridge of her collarbone.

"Did you take a shower?" he asked.

"Before I went out."

He kissed her mouth, and underneath the mint of mouthwash his
breath was faintly sour. Sex for Malcolm was methodical and deliberate; she could have diagrammed the stages. He was vain, sure of his
ability to satisfy, and Caroline let him do that, first for her and then
himself; he wanted only her compliant presence. Afterward he lay on
her, sleek and solid, a sheen of sweat on his neck, and he told her he
loved her.

"You're crushing me," she said, fighting back tears.

"Tell me that you love me."

"I can't breathe."

"Tell me."

"You know I do, Malcolm."

He raised himself onto his elbows. "Why are you crying?"

"People are sad after making love. Somebody said that in Latin."

"Latin's dead." He sounded defeated. He rolled off her, went to the bathroom, and returned, wrapped in a hotel bathrobe. She curled up on her side, and he pulled her by her shoulder onto her back. "Caroline, look at me. It's time we had a baby. I don't want to be so old that my child thinks I'm his grandfather."

She lay rigid, appalled. "You want me to give you a baby for our anniversary?"

"I was thinking about it the other way around. It would be for you."

"What if that's the last thing in the world I want?"

"You're not getting any younger either."

"Thank you. Do you want to trade me in for a newer model?"

He closed his eyes and lowered his head. "Look, I never see my daughter. I want to do a better job this time around — a better job than my father did, or yours —"

"How do you know what kind of father he was? He was dead before you met me." She sat up and pulled the sheet up around her neck.

"I know what you tell me."

"I never said that he was a bad father."

Malcolm stood. She slid into the space he had vacated on the bed and turned away from him.

"What are you saying?" He bent over her.

She rolled flat on her back. "That I don't want a child. With you."

He started. In the decade of their marriage she had never defied him so directly. She lay tense, fearing that he would harm her; then she regretted having harmed him. "You don't want a child, Malcolm. That's what I meant. You want something else."

"And what do you think that is?" he demanded.

"Me. The way I used to be, the way I was."

"You've changed."

"Haven't we both? People do change."

He shook his head. "I've given you everything you wanted." It was a plea and a defense.

"And I've given you everything."

But she had withheld this. If she had a baby with Malcolm, he would own her past redemption. With a child as hostage, nothing, certainly not the child—could remain her own.

Malcolm paced to the corner of the room; he had a lumbering, pigeon-toed walk, from a badly set broken ankle in childhood. She went on: "I wouldn't be able to give you so much. There wouldn't be enough of me." She shifted tactics, blaming herself. "What would I do with a child?" She knew the answer to that question, and longing made her angry. "What would you do, Malcolm? With a real baby, with diapers and crying, not just the idea? A baby changes everything."

"So what do you mean? What do you want to do now?" he asked; it sounded like a dare.

"Sleep," she said. "Just sleep."

MALCOLM WATCHED her; like a child, she could sleep anywhere. What she had said was true; he wanted her the way she was when he first knew her, grateful, naive, with a child's malleability.

It had been okay. A five, maybe a six. No, a five. She wasn't there with him, and he did not enjoy having to work to persuade her. Ten years ago she had been ready all the time, and he had worried, not too seriously, that he couldn't keep up with her; now she just went through the motions. But then, years ago he was ten years younger. Did that have anything to do with it? He tensed his thigh muscles; he flexed his bicep. He wasn't losing mass, though the hair on his shins had rubbed off. That had happened by the time he met her. No question, you slowed down with age. He needed food; he dialed room service and ordered a club sandwich. He thought about ordering for her, but she was down for the count.

In the beginning, that first year, sex was often a ten. Not a technical ten—he'd had women who were willing to try anything to amuse him and themselves, and lately he'd been feeling nostalgic for an uncomplicated, unencumbered, just-for-the-hell-of-it fuck. The one he'd been seeing when he met Caroline and had kept around until he was sure where things were going: that one was a gymnast. Her body was probably shot to hell by now; big tits didn't last. But he'd never had anybody who enjoyed it more than Caroline did. Once. Ten for enthusiasm, and he had loved the little barrier of reserve he had to break through, the little bit that she hid. It was like shame; he had to get past it to bring her to pleasure, and it was more erotic than any position.

He bent down and tickled Caroline's cheek near the corner of her mouth, as he had once tickled his infant daughter when it was time for her bottle. He had always liked the baby better asleep, and recently he had been feeling that way about Caroline.

She cost a lot to maintain. He hated thinking like that — it was a holdover from his first marriage. He still seethed at how his wife had belittled him, as if she had been responsible for his wealth because her father lent him the money to make his first investments — as if that money, which he'd repaid, represented some primal, unredeemable debt. She had taught him money, she claimed. What if she had? He had learned. Funny how when he thought "wife" he thought "Irene"; he had determined never again to allow someone to exert that kind of control over him. "When I'm thirty-four are you going to trade me in for two seventeens?" Caroline teased him. But he could do exactly that, if he chose. Next year she would turn thirty-four.

Malcolm had not let her bring even a pair of sneakers with her when she moved in. He had wanted her to owe him everything. They'd had seven good years, he figured, and then she started taking herself seriously.

She had made him feel that his business wasn't sufficient — that it was ultimately boring; she had encouraged him to publish the newsletter. Financially, it was a bad deal, but he could still afford it — not that she needed to know. And in time — who could say? — it might succeed. But he feared that he had lost the instinct for when to cut his losses.

He yawned, but he did not want to give in to sleep. The market was bad; his mood was bad. Ten years earlier, Malcolm had believed in a future as infinite as the expanding universe. But with a president who lusted only in his heart and didn't have the guts simply to lust, what could the country expect? There was no opportunity in this market; even gold was risky. He wanted out; he wanted his money safe.

And he had wanted Caroline almost from the moment he saw her in Sam Gruson's class at the Museum School. Caroline, beautiful and unfinished, put him in mind of what he was missing: a complete and tender connection, a place — strange that he saw what they had as a place, as occupying square feet, acreage — where he could relax the guard and the calculation that had gotten him where he was, where he could live in safety.

"SO WHAT do you think of her?" Malcolm asked Sam Gruson after class. Sam had taken him to a bar across Huntington Avenue, a dark hole with a sticky floor, apparently his way of reminding Malcolm where they both came from.

"She's got talent . . ." Sam hesitated.

"But?"

"Why are you asking?"

"I liked her work, but I don't know shit about art."

"That's why you buy my stuff? Because it's perfect for the ignorant collector? Is that what you're saying?"

"You do fine, Sam. You don't have to teach."

"Actually, I do." Sam finished his beer and motioned to the bartender to bring another round. "She's probably the most talented kid in the class. Ambitious, too. But — here's your *but* — she has doubts. Some of that's fine. It's what makes the good ones better. But when she does something that works, she thinks it's magic; she doesn't trust herself. She needs — listen, I don't know her at all. I only see what she does in class. You want to buy something? Support a young artist? Ask her. I'll ask her if you want."

Malcolm nodded.

"Mal, what would you have said if I told you she was hopeless?"

Malcolm smiled. "I wouldn't care."

"She deserves a break," Sam said.

"I could help."

"What are you going to do?"

"Marry her." Malcolm was unprepared for what came out of his mouth. A rush of emotion, hot, sweet, and unlike anything he remembered feeling, brought him close to tears.

Sam put down his beer. "You don't mean that, right? She's twenty years younger than we are — than you are."

"I'm not going to hurt her."

"Mal, she's just beginning. You're cooked. You're done. Let her be."

"So you won't come to the wedding?" Malcolm pulled out a sheaf of folded bills from his pocket and threw a twenty on the table. "All I'm looking for is to be happy."

Sam had come to the wedding. It was Malcolm's experience that in the end people did what he wanted them to do.

CAROLINE MOANED and rolled onto her stomach. A shiver of suspicion raised the hairs on the back of Malcolm's neck. She'd started sketching those figures after that boy — what was his name? Lucas, Will Lucas — after he died. He knew about that boy, what she had told him and what she hadn't. She'd get over him; then there might be somebody else. Maybe Sam was right. She hadn't been cooked.

He had bought her that damp stone house on the Hudson, he submitted to concerts — they were worse than Yom Kippur. Music made him think of all the things he'd done wrong. And he went to the ballet and to openings; he contributed to the annual funds of museums she liked. Venice was for her, too, partly. Her love for Venice was the irrational motive that justified establishing the fund. The world credited his analytical intelligence, but his instinct for the irrational had made him rich, at least until recently. Try to put that in his newsletter. He was hot; he turned up the air conditioning.

Where was his lunch? Traveling, he wore two watches, one set to New York time, one to local. Both were plastic, one of his eccentricities; they amused his Swiss colleagues. They respected him as a money man, but Caroline gave him mystery; there were no children, so she loved him for himself and not for his fortune. As he had concluded ten years ago. She did love him — she had, and the painful sweetness that had overcome him when he first realized that he wanted to marry Caroline returned.

The doorbell rang: lunch, finally. He ate his sandwich while he checked in with the office in New York. He still wanted Caroline. But it was time for a child, time for proof of love.

"WAKE UP." Malcolm shook Caroline's shoulder. Disoriented, she listened: no motors, only footsteps and voices bouncing against stone. Venice: this morning's palpable gladness took on the vivid dislocation of a dream. She and Malcolm had to find a way to continue; she was not prepared to act on the implications of what she had said.

He was dressed. The dim light shadowed his features, giving them an ascetic cast. She smiled, masking her wariness; she could show him what she loved. "Let's go out," she said, "and walk around."

"It's seven thirty," he said. "The party starts in half an hour."

"A party? What's the party for?"

"Us."

"What if at Heathrow I'd said I wanted to go home?"

"You didn't."

She lay back. "Do any Venetians know about your plan for Venice?"

"That's what the party's for."

"Who's giving it?"

"A friend of the Heismanns'. A Venetian. A count. In a palazzo. You can speak Italian. Then dinner at Harry's Bar."

"How can you want to save a city you've never really seen?"

"It doesn't really matter, does it?"

She put on the Fortuny tunic and inhaled its musky, soapy perfume; it was ideal for a palazzo. She was grateful for the evening; it was easier to show love for Malcolm in public.

"MAGGIE, dresses aren't art," Samuel Edgar had declared. "Why do you want a book about dresses?" His voice made his pronouncements difficult to contradict. In the army he had sung bass in a choir and seen little combat.

"Fortuny dresses are art. At least I think they are," Margaret answered. "And this book is as close as I'm ever going to get to having one."

"I wasn't telling you not to buy it. If you're spending your father's money, you can do what you want."

That summer their expeditions sometimes ended in a secondhand bookstore or the antique shop where Edgar scrutinized small classical bronzes displayed in cabinets with glass doors. "Freud collected ancient sculpture," he informed Caroline. "But there are a lot of forgeries around; you have to watch out for fakes."

The following afternoon, after much consultation with the proprietor, Samuel bought a little bronze figure with incised eyes, an up-raised hand, and what looked to Caroline like a bronze dishtowel draped over his other arm. "It's Hercules," her father explained, "with the skin of the Nemean lion. Killing the lion was the first of his twelve labors. He once had a club, but it's broken off."

"Honey, now why is that art?" Margaret asked when Samuel came home with it. "To me it looks like a worn-out little toy. And how do you know that it's real?"

Samuel growled, "If you don't want it, you take it back—tell Giuseppe that you think it's a fake." He left it on the piano and closed himself into the small back room he used as an office. Margaret continued slicing tomatoes for a salad.

"It's real," Caroline said.

"Sure it is, honey. Anything's real if you want it to be."

Caroline would like to see that crude little figure again, knowing what she knew now, and she wondered what Sheryl had done with it.

Margaret's precious purchase still lay flat on a high shelf in the house in Northampton, beside Samuel's books: two volumes of poetry and one of criticism. There was *Situation Normal,* the war poems that made his reputation. *Ashes Blown South,* his Venice poems, had been a disappointment. In the months after her father died, Caroline dared not touch his books, perfectly vertical and precisely aligned with the edge of the shelf, a shrine. One Saturday afternoon in March—she remembered the dazzling snow outside the window—she stood on a chair to take them down. Hidden behind the slight cave of shadow between the Fortuny book and the shelf, there was a brown manila envelope. Caroline unwound the string holding the envelope closed and pulled out a sheaf of poems in longhand, written and revised.

They were love poems; they spoke of a woman's body; they were specific and beautiful; they were horrible. To Sheryl, they had to be; he must have written them that summer in Venice.

Caroline did not hear her mother's car. The back door slammed and Margaret came into the living room. When she saw what Caroline was trying to hide, she stood silently and shook her head. The rims of her eyes grew red.

"I'm sorry," Caroline said. "I'm sorry."

"I'm sorry, too, for both of us." Margaret held out her hand, and Caroline gave them up. Though later she searched, she could not find them, and she did not ask how her mother had taken those poems from her father.

"WHAT ARE you wearing — a curtain?" Malcolm looked up.

"I paid for it myself."

"I don't care if you stole it; it does nothing for you."

"It's a work of art."

"Then art makes you look fat." He went back to reading.

"I'm ready to go," she said.

He put down his papers. "That dress — or whatever it is — is wearing you. Go look at yourself."

She frowned into the dressing room mirror. The pleats made her body columnar; the jonquil yellow turned her olive skin sallow. This was the color her blond mother had desired twenty-five years ago. Angrily Caroline pulled it off and put on a white suit: a spare jacket and pants approved by Malcolm, who loved her in white. Now she looked like a stone: the marble wife of the marble donor on a Renaissance altar. She sucked in her stomach and spread her fingers across the span of her waist. She wanted no room, not the smallest space for anything to grow.

A gondola was waiting at the Gritti dock.

"This is for us?" Caroline asked.

"I thought you'd like it."

"We'll look like real tourists showing up at the party in a gondola."

"Isn't that what we are?"

The gondolier muttered, "*Che bella signora*" as he helped Caroline into the boat, and she smiled and said, "*Grazie tanto*" with an operatic rolled *r*. Malcolm did not take the gondolier's hand and stepped awkwardly, half falling onto the cushions on the bench. "What did he say?"

"Just that he thought I was pretty. He probably says worse if you don't speak Italian. Where are we going, what's the address?"

"I don't remember. I told the concierge to take care of it."

Ahead of them a sunset flared orange in the blue-gray sky; the boat rocked slightly as the gondolier shifted his weight from back leg to front with each stroke of the oar. Malcolm stretched his arm along the back of the seat; he sat rigidly, his legs braced. He had tried to please her. The lavish sky, the little waves lapping the prow of the gondola, the languid, rhythmic rowing: Malcolm resisted these pleasures, and when she was with him, so did she. He mistrusted delight, as if it would leave him undefended. She could not go on working to understand.

"*O sole mio.*" With superb irrelevance the gondolier began the Neapolitan song. After two verses he swung the boat in an arc across the Grand Canal and nudged the prow against pilings at the entrance to a Baroque palazzo — pitted marble columns and arched windows. Caroline clambered out. Malcolm waited until the boat had stopped rocking and accepted the gondolier's steadying hand. On the landing he gripped her arm.

"What is it?" asked Caroline.

"I don't like sudden movements, that's all."

"We should have walked."

"By the way, thanks for changing. You look terrific."

From the courtyard they passed through an arched open doorway leading to a grand staircase with stone treads hollowed by centuries of feet. At the head of the stairs a man, about Caroline's age, awaited them. Slim and fair, with blue eyes and a delicate, thin-lipped mouth, he bowed slightly as he introduced himself: "Massimo Farsetti." A name attached to a palazzo: possibly this one.

"*Carolina Spingold. Buona sera. Questo é mio marito, Malcolm Spingold. É questo il palazzo Farsetti?*"

The young man laughed. "*Magari. Oggi lo storico palazzo Farsetti appartiene alla città. Abbiamo un appartamento qui. Ma lei parla italiano.*"

"*Un po', ma non molto bene.*" She said to Malcolm: "Sorry. I was asking if this is the palazzo Farsetti."

Massimo Farsetti turned to Malcolm. "Signore Spingold. I was eager to meet you. Your plan seems very — original." He spoke with a clipped English accent, and Caroline heard a suggestion of irony.

"It seems obvious enough to me," Malcolm answered dismissively.

"Obvious and original are not contradictory ideas. I am sorry my uncle could not be here." Massimo Farsetti's smile was both polite and imperious.

"Your uncle?"

"He has organized a committee to study the economy of Venice. Not unlike what you are proposing."

"Lorenzo Zorzi? He isn't here?"

"He had to be in Padua; he sends his apologies."

Caroline felt Malcolm's displeasure. He expected attention. They followed Farsetti to a small chamber paneled in walnut. From high windows pale light the color of white wine spilled onto the dark wood. Caroline recognized the Swiss financiers, Artur Heismann, with his second wife, Costanza, and Jean-Claude Farge, who was a director of the bank his wife's family owned.

Artur, short and puffed as an éclair, kissed her on both cheeks and aimed a third kiss at her lips, which she dodged. "You are so thin, Caroline." He pronounced her name as if it were French and kept one hand on her shoulder, the other on her waist. "I would prefer a little softness, a little belly . . ." His breath smelled of Scotch.

"Yes, I've noticed." She smiled into his eyes.

Artur released his grip as Solange Farge crossed the room toward Caroline. The women exchanged kisses. "I could never wear pants," said Solange.

"I adore your Givenchy," answered Caroline. Charm was easy, though she would have liked to advise Solange not to dye her hair such an uncompromising black. She embraced blond and rangy Costanza Heismann, who had gained weight, perhaps because Artur had asked her to.

"Where are your beautiful twins?" Caroline asked.

"They are in Brittany with my parents. Artur insisted I come with him. And Venice, it is lovely and calm, don't you think? Who can resist — and perfect for an anniversary."

"I had no idea where we were going. Malcolm didn't tell me until we were on the plane."

"I wish Artur would surprise me. So romantic. But with children . . ." Costanza smiled at her twin shackles.

"Yes." Caroline mustered a wistful tone. Children, babies, bellies.

These wives had ambition, too, but it was domestic and dynastic; they made her question her own. *A marriage needs children,* she could hear them telling their husbands. These women, in their comfortable lives, had no appetite for the tense complications of love.

"AND HOW was the good rabbi today?" Massimo Farsetti asked Gilbert Pryce.

"I went to the Scuola Grande Tedesca, and I think I found the beginning."

"In the dust?"

"It's depressing there, Mimo. It's falling apart."

"Maybe you could persuade this Spingold to restore the building."

"I wonder if he's Jewish." They walked slowly up the stone stairs. "But you said he didn't want art."

"Call it history. And thank you for coming. My uncle — he was not pleased that my uncle did not come back from his villa. I don't understand what the American gets out of this."

"Taxes, probably. Sheltering or avoiding."

"Is it legal?"

"In Switzerland, probably. Probably not in America. Why?"

Massimo said, "I'm curious; my uncle is, too. And, Gilberto, I want to leave early — I'm meeting Sylvana."

"Again? You saw her at lunchtime."

Farsetti smiled. "After an afternoon with Aretino — in one sonnet he decides that heaven is full of beds. And Giulio Romano's woodcuts — those Renaissance pornographers — I'm having more fun than you are, my friend."

"Will you be able to play tomorrow?"

"Why not? Call me — wake me up."

"Mimo — wait." Gilbert put his hand on his friend's shoulder and pointed at Caroline. "Who is she?"

"That woman? She's the wife. Mrs. Spingold. Speaks Italian."

"I know she does. I saw her this morning — actually, she saw me first. She thought I was somebody else. I couldn't figure her out."

"She asked if this was the Palazzo Farsetti. When I saw her I thought she would be a — what is the American word? — a bimba?"

"Bimbo. So she's married to the American?"

"Too bad, no?"

So she was one of those spoiled women, exempt from paying bills, from waiting, from decisions — a woman who had the luxury of being silly, while people had to pretend to take her seriously. But she hadn't appeared silly today, except that she had burst out laughing when she knocked that college girl down. "She was in a *motoscafo*," he said. "I ended up following her to San Marco — she knew the shortcut."

"Forget it," Massimo said. "First you want nobody. Now her, and she's impossible."

"I'm not interested in her."

"I see. But you followed her."

"It happened, that's all."

"If I didn't know that you were incapable of it, I would think that you were lying. Tell me something — do you have one of those complexes? Have you ever been in love?"

"Not really — well, at least not enough. Don't shrug. Listen, Mimo, for you love is easy. But I'm not like you. Come on, let's get this party over with." He had not loved Sarah enough, which had to be his fault. Until that was resolved he needed distance, something else that Massimo would laugh at. But Gilbert had an idea of what love could be.

CAROLINE DISENGAGED herself from the chatter and examined the carving. The edges of leaves and the rims of blossoms had chipped; there was so much beautiful in this city that this decoration seemed minor. A lizard clung to a twig; a butterfly landed on a flower. But this was made at a time when — she heard her father's voice — art mattered. It still mattered, she argued with his voice, it's just our understanding of the nature of the cosmos has changed, and human endeavor has been reduced to insignificance. So art has changed, too.

For Malcolm, art was a diversion, an impediment to his concept of a revived Venice. "The only jobs are in the tourist industry. Venice is stagnant; soon it will be dead — soon only foreigners will own apartments here. Is this what you want, a city of empty buildings with flaking pretty pictures painted on the walls? A city of waiters and chambermaids? What about a city of ideas, a city of new electronic technologies, of industries we can only begin to imagine, which require only communications equipment to grow?"

Caroline tried to detach herself and pretend to see him for the first time. His square shoulders, his graying hair combed back like a hawk's feathers: he claimed and commanded attention. He persuaded. But she was disturbed by a new stridency in his voice.

She was standing in front of a pair of large, carved doors. She pushed them open and entered a dimly lit room, frothy with white and gilt. Rosy putti cavorted in the angles of the painted ceiling and dangled from carved ropes of flowers. Over her head, little angels surfed clouds, and a painted goddess in a golden chariot soared triumphant through an aquamarine sky.

At the apex of the ceiling the clouds thinned to a silver cirrus. Again, that happiness, that alien, weightless joy and desire: was this an emotion accessible to her now only through art? She lowered her eyes, defeated. From the other room she heard applause.

Just below the angle where the wall and ceiling joined, at the horizon, the cloud thickened to a dense, smoky orange, and a swarthy man, distracted from his work, glared, helpless and furious, at the escaping goddess. The smoke from his furnace billowed into clouds. The man stood awkwardly, weight on one leg, the other foot turned in; he was lame. Venus and Vulcan. Caroline choked as if she had inhaled that smoke.

The lights in the room went on, startling her. Massimo Farsetti said, "*Sia la luce! Guardi, signora, guardi!*"

She lifted her eyes again and yielded to the ecstatic sky, the swirling vision of illicit escape.

"I turned around and you were gone." Malcolm's hand clamped around the back of her neck as if she were a kitten.

She freed herself. "Where could I possibly go, Malcolm?" she demanded. She looked up again, briefly, but in the bright light the frescoes appeared suddenly faded and dulled with soot.

He tilted his head back briefly and grimaced. "I'll throw my neck out. Maximo said something about the ceiling. Said it was worth a look. I forget who painted it." He prowled the room, glancing at the walls.

"It has to have been Tiepolo. Let's go." As she turned, she saw the man again, the man who was not Will, standing in the doorway beside Massimo Farsetti. Her first, defensive instinct was to smile: her bright, impenetrable expression. The man kept his eyes on her.

Malcolm nodded. "Tiepolo. That's right, that's what Maximo said. Who's that?"

Malcolm was looking at the wall.

"Vulcan," she answered.

"I like him."

"You would." She started to walk away.

"And who is that — that man, the one you were looking at — next to Maximo?"

"Clark Kent, mild-mannered reporter? I don't know. Ask him. Introduce yourself. I want to find out if these are what I think they are."

"Thank you for the light," she said to Massimo Farsetti. "I've never seen a photograph of these frescoes." She kept her eyes and her smile on Farsetti. "They're Tiepolo?"

"*Non sono conosciuti.*"

"I thought nothing in Venice was undiscovered."

"They had been covered over until very recently."

"Who found them? How did it happen?"

Massimo Farsetti put his hand on his companion's shoulder. "I think that you have almost met?"

She could no longer not look at him. He was nothing like Will; strange that she should have mistaken him. His hair was brown, his eyes a paler blue. Although he was lean, there was a denseness about him, while Will had been insubstantial, light. This man appeared distracted and ill at ease.

"Gilbert Pryce," the man said. He wore a boxy American blazer.

"Caroline Spingold."

"I saw you this morning. You know your way around Venice."

"I lived here for a summer with my parents. I was eleven."

"And how do you find it now?"

"What I found was myself, when I was eleven."

"And where were you hiding?"

She laughed. "Everywhere, really. But this morning, coming in from the airport, it was hard to believe Venice was real."

"It's not real to me yet." Malcolm had come up behind her; she stepped away, preventing him from claiming her by her neck or her shoulder again. "All I've seen so far is the hotel, a couple of canals, and this palazzo. Everything's a palazzo, my wife tells me. And you are?" he asked.

"A friend, a scholar," said Massimo, and introduced Gilbert.

"What do you do?" Malcolm asked.

"I'm writing a life of a seventeenth-century Venetian. A rabbi."

"Why?"

Gilbert smiled. "Complicated reasons."

"The simple version."

"Because I want to. And I'm lucky; I can."

"Are you getting paid to do this?"

"Not really."

"Then what do you really do?"

"I'm a lawyer. Tax law."

Malcolm's eyes widened. "Italian tax law?"

"Some. Why are you interested in Venice?"

"Simple reasons. My wife loves the city. And it seems like a good investment. Let's have breakfast. Tomorrow, at the Gritti. Seven thirty. You could be helpful. And you could show us Venice."

"Your wife can show you Venice."

"Not the art, the city. What it's like now. Bring Maximo."

"He has to teach, and I can't make it that early."

"Eight? I'll send a boat — a taxi. Give me your address."

"I'll be there."

Malcolm smiled at Gilbert, a smooth and practiced contraction of his facial muscles. "Good night, Maximo." He took Caroline's elbow.

"Massimo," Caroline said, "those frescoes —"

"Caroline," Malcolm said. "We're going to be late."

Restraining her anger, she followed her husband down the stone stairs. At dinner, they drank Bellinis and champagne and ordered beautiful, and faintly repulsive, platters of *frutti di mare*. While Malcolm and Jean-Claude speculated sourly on the American economy, Caroline endured Artur's mild lechery, Costanza's musings on motherhood, and Solange's opinions of various precious stones. The way these women talked, even children seemed like earthly possessions.

Earthly possessions: she should not underestimate their value. Her parents' marriage might have thrived if there had been more money. But hers had not.

After dinner, dizzy with drink, she and Malcolm walked back to the hotel. "Why did you ask him to show you Venice?" Caroline demanded. "Don't you think I know it well enough?"

"I thought you would like it," Malcolm answered, with what seemed like sadness.

Later, half asleep, she jerked awake. If this marriage were to end — the thought was as insubstantial and terrifying as a nightmare. How would she live?

AT SEVEN FORTY-FIVE in the morning the Grand Canal rumbled with barges laden with vegetables, copper pipes, a dishwasher in its carton, a rust-stained toilet, pallets of bricks, even a pinball machine. Caroline watched the progress of commerce from the terrace of the hotel. The heavy wakes of scows splashed against pilings and spilled over the dock. But there was something intimate and even romantic about it: Venice in dishabille, a great lady privately and serenely vulgar. Gondoliers at the *traghetti,* the crossing points of the Grand Canal, had taken up their posts, and they and the barge crews shouted jovial obscenities back and forth across the water. The day, too, was lighthearted, the sky white-blue, luminous as a Tiepolo. Caroline observed the glory; it could not cheer her.

When she awoke again, Malcolm was already sitting at the desk in the living room, the phone cradled on his shoulder, listening and making notes. He glanced at her and went back to his call. She took a deep breath to calm a resurgence of panic. "What's going on?" she asked.

"The yen — somebody in Hong Kong fucked up a big trade."

"You made an appointment for breakfast."

"That kid? You go down. I'll try to make it." He spoke into the phone and looked up again. "What was his name?"

"Pryce," she said. "How does he spell his name, do you think? Like Vincent? As in everybody has his? That's what you say. Malcolm — did I have my price?"

He hung up. "You were cheap."

"I was?"

"You cost me a little bit of silver, that's all. When silver was cheap. Nobody had ever done anything for you. It was easy."

She felt sick. "Was I worth it?"

"You were the best thing that ever happened to me," he said gently. He held out his arms, and she came to him. He held her around her waist and pressed his cheek hard against her belly.

"I'M NO ARTIST. I'm not here to talk to you about art; that's Sam's business. My job is to talk to you about the dirty work. The metal. The raw material." Malcolm Spingold twisted his vowels and flattened his *r*s: a pure Providence accent.

"I grew up across the street from the guy," Sam Gruson had told his students. "After school we'd play in his dad's junkyard." Caroline had expected a short and thickset man in rusty khakis, not elegant Malcolm.

"Casting in bronze is like working in hell," Malcolm went on, speaking as the junk man, and Caroline felt the art in his performance. "It's hot and dirty and dangerous. Those little statues across the street in the museum — you know them better than I do — or you should. The twisted lady with the tools."

"*Astronomy*. With Gianbologna's signature stamped on it. That twist — it's called contrapposto." Caroline let him hear her skepticism. He was pretending not to know, and she did not approve.

His narrow golden eyes focused slightly. His black hair was combed back, thick and straight, long over his ears. With his jeans and sport coat and open-necked shirt — a dress shirt that fit him perfectly — he looked more the artist than Sam, who kept his hair cropped short and wore baggy flannel shirts as if he were still in college.

"*Astronomy*. You admire her hair, her fingers and toes — and the rest of her, you wonder how the hell she managed to get herself into that — contrapposto. You know what I see when I look at her? I see copper and tin. That's all she is, with maybe traces of lead and zinc — the tin hardens the copper, makes it durable and easy to melt. Cellini — you know, the murderer — he nearly killed himself casting that statue in Florence. The one outside" — he looked straight at Caroline.

"You want me to tell you what that one is, too?"

He smiled, infuriating her.

"*Perseus.*"

"That one. His crew screwed up and made the fire too hot; the tin burned off, so Cellini heaved all his pewter dishes into the crucible. Hundreds of them. Pewter is mostly tin. But then the crucible exploded. F—" He caught himself. "Fireworks. One man died and it nearly killed Cellini. It's in his autobiography—which should be required reading for this course."

He paused and glanced at the work tables, at the lumps of clay and wax and coils of wire, the anvils and the blackened tools. "This stuff makes a mess." He shrugged. "Maybe that's what art is—it fools us into thinking that what is terrible is beautiful. What is gross is delicate. What kills us gives us pleasure. But I don't know; that's not my problem."

"Art doesn't fool," Caroline protested. "It transforms. It makes the mess bearable."

"Maybe," he said. He stared at her; she met his eyes until he looked away, smiling, and she had the sense that he was letting her win. "Fool. Transform. I'm not so sure there's a difference."

First you hate what you come to love. He crossed the room to her. A clay figure of a girl lay on her work table.

"May I pick it up?" he asked.

She said yes, though usually she hated it when people handled her models.

"What are you going to do with it?"

"We each get to send one piece to the foundry in Rhode Island."

"To Joe Fornari's. I grew up with Joe, too. I only go back to Providence when I have to."

"What about the junkyard?"

"The junkyard runs itself. On Saturdays I let artists in—to take anything they want to salvage. It was Sam's idea." He cradled the little figure in his palm. "Pretty," he said. "Not that I know anything."

"Why do you lie about that?" In the beginning, she wasn't afraid of him.

He laughed and tilted the model from his palm to hers to avoid marring it with his fingerprints. The edge of his hand was muscular and warm. She had imagined the girl in silver, which she could not afford: one of a series of silver children.

The following week Sam Gruson handed her a small box wrapped in tape. "Malcolm sent it," he told her with a puzzled smile. "Malcolm Spingold. He asked me to give it to you."

"It's not a bomb, is it?"

"I have no idea what it is. If it's from Malcolm, it could be anything."

Inside the box were two ingots of silver and Malcolm's business card. *I thought this might make you happy,* he had written on the back. She waited two days before she called him in New York to thank him. The hair on the back of her neck stood on end as she heard the corporate double ring. His secretary put her right through.

"How did you know that I wanted the piece to be made of silver?" she asked.

"I want her, I want a cast. And I want to have dinner with you tonight."

"You're in New York."

"It's half an hour to Boston on the shuttle."

"I have to work."

"Where?"

"In the registrar's office."

"That closes."

"But then —"

"The boyfriend," Malcolm said. "Get rid of the boyfriend. Tell him something; tell him it's about school. Something due tomorrow. It won't be hard."

"Do you pick a girl every year?" she asked.

"No," he said. The metallic, bantering edge in his voice had gone. "No," he repeated. "I have never met anyone like you. Please, get rid of the boyfriend tonight."

The boyfriend of the moment, a pianist, a student at the New England Conservatory, lived in a dingy apartment behind Symphony Hall. His bed was wedged against the wall. Waking up to the sparse branches of a street tree through his streaked, dusty windows, she recoiled from her need: this was not love. In the bleak morning she felt weary and unclean.

But Malcolm saw her as pristine. At their first dinner he said, "I'll wait for you as long as I have to." She spoke to him about whatever was on her mind: art, music, ambition, her friends, her eagerness for experience, her mother. Malcolm made her bold; he knew he had her, and she liked that.

He described his business, its combination of research, intuition, and luck, how trading depended on currents of politics and economics, fear and optimism, even weather. He was a new kind of prince, a ruler of calculation, of interest rates and currency rates, a prince whose domain was money itself. As she described her friends to Malcolm, they seemed fumbling, preparing to settle for small lives, making accommodations she couldn't abide.

Awakening in Malcolm's big bed in his apartment on the East River, she saw the sky and nothing else: a clear precious blue through glass so clean it seemed nonexistent and so thick that no sound could penetrate. She was in heaven.

CAROLINE HATED waiting, standing around with nothing to do, watching the waiters scurry. Her queasiness lingered: wine or half-dream. So that's how it began: silver, a couple of ingots. A transaction, a bargain, the price of love. She thought to call her mother, but Margaret Edgar had a sharp ear for misery. *Caroline — you're where? In Venice? What have you seen? How does it feel being there? Tell me everything. Have you been to see our apartment? I wish I could be there, I wish I could be there with you. Malcolm must be terribly busy; I could keep you company, we could walk around together the way we used to.*

We could alter what happened, Caroline would add.

Her mother would ask what she was wearing.

Just jeans and a T-shirt.

You must look gorgeous. Caro, is something wrong?

"CARO, IS something wrong?" Margaret came to the door in a voluminous brown tweed coat that camouflaged her smallness; she held it wrapped close around her. "I didn't expect you."

"I thought you'd just be getting home from work."

Margaret laughed her Southern flirtatious laugh. "They've asked me to teach ballet at the college. To beginners." She rolled her eyes.

"You didn't tell me."

"I haven't heard much from you lately." Margaret stepped back inside and her coat fell open over black tights and a pink tulle skirt. "Oh, honey, what a surprise. I'm so glad!" She saw the little red MG Malcolm had given Caroline blocking her Volkswagen Beetle. "What is that?"

"I'm getting married," Caroline said.

"Oh, my! My little girl! And you're so tan!" Margaret stood on tiptoe and wrapped her arms around her daughter's neck. "I'll call and cancel the class — they'll be relieved. I work them hard, my hopeless little elephants." She looked doubtful.

"Don't cancel," said Caroline. "I'll take you."

Margaret hesitated. "I have to make a quick call. I'll meet you in the car."

With a dancer's graceful pleating, Margaret Edgar sank into the passenger seat of the car. "You look so elegant! Now tell me everything!"

Caroline described the class, the gift of the ingots, the dinners.

"He's a generous man," Margaret said.

"And smart."

"Does he have a sense of humor? Sam was funny. *Situation Normal.* I loved that title — funny when you thought about it. Even when he was miserable, he thought it was funny. I loved that about him."

"Malcolm's funny, too." But he did not make fun of himself.

"Daddy thought I was too young to get married, but twenty wasn't so young in those days."

"I'm twenty-three, Mom."

"I wasn't talking about you, Caro. Your father didn't want me to work."

Caroline accelerated hard into a curve.

Margaret clung to the passenger's grip. "Caro! Be careful!"

"I know what I'm doing."

"I'm sure you do. Turn left here, sweetie. What are you going to do while I teach?"

"I'll watch. Do you mind?" Caroline sat on the floor in the corner while her mother talked her class through their barre and their simple floor work. She danced the combinations with her hands; moving, Margaret seemed young, not yet filled out. Sketching, Caroline attempted to see her mother; she no longer knew her. But her drawings seemed to her crude and awkward reductions of what she imagined in three dimensions, of what she yearned to understand.

"I've never seen you dance, do you realize that?" Caroline said as they drove back to the house. The call, she guessed, had been to the married professor who Margaret pretended was only a friend. Caroline for a moment imagined that she could sweep her mother up with her into this new life.

Margaret shook her head. "I wasn't really dancing. I can't dance anymore. Does Malcolm's daughter like you?"

"I've never met her. Her mother won't let her see him."

"Is that what he told you?"

Caroline stopped the car at the top of the small hill that sheltered the house from the north wind. Leaf buds blurred the branches of the maples, but the landscape was still transparent: the dark contours of the ridges, the crumbling vertebrae of stone fences crossing the fields, and the second-growth woods. "Mom — what are you doing? What are you asking me?" A mourning dove cooed.

"Your Malcolm would probably call it due diligence. It's what parents are supposed to do. I just want you to be happy. I'm sorry. Even I can tell how corny that sounds. It will be fun to plan the wedding; it will be wonderful to have a wedding here."

"It will be in New York. Nothing big, just a few people, friends."

"Am I invited, then?"

"Of course you are. Why are you upset with me?"

As they went inside, Margaret asked, "Would you like tea — for dinner there's a chicken — I roasted it, more for the cat than for me."

They sat at the scrubbed table in the center of the kitchen, with its brick-patterned vinyl floor and yellow Formica counters. A jelly glass with a sprig of forsythia and a daffodil decorated the windowsill. Her mother's gray tabby circled her ankles. Though the cat had come to the door here a week after Caroline left for college, he regarded Caroline as family and demanded attention. Sabotaged by sadness, she patted his broad head; she had expected to feel liberated from the dingy house and her mother's small means.

Margaret put the chicken on the table. "When your father walked into a room, even after we'd been married for ten years, I just lit up; it was like the first time I saw him."

"So what happened?"

"I don't know. His work wasn't going well, maybe it was that. She was different, she asked things of him. I didn't have a chance." She blinked away more tears. "I'm just so happy for you, Caro. I hope you are, too."

Her mother had guessed that there was something problematical about this happiness. Caroline was not sure precisely why: the difference in their ages, the transformation that would be required of her. She did not invite her friends to the wedding; she could not imagine them in the company of Malcolm's accomplished colleagues. She had an address for Will and wrote him a note, which he did not answer. She sent an announcement to Deirdre, who sent a present in return: coffee mugs, too brightly colored.

Caroline was married in a short gray linen dress. It was not as if they were both starting out together; she was jumping onto his fast-moving life. Of course his daughter was not there. At the reception at Malcolm's club, Margaret offered a toast to her daughter: "May you have as much happiness in your marriage as I had in mine."

All Malcolm's associates knew was that Caroline's father was dead, but Malcolm was distressed. "How can she say that?" he whispered.

"She adored my father." Caroline heard in her mother's words a wish, a prayer, for luck in love. When she and Malcolm were saying their goodbyes, Caroline, intending to embrace her mother only as much as necessary for good manners, clung to her and burst into tears.

"She's going to want things from you," Malcolm said on the way to the airport for their flight to Paris. He meant money.

"I wish she had somebody," Caroline said.

"You can't make her better."

GILBERT PRYCE was late. Annoyed, Caroline paced from the hotel entrance to the dock and back again. She decided to give him another five minutes. The waiters watched her covertly; she wasn't wearing ordinary jeans, but white Italian denim that had not been cut to fit a cowboy, and she wore a Japanese T-shirt with an asymmetrical hem and cutouts under the arms.

The T-shirt would make her mother laugh; Margaret did not approve of messing with the basics. If her mother were here they would speculate, as they used to on the *vaporetti*. Who was the man eating alone and wearing a suit of fine wool with a silky sheen? An art dealer? *No, a professor who bought his clothes with inherited money, a professor of linguistics, here for a conference.* Mom, a linguistics conference at the Gritti? She could see her mother shrug, cheerfully conceding. That couple — the round ones with dark hair. Don't they look like salt and pepper shakers? *They're Turkish.* How do you know? *I just know.* And that elegant Japanese woman sitting alone, looking out on the canal — did you see? *Perfect — she waved to the gondolier, and look what he's doing — he's making his hand into a telephone.* He's telling her to call him. *No!* I'm afraid so. It used to be that Caroline denied similarities with her mother, but here she was carrying on both sides of their conversation.

The five minutes were up. As she started inside, she saw Gilbert Pryce coming out. He ambled; he was wearing the same blazer he had on the night before. His hair was wet. "Good morning," he said, without apology.

"I'd given up."

"Sorry. Massimo and I play tennis most mornings before he goes to Padua. I'm not that late, am I?"

"It's twelve after eight."

"You haven't set your watch to Venetian time, have you?" He smiled, and Caroline felt foolish.

"What is that? Ten minutes behind mainland time?"

"Twenty. I'm early."

"I'll tell my husband you're here." The phone in the living room was busy; she tried the bedroom and let it ring until Malcolm picked up. "I can't make it," he said.

"So what should I do?"

"Take him to breakfast and talk about Tiepolo. Or was that with the other one? I'm on another call. Do whatever you want. Say you're sorry and come back to the room. It doesn't matter. He'll be fine."

Gilbert was sitting at a table for three. "He's not coming," she said. "Something having to do with yen. Money—not desire." She blushed.

His expression reflected her frustration. He stood.

"Don't leave," she said. "If you don't mind having breakfast with me."

"Actually, I'm starving."

She sat down. "Is Massimo a lawyer, too?"

"A professor. He's working on a book about Renaissance eroticism. The love poems of Aretino and Giulio Romano's dirty woodcuts. He's having a good time."

"I bet. I've seen the woodcuts."

"Massimo was impressed with you. Not too many people guess that those frescoes are by Tiepolo."

"It's like learning a language when you're a kid. It's in your brain. It's what I know."

"You're an artist?"

"I make sculptures, small things in silver. Figures. I've wanted to since I was eleven; I decided here, in Venice. Hard to explain."

"Do you show your work?"

She laughed. "I have a show in September. Yes, I'm for real."

"Why would you think that I'd think that you weren't?"

It sounded like a reprimand. "Malcolm doesn't, that's all. Who is this rabbi you're writing about?" she asked.

"He would have been a contemporary of Shylock—of Shakespeare. I didn't find out that I was Jewish—half, really—until I was sixteen."

"What? How couldn't you know?"

"I wasn't who I thought I was, and neither was my mother. She hadn't spoken to her parents since she was married."

"How did you find out?"

"I asked my mother where her parents were buried; she figured I was old enough. They were living in an old-age home in Baltimore."

"How strange."

"It's not supposed to matter anymore—religion, but it's bedrock, it's where you come from. It was not so great to be Jewish when my mother was young. And I love her—"

"Still?"

"Some people have the heart of a lion and some people have the heart of a lamb. She's a lamb."

"I'm Jewish, too. My father. My mother converted."

"Where do they live?"

"My father died when I was sixteen."

"I'm sorry."

"Yes." Today was the kind of bright day her father would have chosen for a trip to an island, maybe to Torcello, deep into the lagoon. She swallowed, and buttered her roll. "My parents were divorced." She signaled the waiter to bring more coffee and smiled as if these facts were unimportant. "So you're writing about Venice from a Jewish point of view. It must be a difficult story. Ugly and hard to piece together."

"He lived on sufferance; the circumstances of his life were arbitrary. Was it good for the Jews or bad for the Jews? I think about it in terms of emotion, the rabbi's. Anxiety, despair, helplessness, hope, intellectual arrogance — a sin in the Catholic church, did you know that? — and a kind of exaltation."

She listened with wonderment to his list of feelings. She put down her coffee. "Venice — the light here — it magnifies emotion."

He said nothing for a moment, and she wondered if he thought she was being silly. Then he asked, "Who did you think I was yesterday?"

"Somebody you couldn't have been. It doesn't matter."

"I've never seen anybody look so happy."

She smiled and looked away. "I was, yes. Until I realized that I was wrong. You saw." She shrugged. "Where would you have taken Malcolm, if he'd been here?"

"The usual."

"But it's only me — what's your favorite place?"

"Not a place. It's two things, but you probably want to see sculpture. A church — Giovanni e Paolo, I bet."

"What if I wanted to see what you wanted to show me?"

"This morning — if I hadn't had this very important breakfast meeting that didn't happen — I was going to go out into the lagoon."

"Why?"

"I shouldn't tell you. It's better if it's a surprise."

"Do you still want to go?"

"Sure."

"What's the other thing?"

"We can do that after; it only takes a minute—or an afternoon, depending on how you feel about paleontology."

"I adore paleontology."

"You're joking, right?"

"Maybe."

"Well, if you're not, they're in the piazza."

"We can take the *vaporetto* from the Piazzetta. I used to take it with my mother, almost every morning."

Gilbert shook his head. "I have a boat, a Boston Whaler. It's not a gondola, but still. We can go to San Marco afterward."

"Your own boat?" She laughed; on those mornings when she was eleven, she had wished more than anything to skim the water in a sleek boat, free to go wherever she chose.

Chapter 5

The Journey Home, June 1880

THE CLACKING WHEELS of the railroad train car acted on John Cross like chloral, lulling him into a stupor denser than sleep. A sharp sway jostled him half awake. Marian was beside him at the window seat, looking out; opposite, his brother Willie dozed.

"Where are we?" he asked. Though he was drowsy and the light was dim, he saw vivacity fade as his wife regarded him.

"Approaching the Brenner Pass. The curves woke you." She made her voice soft and crooning to soothe him and turn him back toward sleep, where, he suspected, she wanted him.

She drew the blanket close against his neck; at this altitude the air was as raw as early spring.

"We have fallen back a season," Marian said.

"That is just what I was thinking," he answered. "We think alike." For three days she had been describing the sights to him as they left the plain of the Veneto and followed the Adige to Trent. When she had last been in Venice, the railroad across the Alps had not been built, and the feats of engineering fascinated her; he heard her discussing trestles and tunnels and grades with Willie. Johnnie knew something about the subject of railroads — he had invested Marian's proceeds from *Middlemarch* profitably in railway construction in

America — but he could not organize his mind to join in the conversation and inform them that there were no tunnels on this route. He felt stupid, due partly to the state of his health; nonetheless he could not help but compare himself to his wife and suffer in the comparison. Before they married her mind had seemed to him a holy object, but in Italy it had become demeaned and sensual, an aspect of her corporeal being. They were traveling north now, every day getting closer to home and farther from the place that had inspired this aberration; soon she would be entirely herself and they could forget the Venetian nightmare.

"Johnnie, can you see outside? There is a fortress, a ruined castle clinging to the rock. You can hardly tell it from the crag."

He tried to open his eyes, but it took too much effort; his wife's vitality sapped his own; even seeing what she saw was too difficult. For the past fortnight she had been a saint; experienced at nursing, she had been tireless. It was just this physical energy, though, that had unnerved him in Venice. He sighed. "Don't try to look," she said, grave with concern; he had his limits, and he hoped she was learning them. She patted his arm in a gentle rhythm, coaxing the staccato wheels into a cradle song. He relaxed, enshrouded in the goodwill of his wife and brother. Since Verona no other traveler had entered their compartment. Because he had desired it, they had quit Venice as soon as possible. He could not breathe in that city's fetid atmosphere; he could not stomach the stench of the canals. A poisonous lassitude had seized him. That was how Marian had described it to Willie when he arrived in Venice and what Willie had apparently accepted.

If Johnnie's brother suspected a connection between this collapse and that episode in America so many years ago, he had not spoken of it. Hoping to cross the North American continent on its new railroad, Johnnie had gone as far west as the Mississippi. Rough accommodations, brutal heat, solitude: it had been too much; that was how Johnnie explained it to his family. He felt himself drifting off again; this was always the difficult moment, when his mental defenses ebbed, when what had happened in St. Louis overwhelmed his thoughts. He tried to concentrate on the chaste and comforting pressure of his wife's hand on his arm. He had imagined marriage to be this: friendship intensified, a deepening of mutual devotion. Marian's tenderness illuminated him as the sun lit the moon. The notion pleased him — he thought he might share it with her: he orbited her, held by her gravity and reflecting her radiance.

But the simile had its dark side. Her incandescence had flamed into demands and threatened to extinguish him; it had revealed in him an active revulsion. She removed her hand. St. Louis. Flora — Florie and Talmadge; the names rose into his conscious mind — Florie was all right in the beginning, though nothing happened, nothing really. Nothing. Nothing had happened in Venice, either. He shuddered; he felt vile and violated; he choked on the shame. He coughed, nearly retching at his failure to forget.

His wife and brother immediately sat at attention, offering water, brandy, biscuits. Johnnie took the brandy. The tracks straightened, the light in the car brightened though the day was overcast and a few flakes of snow burst into droplets against the carriage window. "And it's midsummer!" Marian exclaimed. "I can't tell if I'm looking at snow or edelweiss." The train slowed as if exhausted from its climb, and Marian asked Willie to open the window. Eagerly she leaned out. "Ah, here is the marker," she ducked back inside to announce. "We have reached the summit of the pass. One thousand three hundred and seventy meters."

Johnnie was cold; he could not catch his breath. His wife greedily gulped the thin, pure air that burned his face like ice. He hated his helplessness, his lack of appetite; he had arrived in Europe a vigorous man. "Marian, please," he whispered. She did not hear him, but Willie did.

"What is it? More brandy?"

Johnnie imagined that he could hear in his brother's voice frustration and disapproval. He nodded and pulled the rug closer about his shoulders. Willie handed him the flask. Surely Willie could not have guessed what had made him lose his balance. It was better to think of it as a fall. He had to forget the rage and shame, his incapacity to be — otherwise. But nothing had happened, nothing had happened. It was lack of exercise, too much indolence, hours spent lazing in a gondola when he could have been rowing on an English river, too much passive sightseeing, too much heat and bad air. He waited for Marian to tire of her breathing exercises.

"Johnnie, do you think you could stand? The air is so sweet and sharp, so refreshing; it might do you good."

He shook his head. "Close it, please, the window. You'll catch a chill." She obeyed and resumed stroking his arm. Surely his brother could see how devoted they were. The train lurched and groaned around the switchbacks, beginning the steep descent into Austria. If Marian thought she was breathing sweet air, she had willfully ignored the sickening engine smoke that had entered the carriage. The wheels clacked an obscene rhythm. *Florie and Talmadge and Florie and Talmadge.* In the hiss of brakes slowing their speed he heard laughter. The girl had laughed, scoffing at his reverence, his need to leave her inviolate. Forget, he commanded himself, but he could not forget how she had laughed. Her hands, which he had thought so gentle, gripped her brother's small shoulders like the talons of a hawk, her sweet features screwed into a lewd grimace. "Try him! Try him!" He shut his eyes. She was a hawk; her laughter a keen of dirty triumph.

Willie and Marian were bolstering him against the turns. "Shhh," Marian whispered. "Shhh." She began humming, crooning to him, her hand restraining his shoulder. He tried to breathe to the beat of her hand. Breathe, forget. Her hands were worn, the veins stood out on the backs of her palms, and she had a permanent callus on the little finger of her right hand. He should be caring for her.

THE SNOW at the pass had turned to rain in the valley, and low clouds had hidden the mountains ringing Innsbruck. But the emerald green pastures shimmered in the wet light, and from the spring melt the river Inn rushed, brimming its banks. In the lingering drizzle Marian paced the terrace, getting what exercise she could. Mist clung to her skirts in opalescent beads and cooled her hot face. Johnnie needed to gather strength, and she and George had not been to Innsbruck; here no memories would ambush her. She walked quickly; at any moment Johnnie, fretting, would send somebody to fetch her inside. It gave him solace to believe that she, too, required coddling. He wished her well; she could not afford to forget that he wished her well; it was all that saved her from drowning in anger.

Birds emerged, chattering and calling. In the west it began to clear; she regarded the white shafts of sunlight lifting mist from the peaks. All her life she had responded to a brightening sky. Her spirits were a barometer raised by increasing pressure. But today the gauge had gone awry, the mercury leaked; she remained depressed.

How foolish she had once been to worry that she might be forgetting George — but for her, a measure of guilt accompanied love. If her marriage — if things had turned out differently — the pain of his death might have diminished, but never her memories of their time with each other. George was bound into her being. Forgetting was not in her nature; her mind and her heart retained incident and feeling. Love, anger, grief, delight, shame, pride, jealousy: she had held them up to the light and filled her books with their refracted images. Refracted: ordered and shaped, given form and resolution by a story, memory transformed, split off into characters. She depended upon memory; she guessed that Johnnie found it dangerous.

Across the river, the tile roofs of the old town spilled like slides of red stones. She would have liked to walk those streets, and earlier at tea Johnnie had suggested that Willie accompany her if the weather improved. But she sensed a dare in that urging. Johnnie was testing the strength of duty against pleasure, and she refused to leave him, fearing precisely the pleasure she might feel apart from him. "Tomorrow if the weather improves we will drive out together in a carriage," she said.

A servant approached to say that her husband had asked her to come inside. In German she replied that since the rain had stopped, perhaps her husband might like to join her on the terrace. That, too, was a dare.

She hurried to the door to meet him. "I am so glad you've come out," she said, and took his arm. They strolled the length of the terrace, though she could see that it was an effort.

"I think I had better sit down," Johnnie admitted. He gestured to the servant to dry the sodden frames of the chairs and fit them with cushions and blankets. They settled themselves facing south, looking toward the mountains. The sun beneath the lifting clouds colored the peaks purple and spread a wash of gold on the pastures.

"You must feel better now that the weather has improved," Johnnie observed. "You like this time of day."

This moment of stillness: it should make her happy. In a flash of annoyance she thought how arbitrary her husband was to ascribe emotion to a natural phenomenon, to the effect of the planet spinning toward night. But how many times had she told him that she enjoyed clearing skies and the late afternoon? Only not today. She could not be offended. She would like to abandon Johnnie on the terrace and walk off her sadness, striding through sodden grass until water penetrated her boots and weighted her skirts, until each step took effort and she was exhausted. But she was leashed to him.

In Weimar, she and George had tromped across the fields even in the rain; on sunny days they had lain on the hot, dry meadow grass beside each other, teased with desire until they could endure no more and hurried back to their lodgings. They did not arise until the evening. Now she watched as the golden light spread and deepened. The birds quieted; even the river seemed subdued.

"*Über allen Gipfeln ist Ruh.*" She sang to herself the first line of Schubert's song, Goethe's poem.

"You're singing," Johnnie said.

She stopped.

"Please go on. The salon is empty. You could play. You could sing. I would like that. Remember when you sang for me?"

She said nothing.

"I'm afraid that I'm cold," he said after a few minutes.

"Yes," she agreed. She heard in his voice that he had caught her sadness. It was almost exactly six months ago that he had persuaded her to sing for the first time after George's death; it had seemed then — she had allowed herself to hope — that Johnnie had given her back her voice.

She stood. "The colors are fading."

He smiled and took her hand. "You're like ice. It's not pleasant here."

His hand was colder than hers. During the past two weeks they had resolved the touching; she took care not to encroach, and he no longer flinched.

"Marian, I think only of you."

She gazed at him sternly. "You must think of yourself, too. Take an hour and rest."

· · ·

ALONE INSIDE, she sat at the piano. Music might alleviate anxiety. She started the introduction to the "Wanderers Nachtlied": the lure and threat of peace, of death, contained in a brief minor interval. But her throat clamped shut. She had learned that song for George; she had sung it with Liszt. Liszt had admired Schubert — and Wagner. She preferred Schubert.

Musically, she had described herself as a tadpole, her taste not evolved enough to appreciate Wagner's grandiose constructions. She searched the scores stacked on the shelf and chose an album of Schumann's piano pieces. People were saying now that George Eliot was conservative. It was true that she had always written looking backward over her shoulder. She looked back to throw the present into relief. She needed distance; it made memory bearable.

It was growing almost too dark to see. She opened *Kinderszenen*, "*Scenes from Childhood*." She had played those little pieces for George when he was ill; she could not touch them now. A maid lit the lamp. Was there anything she required? A cup of tea or bouillon? Was she looking for something? *Nein, nein. Bitte, danke.* She attempted to adopt the girl's soft Austrian pronunciation but could not eradicate the northern accent. Every German word in her mouth tasted of her honeymoon with George.

THOSE THREE months in Weimar. Nobody knew or cared that they were not married; they were received everywhere. They were introduced to Liszt, who had invited them to lunch the following afternoon, the great Franz Liszt living notoriously unmarried in Weimar with Princess Carolyne Sayn-Wittgenstein. Liszt, with his long nose, delicate mouth, golden eyes, and his luxurious mane beginning to go gray. He and the princess had taken in the Leweses — Marian called herself by George's name — and become their friends. On their first visit Liszt had played for them — one of his pieces from *Années de pèlerinage*. Marian had fallen half in love with him. That season love was suddenly abundant.

On the last Saturday in October, at the end of the Leweses' stay in Weimar, Liszt and the princess had invited them to a musical party.

"Clara Schumann will be here. You will adore her," the princess announced to Marian. "You, especially, because you are so musical." The princess spoke with serene authority — her ancestors had long since bred doubt out of the line — yet the effect of her self-assurance was not arrogance but freedom. She was a writer, the author, they had been given to understand, of several books to which her brilliant lover had signed his name. She was generous, she was curious, she was rich. She was also plain, short, and alarmingly buxom, with coarse lips, a prominent nose, and unfortunate blackish teeth. She blithely ignored the gross facts of her body and dressed as if she were a beauty; her bodice of sheer lace threaded with silk ribbons clung to the precipitous contours of her *poitrine*. And there was something beautiful about her; her dark, healthy hair and her large eyes, alert for amusement. She was a connoisseur of genius and of folly.

"I wonder if her friend will come with her," the princess mused.

"Her friend?" Marian asked. "But she is married to a great man — and she married for love."

The princess smiled wickedly; she did not care who saw her teeth. "Yes, but her husband is locked away in an asylum." She shook her head so that her curls quivered. "Herr Brahms — Schumann's protégé — he adores Clara; it's marvelous to see. And rather sad."

"And does she adore him?" Marian fought her provincial impulse to be scandalized; were not she and George the scandal of the moment in London?

"She is fourteen years older than he and has all those children — there is no time for anything besides supporting them — and her husband. But of course duty is never what makes dalliance impossible." The princess smiled beatifically, as if adultery were a game for angels. "And though I think Brahms quite handsome . . ." She paused and turned toward Liszt. "Not, my dear, at all like you; he's good-looking in a coarse sort of way, but he is prickly and graceless, and too conservative, strict — he writes looking backward over his shoulder, frightened of Beethoven, of being trampled."

Liszt had laughed. "Why not look forward and outrun him instead?"

The princess had taken his hand. "Not everyone is as fleet as you."

Liszt had raised her little paw of a hand to his delicate lush lips and kissed each finger. And Marian had trembled with delight to be in the company of a man public in his desire and blithe in his ambition.

. . .

BUT ON THE Saturday of the musical party, Marian retreated and stationed herself by the doors opening onto the terrace of Liszt's music room. The low, weakening sun laid down a pattern of parallelograms on the floor and across her feet. Across the lawn a great oak was half bare, and its fallen leaves rose and danced in the wind to unheard music; at first she thought their brown shapes were birds. The tree spread like the oak at Rosehill — on fine summer days she had sat under its branches with the Brays and their visitors as they opened the world to her. In its shallow valley beside a meandering river, Weimar reminded her of Coventry, where she could not return. This afternoon despite the promise of music she was deeply ill at ease.

"She is not fitted to stand alone," the eminent phrenologist had announced to Charles Bray, but no observant person need map the bumps on her cranium to recognize her ardor. How much had happened in the three years since she had left Coventry for London. She had found work, and she had found love — she was an anonymous editor and an illegal wife. In both work and love she bore no name. But she could not have wished for a better love, or for a happier summer and autumn, days replete with pleasure and the task of helping her husband write his biography of Goethe. It was the fulfillment she had dreamed of; she had never reckoned the cost.

This was a large gathering; everyone wanted to hear Clara Schumann. She entered the room — a small woman grown plump and tired, her beauty sunken beneath the surface. Dark circles ringed her large melancholy brown eyes, but her smooth, shining hair and slight smile, grateful and distant, echoed with a beautiful girl's consciousness of bestowing pleasure.

She tilted her head when she was spoken to, and her responses were short. George was beside her, easing her passage, bending his lively face toward her and giving her his sweet attention. Marian felt a shameful pang of jealousy: Schumann had eight children, she was married to a genius, she was herself a pianist — among the most celebrated in Europe — and a composer, and all her life she had been trained and encouraged by her father.

Marian closed in, taking refuge in her old shyness, in a sullen, truculent state of mind she thought she had conquered. Perhaps it was because soon they were leaving Weimar, where Goethe had lived with his Christiane for sixteen years before marrying her and where Liszt and the princess flaunted their irregular connection. The Leweses' landlord certainly did not suspect that his soberly dressed, diligent tenants were not married. In three days she and George were going to Berlin for the winter. Half of their honeymoon had passed; when they returned to England it would be far more difficult for her than for George. She would be cut off from home, once her brother learned what she had done; already she was alienated from the Brays. She could count on being isolated, erased. Respectable women would not visit her.

Servants were passing champagne, which she refused. Liszt, elegant and tall, and the round little princess were flanking Frau Schumann now. Marian did not want to hear her play; she wanted Liszt. If Frau Schumann were not here, Liszt would invite Marian to stand beside the piano; its sound would vibrate through her body. Here she had felt the intimate mystery of music, and she feared that she would never again have that chance.

Liszt began playing one of his transcriptions of Schubert songs, in which he combined the vocal line and accompaniment, his own sensibility inhabiting and expanding Schubert's. He started quietly; with each verse the music enlarged, and dissonant chords broke and foamed into resolution, trailing filigrees of ornament. Beside the piano, the princess closed her eyes in rapture. Liszt reclined in his specially made low chair, holding his torso taut, his arms straight, and his long legs outstretched to reach the pedals, his body joined with his instrument.

When he finished, flushed and radiant, he rose and ceded his place at the piano to Frau Schumann. She gestured toward his peculiar chair, and Liszt laughed and replaced it with a bench. Clara Schumann adjusted its distance from the keyboard and settled her skirts. She bowed her head for a moment, then addressed the audience. "I am going to play *Kinderszenen.*" Her high voice carried, resonant and breathy as a flute.

Marian crossed her arms, preparing to render herself impervious. The first piece began with a simple tune; after the opening measures, Marian, eager to deprecate, decided that Robert Schumann had written it as an exercise for his children to play. It was wise, she conceded, for this woman not to try to compete with Liszt; Clara Schumann's playing could never equal such flamboyant, impetuous intensity. The pieces continued, innocent, foreboding. They conjured a territory bounded by garden walls, a place where childish delights and sorrows predicted larger ones. In this music, joy and grief — especially grief — mingled in recollection. The music touched Marian's regret and fear and doubt; she understood this woman's capacity, her genius. Clara Schumann was a muse, a conduit of emotion; she was at the same time a musician capable of infinite expression. Though Marian would have given the world to dismiss her, she could not.

Clara Schumann barely acknowledged the applause but consulted with Liszt as they sifted through albums of music. Several times she shook her head; finally she nodded and said something in her quiet voice that provoked laughter among those nearby; Marian recognized George's cheerful bray. She hated Frau Schumann.

Liszt placed his chair to the left of Frau Schumann's; he would play the second part of a four-hand piece. They turned the pages of the score, their hands beating time, setting tempi. When Clara Schumann paused to fan herself with a small black silk fan, George Lewes walked to the back of the salon and opened one of the doors a crack. "Would you join me?" he asked Marian. "There's a place. It will be too cool here, with the door ajar." She shook her head no. "Then may I stay with you?" Again she shook her head; she was near tears. George squeezed her hand and returned to his seat.

Liszt announced that they would play Schubert's *Divertissement à l'hongroise.*

"This is because I have practiced it," said Clara Schumann, with a note of humor in her voice that Marian wished were absent. "And Herr Liszt has not. So we will be equals."

Everyone laughed. "But of course you know," she added, "that he, when he wants to hear this piece, plays all the parts by himself. I will try to do justice to my half."

"And I will try to be worthy of you." Liszt bowed to her and opened the music, then settled himself in his chair, testing the distance from the pedals. He craned his neck and searched the room;

when he found Marian, he beckoned. She understood that he wished her to turn pages for them, but she could not. It represented too closely what she feared herself to be: an amanuensis, invisible, ignored, though she might be standing before an audience. Princess Carolyne, who never doubted the effect of her presence, adjusted her lace bodice and smoothed the first page of the music.

Marian knew the opening theme; earlier in the autumn, Liszt had played it for her. He had spoken to her often of Schubert — how she had treasured those discussions — of the poetry of his melodies, his instinct for the emotion of modulation, the fleeting changes of mood: how he could make grief blossom from happiness, wring peace from anxiety. Schubert, Liszt told Marian one evening, had heard a servant girl whistling this melody during a summer he had spent at an Esterhazy estate in Hungary.

"When I heard this, I decided to write my Hungarian rhapsodies," Liszt had said. "As a child I lived at Eisenstadt — in an Esterhazy palace."

"Where Joseph Haydn lived?"

"Where Haydn was in service."

She hesitated. "My father was the agent at Arbury Hall; he managed the estates. I grew up there."

Liszt laughed. "And my father was a steward at Eisenstadt, though I went to Vienna to study when I was very small."

"But our first memories root us; we are made from them."

He had looked at her with surprise and recognition; that exchange had marked a new understanding in their relations, an acknowledgment of connection, a modulation into friendship.

Liszt might have chosen that piece to show her that he remembered their conversation, but she rejected the idea. It had been Frau Schumann's choice. Marian was caught up in the melody shifting between yearning and fulfillment, the frivolous dances, improvisatory tremolos and runs interposed with the wistful folk song. Her throat tightened. Schubert was for the end of summer, for the season of loss and longing.

Liszt and Clara Schumann began the third movement at a thundering, galloping pace, but suddenly Frau Schumann stopped. "No, no, no!" she declared. She beat a slower tempo with her long fingers. The guests murmured, apprehensive and thrilled to witness a clash of musical opinion. Liszt bowed his head, and his arms hung at his sides. Was he refusing to go on? Marian took a step forward, perversely wishing that he would overrule Frau Schumann. But he shook his hair back from his forehead and smiled, the sunny, generous expression that Marian had come to love. He whispered to Clara Schumann, and she nodded in an intimate accord. Marian closed her eyes against them.

They started again, more slowly this time, and a melody that had seemed raucous turned tender, its passion, its headstrong impulsion tempered by hope and disappointment. Marian could not bear to watch them play; at the same time she could not bear to hear the music end.

The melody repeated one last, slow time, resisting, reluctantly sounding the final desolate notes. Unable to endure any more, Marian slipped out through the open door. A cold mist displaced the day's lingering warmth. It was almost winter; it was almost dark. She shivered, but she could not go back. George would have to search for her; what if he didn't notice her absence; what if he was enthralled with Frau Schumann? Then she would freeze.

But almost immediately he found her. "What is wrong, my Polly?" George grasped her upper arms and drew her close to him. "You're shivering. Come inside! What are you doing here?"

"I have a headache."

"Would you like something to drink? A brandy?"

"I must go home."

He nodded. "Oh, Polly, I'm so sorry. Should I ask for a carriage?"

"I prefer to walk."

Keeping to the margin of light, she crossed the lawn to the front of the house. George soon emerged with her cloak. "Liszt asked us to join him and the princess tomorrow for breakfast — for our farewell. He missed your company this afternoon."

"He has company enough."

"He wanted to talk to you about the performance — the tempi, especially."

"I'm sure I shan't be well enough to go."

"You did not speak to Frau Schumann."

"No. Her melancholy put me off."

"I found her charming."

"I could see that. To me she seemed quite sour."

"She was not, not at all; she was modest." George studied Marian from the corner of his eye. "I deserted you."

They walked along in silence for a quarter of a mile. The wind had subsided and leaves lay dead in drifted piles at their feet.

"But she is interesting looking," Marian said, despising her own selfishness. "She has enormous eyes."

"She was a great beauty, they say."

"Not anymore." She could not curb her bitterness.

"You're being hard, Polly."

"I'm reporting what I observed. It's understandable. She has eight children."

"Seven," he corrected. "One died."

"I'm sorry for that."

"And she has a mad husband," he added.

"At least she has a husband."

George ignored her remark. "She plays brilliantly."

"But she can only play. Not like Liszt. Listening to him I am drenched, I am soaked in his invention. When he plays I want to *be* his music; I want to become his sound."

"They are different kinds of artists. I liked the *Kinderszenen* — how she played them so simply, yet how much emotion they contained. I was glad of the chance to hear them."

"They are better than I expected."

They reached the park surrounding Goethe's summer house and crossed its darkening paths.

George said, "Liszt admires you, don't you think?"

Marian removed her hand from his arm. "How could he admire me? He has his princess, and anybody else he cares to have, as well."

George laughed, infuriating her. "He calls on you, he gives you libretti to read, he invites you, particularly, to the opera to hear him conduct, he cares to know what you think of his compositions. He tries to convert you to Herr Wagner."

"He invites us both. He calls on us both. And the princess calls on you; does that mean that she admires you?"

"He talks to you about music because you understand. And because you are beautiful."

"I am not beautiful. I don't understand why you say that to me. You are tormenting me, George." She was close to tears.

"You torment yourself, Polly."

"I don't know how you can bear to be with me." She kicked at a pile of leaves. "I have nothing. The princess has a husband and a daughter and she has money."

George grasped her by the shoulders. His eyes were pale in the blue evening. "Polly, you do not see yourself when you listen to music. While Liszt was playing this afternoon I watched you, and you were beautiful. You *are* beautiful — to me. I wake up to you every morning. Your mind, your spirit — they are beautiful, too. You do not have a husband, that is true. But you could have, if you want. I cannot be that man, but I assure you, you could find one if you wished. A rich one, too, if that is what you require. Polly, don't turn away. It's a child, too, isn't it? We could manage — we would manage. We would give it the best life we could, we would love it enough so it would not matter what the rest of the world thought. It's been done before; I — it's not impossible. But that must be your choice."

She could not staunch her misery. "I have done nothing with my life. I am the same age as Clara Schumann, and look at me. Everyone worships her."

"She is the sole support of her children and her husband. And don't say again that at least she has a husband. She also has her sorrows, Polly. We all do. It is what we do with them that defines us. And look what you have done — your translation, your editing, your articles —"

"I am anonymous."

"You have been — that is what is making you despair."

She sobbed, standing on the gravel path, with dampness seeping through the soles of her shoes. She knew him to be wrong about her beauty and her chances for a husband. She knew also that he was correct about a different truth that had to do with her desire, and with his disregard for circumstance.

George handed her his handkerchief, and though she tried to elude his arms, he embraced her. "Don't run away from me. Nobody will see us." He kissed her, and despite her misery he was smiling. She remembered how, when she first knew him, his laughter had irritated her; loud and flippant and careless it seemed, and she had thought him callous and shallow. George reached for her fist clenched at her side and kissed it open, kissed it again and again. He whispered, "My darling, my own poor dear anonymous love!"

IN THE HOTEL at Innsbruck, Marian turned off the lamp to see the last of the evening. She expected that Johnnie would come down soon, and she did not want him to find her at the piano. She played again the opening chords of "Wanderers Nachtlied." Goethe had written those lines, remembering the Alps. Marian looked out to the slow crystalline darkening calm. Shreds of clouds flared gold, and the mountain peaks had become insubstantial, a jagged wash of blue against the pale sky.

She sang the song through, barely touching the keys, almost in a whisper. *Ruhest du auch.* Peace. You, too, will have peace. She could have been singing to George; he could have been embracing her still.

MARIAN STROLLED with Johnnie and Willie under the linden trees lining the Kurplatz in Bad Wildbad. Here everyone proceeded with measured dignity and breathed conscientiously and deeply. Guests inhaled well-being and speculated on the lineage, financial stability, and health of their neighbors. The Trinkhalle, the ornate cast-iron pavilion where they repaired every morning at ten to drink from the restoring spring, stood to one side of the square, and behind it extended a conservatory.

What an odd little party they made — two younger men who spoke no German and an elderly lady who did. Perched on the steep shoulder of a valley in the Black Forest, Wildbad attracted few English visitors. *Die Engländers:* that was how, Marian was sure, the families staying at the Hotel Klumpp referred to them. Clearly they were prosperous — her brooch attested to that — and the taller of the men seemed unwell, but how were they connected? A mother and her sons? Unlikely: there was no resemblance between the handsome men and the homely lady. An aunt and her nephews? More probable. But how to understand the proprietary way that one of the young men—the one who was ill—insisted on taking the woman's arm? Did she have the money? Would it occur to anyone that they were husband and wife? Marian took a deep breath and exhaled in a sigh.

"My dear, has something upset you?" Johnnie asked quickly, as if he had been monitoring her condition.

"I am only breathing in."

"The air is invigorating, is it not?"

She nodded. It certainly had invigorated Johnnie. The altitude, the crisp mornings: after only three days he showed improved energy. But his face was still gaunt, his eyes shadowed, and after their gentle circuit of the square his cheeks were flushed with effort.

In the bandstand an orchestra, which had been tuning up, began playing an overture by Weber. Most of the sound evaporated in the thin air, leaving drums and horns to echo against the mountainside. Marian smiled at the unmusical effect, its inadvertent humor, and how the crowd in the square, almost as one, began marching to the rhythm. Beside her, Johnnie adjusted his step. He patted her hand. "You're smiling. It's the music, isn't it?"

"Why yes, it is." It unsettled her, how unfailingly attentive to her mood he had become, and how mistaken his interpretation.

Willie consulted his pocket watch. "This air has given me an appetite," he announced. "And my train leaves in less than two hours."

At the hotel they had taken a table near a window overlooking the mountainside, offering a glimpse of the river running silver at the bottom of the valley. "You are certain that you do not need me?" Willie regarded his brother with concern.

Johnnie smiled reassurance. "You can see how much better I am. Every day I am stronger. We shall stay a week, and the journey home will take us only another week."

"I have made all the arrangements," said Willie, handing Marian a packet of tickets.

"I'll take those," his brother said.

"Johnnie, you must not trouble yourself," said Marian, slipping the packet into her pocket. "Not yet."

"Please, my dear. The farther I am from Italy, the stronger I feel."

Willie pushed his chair back from the table. He had been imperturbable, and he had not speculated. His questions had dealt with

what could be controlled, with doctor's visits, medications, timeta-
bles, hotel accommodations, luggage. Like his brother, Willie was
kind and, unlike his brother, he was not complicated. "We will miss
you, Willie," Marian said.

They saw him into the coach. Willie's departure had been noted
by the hotel's guests; perhaps they were revising their speculations.
Marian felt suddenly unbalanced, as if Willie had been the stabiliz-
ing third leg of a stool. Alone with Johnnie, she did not know what
to do.

Johnnie helped her. "I think I might rest," he said. "And you?"

"I do not know." She watched the empty road with a childish
bleakness, a swift and desolate sadness.

"We have not had our coffee," said Johnnie. "That is one thing I
did like about Venice. I liked Florian's; it was cozy inside. Come with
me to the conservatory; we can drink our coffee in peace there. On
such a fine day, everybody will be out walking."

Or they will be in their rooms resting during the private hours
of the early afternoon, she thought, with a spasm of physical longing sharp as a cramp. *Resting:* that was a word they had used between them, she and George. Johnnie stopped. "Marian, tell me, do
you wish that you were walking?"

"Perhaps later in the week you will come with me."

The splashing fountain in the conservatory did a fair imitation
of a brook, and potted ferns clustered at its base suggested the green
solitude of the forest. Marian willed herself to be content. Johnnie put down his coffee cup and crossed his long legs. His thighs
were thin; his trousers hung loose over the knobs of his kneecaps.
"You might begin, you know," Johnnie said. "While we are settled
here."

"Begin?"

"Your memoirs. Your memories of childhood."

He was, she reminded herself, only being kind, only looking after
her; it was not worth anger. "While we are here I will be with you,"
she said.

"I seem to need a great deal of rest. I wish it were otherwise. While
I'm resting you could begin the planning. And we could talk about
it." This was not the first time he had broached the subject. But what
was his intention: that she write her memoirs, or that he help her?

"Johnnie, my childhood — I described it to you because you were — you are — my friend. It was not very interesting."

"But what wonderful characters there were in your family — your father and mother, your brother Isaac."

"They were ordinary people but for the fact that they were the center of my world. That does not make them interesting to anyone but me."

"They are interesting *because* of you."

"My mother was ill for such a long time. She died when I was sixteen, and I remember only her illness."

"You cared for her. That is a wonderful story."

"There was nobody else. It was my duty. A story repeated all over England, Johnnie. It is commonplace."

"But your books tell the extraordinary stories of commonplace people."

"Oh, Johnnie, thank you. They are fiction, altered and heightened, improved. I keep my life to myself. And I could not write about George." She scanned his face for evidence of hurt; Johnnie was too tender for confrontation.

He lowered his head. "I did not mean to offend you. I was speaking of your childhood."

"It was not always happy."

"But you could make it so. You are so good."

"My life has been far from exemplary." She concealed anger in a tone of self-reproach.

"How can you say that? *You* are exemplary."

"I am an example for nobody. Johnnie" — she held back from laughing at the idea that she was defending her own lack of virtue — "oh, Johnnie, never mind."

"What were you going to say?"

"I cannot expect that readers — sometimes not even my friends — will understand my life. My life — any life — is not a plot."

"You are being hard, Marian," he murmured. "I don't know what to say when you are like this."

She was being hard. They sat. Johnnie took several deep breaths, composing himself. "When we are back in England there will be days when I shall be quite busy — with business, and with the alterations to Cheyne Walk. Since we are home, I shall supervise the work. If you prefer, we can take a house in town."

Relieved that he had dropped the subject of memories, she answered quickly: "Oh, no, the country will be delightful." Then she hesitated. Was he suggesting that her house might hold too many memories of George? Did not the entire world? She hoped obliquely to reassure him. "It will be too hot in town, and you must be careful in the heat. You mustn't work too hard, Johnnie, you mustn't risk becoming exhausted again." Exhaustion: that fiction exhausted her.

He sat forward in his chair so that his thin knees almost touched hers. "Marian," he said, "in the evenings, when I am back from town, I will listen to what you have written during the day. I will be able to help you. You've taught me a great deal, you know."

The hothouse fountain seemed to be laughing. "I am not sure I could live up to your intentions," she said.

"It will sell, I promise you. It will sell."

She laughed out loud; when he revealed his true feelings, he was endearing. "I was not aware that I needed the money. I must ask my financial adviser."

"*Theophrastus Such* did not sell."

"Are you now managing my reputation?"

"I am only concerned with your happiness."

She exhaled anger. The air was oppressive with the smell of heliotrope; pots of them purple as thunder clouds bloomed along the perimeter of the conservatory. Johnnie liked projects; he might decide to build a conservatory. He might intend to encourage in his wife an interest in cultivating tropical ferns. Palm trees, too, and she might also develop a curiosity about monkeys and import a pair to swing from the palms. She smiled.

"What are you thinking?" Johnnie said, vigilant, alert for a reconciliation.

"Nothing." She shook her head. "I was smelling the flowers."

"I was thinking that if we added a small conservatory to Cheyne Walk — added it to the back of the house, we wouldn't lose much of the garden."

"What a lovely idea." She smiled mischievously.

"You could grow ferns."

"And keep monkeys."

"They spit, I've heard. And they are not very clean. But—" He would do anything in his power to make her happy.

She sighed. "Johnnie, I feel a headache coming on. I think I must rest."

He took her arm and returned her to the Hotel Klumpp and its soft, not at all Germanic beds. George would have enjoyed these beds. Oh, George. She stretched, anticipating the voluptuous, soft sweetness of memory. She would close her eyes and pass the afternoon remembering.

DOVER'S CHALK cliffs lifted from the sea austere and white in the morning sun, and above them the fortress castle frowned, offering no welcome. Marian had not slept and had come above deck at first light. On her first crossing to the Continent with George twenty-five years earlier she had not slept either, nor had he — how could they? They were adventurers embarking on an expedition, sleepless with audacity, with consciousness of the dangers of their course of action and its cost, but mostly with reckless joy.

It was July then, too; they had passed the short summer night on deck, in the few hours of starlight gazing at the constellations pivoting around the polestar. That had calmed them, the ancient practice of arranging the random scatter of stars into heroes and monsters, a queen, a faithful dog, a winged horse: ordering the unknowable universe into stories. At dawn, the hazy atmosphere turned rosy gold; the low shore of Belgium shimmered, a solid sliver between the sea and sky, a place of deliverance. She had never forgotten that bliss, colored with sunrise.

Eight months later, on the voyage back, sleepless again, this time with trepidation and defiance, she had watched the March sunrise illuminate the Dover cliffs. That morning, too, the gray stone castle keep had appeared to her inimical, a fortress of opprobrium. It had not daunted George. He was fired with the freedom of Europe and with the prospect of selling his biography of Goethe. The evening before their crossing, at their hotel in Brussels, in the lobby after supper, they had glimpsed Hector Berlioz, hollow of cheek and wild of eye; George wanted to approach the great composer.

"What will you say to him?" Marian demanded.

"Why, we will talk to him of Liszt, and of Wagner's operas."

"We have no introduction."

He had dismissed her objection. "We are all travelers."

That evening she had resented his energy for the same reason she had once disliked his laughter: he seemed to be refusing to acknowledge the gravity of the business at hand. In two days he would be off to London, alone, while she remained at Dover. Too much was uncertain.

"Polly — what is it?"

He listened while she removed sandbags of rational explanation — the bulwark surrounding her tenderness — and she broached the truth. "I am jealous of you tonight — our last night away from England. Our last free night. I feel England closing in on me."

"We must think of it differently, Polly. We must think of this as a beginning."

"A continuation."

"Yes, a continuation. Now, come, Mrs. Lewes — which is your name, which is who you truly are — let us continue in a soft, large, comfortable Belgian bed."

The next afternoon, after they deposited their luggage at a hotel in Dover, George insisted that they climb the castle hill to explore the looming fortress of English rectitude.

"Should I not find lodgings first?" she asked.

"First I need a walk."

As they climbed the cliff, George declaimed in his resonant actor's baritone: "'How fearful and dizzy 'tis, to cast one's eyes so low! The crows and choughs that wing the midway air show scarce so gross as beetles.' It's not so bad to be home, is it? There's a comfort in speaking English again."

From the summit the gulls and swallows swooped below them, black and delicate as insects; ships rocked like dories, dories rode the swells like buoys; the fishermen on the beach scurried small as mice along the line of silent surf.

"It makes me dizzy; it makes me want to jump." She held her bonnet against the wind.

George secured his arms around her waist. Below them the Channel shaded from blue to gray and back again with the scudding clouds. "You do not mean that, Marian."

"I am afraid. What are you going to say to your wife?"

"The truth: that I love you and that I am going to live with you."

"She will not accept that."

"She has no choice."

"You must assure her that you will continue to support her and the children, at least the ones that are yours, and the others, as well, if it comes to that. Our loving each other is not important to her. You must make it clear that you do not intend to abandon her."

He loosened his embrace. "Don't you think she knows that? Polly, if I had not behaved so well, it would have been possible for us to marry."

"If you had not looked after her so well, I would not love you. Even so, it is in her power to give us what we want. You have to reassure her."

"Agnes is not as bad as all that."

"You must be better than good."

"I'm sick of being a saint." He had walked away from her then. In Germany these matters had seemed abstract and even amusing. He paced the cliff; she watched his wiry body with an ache of longing for their German idyll. He said, "I hate depending on her for my — for our — happiness."

"She must understand that our happiness will not change her circumstances, that's what I was saying."

The wind had turned chill, a spring wind carrying remnants of winter, and she clutched her shawl tightly around her shoulders. That winter in dank and snowy Berlin she had been blanketed in love.

"It will be difficult to manage, if we are to support ourselves and Agnes and an ever-increasing flock of little bastards —"

"Foolish woman."

"Oh, Polly," he sighed.

"What *are* the benefits of sainthood?" she asked.

"Neither of us will ever know, will we?" He shrugged and smiled, but his smile was brief. "I was saying, I shall sell Goethe, I'm sure, and we will sell your Spinoza translation, too, when you finish it. I will see to all of that when I get to London. And in the meantime Chapman will take anything you write."

They had resumed walking again, arm in arm. "At least *he* doesn't claim that he is offended by us — by me," she said.

"How could he dare to be — the randy old goat!" George had exclaimed with some vehemence, and she blushed, remembering her connection with Chapman. In men the ardor of love and work was not so intertwined.

But Chapman had remained true to her intelligence, possibly because he depended upon it. When she told him of her plan to go to Weimar with George — she had confided in Charles Bray and Chapman — he had encouraged her, surely in part because it assuaged his guilt.

"I'll work on Spinoza while you're in London, and I'll write a piece about Weimar for Chapman. I will have nothing else to do but work and walk."

"It won't be for long."

"No. I hope not."

"What will you read?"

"Shakespeare."

"*Lear?*"

"Perhaps *Venus and Adonis*. Speaking of randy."

" 'Sweet bottom-grass and high delightful plain, Round rising hillocks, brakes obscure and rough,' " he quoted, and kissed her. "Polly. I'll miss you."

The wind died, and her apprehension of danger subsided. That afternoon Marian had understood that she and George inhabited an imagined paradise, a garden enclosed where they saw each other clearly: unencumbered, truthful, naked. That was their marriage, and she willed it to endure. She said, "Tomorrow night, when you're gone, I'll take the poem to bed with me."

THE DRY SUMMER land breeze blew across the Dover cliffs. On board the ship, passengers prepared to resume their English lives; they chattered excitedly and pointed to the Union Jack rippling atop the castle ramparts. Now Marian watched with trepidation as the crenelations grew more distinct. After they docked, she and Johnnie would take the train to The Heights, to the house in Witley she and George had bought only two years earlier, the hospitable house Johnnie had found for them near his mother. Johnnie's unmarried sisters were living in his mother's house now; the newlyweds would have their frequent company.

A quarter of a century ago, approaching the English coast, she had not known how she and George would live, and she had waited, depressed and lonely, six weeks in Dover while he arranged for them an existence that would not prove too awkward or too brazen.

Now she did not know how she and Johnnie would live. In Weimar she had learned the luxurious pleasure of married love; on this sad honeymoon she understood that she did not know how to love Johnnie. Before they married, she had assumed that life would continue as it had been. And how had life been? For six months anticipation and nervous apprehension had sustained her as she prepared for her secret marriage with its great rescue and its small guilt. She had dreamed the sensations of married life: bliss, bodily comfort, happy congruence, or rather, happy incongruence. But she had assumed — she had been rash to assume; she had mistaken Johnnie's passionate solicitousness for passion itself. That misjudgment infected everything. Johnnie had assumed that as her husband he would know what was best for her. Evidently he had decided that she was to work at reminiscence.

"Marian, I thought I had lost you — I searched for you everywhere." Johnnie approached, balancing against the roll of the swell.

"I was up early."

"You should have awakened me."

She shook her head. "You need your sleep, still."

"I feel so much better, breathing English air. I can smell land. We shall be home this evening."

Home: her home was now his. Johnnie smiled with his old, hearty cheerfulness, Europe forgotten, or dismissed. But she could not forget what he had done — what he had done to her. Though still weak, he no longer required pity. He was going to recover, and she could not ignore how monstrous that leap had been. It almost certainly could not have been an attempt at suicide. Suicide she understood; it was never an unconsidered act. But by jumping Johnnie could not have achieved death. He knew how to swim; he enjoyed swimming. Perhaps she was wrong, and he had been so distressed and deranged that he had convinced himself that when he hit the water he would turn into a stone, and his arms and legs would forget how to move.

But Marian had distressed and deranged him; whatever his intention and whatever the result of his action — the power he had gained over her — she had caused him to jump. She had acted on him like poison, and for that there was no antidote. Their union could not be undone, and they could not live separate lives. The headlines of her marriage had not lost their novelty; she could imagine the sensation, both public and private, if the bride and groom lived in their respective houses. She could not do that; she could not go that far. She was not prepared to return to England and face her friends. She turned away from her husband, took a deep breath, and exhaled in a sob that was lost in the wind and the ship's whistle. She would not trot him out like a new puppy; she preferred solitude to that pretense. But she could not hide indefinitely. She would have to learn to dissemble, to affect the new happiness that she would be required to put on display.

JOHNNIE INSISTED that she take the seat by the window. She dozed while beside her he exclaimed at the deep green hedgerows, the golden meadows — Kent's gentle pastoral — and he had to awaken her as the train neared Godalming. The coach met them and they were driven the two miles to the house at Witley. The tall rosy brick chimneys of The Heights emerged from behind the elms lining the drive. Marian had not lived in the house long enough to feel the familiarity of a homecoming; it was more the happy surprise of new possession — or rather a memory of that surprise. It was a beautiful midsummer afternoon, dark and cool under the trees, bright over the distant downs.

Inside the floors and furniture shone, polished and gleaming for their return; she mustered the enthusiasm to accept the staff's congratulations. Afterward she remained in the hall, unsure of where to go, conscious of a profound and nervous languor. She put up her hand to quiet the hammering of her pulse in her temples. "Do you have a headache, my dear?" Johnnie asked. "Would you like tea? A rest?"

"No," she said. "I require nothing. There are accounts to settle. I should attend to them."

Instead, she walked from room to room, scrutinizing each one for changes, as if these possessions — hers and George's — must somehow reflect the monumental alterations that had occurred in her life. Johnnie followed, pausing at each threshold. She touched the covers of the books that remained stacked on George's writing table. The parlor maid had dusted each volume as it lay. Nobody had dared return them to their shelves. Marian shut her eyes against this pretense of death as temporary interruption.

"Why has this been dusted?"

"I asked that nothing be moved," Johnnie said. "In May. Before —"

"A shrine."

"Yes," he answered. "I thought that was what you would want."

"George is dead. He does not need these books. I finished his work as best I could."

Her husband drew himself up. "That was not my intention."

"And what was your intention?"

"I thought you wanted to preserve his memory."

"His memory is not your concern. By marrying me you did not come into possession of his memory. Or mine, for that matter." She flicked the cover shut and gathered up the stack of books. As she struggled to replace them on the shelves, Johnnie hurried to help and tried to wrest the books from her. She resisted and held on to them, and they scattered onto the floor, pages crumpled, bindings splayed.

"How can you speak like that?" His voice was constricted, a furious whisper, as he stooped to rescue the books.

"Leave them," she ordered, stepping between him and the disorder. "There is a great deal I cannot speak."

He gazed up at her, appalled and transfixed, and she understood that in his eyes she might as well be a gorgon, with graying hair spitting from her head like snakes. "I am not what you imagined me to be, and there is nothing to be done," she said, and she hid her face in her hands.

He did not reply, but then she had not asked a question. The floorboards creaked; he stood. "Marian," he whispered. "Marian, please. Look at me. You must."

She lowered her hands. He braced himself with his hip against the edge of the writing table, and extended his hand toward her. It was trembling, she saw, and she thought, cruelly, that at least he hadn't turned to stone. He spoke in a low voice, but its sharp edge cut into her consciousness.

"Marian, I promised you peace. And I can give you that. Peace. That is not inconsiderable. Is it?"

She had wondered — to George — how such a kind man as Johnnie could succeed in the harsh and uncertain world of finance. Here were his terms: the bargain, the offer.

"Answer me," he commanded. "Is it?"

She looked at him with reluctant and bitter respect, admiring his effort, fearful of his resolve. "No, it is not."

"Well, then. Come now. This has unsettled you, this return is difficult. But tomorrow Eleanor is coming — she'll welcome you properly as her new sister, and you will feel better, I'm sure of it. And Charles Lewes and Gertrude are arriving the day after tomorrow. We will see only family. We will be happy. Now, come, Marian. Come with me. Leave this room until you are prepared to take consolation in it."

She balked. "And how will I do that?"

"We left my mother's room untouched. Before I" — he hesitated, compressed his lips as if trying to hold back a secret. "Before I asked you to be my wife, I went into her room and sat in the little chair beside her bed, the chair where I used to sit during her illness, and it was as if" — he glanced at her fearfully, then bowed his head and went on — "as if she were there, advising me, comforting me. I was reassured, I knew that I had made the right decision."

It was not so different from what Marian had done on the morning of her marriage. But George had not been her father. She bit her lip, resisting the defiant urge to laugh.

"And I continue to believe that I have done so," he added, as if from the play of expression across her face he guessed that what she had wanted to say was not kind. "Our tea will be ready." He raised his arm, elbow crooked for her to take, and she bent her head and went with him. He shut the door behind them.

Afterward she walked outside to the terrace and sat in one of the chairs she and George had placed for the view, for the sight of peace. A thrush sang, silvery falling notes. She heard a rustling behind her like footsteps, and for a moment she permitted herself to believe that it was George coming around the house with a posy from the cutting garden. But she would not look. The rustling continued, punctuated with a loud, trilling chirrup. It was natural, this willingness to be fooled, but she could not suppress a flash of disappointed anger at the squirrel scrabbling through the shrubbery.

AND THERE was peace. Johnnie's sisters visited from Weybridge the next morning, bringing with them in the carriage cases of their brother's claret and welcoming their new sister with sincere and abundant goodwill. Eleanor vowed that she would never unclasp the locket Marian had brought her; Frances declared she would treasure the exquisite lace handkerchiefs and never let them anywhere near her nose. It was a familial trait, this capacity to delight in the moment, to find amusement and cheer in the smallest and most ordinary occurrences. It had drawn her and George to Johnnie and his mother when they first met in Rome; it had led the Leweses to search for a summer house near Weybridge and the Crosses.

In the presence of his sisters, resting against the cushions of their gentle concern, Johnnie revived. The couple's early return from their honeymoon was never discussed; his sisters' instinctive delicacy curbed their curiosity. There was a lesson in that, Marian saw, a lesson she had better learn. What was the value of understanding motive? It did not alter the effect.

As Eleanor and Florence drove off at the end of the afternoon, Marian's spirits caved. She had contaminated Johnnie's grace. Alone, she feared that they would revert to a civil wariness worse than solitude: that was what peace would entail. But Johnnie's sisters had left behind sufficient cheer to last the Crosses the evening. The next morning Marian did not see Johnnie until lunch; he had letters to write and business to attend to. Then Charles and Gertrude arrived for dinner and stayed the night, and Johnnie was once again delightful; to accompany the gifts, he had composed verses, whose ineptitude, combined with claret, kept them laughing:

> *This little present is*
> *A lacy shawl from Venice.*

And:

Puppets here for Gertrude
To bring home to her young brood.

When Charles inquired as to Johnnie's health—and Marian thought she heard in her stepson's question a hint of warning, a whisper of threat—Johnnie spoke of his exhaustion, blaming it on the heat and the absence of French wine, diminishing it to anecdote, bad luck, uprooting it so that it withered into eccentricity.

MARIAN AWOKE early and walked through the warmth of the kitchen garden, whose pink brick walls had already collected the heat of the summer sun. Ripening tomatoes hung dense and solid from their vines, and she cradled one to feel its warm heft. She brushed her palm along the branches of tickling, feathery parsnip and carrot tops almost as high as her waist. How George used to laugh at vegetables' evocation of anatomy. There was peace here, and a fertile and familiar sense of blessed abundance. When she was a girl, on cool mornings she had played in the kitchen garden at Griff with her brother, absorbing light and heat like a growing plant.

What a hungry child she had been, ravenous for love. But would she have loved Isaac so well if he had returned her regard in equal measure, if he had not indentured her to earn his affection—as if her love for him in some fundamental way chafed at his identity and irritated him? In order to love did she require some element of difficulty or irregularity: something to be overcome?

She had foreseen that the twenty years that separated her and Johnnie would incite gossip, if not exactly scandal; she had not guessed that the true difficulty—worse, the terrible impossibility—would lie elsewhere. Yet these first few days with family, these small celebrations, had passed more happily than she had anticipated. The cheer was all on the surface, light reflecting off water; the bright appearance all that was needed.

Globes of cabbages were swelling taut as bellies in their nests of leaves. Marian stooped and stroked the silvery skin. Small beauties could sustain her.

"*Mutter.*" Shocked, she straightened up, unprepared for her stepson's voice, its lilt so like his father's.

"I startled you. I'm sorry." Charles took her hand and helped her up. "I hope I'm not disturbing you."

"You never could do that," she said. "No. I was just admiring a cabbage."

"'The time has come,' the Walrus said, 'to talk of many things: Of shoes — and ships — and sealing wax — Of cabbages — and kings —'"

Marian laughed. "'And why the sea is boiling hot — and whether pigs have wings.' What is Lewis Carroll's real name? Dodgson, isn't it? Charles Dodgson? Your girls love *Alice,* don't they?"

"They do indeed, and so do I."

"I imagine a resemblance between me and the Red Queen. When you bring the girls to visit, we will play charades, and I shall be the Red Queen."

Charles shook his head. "*Mutter,* I'm glad to see you laughing. I was concerned."

"Why should you be?"

"You seemed tired, burdened. Even last night, when we were so jolly. There was something — it could have been my imagination."

"I do worry about Johnnie; he is not yet well, but, otherwise — no. I have no burdens." She bent her head; the sun was suddenly hot and the garden confining. "No burdens." She took his arm and led him out of the garden and under the shade of the old oaks. "Though I am still not quite used to being married. I feel as if an old pain has suddenly ceased. I expect it, yet it is not there. It even makes me walk differently. Have you noticed?" She smiled and looked up at him, radiating brightness.

"I'll be sure to watch you." He laughed, believing her, and she was reassured at her success in persuading him that she was content. This was an unaccustomed exercise. It was not precisely lying; it was what was required of her now. They walked for a while. In the shadows the grass was still wet from dew. "Your step does seem lighter," he said, and added, "It is lovely here, if memory doesn't make it painful, and it seems not to have done so. I cannot say how happy I am for you." He pressed her hand, and she could not repress a small shiver at his warm, generous touch. He did not seem to notice.

· · ·

"IT HAS BEEN a lovely homecoming," Marian said. "Our families have made great efforts." In the hour before dinner, she and Johnnie sat side by side in the chairs overlooking the downs. They had driven out that day, which had tired her husband. She had thought he might be asleep, but he answered.

"Then, Marian, I have done something that I hope will make you happy."

"What is that?" She was drowsy, too, with a pent-up tiredness that, now that they had settled in, was beginning to overwhelm her.

"I have written to your brother. I have written to Isaac."

"Isaac? You have done what?"

"I have written to invite him to visit us at Cheyne Walk in the autumn when the house is ready."

She stood, her hands clenched. In the evening light, her shadow spilled down the lawn. "I see. And what has he answered? Has he answered?"

"Oh, yes, he has. But he's a strange one, your brother. He writes that he will wait to receive an invitation from you."

"Ah," she breathed, reprieved. "He is a stubborn man."

"You'll write, won't you?"

"When the time comes, we will see."

"You are pleased, of course." He had not noticed her agitation. "Pleased that I wrote. I thought you would be."

"Oh, of course I'm pleased. Always, Johnnie. Always."

Chapter 6

August 1980

CAROLINE KNEADED the mass of clay, heavy as flesh. "You have hands like a bricklayer's," Malcolm had complained. The polish from her Venetian manicure had chipped off, and clay lodged under her fingernails in dark crescents. "*Peccato, queste belle mani,*" the manicurist had exclaimed, shaking her head as she picked at granules of clay, and Caroline had answered, "*Sono una scultrice. Faccio piccole statue.*"

I make little statues: the diminutive was key. As to what she was: she would not say in English that she was a sculptor. But that reticence was a dissembling modesty. When asked what he did, her father had answered, "I write poems." Sometimes Malcolm said, "I play with money."

I play with clay. It was just ten; she had been at work for almost three hours. The night before Malcolm had called to say he was coming up for the weekend, bringing the Heismanns. "They're your friends, too; they want to see you."

Pollen filmed the big window and dulled the morning light. Caroline had told the caretaker to leave her studio alone, but now she was irritated that he should have let the window get so dirty. She slammed the clay down on the work table. It made a noise like a slap against skin, and she was ashamed of her petulance. Since Venice, she had stayed in the country, while Malcolm spent the week in the city.

"I have to stay here," she said. "I have to make these sculptures."

"If that's what you want."

"It's what I have to do."

It might have been, she thought, a relief for him, too. The first days, solitude had unnerved her. Sitting in the kitchen or lying in bed, she was threatened by the silence and felt tentative, as if she required the noise of another person to confirm her own existence. But by the third evening silence had softened, fitting to her movement and responding to her breathing. She felt the shapes of ideas emerging against it, and with them her self, unaccompanied, both familiar and strange. Night sounds comforted her: the rustling of a raccoon outside the open window, the sighs and creaks of the house settling and shifting in the dropping temperature.

When he returned the first weekend, she reluctantly molded herself back into a shape he expected; she felt it as a physical pain, as if she were being bent in an unnatural way. After Ricky drove Malcolm back to the city, she turned off the air conditioning and opened all the windows.

THAT MORNING in Venice, heading toward the worm-shaped mounds of the barrier islands, Caroline stood beside Gilbert at the wheel of his Boston Whaler. They had left the canal traffic behind and encountered only fishing boats and a barge carrying a derrick. Gilbert had taken off his blazer and stowed it under the seat; he had golden hairs on his forearms. It was hard to talk over the engine. Fifty yards from the boat, men and women in waders were prodding the silt for clams and periwinkles. "They look like they're walking on water," she said.

Gilbert cut the engine so she could hear him. "They know where the rocks are." He went on: "Seriously, the lagoon is only about a foot and a half deep. It wants to silt up. Those dredgers keep the channel open."

"I like what you know," she said.

"If I bore you, just tell me," he answered.

"I told you, I like it."

Behind them she heard the warning whine of another motorboat. Caroline started to turn. "Don't," said Gilbert. "Don't turn around — not yet. Don't look yet."

The other boat, a water taxi, careened past them, throwing up a fin of water. It spun in a tight circle, its deck awash, and headed back in their direction.

"Go back, please. We have to go back," Caroline insisted.

"Why?"

"Please." She had no explanation, but she was convinced that the other boat had to do with Malcolm. She had not seen Ricky this morning.

"Please!" she repeated. The boat cut close to their stern.

As they rocked in its heavy wake, she lost her balance, and Gilbert caught her shoulder. His arm, hot from the sun, rested across her back. She flinched, startled with pleasure and surprise. Gilbert removed it quickly, as if he had offended her.

Gilbert swung the Whaler around, and she saw the gray massif of the Dolomites rising behind the city, sudden as a thundercloud. "Oh!" she gasped, dizzy with desire, remembered and new. She lifted her arms, and Gilbert turned toward her, as if he imagined that she was going to embrace him, but her fists were clenched.

He drove past the landing at the Piazzetta. Caroline started to ask what he had wanted to show her there, but he did not glance in her direction. It was a chance lost, an encounter gone wrong. As they approached the hotel dock, Caroline saw Malcolm sitting at a table on the terrace, and her anxiety returned. Malcolm took off his sunglasses and squinted into the sun. Gilbert nudged the boat against the dock, she jumped out, and hurried toward Malcolm.

"You forgot this," Gilbert called, holding up her pocketbook, which he had stowed under the seat.

She ran back, and he tossed it to her. "Thank you," she said, "for everything."

"Good catch," he said, and drove off.

"I didn't know he had a boat," said Malcolm. "He could have shown us around."

"It's too late."

"It's you and me, then. Show me Venice."

Relying on memory, she led her husband through the hot streets; she walked in trochees to induce yesterday's exhilaration: *I* am *hap*py. But there was a limit to what she could control. Each step reminded her of time passing and who she had once been.

"How far is it?" Malcolm asked.

"Not far," she answered.

"I hope it's cool inside."

"It always is."

"Are you sure you know the way?"

"No. It's been a long time."

He stopped. "We could have hired a guide."

"You can always go back." Soon enough they turned a corner and came upon the brick façade of the church of the Frari. In the church she stood Malcolm in front of Titian's *Assumption*.

"Tell me about this," Malcolm said. "Tell me what's so great about it."

"Faith made tangible," she said. "A miracle real."

"So that's God?" He pointed at the dark cloud of a foreshortened old man attended by angels.

She nodded, numb. When she had been a child, she had gazed at the ecstasies of Mary and longed to defy gravity, too. The destination — sky, heaven — was unimportant; it was the float through the clouds. *Ask your mother what it's about*. The paintings were inhabited by a wind that stirred the drapery and the emotions — a spirit, an exaltation — and she heard her father again: "Caro, in Hebrew the word for 'wind' and 'spirit' is the same." She did not feel those currents now.

Titian had painted the wind that teased off Europa's drapery: a breeze off the Lido, with the Dolomites in the background. She had felt it this morning.

"Have you seen enough?" Caroline asked.

SHE LEANED her elbows on the work table and put her head in her hands. It wasn't that pollen clouded the windows or that Malcolm was bringing the Heismanns for the weekend. She pushed her shoulder against the screen door and went out onto the brick terrace. The flowers of the white nicotiana Caroline grew in pots for its evening perfume were shriveled shut, refusing the sun.

Light embraced her like a weightless body hot with pleasure; it pressed its summer glare against her eyes, making her dizzy. She lifted her hands; clay was baking white onto her forearms. Her fingers could be sprouting leaves; she could be Daphne chased by

Apollo, Daphne turning into a tree, caught in Bernini's marble. Her mother had kept a postcard of the statue stuck in the frame of the mirror over her dresser, and when Caroline was a child the image had repulsed her: the god's laughing lust, the futility of Daphne's attempt to escape. There was something heedless and cruel in the delight with which the sculptor had portrayed the girl's agony, the specificity of the transformation: hands reaching into branches, toes elongating into roots, thighs roughening to bark. Daphne's refusal — her god-fearing virtue — had led to annihilation, unless there was virtue in turning into a tree.

"I hate that statue. It's disgusting. Why do you have a postcard of it?" Caroline, seventeen and truculent, had demanded.

Her mother had been chopping an onion. "Do you want to know, or do you want to hate it?" she asked.

"Tell me," Caroline had answered.

"It's like dance. Daphne looks like she's running away, but really Apollo is supporting her. He's helping her jump."

"She's not jumping anywhere. She's turning into a goddamn tree."

"Caro, don't use language like that." The tendons on the side of her mother's neck were rigid. "I'm making spaghetti sauce for dinner." She wiped an onion tear from her cheek.

"I'm going out."

Below the terrace the lilac blooms dangled brown and withered and unpruned, an island of disorder. Little needles of heat jabbed at Caroline's scalp along her part. Her hands itched from the clay that was crumbling and falling in a gray powder onto the bricks. Ten years ago she had craved a dissolution of self, as if love were an alembic, a means of purification. Ten years ago she had equated legitimacy — marriage — with happiness. She had reveled in legitimacy. Those two girls in Venice — those brash, annoying, beguiling girls — they had kept love down, reduced it to something you could take or leave — preferably, leave. She should strive to be like them; she did not think she could survive alone.

But married to Malcolm, she had ceased to feel. For him, she had become a precious object sealed off from the mess of existence, from mistakes and pain, ugliness and loss. Her marriage had been a cabinet of wonders where she could lock herself away, immune to change and time. It was worse than being alone.

Something moved near the lilacs, something red and larger than a squirrel — maybe a fox. The caretaker had said that there was a den of foxes on the property. "My father told me that if you see a fox," Margaret had said, "it means somebody's going to die." Caroline ran to the house for the binoculars, but when she got them focused, whatever it was had moved on.

She went back inside and picked up the lump of clay again, caressing it into an oval, pressing it and rolling it around a steel armature, rounding and tapering it into the form of a thigh. Malcolm had been her armature; without him she had believed that she had no strength. She was making a man's sinewy thigh, leaner than Malcolm's; his was dense with muscle and flesh.

Adam. That was the Hebrew word for "clay, earth"; its letters formed also the root of the Hebrew words for "red" and "vegetable." Her father had taught her that; her father, with his ambition and doubt. His presence inhabited her when she worked, encouraging and questioning: *What are you doing — making a man out of clay? Who do you think you are — God? But this isn't so bad — it's Icarus — or Lucifer, after all, you're half a goy. Use that, use it all. Give it wings, Caro, what are you afraid of?*

"I don't like it." Malcolm's criticism had stayed with her — she fought the habit of believing him. She would not let him see these pieces. She felt her body collapse. Could she model that posture? She laid aside the thigh and tore off another lump of clay, pinching a waist and squeezing it downward into the breadth of hips. No armature; she wanted this pliant. She bent it inward, trying for the vulnerable bulge of belly and droop of breasts, suggesting the flexible knobs of backbone. The figure was cowering, or bent over some internal female pain and shame.

There was a moment, a hinge — an awakening — when shame turned to pleasure, repulsion to desire. Caroline pulled the figure into the opposite direction, arching the back, stretching the torso. Daphne's back had been arched; Apollo's fingers indented her marble flesh. Ecstasy and terror, like Europa, too.

A draft blew through the studio window and kicked up clay dust. It was close to eleven, then; that was when the wind came up. She listened for Ricky's car on the gravel driveway; he was bringing lobsters and peaches from the city. It would take most of the afternoon to prepare for the weekend. The lobster had to be poached, the meat picked out and bound with aioli, caponata concocted, bread baked. The bread needed three risings. A cold meal for a summer evening, everything produced by her. And muffins for breakfast. A weekend was a performance, a wifely duty, a penance.

She had to make time for a swim. Malcolm would find this figure repugnant, too, this suggestion of softness and fat and fecundity. Or was she the one who was repelled; was she modeling what she feared? Malcolm had wanted her to be a child: how could he want her to have a child?

This woman, this big rough clay as large as the falling man, was balancing, arched or bent, precarious at the edge of revelation, awaiting some dangerous knowledge. Or she could be dancing. She could be young, at that hinge: the turning where ardor flowered into desire. Or she could be older; in one of Caroline's sketches of her mother, Margaret was bowing, a *révérence,* the end of class, an acknowledgment of ceremony.

Caroline squeezed her eyes shut. She could not get at what she had to know, what she had to see. It had to do with her own power, her own ability to act and not to be acted upon. Anxiety prickled at the base of her skull. The clay resisted her. She was proceeding without knowing, searching for what it was going to be, for what she felt. She caught her breath with excitement and apprehension. She wished that only her hands—not her brain or her heart—could know.

There might be two figures, bent and arched: the same person. She set a ball of clay on a stand and pressed it between her palms to taper it to a chin; she dug the ridge of her palm in a diagonal to make the hollow under a cheekbone, scooped eye sockets with her thumb, and pinched protrusions for lips. This was another thing entirely. This stopped at the shoulders, a smooth and sexless swelling. There was nothing precarious about this. She would turn it into a vessel, a reliquary: a bust, like the pure and beautiful princesses Francesco Laurana had carved in the sixteenth century from veinless white marble. They had been painted once: polychromed. Her father had loved that word.

Maybe she could send it off to Carrara to be carved, as those nineteenth-century American lady sculptors had done. Hawthorne's marmoreal flock: condescending, implying failed aspirations. Lady sculptor: that designation was what Caroline had feared — becoming one of them, making anachronistic statues, unable to see anything more than what had already been seen. She would turn that fear inside out. Instead of marble, she would cast this in silver: brash, polished silver to reflect everything. If it was a reliquary, what did she intend it to contain?

She thought she heard tires crackling on gravel. The day Will had come to the house, she had heard that sound and thought Ricky was arriving. It had been a Friday, too, and she had been working, her mind flitting between the small figure she was modeling and the pumpkin soup served in pumpkin shells that she was planning for dinner. Yet another dinner.

Ricky made no concession to the change in surface from road to driveway, and his tires sprayed pebbles like bullets. The day Will had come, she had wondered why the car's approach had sounded so tentative.

UNIFORM PUMPKINS, she had been thinking that Friday in October; at the farm stand she would have to find eight small sugar pumpkins of uniform size to fill with soup. It was a warm Indian summer day, and her mind had flickered over Will. It never more than flickered; she was a cautious moth.

A fall day years earlier: she had cut classes and they had driven to Crane Beach in Ipswich. The beach was empty, the ocean nearly flat. Holding hands, they had walked into the water. "This is the time of year when the ocean is warmest," Will said, and released her hand and dove. Caroline followed his bubbles, feeling as if his breath were her own, and dove in after him. They cavorted like seals, sounding and surfacing. Glistening with sheets of water that flattened his thick hair, Will gasped. "Have you ever heard a seal burp?"

"Seals don't burp."

"Yes, they do — like this," and he belched an imitation before diving under again, arms tight to his sides like seal flippers.

Driving back to Boston, they took the coast road through the salt marshes toward Essex and pulled off onto the shoulder at a stone wall bordering a mown field. Sprays of white and purple asters drooped over the wall, and the tall mauve tassels of joe-pye weed bordered the margins of the field. She and Will, arms touching, leaned against the fallen stones warm from the sun. Heavy bees drunk with nectar browsed close around them, pale pollen clinging to their black bodies. Crickets sang, and fat robins waddled in the bright grass; the field was tinged pink in the low light. Caroline stretched, Will's skin against hers, warmth against warmth, wanting him and loving her desire. There was plenty of time.

"Crickets sing before they die," said Will. "Did you know that?"

"Crickets sing and seals burp. You know a lot about animal sounds," she answered him, smiling. But his voice had changed, something slight, a loss of resonance, as if his words came from some closed-in place. He rolled toward her, the sun in his blue eyes, threads of salt in his black hair and along the down on his cheekbones, salt like pollen, she thought, and he kissed her. They moved behind the wall, flattening the aster and the joe-pye weed, giving no thought to poison ivy.

"I'm going to Chicago," he said, when they were in the car, driving home.

"When?"

"Friday. The day after tomorrow." He kept his eyes on the road.

"Oh. How come?" She pretended to be casual, asking about unimportant details. "For how long?"

"I don't know yet. Maybe a month, maybe a year. Caro, Caro, it's not you. It's just time. I have to go."

SHE HAD NEVER thought that Will would stay with her; what they had could not have lasted. Their time together had been an idyll, its intensity impossible to sustain. But she had always imagined that he might come back. In her studio that morning in October, she had been preoccupied with pumpkins when she heard the car. She looked out at the bright maples; this week was the peak of their color. She had Malcolm now; she would live in the same house next year and the year after that; she would watch the seasons from her windows. If she felt the effort of holding on to that certainty, or felt a twinge of dismay at her fixed future, she ignored it. The car stopped.

She had been working out the angle of a woman's waist, slightly bent and twisting to the left: bowing, submitting. She held to an ambivalence in her figures; they desired or not, they watched or they looked away, they were lonely or self-sufficient, they might have been asking for help, with their chores, their children, their souls. They suggested a story or they were abstractions, experiments in form.

She went outside into the hazy sunlight. It might be better to serve the soup from one large pumpkin, easier than hollowing out eight separate shells. An unfamiliar car stood in the driveway. The door opened, and Will got out and looked up at the red and yellow trees.

"William!" she called, her voice thin and unsupported, joy and incredulity mixed. "Is that you?"

"Caro."

He found the stone path that led to the terrace. "Caro, hello." He smiled, his deep blue eyes tender.

Her agitation subsided. "How did you find me? How did you know where I was?"

He shrugged. "I have my ways. I came by yesterday, too."

"We — I'm in the city during the week. I drove up last night. Where are you staying?"

"At my grandmother's old place — we're selling it."

"I'd forgotten that it was around here." She had not forgotten, and it was not close — an hour away. "I'm glad you came back." She glanced down at her hands encrusted with clay. Her wedding ring seemed organic, a burl at the base of her fourth finger.

He followed her eyes. "I'm not disturbing you?"

"No, no, no. Will." She had loved how his name felt in her mouth, like a kiss. She said, "I was thinking about you this morning. And now you're here. Tell me everything; I want to hear everything about you."

He'd gone from Chicago to California; he had studied geology; he had returned to New York and was working for his father in the family's real estate business. "It helps to know what your assets are sitting on," he said.

"I wish you hadn't stopped painting."

He smiled, his old expression of bemused mystification. "It's ridiculous, isn't it — to spend your days smearing colored mud on scraps of cloth?"

"About as bad as making mud pies."

"We should do something useful; at least I should, Caro."

"You don't really believe that painting wasn't useful."

"I wasn't good enough."

"You can't believe that, either."

A bleak expression supplanted his smile, but only for a fraction of a second. He looked at her hands. "You're still at it, though. Would you show me?"

"Oh, yes." She took him inside; she wanted his eyes on her work, her bodies.

"May I?"

She nodded, and he stood the bending woman gently on his palm, with his fingers against its back as if he were dancing with it.

"What if you made this larger?" he asked. "You've figured out the small ones."

"I don't know if I can."

"When I think of you, I think of big things. Try it, anyway."

"How will I know if it works?"

"You'll know." He put the little figure down, and Caroline wondered if he had left fingerprints in the soft clay. He asked, "You're happy?"

"Of course I am. Are you — do you have somebody now?"

"Yes," he said.

"Lucky woman."

"You think so? Why?"

Why not, why not tell the truth? It didn't matter. "Because you were wonderful. Making love with you was wonderful, that's why."

He regarded her with an amalgam of amusement, yearning, and that bleakness again. "No, Caro. I wasn't wonderful. We were, you and I together. I've never had anything like that again."

"No. Neither have I."

"It was luck, pure luck."

She reached for the little figure, and he stroked her wrist; he could have been dusting off the clay, longingly brushing away layers of time to get back to what had been.

"Let's go outside," she said.

On the terrace he said, "This is like your mother's house, only better. In the country, on a hill."

"But we have the river. My husband just cleared the view—for me." *Husband.* She felt strange saying that word to Will, who knew her bedrock. *And what was it? What did he know?* "You can see the Palisades from here. Geology. The Hudson River's a fault, right?"

"No. It's not tectonic, it's glacial. Technically it's a fjord. You'd love it, Caro, geology. There's so much time—millions of years."

How long would it take for that swath Malcolm had bulldozed to appear consonant with the landscape? They could help it along and plant rhododendron and mountain laurel, dogwoods and wild pink azaleas. But Malcolm was not so interested in planting.

"What are you thinking about?" Will asked.

"Nothing. Gardening. Time. We can walk down to the river—to the fjord, I mean." They followed Malcolm's cut, the margins littered with severed roots and small stumps. "Sorry about the devastation." She stood at the brink of the cellar hole. It was walled with flat-faced boulders, green with moss. A small oak, which retained its leathery leaves, grew from the center of the floor, and vines of bittersweet heavy with red berries twined around its trunk.

"Have you ever gone down into it?" Will asked.

"I'm afraid of what might be there. Snakes, or something."

He nodded seriously. "Or the bones of little children."

"Will!"

"Or little animals, like the ones you're making."

"Those are what I see from my window."

"So you keep your distance, Caro?" He peered into the hole. "The Pueblo make drawings of what goes on underground—in the Southwest there are cuts, gorges—like the Rio Grande canyon. I went there once when I drove across the country—and you can see the strata, all the bones and the spirits."

"And what were you smoking?" She could say that lightly, now.

He smiled. "Not smoking. Mushrooms." He peered into the hole.

"It's really early, they told us when we bought the house, then it was abandoned for the new one up the hill."

The lilac leaves were tinged with rust; it was almost impossible to remember their springtime translucence, their profligate blossoming. "I wouldn't let Malcolm cut down these lilacs, even though they block the view."

"So you still love lilacs, Caro," he said, with his bemused, sad smile, and placed his hand against the back of her head. She stood rooted; she lifted her arms to his shoulders; she was flowering.

Eyes open, they kissed. Shaking, from desire or from the pain of memory, she stepped backward out of his arms. He caught her hands. "Careful," he said. "Don't fall."

"I won't." She would have liked to tumble with him into the cellar hole, with dead leaves and snakes and tangled bittersweet vines, and become for half an hour a relict of past time. She held his hands and saw small crow's feet bracketing the delicate curve of his top lip and at the corners of his eyes, a crinkling of his eyelids, the same slight signs she found in herself. She pitied them both, for what each had become, what they had given up. She started to rest her hand, her head, against his chest, but she dropped her arms to her sides.

THAT NIGHT, while Malcolm squeezed toothpaste onto his toothbrush, he had complimented her on the pumpkin soup.

"I don't know if it was worth it, all that scooping. Mal, a strange thing happened this afternoon. Will, remember I told you about him?" She held the shape of his name in her mouth. "Will Lucas? From the Museum School? He came by today, he just drove up the driveway."

"And?" Malcolm had looked at her in the mirror, his smile crooked and skeptical — altered by the reflection, she thought. He must have been amused that one of those boys from her little list would show up.

"And nothing. It was nice to see him. He didn't stay long. I just wanted to tell you. Nothing." She laid that report at her husband's feet, an offering.

SHE HAD NOT touched that little figure since the day Will had held it nine months earlier. That day she had seen in Will's eyes the cloudiness of longing, and she had refused him. She was married. Refusing him had been an act of self-preservation, and it had been cruel, too, a little revenge, a wish to show Will that she had survived. He would come back again, she was sure. She had needed more time. If she had known that there was none — she could not have known.

The reliquary was to hold desire.

The sky was filming with haze; the wind had turned humid and languid: good for clay, not so good for mayonnaise. Venice had been like this the last few days, the clarity gone. The dollar fell against the lira; Malcolm was unhappy; she could not wait to leave. She had wanted Gilbert; she might want anybody now. She was losing control.

The leg she had begun lay on the table. He would be a man resting on his right side: a narrow body, a young man, thin waist, protruding hip bones, the lovely long line of his thigh and groin. He could be an Etruscan effigy — those smiling figures, carved as if they were alive and feasting.

"Caro, we could be the lid of a sarcophagus." Samuel Edgar reclined on the bed in the apartment in Venice and propped his head on his hand. Caroline lay beside him, happy in his warmth against the length of her. "You've gotten so big." He rested his hand on her shoulder, and she grinned up at him as her mother came into the room with a stack of typed poems. He pushed Caroline away. "Get up now, get up. I have to work."

"YOU'VE GROWN, Caro, in a week, I swear, you've grown. Each time I see you, I hardly recognize you."

Caroline tossed her duffel bag on her father's living room floor; his house was not orderly. There was no doormat; her sneakers left wet prints on the rag rug.

"I haven't grown. And it's been two weeks. Mom says you don't want to see me."

"She makes it hard."

"You could get me a car."

"You don't even have your license yet."

"I will. I have my test in a week."

"I can't afford to — you know that."

"Where's Sheryl?"

"She's supposed to be home. I don't know where she is."

"I'm hungry." Caroline flopped onto the sofa, tearing the Indian print bedspread covering the back. "Sorry," she said. From where she was sitting, Caroline could see into the bedroom, the big bed with sheets and pillows in a flagrant tangle.

"It's not worth anything."

"Dad, do you like this place? It's like a cabin in the woods, like you're camping out. Like you're not going to stay."

"For the foreseeable future, I am." He settled into a canvas chair beside the sofa. His big hands rested on his lean thighs; Caroline studied the dark hair on his wrists. Since he remarried he had been sparse with his touch.

"What are you reading?" her father asked.

"Books."

The smells of rain and spring drifted in through the open window. Caroline got up and stood beside his chair. "Dad—I want to come and live with you and Sheryl."

He shook his head. "What about your mother?" he said finally, and stood. "Don't you think I've hurt her enough?"

Standing, Caroline was almost as tall as he was. "What about me? I'm talking about me, about what I want."

"Caro!"

"It's Sheryl, then, isn't it?"

He did not answer.

"She doesn't want me."

"She's here," he said.

The front door opened, and Sheryl hurried in, breathless and blowsy, her hair frizzy with raindrops; she was laden with books and bags of groceries. "I'm so sorry—"

"Where were you?" asked Samuel. Caroline recognized that tone of voice; he was annoyed and disappointed.

"I was grading midterms; I lost track of time. And then I had to go shopping—there's nothing in the house, and I forgot she was coming. I wanted to get something nice for dinner. I should have called. I'm sorry." As she started across the room, one of the wet bags split, spilling oranges and grapes and cans of tomatoes across the floor. "Oh, damn! What a klutz!" Sheryl tumbled the rest of her load onto the counter, threw her dripping coat over everything, and bent down to retrieve her fruit. "Hi, Caroline." Harried and anxious, Sheryl looked up and smiled. "I'm glad you're here."

"Hi," said Caroline, with resentment and sympathy. "Thanks."

Samuel reached for an orange that had rolled under the sofa. "Aren't you going to help out?"

He had been worried; Caroline wanted to tell Sheryl that he hid concern with annoyance. But it was none of her business — and what would that be doing to her mother? *How can this child's body know?* That was a line in one of the poems that Caroline had found. She stepped on a loose grape, squashing it into the rug.

DID SAMUEL EDGAR think that Sheryl would revive his art? Or did she have nothing to do with his mind? Was leaving his wife for her a terrible, useless indulgence? Those last years, he published nothing. And was Caroline's own dissatisfaction a similar thing? Was she indulging — and damaging — herself? After they made love the first time, Malcolm had whispered, "I never thought I'd have a young body like this again." His wonder had seemed to her a triumph; now it repulsed her. But that was ten years ago.

Ricky must be here; she had to start cooking. She had the rough shapes, though: the falling man, the reclining man, the women, the reliquary. She considered the woman with the arched back. She would be half woman, half tree: Daphne alone, pulling her feet from the ground, uprooting herself.

Costanza Heismann wanted to see Woodstock — the field, not the town. Maybe she thought its soil contained the lingering fumes of recreational substances that would alter her consciousness, or her husband's. That would be nice. Caroline started wrapping the clay in burlap. Through the screen door, she saw a movement, a shadow — the fox. She put down the burlap and pushed open the door. Malcolm stood on the terrace. She started. "What are you doing here?"

"Am I interrupting you?"

"Only my work."

She had meant that to be funny, but he did not laugh. She said, "Where's Ricky? And the Heismanns?"

"He's coming. They're taking the train. They like trains."

"When is Ricky getting here? I need those lobsters. His cough isn't better; he won't see a doctor." Caroline remembered to kiss Malcolm's cheek. Arranging schedules, organizing food and excursions: the inconsequential was reassuring. She felt acutely the deep tracks of connection to Malcolm, worn into her mind and body, deep as love.

"It's hot out here," he said, and opened the screen door. She blocked the way.

"Then let's go up to the house. I'll meet you; I have to finish up."

He pushed past her. Inside, his amber eyes moved methodically from object to object: the cork board crowded with postcards, the shelves holding her models, bags of clay, her tools. "What's this?" he asked, approaching the table.

"What you interrupted."

"Who is it?" His voice was pinched.

"What are you asking?"

"That's not me. I'm not built like that."

"It's a product of my imagination." She flushed.

"That's not imagination."

"Actually, it is. Not everything comes from life. That's not how it works, Mal. There's distance." She held her arms clear from her sides. "There's wishful thinking."

"I think I know how it works, Caroline." His bottom lip was drawn tight against his teeth.

"Then tell me how."

He looked at her as if figuring some equation of profit and loss, some calculation of love. He opened his mouth and closed it again, tasting the sound of his answer and rejecting it. "You've got clay in your hair," he said.

Caroline swiped at it.

"You're making it worse."

"I know."

"Gold is way down. I made a mistake; I didn't get out in time."

"Gold goes up and down every day."

"This is different. It's huge."

"That's hard to believe." She smiled.

"I'm not lying."

"That was supposed to be a compliment. Jesus, Malcolm, can't I say anything?"

"You're not listening. I put too much into gold."

She nodded, but she did not know whether to believe him. Even six months ago she would not have thought to doubt. Six months ago, he would not have bet so recklessly.

She said, without compassion, "Why did you do it?"

He slumped, as if the armature of his spine had ceased to support him. He splayed his fingers along the edge of the work table, well-kept thick fingers, the nails neatly trimmed, and he said quietly, "I love you. Sometimes I don't recognize you anymore."

"I'm working—is that the problem? That I'm not in your pocket anymore? It is, isn't it?" The studio was growing close. The light had turned milky, diminishing shadows. Tonight there might be a thunderstorm, or it might only threaten.

"I miss you," Malcolm said. He unbuttoned his cuffs and pushed his sleeves up. "I want you, Caroline. Look at me." He spoke sharply, calling her to heel.

She used to believe she could assuage what she saw in his eyes: she had called it sadness, loneliness. What if it was emptiness?

He said, "This isn't working."

She picked up a length of burlap stiff with clay. She shook it hard.

Malcolm retreated from the dust. "It's not what you do; it's what you're turning into."

"And what is that?"

"I don't recognize you."

"Then look at me."

"You're hard, Caroline. You're losing—"

"Losing what?" she shouted.

"Your softness. You're getting to be like everybody else."

"Is that so bad?"

He prowled the room. "Where are the binoculars?" he asked. "They're not in the house."

"Here. I brought them down." Something safe to talk about. "I thought I saw a fox this morning, near the cellar hole. Ray says there's a den."

"I wondered what happened to them."

"I didn't know you used them."

He looked at her models, the small figures, a group of birds and animals: hawks, foxes, rabbits.

"I might have to sell the house."

"I wouldn't like that."

"The house is in my name."

"Everything's in your name."

"What's this supposed to be?" He picked up the woman Will had held, the woman bending. "Do you think this will sell?"

"Leave that alone," she ordered. "Leave it."

Startled, he closed his fingers around it. She pried the figure from his hand and laid it back on the shelf. "Go," she said.

HE TOOK the binoculars with him. He'd put a treadmill in a little room off the garage, along with an air conditioner and a tape player. He turned up the cold, put Herb Alpert on the stereo, and strapped on the monitor. Anger pushed his heart rate up. Stepping on the treadmill, he thought of his father — if the bastard had exercised, he might have lived longer. Not that it would have made a difference. All he'd gotten from the old man was half a junkyard and genes for a bad heart. Maybe his wife was trying to give him a heart attack. A five-minute warmup, then a jog for twenty: his regimen, raising his heartbeat, but not too high.

Caroline swam in the pond despite weeds and snapping turtles and water snakes; sometimes she emerged streaked with brown slime and laughed at him as if he were some weirdo germ freak. She wouldn't let him build a pool; it wasn't worth fighting for. He'd be glad to get rid of the house; he would if he had to.

At six minutes, just about right, he began to sweat, but he couldn't settle into his stride; he was hyperventilating. He had let her know what he could do. There was always a component of fear in love, an imbalance of power and money. He'd been afraid of Irene; God knows he'd been afraid of his father. He edged the treadmill up two notches.

The first time they fucked — he'd taken her to the Virgin Islands — he'd wanted time. Breathe, he reminded himself, breathe. He'd figured there was a chance she'd back out, and protecting himself because he wanted her so badly, he'd lined up a substitute. But Caroline showed up at the airport. When he told her about the replacement, she'd laughed; she liked to win. As soon as they got to the room they made love. For a week she swam and played in the sea, her shiny black head — her hair was long and he wished she hadn't cut it short — breaking the surface like a dolphin's, and he watched, getting used to it: he'd made her his.

She'd been practically a child when he married her; Gruson had warned him. He felt better knowing that he was far from the first. Her ardor had made him forget a numbness at his core, a lack. It had been strange, catching her through the binoculars with that Will Lucas out there under her damned lilacs; it was like listening to her confessions. He had felt that same urgent, obscure excitement; he had wanted her more. Sure, in the last couple of years, they'd cooled down; still, they had more than most people. He'd begun to believe that he'd gotten lucky.

But she was pulling away. She no longer believed in him — and he was beginning not to trust himself. Even in business, he was defending against losses, reacting, not acting. Gold had fallen more than he'd predicted, though he'd recovered much of that mistake. Those misjudgments had to do with her. He no longer held the center of her life. It wasn't the men; it was the work.

He inhaled deeply. She could not leave him. He was imagining the worst. Seven and a half more minutes, then three to cool down. She had changed the rules. Fine. Love was no different from money, and he'd already hedged his bets.

CAROLINE DROVE her station wagon across Connecticut, up the interstate along the industrial coast to Rhode Island, speeding, weaving relentlessly in and out among the semis. She had to keep the windows open; the air conditioning was not working.

"Cleopatra arrives in her barge," Joe Fornari exclaimed. "How long did it take you?"

"You don't want to know. Malcolm gave me a radar detector. It's cheating, I know."

"Not if you get away with it, he says." Joe opened the rear door.

"The theory of laws as challenges, not rules."

"So now it's a theory?" Joe was a slight man in his early fifties, with large hands and small features; his skin was ruddy, as if he had been roasted by his furnaces.

"How's your dad?" asked Caroline.

"Bored. When he's in Florida, at least everybody else does nothing, too. Up here he sits around feeling useless, but when I ask him if he wants to come in to work, he says it's too hot. He doesn't want to get in my way."

"He's a sweet guy."

"Yeah. How'd you load these things up by yourself?"

"I'm strong."

A small window in the office looked into the furnace room. While Joe's workmen unloaded the models, Caroline watched a crucible of molten metal spill in an alluring red arc. She had loved how Malcolm had described the hazards of casting bronze, welding danger to art.

"Tell me what needs to change," Caroline said.

"Well, princess," Joe said, "change how? To make them easier to fabricate? That's my job — the molds, the casting, the patina. These are really nice."

"You say that to all the girls."

Joe shook his head. "Nope. And not to the boys, either. Who is this?" He rested his hand on the clay knee of the reclining man.

"That's what Malcolm wanted to know."

"I bet." Joe pursed his lips. "Bronze?"

"Everything but the bust. She's silver."

Joe nodded. "Like a reliquary, you mean?"

"Exactly."

"Why are you messing around with the remains of saints?"

"Just a place to put things. Intangibles."

"Silver — for something this size, that's going to cost." He lowered his eyes. "I've got to ask for a deposit."

"What's the problem?"

"Malcolm takes his time paying the invoices."

"I give them to Ricky and assume they're paid. How long do you have to wait?"

"I shouldn't have said anything — but I can't carry the cost of the silver."

"Months?"

Joe nodded.

"At least there's interest."

"He doesn't pay that. It's not worth it to go after him."

"Oh, Jesus. I feel awful."

"You're surprised? That's who he is."

"I thought you liked him."

"I've known him too long to like him or not. You never met his dad. A bastard, a real bastard. It wasn't easy for Mal."

"Malcolm isn't easy. I'm sorry."

"I'll tell you something — when he asked me to cast your first batch of stuff, I was going to say no. I didn't want to do business with him. But then I thought — I don't know — I didn't think that Malcolm would go for a person like you. I thought maybe I was wrong about him, if you want to know the truth."

"Just send me the invoice, okay? He doesn't have to subsidize this anymore. It's between you and me now." The price of silver had risen. "Malcolm doesn't think these will sell."

"Forget what he says. He told me that this foundry would never make any money — that art was over. So, how are we going to do these?"

"A black patina — I want them to be like those Renaissance bronzes that were made to look like Roman statues — like Antico. And I want eyes, in the animals, too. Silver eyes, inlaid. I want them to look alive. Maybe onyx eyeballs. Will they stay?"

"We can use epoxy to glue the stones. Why not? And the silver?"

"Gold eyes. Vermeil — just a thin coat of gold. So it tarnishes eventually. And a polished finish on the silver; I want it reflective."

"You'll lose the details."

"You'll have to look closely. I'll probably want to work on them after they're cast. Chase them."

"We'll be seeing a lot of you."

"Do you mind?"

"Are you kidding? Want a beer?"

They sat outside on a bench against the building. The wind had shifted to the northwest, and the haze was clearing, a premonition of fall.

"I'm taking Joey — my kid Josephine — to the game tonight. The Red Sox."

"Lucky girl. But the Sox are stuck in fifth. I can't stand to listen; it's too painful."

"Malcolm's a Yankees fan," Joe said. "Always was."

"So? On Saturdays when I was a kid, my father drove to Boston and took me to the Museum of Fine Arts in the morning and to a ball game in the afternoon. We walked from the museum to Fenway Park." Three Saturdays, but the third time he took Sheryl along. When he asked again, Caroline refused to go. She took a swallow of beer. "He loved Ted Williams. He said he was thinking of writing a poem about his swing, but he never did."

THE FIGURES lay on the floor of Deirdre's gallery. Deirdre said, "Only one set of wings? I thought I'd be selling angels."

"People don't fly," said Caroline. "They fall."

"How are we supposed to show them?"

"Bolt them into the studs. Joe recessed the hooks."

"Hanging? No bases?"

"No, not for the falling ones."

"What if people don't want to put holes in their walls?"

"Talk them into it. All the eyes are onyx. Do you think anybody's going to want these?"

Caroline considered her work: the kicking legs, the fluid stretch of the fox's belly, the hawk's chased wings, the filaments of roots trailing from Daphne's feet. They were complete now, separate from her.

"They're disturbing," said Deirdre.

"Is that good or bad?"

"Good or bad? Caro, I'm way past that. I don't want to see what they're seeing."

"It's hard."

"They're not easy."

"They look so set. Done. I can't change them. That's such a strange feeling."

"There's nothing you need to change."

"I'm afraid I'll discover some terrible mistake. I see things that could be different."

"You always will."

"It's like death — when change stops."

"You can make other things."

"I didn't believe I could make these. I still don't believe it." She walked toward the little back room, overwhelmed, empty.

"Caro!" Deirdre followed her. "Aren't you happy?"

Caroline shook her head. "Yes. Very. No."

"Do you want coffee? The installer won't be here for an hour. Come on."

The last day in August was as warm as midsummer, a soft deceit. Caroline said, "I'm so afraid."

"Afraid? I don't understand — afraid of what?"

"Of those. Of me — of what I'm capable of. Of — what's going to happen next."

"Malcolm?"

"I don't know what to do."

"I was wondering. Concerned. I didn't know how to ask."

"He's given me the summer off, it feels like, to come back to him. Come back to him the way I was."

"How's that?"

"Soft, he says. What was I like before I met him?"

"You were — it's hard to describe — I know this sounds terrible, but — you were skinless. There was nothing between you and the world — you let everything in and you let everything show. It was scary how happy you were when —"

"When I was with Will."

"I almost couldn't be with you."

"I'm sorry."

"It wasn't you — I thought you were flaunting him — but it really was that you had something I knew I never would."

"Deirdre —"

"It's the way it was. But you were tough, too."

"Tough and skinless, a strange combination."

"It's probably why you're the artist and I'm the dealer. What I mean is that one minute I thought you were a lost soul and the next I was sure you could take care of yourself."

"I thought you had everything figured out."

"You went after what you wanted."

"Didn't you?"

"I slapped sheets of steel together with a welding torch and went out to dinner with Geoff." Deirdre looked away quickly. "What I thought I wanted."

"Has that changed?"

"Hasn't it? Doesn't it?"

"Malcolm wants to give me things, but I can't ask for them."

"He's given you an amazing life."

"So I have no right to ask for anything more?"

"Like what?"

"Intangibles. He's not a big fan of intangibles."

Deirdre laughed. "I remember the first time we went out to lunch, after we met again—Jennie was just born—you paid, and you didn't even take the receipt. You crumpled it up and left it on the table. You didn't have to keep track. And with your rings and your clothes —and Ricky sometimes to drive you around—it made me feel poor. And more than that. It was weird, out of whack, as if you'd skipped out of our generation. Jumped forward in time. Do you know what I mean? I even wondered if I should ask to take you on—you might think I wasn't an important enough dealer."

"I'm sorry."

"I'm not telling you that to make you feel bad. It's the way it was."

Caroline nodded. "Malcolm came ready-made—like Duchamp's urinals."

"Caroline!" Deirdre went on. "But, Caroline, I wonder how you'd live if you didn't have money. It would be hard—and Malcolm knows that. It comes down to money."

"Not all of it."

"Then what?"

"Promises. My father left my mother. Loving, honoring, obeying. I saw Will a year ago; he found me. I've been faithful."

"Oh, Caro." Deirdre touched her shoulder. "I wouldn't have been."

"Maybe I wouldn't have been, either, if—"

"And you really said obey?"

"Didn't you?"

Deirdre laughed. "I guess I did. But things never turn out the way they were supposed to. Then what do you do? Whose fault is it?"

"Are you talking about me or about you?"

"This morning we're talking about you. At least you don't have children."

"In Venice he said he wanted me to give him a baby. A new toy. You don't give anybody a baby. He wants everything his own way. He wants me his own way." Caroline put her head in her hands.

"At least he wants you," Deirdre said.

"He wants his idea of me."

"You don't love him, do you?"

Caroline finished her coffee, got up, and left a ten-dollar bill on the table. Malcolm wouldn't wait for change. "Don't we have to get started?"

HER HAWKS flew, round eyes tracking the scuttle of a vole. Her animals held the memory of the liquid bronze in the flow of their muscles. Her men fell, spinning, eyes fixed on the rejecting sky. Her women bowed in submission and arched their backs, possessed. Her bronze man reclined, anticipating love. Daphne — uprooting herself, she might not survive. And her reliquary waited empty, with golden eyes: Malcolm's eyes, until they tarnished and darkened.

"I'm exhausted," said Deirdre. "I should have been home an hour ago."

"To change your clothes and turn into a wife and mother."

"You make it sound funny. It's not."

"Sure it is." Caroline embraced her friend. "A change of costume, a change of heart."

A tall, thin man rang the bell at the gallery door. "Anthony!" Deirdre said, pleased. "I didn't expect you today — we were just leaving."

"I was at another gallery; I thought I'd come by and see if the show was up." His thick blond hair fell over his forehead, giving him an appearance of boyishness, but his prominent cheekbones made his face gaunt. As he looked at her, Caroline saw a little tremor flicker across his thin mouth, shifting his smile from polite to interested.

"You're C. Edgar Spingold," he said. "You made these."

"I made them!" Caroline spoke so ardently that she laughed at herself. "In real life I'm Caroline."

He held out his hand and she took it. "Anthony Reardon." She knew who he was: a collector with an instinct for the next new thing.

"I liked the announcement. Deirdre told me who you were. You're Samuel Edgar's daughter."

"How do you know him?"

"A girlfriend of mine in college took courses from him — writing and history. She said he was a wonderful teacher; she loved him."

"I bet."

"She liked his poems."

"His poems are hard for me to read."

"Why?"

"There's too much I don't understand."

"How old were you?"

"When he died? Sixteen."

"You were only a kid."

"Yes and no."

"His wife — she wasn't your mother?"

"They were divorced."

"His wife was younger. I met her once. Sexy."

"You would know that better than I would." Caroline did not bother to curb the sharpness in her voice.

In the office, the phone rang: Geoff, probably. "Excuse me," said Deirdre, and ran to answer it.

Anthony Reardon circled the room. "Who is that?" He pointed to the reclining figure.

"If I were a man, you wouldn't ask."

"I'd be curious, though. I like these; I like what you're doing. Tell me about them."

"What do you want to know?"

"What you were thinking about, what they represent — I'm afraid to ask who they are."

Caroline smiled. "Some of them I'll tell you." She walked around the room, talking about Daphne, Icarus and Lucifer, seraphim and *molochim* — God's messengers, she explained, thinking of her father's voice as she rumbled the guttural *ch* in the Hebrew word.

"I like them. I like what you've done with the eyes. Your prices are low."

"So I've been told."

"Do you want to go somewhere for a drink?"

"I'm sorry, but"—Caroline hesitated. "I have to meet some people for dinner."

"I'll take you. I have a motorcycle. It's the fastest way."

"They're dangerous." She was weary.

"They can be."

Deirdre came back from the office, her mouth tight and angry, her curls spiky. "I'm afraid I have to close up." She shook her head. "I'm so sorry."

They left the gallery together. Deirdre locked the door and hugged Caroline quickly. "I'll call in the morning."

The black and chrome BMW was parked at the curb. Anthony kicked the starter, and the engine rumbled. "Well?"

"I don't think so." It would be too convenient; he would be like the others she'd confessed to Malcolm: a name on a list.

"Another time?"

She hailed a taxi. "Maybe. Another time."

THE MORNING of her father's funeral, Caroline came downstairs dressed self-consciously in as much black as she owned and found her mother sitting, feeble with misery, at the kitchen table. Margaret Edgar looked like an Italian widow: black suit, black stockings, a black beret that she pulled straight across her forehead so that it did not even suggest jauntiness. Her lips and cheeks were white, as if she had smeared them with chalk, and her hand on the table trembled.

"Mom, don't go; please don't go. You'll be all alone."

"You'll sit with me, honey."

"No. I have to sit up front. I will sit up front. He's my father. You can't."

Samuel Edgar dove into a lake near Cummington and never surfaced; the lifeguards had gone; minutes passed before anyone noticed, too late to prevent his drowning. He had had a heart attack. When Caroline's mother heard, she had started to shake. "Where was that Sheryl?" she moaned. "Why wasn't she there?" Caroline held Margaret and stroked her back, though she wanted to crush her to shut her up.

She couldn't cry. She directed a hopeless fury at herself; if she had been there — she was a lifeguard; she could have stayed late to spend some time with her father and his wife — she would have gone after him. She would have saved his life.

The funeral was held the day after Samuel died. His will had stated that he wanted to be buried according to Jewish ritual, as quickly as possible in a plain raw-pine coffin. *Ruach* — spirit and wind. Gone. Stillness. There was no music at the service, no beauty. Caroline sat in front with her stepmother, who embraced her and murmured, "Thank God you're here. I didn't think she'd let you come." Sheryl's hands were hot and her breath rank from weeping. Caroline shook her off, and glancing over her shoulder, she found her mother standing in the back aisle beside the row of Caroline's subdued and frightened high school classmates. Caroline looked away.

Afterward, at the little house, there were one or two friends Caroline recognized and many she did not. Sheryl, surrounded by whispers of condolence and offers of food, sank into the sofa and wiped silent, abundant tears. Caroline took the keys to her father's car and drove to the lake, down the dirt track to the shore. The moon shone fractured through the pines. She stripped off her clothes and dove and swam underwater below the path of the moon. She surfaced, gasping; she dove again, making herself stay deep to the last instant before reflex would force her mouth open and flood her lungs. Home, nauseated and shaking, she tiptoed up the stairs in the fluorescent moonlight and heard her mother sobbing in the bedroom and pressed her hands over her ears.

SHE HAD the taxi wait while she changed — an extravagant habit — and drove back downtown. The cab dropped her at the corner of Fifty-third Street and she gave the driver a large tip. "Money isn't everything," Samuel had said, "but it's way ahead of whatever else is in second place." He had thought that Margaret's family had more than they did. Malcolm's money would have intimidated Samuel; he would have been impressed by Malcolm's theories, his newsletter, his ambition. Malcolm would have found her father silly and credulous, not worth courting.

In the blue fading light she walked quickly, not because she was late, though she was very late, but because she liked the feeling of her long legs striding, balancing in high heels. Her father had loved her when she was a child; he had not understood how to love a growing girl. But he would have loved her statues. She was certain of that. He would have loved the layers of allusion, the deliberate archaisms, the ambivalence. She smiled and a young man, surprised and flattered, smiled back at her. "What I have made!" She said it out loud and laughed.

Malcolm got up from the table when she entered the dining room and steered her back to a corner of the bar. "What took you so long?"

"The installation. I told you it might. Would you have preferred me to show up in jeans? At least I'm here. Malcolm, it's fantastic. You have to see it."

"Who is C. Edgar Spingold?"

"Me."

"Why?"

"Why not? It's a good name, mysterious."

"You didn't tell me. I saw it on the announcement."

"I didn't think you'd care."

"It's my name."

She laughed. "Malcolm, you can't be serious. Come on, I'm sorry I'm so late — I hope you all started."

"One thing." He tightened his hold on her elbow. "Don't talk about your show — don't talk about your sculpture."

Her elation condensed into anger. "Do you have a list of approved topics? Clothes? Real estate? How hard it is to find good help?"

"Please," he said.

She despised herself for her habit of acquiescing. "Let go of me," she said.

"THANK YOU," he said as he got into bed. He turned toward her. "You were great tonight."

"I didn't say a word. I didn't have anything to say."

"You said enough." As he straddled her and tried to separate her legs with his knee, she was repelled by his bulk, by his insistence. She resisted and closed her eyes and saw her reclining man and her woman uprooting.

The first time she and Will had made love, they had laughed. They lay tangled and laughed with a satisfaction beyond consummation, with surprise at what they had done: at the easy conjoining of their two different selves. They had wonderful, temporary luck; they had, for a moment, the world. She had used that, paid for that.

Malcolm let his full weight rest on Caroline's body. He twitched, falling asleep; he had drunk more than a bottle of wine. Reprieved, she rolled out from under him.

Chapter 7

Cheyne Walk, December 1880

THE CARRIAGE STOPPED at Four Cheyne Walk. John Cross helped Marian out and pushed open the newly painted wrought-iron gate. Its heavy arabesques seemed to her more confining than enclosing, but what place on earth could offer ease?

In the six months since Venice, Johnnie had become robust. As he stood back to let his wife pass before him into the garden, his posture was that of a man of property; he had regained his pride.

"At last, I am bringing you home," Johnnie said.

"This requires a flourish of trumpets!" Marian held her fist to her mouth and pretended to blow — that was something George might have done, and Johnnie looked alarmed, as she had known he would.

The garden lay dormant; a few dead leaves hung from the black branches of the great tree of heaven to the left of the gate, and the river's smell, stinging with dampness and decomposition, carried on the chill December wind.

"I have engaged a gardener," Johnnie declared. "This will be lovely in the spring, and by next winter, I shall have built our conservatory."

Marian smiled, mouth closed, lips curved slightly: the mask she wore to conceal poisonous emotions — resentment, frustration, disappointment — from her husband. She stooped and pushed aside the ivy bordering the path by the steps. Two Christmas roses were in bud, the fist of their petals curled just inches from the earth.

"Johnnie, you remembered how fond I am of hellebore."

"They started blooming a few days ago, just in time. I wish I could take credit for them, but they were already here."

"They say that the root is thought to cure madness — did you know that? George thought that distilling it into an elixir might be an interesting proposition, in America especially, where everybody believes in dosing themselves with miracles — and everybody is mad."

Johnnie considered. "I don't have much confidence in that kind of speculation, even in America. Better to stay with industry."

"George said things, Johnnie, without intending to act."

Johnnie bit his lip, sensitive to reproof. Remorseful, she took his arm. In the oblique sunlight the freshly painted white pilasters at the entrance gleamed, and limestone keystones surmounted the tall arched windows like plumes in headdresses. The top of the façade was cut in crenelations, imitating a castle keep. She would be living on the same street as the Carlyles — who had refused to receive her when she and George returned from Weimar. "It is so grand!" she exclaimed. "Fortified."

"I'm only sorry that it has taken so long to be made ready," he said.

"But we're here. It will all have been worth it."

"Please remember, my dear, that the woodwork in the drawing room isn't painted, and the curtains are not yet hung. The final touches, you know, the last decorations. You must not be disappointed."

"Of course not."

"Finally we can begin our new life." They mounted the front steps. She had not yet seen the house refurbished. It was not that she had no interest, but the entire undertaking, the effort her husband devoted to it, made her anxious and sad. For a moment she feared that he was going to hoist her into his strapping arms and carry her across the threshold, more an invalid grandmother than a bride. The time spent in the country had been salutary for him; when he chopped down trees for exercise, muscles flexed beneath his linen shirt, not the ridges of shoulder blades.

She had watched him, recalling her fondness for his energy when she had thought of him as her nephew, and her amusement at his belief in physical exercise. Johnnie had interested George in tennis, convinced that batting the ball around a court for an hour would cure any ailment; it had not. This autumn at Witley, when it grew colder, they had cleared the dining room of furniture and played badminton inside, and Johnnie was laying out a tennis court to be ready by spring. She praised his efforts as if he were a boy, and he flourished. Only half an hour to fell a tree: how admirable that was.

His handsome face had filled out, and his complexion was healthy; she was ashamed of the vestiges of desire. She had deceived herself; her only recourse had been to revert to her old feelings for him. Perhaps with time her disappointment would silt up and become shallow and harmless. Johnnie was full of their future; it was difficult for her to think even a week ahead.

Inside, the house smelled of wax and fresh paint — newly varnished floors, banisters, and paneled walls — and the hall gleamed with a ruddy mahogany luster. Johnnie's Venetian chandelier, swathed in muslin against the dust of painting and carpentry, floated like a heavy cloud above the dining room table. In the back parlor, many of the pieces from the Priory had been reupholstered; in their new plush mohair they resembled matrons in unsuitably youthful clothing. The room seemed naked and embarrassed to be caught without drapery. Although Mr. Armitage of Manchester — Johnnie insisted on the best — had overseen the decoration, Johnnie had reviewed, and occasionally altered, each decision: fabric, furniture, even the fittings for the bath.

"Mr. Armitage has found an excellent library table, my dear," he had announced in October, "more substantial than the old one from the Priory, and the top is a beautiful rosewood."

"Oh, the old one is good enough for me, Johnnie. It's what you would like that matters." Discussing furniture distressed her; it seemed a frivolous intrusion. She was attempting to live in the present, resisting the pull of the past; the future, its conjecture, daunted her.

A new life. In the hall Johnnie had hung Mr. Bunney's watercolors, enshrined in bright gilt frames. She thought she recognized the sconces — of course: she and George had bought them for the Priory.

They had been taken down, polished, and screwed into these grand and different walls, almost familiar — as she herself felt, inhabiting the life of the person who was Mrs. John Cross.

"And the books?" she asked. "Have the books been unpacked?"

In the sunny library, with French doors giving onto the garden, Johnnie had ranged the old volumes in new cases. The room was larger than the library at the Priory, and even with the addition of books from Witley she had packed herself, some shelves stood empty, awaiting future acquisitions. A fire had been lit in the grate, prints from the Priory hung on the walls, and the new table occupied the center of the room. On it Johnnie had laid out Marian's last book, *Theophrastus Such* — with its ponderous ruminations, had Johnnie even read it? — and George's *Problems of Life and Mind,* which she had completed after his death, her memorial to him, work that had kept her alive that first year.

This library held the intertwined histories of their minds; she and George had read many of the books aloud to each other. She took one down, a volume of Herbert Spencer's essays inscribed to her and to George; glancing at its sentences, she heard the cadences of George's voice. She returned the book to its place. Spencer had sent her his new *Sociology,* and she and Johnnie had been reading it together.

Johnnie caressed the table's surface, the rosewood's swirling red-brown grain. "I brought your old chair from the Priory, so you will be comfortable writing."

She laughed. "Writing. You want so badly to see me writing, Johnnie. It is a picture you have in your mind."

"Writing, you are happy."

"No," she said. "I am not."

"I don't believe you, Marian." When he was distressed, he spoke softly, his voice caught in his throat as if he were trying to swallow unpleasantness.

The tabletop was slick with wax; it almost gave back her reflection. She ought to have Mr. Whistler's portrait sketch framed. It would be a pleasant errand; she would find a little silver frame for it and stand it on the table. Johnnie would object, claiming that it would mar his scheme, though in fact, with its presumptive intimacy, the sketch offended him. Rarely in their transactions did she and Johnnie address the truth of their feelings. This light and cheerful room was redolent of memory, but memory rearranged, sterile and disconnected. With a sigh, she smiled and settled into a chair by the hearth, her feet on the fender. "It must soon be time for tea," she said. "And then I shall unpack." Before she packed them, she had dusted the books; it had seemed a ceremony, laying them to rest.

JOHN CHAPMAN had introduced George and Marian at a bookseller's. Just the other day they had worked out the exact date of that encounter, the sixth of October, 1851. Chapman had as yet no idea of what existed between them — nobody had. Marian Evans always the friend, Marian the intellect, too ugly for tender feelings. George Lewes, brilliant and undependable, a cuckold and not to be trusted with women, a man who lived by his wits, whose origins were obscure.

She settled herself sideways in her chair and slung her feet over the arm closest to the fire. When she worked, she liked her face cool and her feet warm. She loosened her hair; pinned, it gave her a headache, and her hair was abundant and beautiful. Firelight picked out gold glints in the auburn, and in an hour or so the sun would shine through the window behind her and do its work, too. Proof sheets rested against her thighs, and the side of her hand was smeared black from her pencil. On his way out after lunch, John Chapman had inquired as to when she would finish her corrections. "It depends, doesn't it," she had answered, without looking up from her pages, "on the quality of what you have given me to correct."

John closed the door quietly, regretting, as she had intended, having disturbed her. She smiled to herself; she enjoyed tormenting him. Though he had spurned her, he had assumed — had it not always been this way? — that she would remain constant, and that he would maintain a hold on her affections. But she had not, and now he needed her help more than she needed his; she kept his *Westminster Review* alive intellectually while he struggled with its finances. He did what she told him to do.

She had deadlines, she should get on with her work, but it was impossible not to think about George. Spontaneous combustion — George had attacked Mr. Charles Dickens's spurious scientific solution to the disposition of an unsavory character. Marian had suggested that perhaps George should not have taken offense; after all, Dickens was his friend, and this was a novel, not a learned treatise. But George was impulsive and reckless; he would slay his dragon and defend his science — defend himself, perhaps. He lived by his charm and by the controversies he provoked. He believed in the future; indeed, he had no past — he had never known his father. Marian saw George without illusion; she could not help but see clearly, though love had begun to soften her judgments. She perceived that beneath his brilliant, combative façade there was concealed an abiding tenderness.

Finally: a knock on the door. "Who is it?" she called, though she knew who it was.

"The sun makes your hair copper," George said, coming in.

"The sun makes yours into a halo, though I think you're less a saint than a clown." She smiled.

"What kind of clown? Shakespearean or pantomime?" As he spoke he crossed the room and caressed the back of her head.

She leaned into his touch. "Touchstone, I was thinking. Your flippancy masks your kind heart."

George puffed out his chest to a comic dimension and declaimed, "Truly, lass, the gods have made thee poetical! And it is true that I have trod a measure — that I have flattered a lady." He laughed. "Polly, are you glad to see me? Or should I call you Audrey?"

"Am I glad? Of course I am glad. And so, Touchstone, my clown, am I an ill-favored thing? Am I your own? Will you take what no man else will?" She heard the doubt and hope and elation in her voice; there was no hiding it, and there was no need to hide.

George answered, "I will take you, my dearest thing, though we will not be well married."

"No, but better married than most." She dropped her proofs to the floor and opened her arms to him.

"MR. DICKENS made light of you because you haven't been to university."

"Neither has he."

"Which might be why he is so sensitive about his own science."

"And Thomas Huxley is like those experts who laughed at Goethe's experiments. You can't learn science at university; at university you attend lectures, you don't experiment, you don't observe. And it is beyond understanding why John Chapman is going to publish Huxley's article attacking me."

"I have protested as strongly as I can—you've seen the letter. I've done everything short of taking John by the shoulders and shaking him and demanding that he choose you. I can't refuse to run that article, though I've said it isn't worthy of being published; if I do refuse, he will suspect, and it will come out—you and I, I mean. George, what are you to do?"

"It will pass. I have a thick skin, Polly, not like you. These disputes trouble you more than they upset me. Oh, I'll make it up with them, eventually. I don't fight with men; I fight with their ideas, and they know that."

For her, George had moderated his combativeness, except where it concerned her; he became her champion. They had everything they could have asked for.

"MARIAN, are you going out?" Johnnie stood in the center of the parlor, directing the curtain maker's assistants, who had set up ladders beside the tall windows. "Watch where you step, my dear; they've rolled up the rug."

"Yes, I can see that."

The noise of hammering had penetrated the closed doors of the library; when the workmen finished in the parlor, they would invade her sanctum. It couldn't be helped; she should have been pleased that Mr. Armitage had rushed the completion of the curtains, but the bustle made her nearly frantic. She felt imposed upon; an edifice was being constructed around her—for her, to display her—while she remained marginal to the undertaking. She had asked not to be consulted, she must remember that: both because she was truly not interested, but also because she could not interfere with her husband's masterpiece.

The drawing room was splendid now, dense with pattern, dark intricacies of color and line, with upholstery woven by Morris and Company and walls papered with Morris's designs. Though Marian's taste ran to the spare rooms of an earlier generation, she could appreciate that this decoration was the height of fashion.

"Stay where you are," commanded Johnnie, "and I'll come to you." He stepped over the carpet and the bundles containing the velvet curtains. The assistants hopped out of his way. Johnnie enjoyed this confusion; he knew how to marshal the forces of domestic transformation.

"I am in search of a picture frame."

"You are going alone?"

"You are occupied with curtains."

"Mrs. Cross, I will accompany you."

"Mr. Cross, our new life has stalled until these workmen are out of the house. Your presence is necessary here." She released a dose of acerbity to deflect him, but it seemed to have the opposite effect.

"I am not required. Let me get my coat and hat." He surveyed the room. "And what do you want a frame for? A photograph? A photograph of George?"

"No." She did not need assistance remembering George, though his features in her mind sometimes blurred; he was growing less distinct and more pervasive. "I nearly forgot. Mr. Bray has written to say that he wants a photograph of you, Johnnie. I told him that you had none."

"Do you wish you had one to send — to advertise me? Am I such a fine specimen?"

"You are, indeed, Johnnie, and you are looking quite well."

He was mollified. "What do you wish to have framed?"

"The little sketch Mr. Whistler gave me, if you must know."

"That scrap of paper? Is it worth the trouble?"

"I must think so; otherwise why would I want a frame for it?"

A bracket clattered to the floor. From the top of a ladder, a young apprentice grimaced with chagrin and scrambled down to retrieve the fixture. Johnnie, his mouth tight with rage, glared at the unhappy boy, who had vague features in a round, white, scared face; he looked as if he wanted to fade away. "You will be liable, you understand, for the repair of damage to the floor." Johnnie turned around to inspect the spot where the metal fitting had fallen.

Marian touched his arm. "Johnnie," she remonstrated in a whisper. "Johnnie!"

He stooped and ran his fingers across the wood; the floor appeared to be unmarred.

"Johnnie, he's a child."

"Then he will learn young the consequences of carelessness."

"But he has done nothing."

"I'm sure that the bracket is dented — ruined."

"We will never see it. We will never know. Johnnie, I don't understand why you are so angry. It was nothing, a harmless mistake. It didn't fall on my head; the boy did no damage."

"I detest carelessness. I detest it. I do not want that boy in this house."

"Yes, I can see that."

He looked at her, wary, uneasy, and tried to smile. "Well, then," he said. "I'm sorry. It probably was nothing. But the shops will be closing soon. Perhaps we should go out this afternoon, or tomorrow."

Marian resisted reconciliation; her husband's pettiness distressed her. She said, "Do you know, Johnnie, I'm not convinced that the hall is the right spot to hang the Venetian watercolors. The light is too dim; you can see nothing but the frames. While the workmen are here, you might move them into your study; you can enjoy them there — you can appreciate them at your leisure." She smiled, bright and hard.

His headache began before dinner; an hour later it had expanded into nausea. He could tolerate no light and refused food. Marian pressed a cold compress to his eyes and held a glass of water to his lips. "It was the move," he whispered. The myriad details, the unfinished work made him distraught; it was not how he had imagined bringing his wife to her new home. She stroked his forehead, easing his anxiety as if he were a child.

But he did not leave his bed until almost a week had passed. "You are not yet strong," Marian murmured. "You must rest."

THE VENETIAN watercolors remained in the hall; she did not buy a silver frame for the little sketch and instead inserted it for safe-keeping between the pages of her journal. When the curtains had been hung in the library — while Johnnie was ill, the workmen muffled their boots with felt overshoes — Marian arranged her papers on the table: her journals, and here was her old unfinished translation of Spinoza. Proposition XXIII: *The human mind cannot be absolutely destroyed with the body, but there remains of it something eternal.* George had been unable to interest a publisher in her efforts. That work had been a labor of love — perhaps she should finish it and end her career with translation, where she had begun. Perhaps. She put it down and opened her journal — here were decades of journals, and she began reading.

Her round and open hand had not changed. She read of her disastrous forays into love; she wept for her ardor, for the unquenchable abundance of emotion aroused by music, by vain and unfeeling men, by dangerous, marvelous knowledge. Suffering was ardor's corollary. When she was thirty, she had prayed — the habit of supplication — to harden off, to grow a shell against love and heartbreak and spoiled expectations.

And then it had come round right. What she remembered most of all from the beginning was laughter, his marvelous levity. George was an actor, and if in memory his features had grown vague, it was because they were so mobile; he was a sprite, a mimic, her marvelous lunatic, her lover. If he had not been able, while alive, to give her his own legal name, he had offered her a habitation for her mind and spirit — and for her body, a home, an exquisite nautilus that shielded her and contained her tenderness, that let her imagination flourish.

While George was ill, she had turned inward and clamored less to be heard. Now, married to Johnnie, ardor had atrophied and weariness had taken its place. Their shell, their connection was pretense, but she was cared for, and she was not alone.

THE DECEMBER days passed in shades of gray; the fog thickened and thinned. Mr. and Mrs. Cross ventured out to a Popular Concert at St. James's Hall. Johnnie listened dutifully to Beethoven and tapped his foot in reasonable time with the beat. He closed his eyes and smiled, too, but never at the sublime moments, the transitions, the modulations, the measures of hesitation and tension, doubt and release. Members of the audience recognized George Eliot: small and severe, her flesh thin over her craggy bones, she entered beside her tall and solicitous husband. If she were not so famous, they would have been tempted to smile. As it was, they gossiped, but she held herself at a remove. She had come for the music.

To appease Johnnie, she pretended to work. The curtains, pale silk to a lady's taste, had been installed in the library. Marian read from her journals: uncomfortable beds, George turning cartwheels in a Weimar meadow, her jealousy of Frau Schumann, her terrible isolation in Richmond during those first years after their idyll in Germany. She read with deep disquiet; though she had omitted much, she felt small, persistent shame, shame not recorded, running remembered through the pages. Writing her novels, she had employed that shame and its corollary, defiant determination, and picked it apart, wrought it into many shapes, into complexities of feeling, anger and bitterness and forgiveness, desperation and resolution. But she had never permitted a character to endure her own circumstances. That would have been self-serving, or worse — dishonest. She was no exemplar; she had been singular.

AT THE PICNIC, the girl had placed herself at a distance, listening. Intense and watchful, she reminded Marian of her youthful self. Johnnie's sister Anna and her husband had organized a jolly afternoon at Sevenoaks; it was early September, just three months ago, a day replete with late summer fruitfulness, a table set under one of the oaks, children and dogs cheerful and underfoot. The visit had been a success; in his sisters' presence, Johnnie became once again a simple and charming boy, entertaining the children, participating in games; he had left Marian's side to play on his brother-in-law's new tennis court. As conversation lulled, the girl, a neighbor's daughter — her name was Annabel — approached Marian and sat at her feet. "What about the plight of women?" she had asked.

Marian smiled. "I was not aware that women had a plight."

The girl's eyes were pale blue, and her skin was freckled, translucent as a chrysalis. "They are little more than chattels; they cannot attend university."

"They can attend the University of London."

"Not Cambridge or Oxford. The world is shut against them — against us."

"There is Girton College."

"It is *at* Cambridge, not part of it. It is entirely separate from the university."

"Women can now divorce."

"But a woman can control only her own earnings, not her inheritance — and how many women are like you, Mrs. Cross, with earnings to control? A widow is at the mercy of her children, or her child's husband. An unmarried woman must depend on her wits, on the whims of her family." She hesitated, expecting to be contradicted, but Marian remained silent. "I need not tell you these things; you know them, you have described them — but you do not lend your voice to the cause. You could help us achieve so much."

Around them, conversations had ceased. Marian had answered in her public voice — and she heard in that detachment defense against her own youthful suffering, a remoteness she had labored for and claimed and was loath — possibly afraid, especially now — to abandon. "I do not pretend to know what is best for all women, and I am not convinced that the needs of women are so different from the needs of men. Dividing the human condition by sex seems — fruitless. And I am only one voice."

"You underestimate your power."

"That is better than overestimating it, don't you think? I am a grandmother, Annabel; I am not so interested in change. I have recorded circumstances, what I observe. Change occurs without me." The girl nodded, crestfallen.

Marian relented. "I have friends who have worked for women's causes — you might become one of them. I am not politically inclined. But you, with your keen interest — with your convictions — you could effect change."

Annabel lowered her head so that Marian could not see her eyes.

Marian leaned forward in her chair and patted the girl's arm. "I mean what I say."

"You are not mocking me?" The rims of the girl's eyes were red; she was fighting tears.

"Not at all." Marian saw Johnnie approaching, exercised and happy, glistening like a horse in a paddock. He appraised the situation — the silence, the girl's flushed face — and launched into an elaborate description of the match: paragraphs of serves and volleys.

"You seem tired, Marian," he announced when he had recounted his final, victorious point. "I must take you inside." As they walked back to the house he said, "I am sorry about Annabel. She is quite ill-mannered. I don't find her at all sympathetic."

"But I enjoyed her; she was like a little caterpillar. I admired her, and I meant to encourage her."

"You were distressed."

"You were distressed. I was engaged." She added, intending to tease him out of protectiveness, "But Johnnie, you did well; never have I heard such a thorough account of a tennis game!"

"And I am sorry for being tedious." He went to his room to change for dinner.

JOHNNIE WAS pleased to see her journals stacked on the library table. "So, my dear, you are beginning."

"Yes." She lied. "I am."

There was nothing to begin. A memoir? How could she? Her particular life: it was too irregular; it lacked shape and resolution. Her mind had not saved her from making errors; her intelligence had not curbed her feelings. She was fallible and flawed. But she had had great good luck in love. It had permitted her to look outward— and see her stories.

"I FEEL LIKE Adam, naming the animals," Marian said to George. "I want to know the names of everything, every zoophyte, every flower, every sort of cloud."

"As do I. We're twin Adams, you and I."

"And we have sneaked back into paradise."

They were walking above Ilfracombe, on the north Devon coast, where they had come to make George's reputation: he intended to write about marine creatures. Observations in the field: all summer long they collected creatures at the margins of land and water. Learning the difference between having eyes and seeing, they grew able to identify and differentiate species. George was compiling a guide. A summer at the seaside, the luxury of meadows, of cliffs and cows, of blooming and fading flowers, green grass and harvested fields. She was preparing to begin.

"What shall I write?"

"What do you yearn for? What do you know? You can write description; now you must come up with character."

"I'll write about Warwickshire, villagers, unlucky wives, clerics."

"Your childhood."

"What I remember — the inhabitants of a neighborhood; I know everything about them; I can see them. I have stories I was told as a child. People who would be overlooked, obscure lives, anemones who wither at a touch, who struggle in shadows. Girls and women. And I'll write about gentlemen — men, at least, some gentle, and some not."

"You'll write about faith, I imagine."

"Why do you say that?"

"Faith, meaning: where we have been, where we are going. Those are the big questions, Polly. You will not be a silly lady novelist."

"What if it's not good?"

"You'll know. I'll know, too. I will tell you."

"I cannot write under my own name; I would be a laughingstock, a scandal."

"You write under your own name now."

"That's different; that's criticism, not my heart."

"Then I will shield you. Nobody will know who you are, except that you are my friend. Let's make you into a clergyman, since you've left the church, and since you are writing about clerics. What do you think?"

"My first name will be George."

He laughed. "Then, George, tell me your stories."

She had written for him; he was her loving audience. Writing, she reclaimed her childhood, its placid landscape, though she continued to long for what she had abandoned, her legitimate place in the clamor of family.

JOHNNIE SAID, "You must write to your brother Isaac. If you don't, I shall again. I feel it is my duty; he is my brother now, as well."

She spoke slowly, as if dictating instructions; she was not angry, only weary. "I have already written to my brother. I wrote to him six months ago; I informed him of our new address, Four Cheyne Walk. If he chooses to call, he may. He may leave his card. I have done all I intend to do. He has not responded. If you wish to make his acquaintance, if you wish to call him brother, you may do so after I am dead."

She would not extend an invitation to Isaac. She had been overjoyed at how eagerly Johnnie's sisters welcomed her, how they extended their love to her. On that September afternoon, married, legitimate, with Johnnie absorbed in tennis, the girl Annabel reminding her of her own youth and her invented Dorothea, the air soft with her sister-in-law's kindness, she had been content. Marriage had seemed a plausible resolution; her satisfaction had not lasted.

VENETIAN MIST, London fog: he was drawn to vapor, to light diffused and to the absence of shadow. In the fog all was tone and muted color; solids dissolved into mood. From the Chelsea Embankment, James Whistler considered the Thames. Metallic with effluents, its waves rolled too oily to crest; molten light pooled and scattered into slivers of mercury. The wind etched its chill into Whistler's cheeks, and he lowered his head against it.

He had delivered his pastels and etchings to the Fine Art Society; his exhibition would not open until the new year. He wished it were summer and not so raw; he would take a rowboat out on the river. He was happiest on water, looking at the land, viewing it reflected and insubstantial. He was an artist of the ephemeral, the shifting: light, emotions. It was difficult being back in London; London was too permanent — indifferent as well. Whistler was choking with nervous anticipation, and there was nothing to do but attend to the business of attracting notice and wait. Two years had passed since the ignominious lawsuit; perhaps the scandal had left a persistent disturbance, a wake, that would jostle the public, and they would come see — and marvel at — and buy — his Venice work.

Darkness fell early here; it was just past three and already dusk and more than a week to go until the winter solstice; streetlights were coming on, the lamps of the omnibuses and coaches were lit, emitting streaks of illumination. In the west, the polluted sunset had dimmed to a translucent wash of mauve. Whistler felt close to invisible; it was not amusing to be desperate in London. Expatriate bravado had worked in Venice, but here his circumstances were perceived to be a moral failure. He had to be patient.

Maud Franklin had come back with him. In Venice, that city of irregularity, their arrangement had been difficult enough. Here, there was no escaping the impossibility of her situation. But he could not abandon her, as much as he would like to. She was pregnant again, and he was angry, irrationally, he knew — not that she expected him to support the child or give it his name. He had not acknowledged the first one. Now she was tired and ill and swollen and lay in bed all day, holding her book close to her eyes because she was shortsighted. She called herself an artist, and he had to maintain that fiction or she would lose the last wisp of self-respect. But she could not see, and he could not tell her that her work was tame and feminine, awkward and pretty.

She wasn't even pretty herself; she was ferocious and pale and long, and he could not resist her white legs and red hair, darkened after the birth of the little girl. Maud: his nocturne in russet and white. And pink, that damned, clear pink: the tips of her fingers and toes, her breasts. He drew her, suggesting by his coat hanging from a hook on the wall his presence and by the disheveled bed their congress; she permitted him anything. Those drawings sold. Married men kept them in portfolios and took them out after cigars and port. He was her artist, she said, and she was his art. He resented her because he wanted her. He wished she would resist him, and when she did, he threatened to leave her. Last night she was after him again to take her with him to America. He could not return in disgrace, he argued; he did not add that if this exhibition was a success, he would not have to go at all. But she knew that.

It was growing too cold to think, but the commerce of the Thames drew him, the hulks of barges, the rhythmic plash of oars. Voices carried in the fog, the river became intimate, revealing. Light took on volume and spread in horizontal rays; lamps wore halos. The water was dark and luminous, the barges like black oblongs of soot, the shore murky, the blocks of houses even darker and opaque. The sky held on to light, deepened now to a bluish gray. If he did not paint quickly, how could he hold these shades in his mind?

At the trial, the speed of his work had been a source of contention — Ruskin claimed he worked too rapidly for the result to be any good. The Venice work had been quick, pastels laid on as fast as perception. But he had worked the etchings over, painstakingly proofing state after state to achieve the tension of space and line until the atmosphere almost breathed: condensing a moment, the intersection of feeling and sight. His work would astonish; it would succeed. He felt his fortunes changing, although there was no sign yet of that. It was slack tide, the moments when movement ceases before the onset of the opposite pull.

She lived near here, George Eliot, Mrs. Cross. He had thought of her often. Their encounter had been intimate, swaddled in a kind of gentle fog. It had been tender in that it was painful, and also in that what had passed between them was not love, but not unlike it. Cheyne Walk: number four. *We are at home on Sunday afternoons.* It was not Sunday. He would call and leave his card; she could write to him if she chose.

The gates at Four Cheyne Walk gleamed with an oily luster; the path and the stone steps were so clean, they appeared to have been freshly honed. Whistler could see his face reflected, distorted, in the brass knocker on the front door. The house embodied George Eliot's public eminence, and Mr. Cross had interests in the City; Maud had told him that. From here, the Thames appeared picturesque; a garden and an esplanade shielded the residents of Cheyne Walk from the river's moil. Whistler could not deny that he envied this solid domesticity. He yearned to be married. To whom — to a woman whose father had prospered, whose father would never countenance a disreputable man like him? He smiled at his aspirations. He would settle for less, much less; all he desired was a woman whom it was permissible to love. The servant opened the door, and Whistler left his card.

JOHN CROSS had chosen to return to Cheyne Walk by foot. He required exercise; it was critical to his recovery, and after the attack of the previous week, he understood how fragile his health remained. He needed a chance to think, as well. The fog, though he disliked its smell, enclosed him in a semblance of solitude. He took stock. Business was good; his instincts were reliable. Just six months earlier he had declined to invest in a manufacturing scheme in Manchester; this morning he had learned that the enterprise had gone bankrupt. As Johnnie had suspected, the man had proved unsound, his resources far smaller than represented. But marriage — he sighed, and his breath plumed and blended with the mist. His marriage would sort itself out; this was a difficult time, a time of transition.

Marian had been sharp with him. Her disapproval, coupled with the moral force it carried — she could not help herself — everything she uttered emerged backed by formidable conviction and caught him by surprise and wounded him; she was a combination of mother and priestess. He could not let down his guard; he tried to anticipate her moods, but she was quicker than he was. In retrospect he could reconstruct what had precipitated her displeasure: at his sister's luncheon party he had been overly solicitous — she could easily defend herself against a girl; last week he had been perhaps too exacting in his own standards of workmanship. The boy — Johnnie had read insolence in his small, wet mouth and a taunting, infuriating vulnerability in his round and not innocent eyes. His own reaction to the boy had made him ill, that and his wife's reproach; he feared she saw into him. He had caved in; it was a sickening collapse; he could not permit himself to think about it.

She had collected Mr. Bunney's watercolors while he was ill in Venice. He had assumed that she had reconsidered her first impression and that she approved of them; fetching them had required a great deal of trouble, an entire morning. For that reason he had the watercolors hung in the hall, and also to show her that he intended to forget the terrible things that had happened in Venice. To do otherwise would be to indulge in morbidity

At other times Marian seemed to desire nothing more than to be with him. Her manner with his sisters was loving; she was eager for Christmas at Sevenoaks. They were to arrive on Christmas Eve, and she was accumulating presents for the children — she was happiest in the country. Perhaps in the new year she would write to Isaac; it would give him great pleasure to witness their reconciliation; Johnnie pictured brother and sister folded in each other's arms in a kind of tableau vivant.

She had been happy at the concert at St. James's Theatre — Beethoven: the emotion, for him, he had to admit, was a bit excessive and a bit loud; the pianist quite banged. That beautiful expression of serenity and utter contentment had suffused her face. He adored her then and delighted in the fruits of his dedication.

But the following day, she had gone from room to room, fretting over the unfinished decoration. That, finally, had been completed; no more workmen disturbed her days. Her unsettled state, he was sure, had to do with the flux of their living arrangements. Women needed a home, a frame, a surrounding establishment, and Marian was an excellent manager; Johnnie had long had intimations of that from their discussions of investments. Organizing a household with economy and efficiency gave her great satisfaction; his mother, too, had taken pride in a smoothly running establishment.

Dismantling the Priory had been difficult; the house held happy memories and painful ones, too: ghosts, not only George but his poor son Bertie, felled by a ghastly African plague. One must concentrate on the positive. And Johnnie was getting a good price for the property. He had stopped there today and found that Herbert Spencer had left his card. Marian would be pleased; they had just finished reading his *Sociology* together; it was rather heavy going, but they had persisted, out of friendship.

The evening before, as a reward for completing Spencer, they had embarked on Tennyson's new poems in *Cornhill*. As she read, Marian's voice lost its resonance and became dull and automatic; Johnnie recognized the pain it concealed. She was remembering George: after George died, she had turned to Tennyson for solace. "You do not have to go on, my dear," he had said, and she put the book down and retired to her bedroom.

It was a positive sign that she was beginning to work; all summer she had resisted his suggestions, his offers of support. When he returned from the City and saw her in her library — such a light, lovely room, and before you knew it the bulbs would be coming up in the garden — reading her journals, organizing her past, he was cheered. She was beginning to turn her mind to another book, a culmination. He understood her qualms about a memoir; there were aspects of her past — the particulars of her marriage to George — but not every wrinkle had to be ironed out. After all, when she and Johnnie married at St. George's Church, Marian Evans Lewes was the legal name she had signed in the register. And if not a memoir, another novel, with a noble heroine, a woman who understood duty.

A novel would be small in scale; he doubted that she had the stamina to complete a book as ambitious as *Middlemarch*. He had to be careful with her; when she objected to his suggestions, he had noticed that she did not contradict him directly but found other means to express her displeasure. He had thought to manage her life as he managed her finances. George had acted as her agent, her filter, the screen between her and the world. Johnnie had hoped to do the same. Marian was a sensitive creature, fragile, if occasionally ferocious.

He stopped for a moment at the Embankment; he enjoyed the sounds of commerce, magnified and mysterious in the fog, the guttural rumble of engines, the deep throbbing of prosperity. This was music to him; he preferred its steadiness to Beethoven. The other evening Marian had asked him about the Embankment, the engineering involved, the underwater foundations, the physical forces that had to be considered. He had explained as best he could, admitting that he understood more about the financing than about the construction. She had asked about the financing, then, bond issues, degrees of risk, rates of return; it was marvelous how quickly she comprehended.

"I quite like that risk can be calculated," she had said, "that it has a price. I must remember that."

She had made him laugh. He smiled now, remembering. He had begun his walk distressed, but his state of mind was improving. Every marriage required time to establish itself, temperaments had to adjust. It was an intimate arrangement; he was worrying unnecessarily; what mattered most was his certainty that he adored her, that he would do anything to safeguard her. He left the Embankment and headed toward Cheyne Walk. By now it was almost dark, and as he approached he saw a figure, a man, closing the gate to his house. The man turned onto the street and headed away from him; in the fog it was impossible to make out who he was.

His visiting card lay on the tray in the front hall: James McNeill Whistler. Johnnie shivered; once inside he realized how cold he had been; he hoped that he would not suffer a relapse. Before greeting his wife, he went into his study and poured himself a medicinal brandy and drank it down. Whistler's card, offensively large and vulgar, was in his hand; he had forgotten to return it to the tray. A loathsome man, Whistler, a flâneur. He must protect his wife. Johnnie stowed the rectangle of cardboard in his desk drawer; he sought out Marian in the library to give her Herbert Spencer's card.

• • •

SPENCER HAD a rigorous mind, though he lacked a heart. It was too late in their lives to abandon their friendship; she ought to invite him to call. And he had visited her and George in those difficult years at Richmond when few others had seen fit to acknowledge them. She had sometimes wondered what combination of curiosity — Spencer would have called it scientific inquiry — and kindness had led him to do so.

"How did you know I was arriving?" Herbert Spencer, hale and rested, stepped off the train at Richmond. "I intended to surprise you."

"And, indeed, you have!" George shook his friend's hand. "We are not waiting for you — no offense, Herbert, but for somebody else — for Barbara Smith, and she has not appeared." They waited until the carriage doors slammed shut and the train left the station. George reached for Spencer's traveling case, and Marian said: "You must come home with us."

"I was intending to call on you; I am on my way from Brighton to Paris." Spencer, with his wintry eyes, looked Marian and George up and down.

"You mean that your curiosity got the better of you?" Marian chided. "Do not examine us as if we were specimens, or at least do not do so here — wait until you see us in our natural habitat, and then you can judge."

She had felt no trace of awkwardness that October afternoon, only a lingering familiarity, a sweet trace of connection. They talked of science, of George's *Sea-Side Studies,* which had appeared in *Blackwood's* and been well received, and they gossiped. Mr. Chapman was pursuing a medical degree, Barbara Smith had declined Chapman's kind and selfish offer to set her up as his mistress — though of course he had not put it in those terms — and to introduce her to the fulfillments of motherhood.

"The man is innocent of conscience," Spencer declared. "That is why we forgive him. And he takes anything you write, Marian. I quite liked your 'Silly Novels by Lady Novelists.' I read it on the train; it made me laugh."

"Why, thank you. I did not think you cared for lady novelists."

"I might if you were to become one."

She had responded without thinking, expansive in his company, shored up with George's confidence. "A novel is exactly what I am writing. I am almost finished. *The Sad Fortunes of the Rev. Amos Barton* is what we're calling it." Horrified, she had turned to George.

He had been leaning against the mantelpiece. He crossed the room and stood tense and pale before his friend. "Spencer, you must never tell a soul."

"Everyone will soon know, if you publish. Unless you use a nom de plume. Of course you will — and what will it be?"

"George Eliot."

"A man? How clever. Everyone says that you have a man's mind, Marian."

"Nobody must know. You must promise."

Spencer had promised. He kept the secret for two years, but in the end he had revealed her as the author. Scrupulous even in betrayal, he came to see them in Richmond to inform them of what he had done.

"Chapman asked me if you had written *Adam Bede.* I could not lie. If I had said no, he would have seen the lie in my face."

"You do not understand what this does to me."

"I think that it rather exalts you, Marian. After all, everybody is reading your book. And that ridiculous Mr. Joseph Liggins is claiming that he is the author and demanding his money, your money. You can't imagine you can get rid of him by writing letters — even though, George, you do write the most stinging letters — and not showing your face." He glanced at George, at the austere little sitting room where few visitors were received.

She had avoided showing her face, her irregular circumstances. Without being aware of it, Spencer had a knack for locating her shame — and her anxiety: that notoriety would undermine her fragile marriage, that gossip and public exposure would drive George away.

"Marian, you are being foolish and stubborn. If I were you, I should enjoy this; I should seize it. You cannot hide like a mollusk and close yourself up in your shell. And I cannot think that you want to; you are dissembling. People talk about you and George already; they will do so whether or not you are the author of *Adam Bede.*"

There was an element of revenge, George said, in Spencer's revelation; it was the act of a man who believed he had failed to recognize and claim a precious object. But George was also angry because he had also failed to protect their secret — though how he could have done so much longer Marian did not know.

THEY HAD reconciled with Spencer, and with Chapman, and with Dickens, and with Huxley. After *Adam Bede* everybody wanted to know George Eliot, though not everybody would receive or call on Marian Evans Lewes. Eventually her fame silenced those critics of her circumstances. Her withdrawal came to be understood as a sacrifice to her art, and her art came to be seen as her vocation. She was perceived as a sibyl, enriched by what had once caused her despair: her ugliness, her brains. George had known the difference between her image and her person; Johnnie did not — or could not.

Marian put down her journal; through the window she watched the arrival of darkness, the opaque and luminous swirls of London fog. Johnnie, fearing that she would catch a chill, sent the servant in every evening to draw the curtains, and Marian, every evening, dismissed her. She promised her husband that she would sit close to the fire.

It was odd to understand one's self retrospectively, to find oneself amused and close to tears at one's own history. She had written down columns of numbers, her books, George's books: volumes sold, monies paid, monies promised. Her father's daughter, the careful steward, she recorded her success: totting up accounts to demonstrate profit. The solid, measurable underpinnings of joy. Accounts interspersed with rapturous descriptions of landscape: landscape was more or less permanent, not ephemeral like success.

Not that the writing came more easily. There was always an element of penance in it, in the headaches and depression, in the loud, unceasing, critical voice in her head, a constant damaging obbligato. George had overridden its objections. He became her writer's conscience, benign, encouraging; for twenty-four years he had contradicted that stubborn, disparaging, mocking voice.

She wished she had been well enough to visit the cemetery on the anniversary of his death. She had told Charles Lewes that she thought it prudent to avoid Highgate's dampness; in truth she was not strong enough to confront what two years had done to his grave: the earth settled, the newly dead encroaching. The ivy was dying, Charles had told her. She wanted more planted, and she wanted a new, high, distinctive fence surrounding the grave; she wanted George apart, singular. When the depredations of time had been repaired, then she would go.

The maid brought the afternoon post. An announcement from the Fine Art Society: an exhibition in January of pastels and etchings of Venice by Mr. James McNeill Whistler. She examined the envelope; the handwriting was familiar. It was Whistler's own. So he was in London. Perhaps he would call; she hoped he would. She would ask Johnnie to attend the vernissage with her; it would give her something to look forward to in the dull days after Christmas. Herbert Spencer had written to say that he would call tomorrow afternoon.

"SO, MY FRIEND, do you like our new home?"

"Marian, it is splendid, just splendid." Spencer's nimbus of fair curls had thinned and turned gray; his icy eyes were now pouched and watery. He had been lithe and dense with muscle; now he was desiccated, his skin a shriveled husk. Once, despairing that her gaze, naked with ardor and yearning, would turn his heart to stone, she had called herself a Medusa, as if by naming the effect she could reduce it. Now she found him difficult to look at. He said, "I enjoy the smell of fresh paint."

"Which I am rather tired of."

"And you are happy?"

"What a question coming from you, Herbert. You should know the answer: I am married; I am happy. I shall abandon myself to the feminine sphere of inchoate feeling and leave men to give birth to ideas. Does that not follow in your thinking as night follows day?"

"Marian! You wish to mock my theories?"

"No, I wish to converse with you." She spoke gently; Spencer's arid rectitude, his punctilious and resistant logic — qualities that experience had only made more unyielding — compelled her to be kind. He had come so close; *evolution* had been his word — as he often reminded her. He had perceived the scaffolding of evolution before

228

Darwin, but not the mechanism, not the accidents of natural selection. He did not allow for chance.

His ideas were important, and they were flawed; she resented his ideas about women. As she saw it, he drained his science of emotion. But he was rigorous; he was honest, and when Marian had first come to London, he had loved her mind, however masculine he deemed it.

"You did everything to help me," he said. He blushed; his thinning skin could not keep emotion from surfacing, and he added, testily, "You have reread my *Sociology*. You have read it several times."

"You have never married — I might accuse you of ignoring your own advice. You are the kind of man who should have children."

"I have never" — he coughed — "it would compromise my objectivity."

"I once asked you never to marry."

"I remember."

"I hope that I did not dissuade you."

"My work has been my satisfaction."

"And it is fine work, Herbert. It is closely argued — and, by the way, there are many typographical errors in *Sociology*, as many as I find in my own books. Why should human society not adhere to the laws of evolution? And I very much like that you call your theory Social Darwinism; you organize the process of natural selection, you give it a moral. The survival of the fittest."

He stretched his legs toward the fire. Earlier, the fog had lifted, but it was returning, swallowing the Thames, the gardens, the streets, darkening the afternoon. The lamps were already lit. Marian would have liked to talk with Herbert of George, but between them the habit of disputation endured. They were like opposing magnets now, and their friendship was prickly with enmity. She went on: "But, Herbert, your notion of 'equilibrium,' that state of perfect adaptation, when every organism in a society fulfills its purpose, reminds me of those medieval paintings of the Last Judgment. Mr. Cross and I made a special study of them in Venice last summer, though we disagreed on which we preferred, heaven or hell. Mr. Cross chose angels."

"He attends church?"

"He did, while his mother was alive. Herbert, I think that you would be on the side of the angels, too: standing in ranks on the right hand of God."

"I do not believe in God. Neither do you."

"No. Nor in angels. But it is a comfort to know that we are heading in the right direction, that the world is always improving."

He sat up, anticipating the challenge.

She said, "But Herbert, don't you think that equilibrium would lead to the end of stories?"

"How do you mean?"

"Stories arise from abrasion, from the conflict between character and circumstance, from the volatile chemistry of emotion. You say we are evolving away from that, toward those uniform angels, who all sing the same song. Even hosanna a million times over might grow tedious. You know, I much prefer the depictions of hell."

Spencer refused to fight. "You would, Marian; hell is far more amusing, and there are better stories in hell than in heaven. Goodness is always rather dull. Perhaps since I am deficient in emotion, I appreciate equilibrium more than you do. But you will not run out of stories."

"I was not thinking of myself. Anyway, I am through with stories."

Spencer looked at her with alarm. "What is it, Marian? Are you tired? Forgive me for saying this, but you look a bit careworn."

She smiled. "And just today I was thinking that I was not as homely as I used to be, that I have grown into my face."

He studied her, and she saw in his pale eyes shades of regret and blame — she thought he resented her still for having been unable to attract him. "I believe that you are right. Mr. Cross must do you good, Marian."

"He is devoted to me. I am lucky in that."

"The move has tired you."

"And the time of year. It is always dark, and the fog — Johnnie tries to keep me cheerful, but I am not easy to humor. I resist. He would like me to write, but I have no idea what to begin. He thinks a memoir. I've been reading my journals."

"Ah." He looked briefly alarmed.

She laughed. "Are you afraid that we will all tell each other's stories for posterity? Leaving posterity quite confused, no doubt, and wondering when we found the time to work. Tell me, Herbert, how is your autobiography coming? Are you enjoying rummaging among your ancestors?"

"I am, quite. But I am doing so in the spirit of scientific inquiry. It will be a setting down of the evolution of my thought. And I am interested in how I evolved myself, physically and mentally — from whom I inherited my qualities of mind."

Marian laughed. "I am sure that I evolved quite miraculously. If my mother had known what I would become, she might have drowned me at birth like a superfluous kitten. I am sure that my brother wishes she had."

"I am not sure if I should laugh at what you are saying."

"Don't you think of me as a sport of nature?"

"Marian, I think of you as my friend." He seemed to struggle against his instincts for reserve and self-defense. He looked at the fire as he spoke. "You have been brooding, I am guessing, about George."

"As I said, it is the time of year. He is always on my mind."

"You must look to the future, Marian."

"I have always looked to the past."

"With George to anchor you. He was the most extraordinary friend. I have to admit that sometimes I think I hear his voice."

"Yes," she said.

"He could make me laugh."

"Yes. I miss that."

"I wish I could comfort you. Do you wish you could work?"

"I do not have the energy — it would be for Johnnie."

"Then that is not a sufficient reason. You cannot write to make someone else happy. Perhaps you are ill."

"I have a slight sore throat, that is all, nothing. But now I am being tedious; I am far worse than angels. You do comfort me, Herbert. I'll ring for tea. You must tell me what you have discovered about your ancestors. Have you reached into the past as far back as the monkeys?"

ILLNESS WAS familiar, she knew its routine, its course, and she welcomed its lassitude. It was preferable to be the patient and not the nurse, not the witness. She was not passive; she resisted submission to the inevitable; she found no beauty—or reward—in suffering. It was not until the end that she had given up hope for George, not until she understood that relinquishing him was all that would give him peace. His eyes—the awful appeal. They did not fade. *Go, go.* A terrible release. She had closed his eyes; she saw them still.

She was not depressed by this illness; it seemed instead a respite from the business of settling into the house and becoming happy. Like fog it obliterated space. She existed in whiteness, and she experienced a gentle vertigo; she spun around pain that began in her throat and spread to her chest, constricting her heart. Pain freed her attention, it released her from time; she had no idea if it was morning or evening, this year or last. She felt as if she were floating, drifting in a medium of air and water without horizon.

Johnnie was not concerned, and neither was she. They had not called for the doctor. It was a sore throat caused by the dampness and the fog. She expected that she would recover in a few days, and then they would be off to his sister Anna and her family at Sevenoaks. It would be good to leave London. It was difficult to talk; the infection thickened her throat. Another voice: the doctor. The heat of fever, incandescent like the sun, burned off the fog. Johnnie gave her hot water and lemon juice and honey to drink. She could not swallow.

SHE WAS HOT. Of course she was. It was a warm July afternoon, her window open on Cambridge Street: shouts, soot, the clopping of hooves, and, floating on top of the grime, a sweet, soft breeze. She was packing her earthly possessions into her trunk. After her father's death this trunk had gone with her from Coventry to Geneva with the Brays; it had arrived with her in London three years ago.

Marian laid her books in the bottom of her trunk: her German, French, and Latin dictionaries—and two copies of her own translation from the German of Feuerbach's *Essence of Christianity,* which John Chapman had just published, her name, Marian Evans, on the title page. *"Life is, in its essential relations, of a divine nature. Its consecration is not conferred by the blessing of a priest . . . Marriage is the free bond of love, sacred in itself."* She arranged her manuscripts and a small portfolio of photographs: her sister Chrissey, an old portrait of Isaac on the cusp of youth and adulthood, before his features had set and his heart had hardened. Her brother and sister had no photograph of her, but she had given Chrissey a portrait; if she never saw her sister again, perhaps that image would supplant memory.

It had been painted by the artist in whose house she had taken lodgings in Geneva five years ago. Monsieur Durade: she had been half in love with him, half in love with any man who showed her kindness. She was not suited to stand alone. Monsieur Durade had cropped her nose and shortened her chin, enlarged her gray eyes; he had made her far more beautiful than she really was. Gentle man, he had been half in love with her.

The dim mirror above her dresser reflected her face, soft, highly colored, feverish with expectation and dread. She saw herself: if not beautiful in her bones, then arresting in her ardor.

Her summer dress, her winter dress, a bodice and fabric for a skirt, linens, stockings, cloak, bonnets, boots, needles and thread; yesterday she had bought a ribbon and a length of lace; she did not know what she would find in Weimar. Her hairbrush she packed in her carpetbag, along with her steamship ticket, her journal, and her volume of Spinoza's *Ethics;* she intended to translate Spinoza. *"A life of good deeds, I call piety."*

Nobody except Chapman and Charles Bray knew where she was going, what she was intending. She had made all the arrangements; she was ready. Months ago she had resigned from the editorship of the *Westminster Review;* and now Chapman would have to pay her as a contributor. He had offered her a regular column: Belles Lettres, at sixteen guineas a quarter; she would review contemporary literature, and in addition he had asked her to write an article on French literary women. An occupation and the promise of an income: it was the least Chapman could do.

She had not told Spencer. What would he — that prince of pure reason — say when he found out? He would be relieved, he would be curious; perhaps he would feel accountable, responsible, by his rejection, for her desperate flight. But her decision was not desperate; neither did it submit itself to analysis. It was not a flight into romance — she could in no way ignore or diminish the difficult consequences of this action. It was — necessary. She needed this man, this connection, absolutely; otherwise she would not survive. She was neither courageous nor foolhardy. That they could not marry in a church was, to her, ultimately irrelevant. To the world it was all that mattered.

She had instructed Isaac to send Chrissey half of the income paid to her annually from her father's trust and to send the other half to her in care of John Chapman. The rent on her lodgings was paid up; her landlady had been sorry to see her go. Marian was sober and studious, quiet, reassuringly plain, and she had played the piano in the parlor. Mrs. Burke had often stood in the doorway listening. Since Mr. Burke's death, she had explained, she had had moments of loneliness. Music eased the pain. "You might understand, Miss Evans; you, too, live a solitary existence."

The maid helped her carry her trunk downstairs. She was ready, but she had hours to wait. She went back to her room and sat on the bare mattress in the warm wind from the window. Yesterday she had posted her letter to Coventry:

> I have only time to say good bye and God bless you. Poste Restante, Weimar for the next six weeks, and afterwards Berlin.
>   Ever your loving and grateful Marian

The steamship sailed in the evening, overnight to Antwerp. An ending and a beginning. She sat and waited. What if George had changed his mind? He would not. What if Agnes threatened a scandal? What if he suddenly had qualms about publicly uniting his life with a thirty-five-year-old spinster with little money and few prospects? What if he tired of her after two months? What if he left her? In her experience, love ended badly. There were no assurances, only faith. If she were wrong, if that faith turned out to be an illusion, she would be publicly ruined. Her friends had warned her that he possessed an indifferent character; she had heard the rumors: his parents never married, a second, hidden family, even more children.

She would have nowhere to go. Isaac would cut her off. Either way, he would cut her off; already their relations were tenuous. Her move to London was suspect, her writing an indulgence; her refusal to come home and help care for Chrissey's children verged on dereliction of duty. Only the contributions of money redeemed her. Isaac kept meticulous accounts. She got up and stood at the window. It was almost certain that she would never see him again — or her sister. Her personal happiness — the words themselves sounded indulgent — counted for nothing, for less than nothing, in Isaac's moral ledger; he entered only sacrifice, obedience, and duty.

Her stomach was hollow and she was lightheaded and thirsty; for days now she had been unable to eat. She began to sing; her voice blew away on the hot breeze. George loved to hear her sing this song. Goethe's poem: "Wanderers Nachtlied." They were wanderers, both of them.

The parlor was dim and still; Mrs. Burke was strict about drawing the curtains against the damaging, fading summer sun. The album of Beethoven lay on top of the piano; Marian had forgotten to pack it. She sat down, opened the piano, and played the slow movement of one of the sonatas, a barcarole, the line rolling and yearning, shimmering between discord and resolution, restlessness and peace, shifting, aching contradictions of feeling. She played, and she wept in the suffocating, hot parlor for what she was giving up, for what was yet to come.

THOUGH SHE had delayed as long as she could bear, still she arrived at the London docks a half-hour early; she was one of the first to board the steamer *Ravensbourne*, bound for Antwerp. After she ensured that her trunk was safely stowed on board, she stood at the railing. It was a warm, bright evening; the lowering sun tinged the Thames a warm, metallic gray. Gulls laughed and wheeled overhead, catching the currents of hot wind, their white breasts and wings luminous in the deepening golden light. She concentrated on the bustle, the final loading of cargo, bales, and bundles, the stevedores calling, their inarticulate guttural shouts more like music than words.

Passengers were beginning to arrive. Ladies and gentlemen, laughing or preoccupied, descended from cabs and carriages, counted their luggage, rummaged for their tickets, paid off the drivers, tipped porters, embraced the friends who had come to see them off. Nobody else seemed to be alone. Ten minutes, fifteen minutes. The river beside the ship lapped in opaque eddies. She sought to lose herself in the pattern, the rhythm, of the water — in the suggestion and the promise of oblivion, peace. If he did not come, she would wait until nightfall. It was not unusual: a small notice in the newspaper, afterward forgotten.

Marian stood at the railing in her sober dress, her quiet bonnet, small and inconspicuous, her breath, her life thick in her throat, her gray eyes fixed on the gangplank. A porter was hauling a trunk up the narrow passageway, and behind his head, she saw George Lewes; he had come, he was here, he was looking for her. He saw her. Weightless, breathless, laughing, capable of flight, she ran toward him.

Chapter 8

Venice, November 1980

MEET ME IN VENICE," Malcolm said. "After you
go to Germany. I'll be in Venice next week."
"I don't know what I'm going to do," Caroline
said. "I haven't thought past today."

Ricky Coelho's coffin rested beneath the altar in a shabby par-
ish church in Providence, a gray stone building on a street of empty
storefronts. Paintings of martyrs in theatrical agonies hung in the
chapels, and it was dimly lit, heavy with retribution. Ricky's large
family occupied the first rows of pews, their heads bowed in the at-
titude of grief though they had not seen him or spoken to him for
thirty years. The ornate coffin was closed, pneumonia listed as the
cause of death.

"There's a statue of John the Baptist by Donatello in the Church
of the Frari — do you remember?" Caroline said as they followed the
pallbearers outside. "I showed it to you. It was wood, painted wood;
you hated it. It's what Ricky looked like before he died. Emaciated.
You didn't come see him."

"I'm here now."

"He isn't contagious anymore."

"I paid for everything, the funeral, the coffin, the plot."

"Of course you did. You read somebody your credit card number
over the phone."

"Would cash have made it better?"

"Forget it, Mal."

At the door of the church, in the soft November morning, Ricky's brothers and sisters thanked Malcolm for everything he had done. They shook Caroline's hand but did not thank her. They did not know, she thought, angry at herself for wanting acknowledgment.

"I'm not going to the cemetery. Drive back to the city with me." Malcolm had lost weight, and shadows shrouded his eyes.

"I have the station wagon."

"I thought your mother would be here."

"She had to get back to Northampton; she'd been gone for a couple of weeks."

"Her professor?"

"Her job, her ballet students — they love her."

He reached for Caroline's hand and she let him take it, against the solitariness of death. His familiar, broad palm was an aching comfort, despite every grievance. "Your hand is soft," he said. "You haven't been working."

A WEEK EARLIER, Caroline, lightheaded with loss and relief, stood with her mother on the sidewalk outside the hospital. The air was acrid from the morning rush hour; traffic on the FDR Drive was at a standstill. Ricky had been dead for half an hour. "Some people are afraid of death," Margaret said. "Don't blame Malcolm."

"Are you apologizing for him?"

"I'm just trying to see it from his point of view."

"When I called to tell him —"

"Where is he?"

"Geneva, putting together his Venice fund, I think. I can't keep track. Anyway, he thanked me, as if I'd done something for him, not for Ricky."

"Well, you did. You took care of Ricky. For him, that was the same as if he had done it."

"Malcolm didn't even want Ricky to see our doctor."

Margaret shrugged. "Ricky's family wouldn't visit him, either."

"Don't you want a cup of coffee?" Caroline asked.

"No, not really. We've had too much coffee, and it's been terrible."

"Come back to the apartment and I'll make you a cappuccino."

"When does Malcolm get back?"

"Tonight, then he's off again in the morning."

"He's been busy."

"Why are you trying to excuse him?"

Margaret hunched her shoulders, bent in on herself, an admission of defeat. "I was brought up to believe that I was the one who had to change. Wives adapt. That's how Malcolm thinks. Not that I'm blaming you, Caro; I try not to blame anymore. My father blamed me. First for marrying Sam and then for letting him leave me. But I believed in Sam and his art."

"I think I married Malcolm because he didn't believe in art."

"But you're an artist."

"Yes, but I thought that would make it easier, for me. Art for Malcolm wasn't such a big deal; it wasn't the beginning and the end, the way it was for Daddy — for my father. Daddy — he took up all the available — space, air, energy — I don't know what to call it. I figured that Mal would give me room, but it wasn't really about art."

"I thought he wanted you to work."

"Ten years ago. I think he thought it was nice that I made little statues. Now it gets in the way. It takes up too much space; I take up too much space. He doesn't like it."

"He's given you a lot."

"And he takes away, too."

"WE'RE LUCKY with the weather," Margaret had said as she and Caroline walked along Fifty-seventh Street the afternoon of the opening. It was the first week of September, a clear, windless day when distant buildings seemed close, and colors, even those of traffic lights, glowed with heightened brilliance. "My father used to call days like this weather-breeders," Margaret said. She patted the shopping bag swinging from the crook of her elbow. "Thank you so much for this suit — I'll feel like a presentable mother, not a dowdy divorcée. Even though I need a refrigerator more than I need a suit."

"You'd look really bad in a refrigerator," Caroline said. "And you're not a divorcée. He's been dead for seventeen years. And you have Jack. Even though he's only a friend." When they stopped at a corner, Margaret looked at her daughter with an expression that Caroline read as a mix of resentment and admiration.

"Caro, what are these statues like?"

"You'll see them at six."

"They're not too huge, are they? And are they—are they very naked?"

"Do you really want me to describe them to you? I won't do a good job; I don't make words." Caroline bit her lip at her mother's ability to infuriate her. "And you don't have to like them—you can think what you want to think." She stepped off the curb and stumbled and caught herself. "Do you still have that folder of poems?"

"I don't have any poems."

"The ones on the shelf in the living room. Under a pile of books, under your Fortuny book."

"I don't know what you're talking about." Margaret paused in front of one of Bergdorf's windows. "Those dresses would look marvelous on you, Caro. Why don't we go in, and you can try them on? You could wear one this evening."

"I saw them, Mom."

"Well, aren't they beautiful?"

"The poems," Caroline said, "not the clothes. I read them. I remember."

Margaret stood primly, her lips composed in a small crescent. "At least let's take a look."

"What did you do with them?"

Margaret pushed the revolving door, and Caroline had to follow. "Did you hear me?" she asked when they were both inside.

Margaret stopped beside the hat counter. "Caroline, I have always wanted the best for you, and I know you think I have no idea what that is. I also want you to know that your father loved you. Always. It was me he stopped loving. Don't you want to try those dresses?"

Ashamed of her truculence, Caroline considered her mother: blond hair streaked with white and wrapped into a dancer's bun, pale skin pleated with fine wrinkles like Fortuny silk, pink lipstick on her thin mouth. "Mom, you need lipstick. What you have on is too bright for the new suit. Let's do that first."

Caroline led Margaret to the cosmetics department, and they wandered from counter to counter, sampling the rainbows of makeup, while saleswomen, faces carefully painted, offered Q-tips and squares of cotton. In a color course at school, Caroline had once made a painting — a figure — with fifteen tubes of drugstore lipstick, three bottles of liquid foundation, and eye shadow. They decided on a brownish pink flecked with gold for Margaret and a deep red for Caroline; she took out her charge card.

The saleswoman cradled the phone between her ear and shoulder while she wrapped the lipstick and cologne in lavender paper. Margaret browsed among the eye shadows, and with eyeliner Caroline drew a bird on a square of tissue. When the saleswoman put down the phone, her stenciled brows knit into a worried chevron. "I'm sorry, Mrs. Spingold, but there seems to be a problem."

"With lipstick?"

"I have somebody in the credit department on the line." She handed the phone to Caroline.

"I'm afraid that the card has been canceled." It was a male voice, chagrinned.

For a moment Caroline did not understand. "When did that happen?"

"I'm so sorry, but it seems that Mr. Spingold closed the account two days ago."

"I see."

She handed the phone back to the saleswoman and reached for her wallet. "I'll pay cash." She smiled and shook with humiliation. The saleswoman, relieved — no scene, a sale — added an extra handful of free samples to the lavender shopping bag before she made change and gave back pennies.

"Let's get out of here," Caroline said to her mother.

"What are you going to wear tonight, dear? Have you decided? We have time, don't we, to look?"

"Black, Mom, I'm wearing black. I can't buy anything."

DEIRDRE, with her slight body and bright hair, looked innocent and severe in her black Japanese jacket. In the gallery's back room, she poured a glass of wine and handed it to Caroline. "You'll need this. People are going to want you to talk about your art — your favorite thing."

"I'm ready. I practiced on Anthony Reardon the other day. Don't you need wine, too?"

"Not yet. I'm working — I have to do the math — you're performing. You know, Caro, you should put this money in a separate account. You don't have one, do you?"

"No." Caroline gulped her wine. "What's mine is his."

"But this is yours." Deirdre took Caroline's arm, and her dandelion curls tickled Caroline's chin. "Okay," she said, "here we go."

In the gallery, Deirdre's assistant, Julian, was setting up ranks of wine glasses. Only a few people had arrived; Deirdre went to greet them. Caroline stood alone in the center of the room; she pulled her shoulders down and tucked in her stomach. "Stand straight," her mother had admonished when she was young and tall and wanted to slouch. She looked at the figures, their onyx eyes, with wonder and anxiety. How had she thought to make them? Doubt shook her, and she flung out her arms to steady herself.

"Are you all right?" Julian asked.

"High heels," she said. "I'm not used to them."

Then she knew. She had seen emotions — terror, desire, anger, joy: the whole array, their sequences, their contradictions — and she had submitted to their postures and proportions. She lowered her arms, balanced, and, as she claimed precarious delight, she heard her father's voice reciting the poem: *their eyes, their ancient, glittering eyes.*

Across the room her mother stood with Ricky, looking at the pair of bronze women, one arching backward, the other bowing. Margaret reached out and touched the figure of the bowing woman: the little belly and slackening thighs, the long neck, the shoulder blades like wings. She turned, found her daughter, and raised an amused and scolding eyebrow, an ability Caroline had not inherited. The little paunch beneath the waistband of her skirt aroused in Caroline a tender and infuriated affection.

Margaret took Ricky's arm with both her hands. His blue gabardine suit hung loosely from his shoulders. Caroline had made him an appointment with their doctor, and she had promised to go with him.

He laughed at something Margaret said; she stretched her arm around his waist. Caroline started in their direction, but two girls were approaching, girls in jeans and boots. One had looped a turquoise silk scarf around her neck.

"You don't recognize us." The girl with the scarf had short red hair. "I used to have a braid. You knocked Perry down."

"In Venice — oh, yes! You cut your hair." Caroline smiled — what was the girl's name?

The girl pulled at her short ends. "I liked yours, it seemed so easy, and I figure it can always grow back."

Caroline asked, "How did you find me?"

"We saw a piece about your show. At least we thought it was you — C. Edgar Spingold. We were so surprised —"

Courtney, that was it. "You thought I made bronze gnomes?"

"No! No, not at all. We didn't know you lived in New York. And that you were such a big deal," said Perry. "We're at Sarah Lawrence, and this is so cool! Really! We had to come! And just so you know — we found the Hôtel de l'Europe!"

"Wonderful," Caroline nodded. "George Eliot's honeymoon, right?"

"Right. Some guy — he was really great — took us there."

"That was nice," said Caroline.

"It's offices now, but they let us in, to see the window he jumped out of. At least I think it was the window."

"Who jumped?"

"Her husband. Into the canal."

"On his honeymoon?"

"He could swim. He lived until 1924."

"Is that going to be your thesis?"

"That's not a thesis; it's just a story," said Courtney.

"I see," said Caroline. She took an invitation from the stack on the desk and wrote her phone number on it. "Here — call me; I'd like that. If you want, you can come out to my studio — it's not that far from you. Now go look — tell me what you think!"

"These things stick out too far from the wall. They're not my cup of sangria," a small woman wearing a thick gold choker announced to her husband.

"I'd be worried if it was," whispered Deirdre's assistant as he handed Caroline another glass of wine.

"Julian, is this your job, making sure my glass is full?"

He laughed. "Think of it as medicine."

She could not find her mother. There was a new red dot beside the reclining man's label: sold. She saw Deirdre near the falling man without wings, talking to Stan Lerner. Will's friend: he remained lanky and boyish. Surprised and shy, she held out her arms to him. "I'm so glad to see you! Stan, what are you up to? Tell me! Are you still playing the piano?"

"Not really — on weekends. In real life, I'm a mathematician, in New Jersey."

"I'm sorry."

"No reason to be." He hesitated. "You know about Will?"

She gestured toward the Icarus.

"I wondered. Last fall Will told me he'd seen you and that he liked what you were doing."

"He told me to make the figures big. So —" She started to smile but shook her head and couldn't go on.

"I wanted to call you when I heard the news, but I didn't know what to say. Will told me that you were still lovely. *Lovely,* that was the word, and then he said, 'I'll go see her again — next year — or maybe the year after.' "

She nodded and closed her eyes.

"I'm sorry. Maybe I shouldn't have told you that."

"No, no, I'm glad you did. It's good — I can't tell you. Thank you."

Stan smiled, and Caroline remembered his unprotected tenderness — he had been unable to comfort her after Will left, though he had tried once; another name — another pianist, Malcolm had said. Now Stan was smiling at somebody behind her. "My wife, Cynthia," he said. Cynthia's belly was bulging.

"How wonderful," Caroline exclaimed, feeling barren.

Deirdre steered her toward another group of people. "Who bought my sexy man?" Caroline asked.

"Anthony Reardon." Deirdre grinned.

"No."

"Yes. Well, I gave him a discount —"

"But he said my prices were low."

"I had to. He just called. He thinks you're the next big thing."

"As long as he doesn't expect me to admire his big thing."

"Maybe you don't need that wine."

Caroline laughed. "I'm fine, Deirdre. So — that's a beginning. Anthony Reardon."

"Who's that?" Malcolm asked.

Caroline flushed. "Malcolm, where did you come from? I didn't think you were coming."

"I tried to call, but you didn't pick up."

"I wasn't home — and you didn't leave a message. Where were you?"

"Boston. About the newsletter. Who is Anthony Reardon?"

"A collector. It's fantastic that he wanted something." In her husband's presence, Caroline felt herself sounding high-pitched and inconsequential. "He said my work was cheap. Maybe I should raise the prices so I can afford to buy lipstick at Bergdorf's. You could have warned me."

Malcolm looked over her head. "I was consolidating the department store accounts. You still have your credit cards."

She gulped her wine. "Would you like a glass?"

"Not this swill. I can't stay long — I have a flight to London."

"Why didn't you fly from Boston?"

"I thought you wanted me here — a command performance."

"Mine — not yours."

"Do you want a quick supper?"

"The opening — my opening — goes until eight."

"Would you like me to leave now?" He sounded affable, asking a simple logistical question.

"Whatever makes you happy, Malcolm. That's what I want."

His amber eyes widened in warning.

She said, "We can leave now, dear — is that what you want me to say?"

"I don't want you to say anything." Malcolm reached for her arm, but she pulled away.

"Oh, Malcolm, here you are! I was so afraid you wouldn't make it!" Margaret leapt in a small glissade between Caroline and Malcolm. "It must have been a terribly important meeting — I know that you wouldn't miss Caroline's opening for the world. Isn't it marvelous? My little girl!" She drawled like an alcoholic belle. "Caroline says you're so busy, with your Venice fund. I want you to tell me all about it! I just love Venice! I was — we all were — we were so happy there! Malcolm, honey, come with me. I'll show you around — it's not so crowded once you get past the bar."

Margaret led him away. Astonished at her deliverance, Caroline started to laugh.

Deirdre said, "So Malcolm made it."

"This kind of thing is not his cup of sangria."

"Nobody knows who he is, that's all. He feels left out."

"And Geoff?"

"The deal is he doesn't have to come to these things. Don't take it personally. We're negotiating."

"Deirdre, that head — what is it?" a tall woman with cropped gray hair and violet lipstick asked.

"A reliquary," she said.

"Does it open? Can you put things in it? Potpourri?"

Caroline considered. "This one doesn't open. But I suppose I could make one. With a screw-on head, or maybe a cork in the bottom. I'd have to think about it."

Deirdre shut her eyes. But the woman nodded, attentive.

"I don't believe that a work of art has to be useless," Caroline said. "You don't either, do you, Deirdre?"

"Oh, no. Certainly not."

"I'm all for form and function."

"Me, too," seconded Deirdre, and hustled the woman toward the hors d'oeuvres. Caroline saw Courtney twine her arms around a tall young man while Perry looked away. Margaret herded Malcolm from figure to figure. Watching them, Caroline leaned against the wall, her pleasure dissolved in the debilitating misery of attachment; she could not remember how she had controlled the alloy of grief and desire and ambition with which she had modeled her work.

Deirdre came back. "Good news and bad news. She's commissioned a head. Without holes, thank God, but — she told me she'd like a screw-top. And the curator for a big collector in Germany wants to talk — another commission. He wants to fly you over to Frankfurt this fall. And lots of the little animals have sold."

"Malcolm's about to leave."

"So let him."

As Malcolm finished his circuit, Caroline rested her hand on the knee of the reclining man, who was no longer hers. Malcolm kissed her forehead, and his face was heavy with sadness. "You've worked hard for this, Caroline. You've gotten what you wanted."

"Yes."

"Enjoy your party. You deserve it."

CAROLINE AND her mother walked from the hospital back to the apartment, slowly. While her mother packed her suitcase, Caroline made coffee. They sat at the kitchen counter. Margaret said, "I've loved being with you these days. It sounds awful, but I don't think we've spent so much time together since you got married. I remember when you came to tell me about Malcolm, when you got out of that little car. You were so polished and ferocious; I couldn't touch you. I thought I'd done something wrong."

"No. You didn't do anything."

"I tried —"

"You could have asked me what I thought I was doing."

"And you would have told me to mind my own business."

"Probably. Some things have to happen."

"It would be nice if you could live in reverse every once in a while. Not always, just sometimes."

"I don't want to undo."

"Your father said that if he didn't make mistakes, he couldn't write poetry. It sounded like an excuse." Margaret lowered her eyes and looked at her watch. "I should get over to the Port Authority."

"I worry about you."

"Malcolm thinks that Jack will never marry me. Malcolm doesn't give me much credit, does he?" She crossed her arms over her stomach. "He doesn't like me."

"Mom —"

"Caro, don't pretend. He doesn't trust people who have no money." She ran her hand over the counter. "Marble, stainless steel, a Mercedes, a house in the country."

"I drive a beat-up old station wagon."

"That's your choice. I have nothing to give you, if — I can't help you. My father helped me."

"I know that, and I wouldn't ask." Caroline put down her cup. "Mom, when I married Malcolm I promised myself that I would never divorce him. I never wanted to be divorced."

Margaret said, "You wanted never to be like me."

"Yes," Caroline said. "That's true. That was true — was."

"One thing, though. Your father and I — and now Jack and I — we — well, we enjoyed each other. You —"

"No."

"Well, then. Is there — do you have —?"

Caroline flushed. "That's not the whole reason."

"No. Never mind," said Margaret. "You never told me very much. I probably wasn't paying attention anyway. There are things I would like to do over."

Caroline nodded. "Mom, stop that. Malcolm — if there's a way — I still think that one day I'll wake up and find him miraculously changed. He wants me to go to Venice. I owe him." She was being only partially honest; if she went, it would not be only for Malcolm. But she was, for better or worse, Malcolm's wife. He had tried to change; at least at the opening he had acknowledged her success. She did not know if trying was enough, but she owed him the possibility that it might be.

"He owes you, too." Margaret slid off the stool. She stretched her spine, aligning herself, measuring space in preparation for a leap. "Honey, those poems. They weren't written about her. Your father wrote them about me."

Caroline stared, shocked, at her mother, and Margaret blushed. "Is it so hard to think about me that way?"

"They're beautiful," Caroline said.

Margaret rested her hand on the edge of the counter as if it were a barre. "I found them after he left — in a folder with old bills from when we bought the house. I don't know when he wrote them. He didn't take them with him, on purpose. He couldn't have published them — it wouldn't have been right — they were too personal."

Caroline covered her mother's hand with her own. "But you kept them."

"Your figures were of me, weren't they? So what am I — just raw material?"

"You used to be a dancer," Caroline said.

FOG DRIFTED IN from the lagoon and rose from the canals; it was like walking through dissolving walls of vapor. Buildings emerged in shades of gray, and as Caroline approached they acquired mass and color. She felt insubstantial herself. In Germany, she had discussed an installation: winged creatures—a gryphon, a horse, birds, seraphim and *molochim,* whatever she wanted to make. The questions the curator asked concerned her desires, her ideas. She was being courted. "I wish you'd come along," Caroline had told Deirdre.

"I can't go, and you don't need me. Don't agree to anything," Deirdre had advised. "That's my job, the deal. Yours is to decide what you can do—what you want to do."

"I'm working on that."

Caroline had caught an earlier flight to Venice, but when she arrived at the hotel, Malcolm was not in the room. She was relieved; it gave her time.

The city was alien in this dark season: empty, monochromatic, depressed, its play of light extinguished. It reflected her state of mind. The past decade of her life seemed a false summer, perpetually bright, unnatural.

Shops were opening for business. Silk, shoes, jewelry: she wanted none of those. She walked along the Merceria toward the Rialto Bridge.

The grille shielding the antique shop was raised partway; it was still dark inside, and the door, when she tried it, was locked. In the small vitrine she made out a bronze salt cellar. As she peered at it, the display light went on, and a moment later a tall thin man with fine white hair combed back from his forehead opened the door.

"*Buon giorno,*" she said. "*Sto cercando . . .*"

He smiled. "I speak English, unless you prefer Italian."

"It might be easier in English," Caroline admitted.

"How can I help you? Were you looking for something specific?"

"A little statue—a boy—you had it this summer."

"The little David?"

"Is that what it is? I thought it could be a saint."

"Or an Apollo."

"You don't have it anymore."

"I do." The man showed her up a flight of stairs into a small room paneled in walnut with a table of embossed and gilded leather in the center. "Excuse me, please." After a few moments he returned with the figure. A boy verging on manhood: his nose and chin still soft and childish, but his cheekbones were prominent and his jaw defined. One arm was raised; he could have been aiming a slingshot or wielding a knife — Apollo flaying the centaur Marsyas. Or St. Sebastian, arm outflung in exquisite agony. Caroline lifted the statue — it was heavy, thickly cast — and studied where it had been chased: eyelids and eyeballs, fingernails and toenails, locks of hair; she found the little plugs covering the holes in the casting.

"Who made it?" she asked.

"Often it is difficult to know."

"I understand. I thought that you might have an idea. A person I know thinks the sculptor might have been Jewish."

"Giuseppe de Levis had a workshop in Verona; he was a Jew. At least we speculate that he was a Jew. There is an ambivalence about his figures; they could refer either to the Old Testament or the New, or to a pagan image — a Roman marble of a boy that had been brought to Venice in the sixteenth century. It is unlikely, though it was a time of freedom for the Jews, that a man would call himself Levis unless —"

"Unless he had to?"

"Exactly. But de Levis signed some of his works, and this is not signed."

"It's very beautiful."

"It does not have the refinement of some Paduan sculpture."

"It has energy. I was sure it would be sold."

"Bronzes are a particular passion. You are a collector?"

"I make them."

"Ah."

"The price?"

"In dollars, seven thousand."

Caroline nodded. She had the money. "May I think about it?"

"Of course. You are in Venice for some time?"

"I don't know yet. I really don't know anything. But I'll be back."

As she left the shop, she saw Malcolm heading toward San Marco, arm in arm with a woman. She thought it was Malcolm; in the fog she could not be certain. He could be a chimera, a fear or a wish, but the chance that this man was her husband made her reel. Foolishly, she had imagined Malcolm faithful, waiting. The realization that he was not dislodged a chock of resistance and loyalty. But she was not prepared for the physical pain of that knowledge, the knot in her stomach that took her breath away.

She did not follow him, but headed in the direction of the Cannaregio, the old ghetto. She had Gilbert's address, but she did not know that part of the city. Before she left New York, she had telephoned his apartment — at a time of day when he would not be there — and hung up when she got his answering machine.

"I HAVE A confession to make," Ricky said to her. "Can you prop me up?"

She raised the head of the hospital bed and slid a pillow behind his back.

"Promise you won't get angry — or at least that you won't get angry at me."

"That's an easy promise."

"Don't look at me while I tell you."

"Okay, I won't."

"He — Malcolm — had me follow you in that boat."

"In Venice?"

"He was suspicious."

"Of me? I have to tell you — I wondered what that boat was doing."

"I tried to warn you; I made the driver cut close."

"You nearly swamped us. Well, I did feel warned. I'm not angry at you — I can't be angry at you. But Malcolm — he sent you to spy on me. How could he do that to me — and to you?"

"He loves you."

"Yes. He has a strange way of showing it. A strange kind of love. How can I forgive him?"

"You forgive what you want to forgive — what you have to forgive. That's who he is. He doesn't change."

"But I have."

"Caroline —"

"What can I do, Ricky? I don't know if I can stay, but I don't know how to leave."

"A lot of people would settle. They'd forgive him."

"A lot of women would settle. But Malcolm didn't—he left his first wife."

"He's not a bad man. He's taking care of me."

"In his way—everything is his way. Your insurance is taking care of you."

"He paid for that."

"He wants to keep me down."

Ricky's eyes, deep in their sockets, measured an imminent distance. "Caroline, I would say that he wants to keep you, that's all. And you don't want to be kept."

"Not anymore."

"GILBERT? It's you? You're the last person in the world"— Caroline was unreasonably glad—and disconcerted—to hear his voice.

"I saw your show, that's why I'm calling. I liked it."

Caroline, who was not averse to hyperbole, was puzzled as to why she was satisfied with his measured assessment. "You're here, in New York?"

"Doing some work for my law firm."

"Your sabbatical is over?"

"Not yet—this has to do with using foreign funds to restore works of art in Venice—transferring money, deductions, the tedious part of funds like your husband's. Massimo's uncle is involved. And it's about assuring the managing partner that I'll come back at the beginning of the year—and trying to figure out if I really will. It's nice to spend the day with people, though. Research is lonely."

"I'd have come with you to the show."

"I wanted to see it alone, in case—sometimes it's difficult to look at a friend's work. What if you don't like it? Then you have to worry about what you're going to say."

"I'd like to see you," she said.

"Yes. I'd like to see you."

They met at the Frick and sat in the courtyard on one of the benches beside the pool. She was struck again by his density, his absorbing gentleness; more than physical, a moral quality: goodness. When she was younger, she had equated goodness with gullibility, but Gilbert was not gullible. Malcolm exploited goodness; her father had not trusted in its existence.

"I'm surprised you called," she said. "After I made you take me back—after I made a fool of myself. You couldn't wait to get rid of me."

"I thought the best thing I could do was get out of there. And I thought I'd see you again—I wanted to. That first day, after you waved at me from the boat—I kept seeing you. Wherever I went, there you were. Venice is like that."

"Not only Venice. You know those girls—the one I knocked over —I guess you saw that—the ones looking for some extinct hotel? I saw them a couple of weeks ago. They came to the opening. They're seniors in college—they're going to rule the world. Or were going to. But one of them has fallen in love."

"That's not good?"

"It weakens your resolve. It blurs you."

"Does it have to? It hasn't weakened yours."

She didn't speak for a moment. "What do you want to see here?"

"It doesn't matter," he said.

"There are Renaissance bronzes."

"You stopped and looked at one, in the window of a shop. It makes sense, now."

"I've been wondering if I should do something else."

"Like what?"

"Like learn to be a good wife."

"At wife school?"

"I'm sorry. I shouldn't say these things. They're just on my mind." But it had to do with him, as if there was a space between them, a permission, where she could speak the truth.

"He's an impressive man, your husband. He knows what he wants."

"He does know that." Caroline stood up. "Let's look at something."

"They also have a show of their Whistler etchings, the Venetian ones." At the entrance to the gallery, Gilbert picked up a brochure. "He showed these in London in 1881. They were a sensation—they are pretty amazing, don't you think?" He studied an image of a canal constricted by buildings and washing hung out to dry. "You can feel the fog—you've never been in Venice in the winter, have you?"

"Malcolm's talking about going back in November—I don't know if I'll go. I don't know what's going to happen. I don't know anything." She moved to another etching, a girl making lace. "I couldn't figure out what else it was you wanted to show me."

"I'll show you if you come back."

"Promise?"

They wandered back into the courtyard. "Icarus — the falling man I made — do you remember it? I made it because of the man I thought you were. In May he was thrown out of his car on a bridge, and he drowned. I think about how he felt, falling, if it was like flying. If he got past terror, if he saw something — I don't know what — the pattern of the waves — if it was wild and beautiful — I hope so."

"I look like him?"

"Not really."

"You loved him?"

"For a while. It ended."

"At least you had it." He took a penny out of his pocket and tossed it into the pool.

"What did you do that for?"

"For luck." Gilbert smiled. "Do you want one, too?"

"You're not here only for business, are you?"

"Somebody told me the other day that I had problems with love."

"A girlfriend?"

"I've known her a long time. We're a good couple, everybody says."

"So what's the problem?"

"I don't love her. Not enough. But I'd do almost anything in the world not to hurt her."

"Including getting married?"

DEIRDRE'S ASSISTANT lifted the figures off their hooks and laid them on the floor. "I hate seeing this show come down," Julian said. "Minimalism next week. Paintings that are all one color. It gets boring looking at nothing all day long."

"Julian, it's not nothing," Deirdre said. "It's spiritual. But the young — that's you — don't know from spiritual. Looking at surface, you learn to see depths."

"Deirdre, sometimes it's better not to explain," said Caroline.

"You have to explain, or people don't buy."

"What do you say about Caroline?" Gilbert asked.

"I tell people that her figures are avatars."

Caroline said, "Aardvarks."

"Do aardvarks have armor?" asked Julian.

"That's armadillos. Aardvarks are kind of bald. Maybe I should make a series of anteaters."

"And bronze ants to go with them," said Gilbert. "With glass eyes."

"Multiples. You'd have to buy a bunch. I love it."

"It won't fly," said Deirdre. "You're suffering withdrawal, Caroline."

"I'm going back to Venice tomorrow," said Gilbert. "To finish my research."

Caroline held her face blank against Deirdre's scrutiny. "Julian, I'll keep you company while you stare at spiritual nothings. Once we"—Caroline paused—"we went to the Rothko Chapel in Houston. Malcolm walked out. He said that if he wanted to look at blank things, he could stare at his TV screen."

"Malcolm's such a connoisseur," said Deirdre.

"He has a way of putting things," Gilbert said.

"What am I going to do next?" Caroline asked.

AT THE END of the Strada Nova, Caroline saw a sign for the ghetto —a new bright blue sign—possibly accurate, unlike the faded signs painted on the walls of buildings. She crossed the bridge over the canal encircling the ghetto. Dust filmed the street; the empty buildings were tall and constricted, façades unadorned: centuries of packed and ugly habitation. Even the open space of the square seemed foul, as if fresh air had long ago been prohibited. A sense of oppression and revulsion survived from her childhood; in the desolate *campo* her father had presented her with his history.

Gilbert's history encompassed a different moment. In these cramped rooms a Jew wrote glorious music for a duke and for a Venetian congregation; a Jew cast bronzes for doges and churches; a rabbi instructed cardinals and ambassadors in the intricacies of Jewish law. After an epidemic of plague and a massacre, her father's version resumed.

Versions: her parents' history, too, had its different interpretations. Caroline had imagined that her mother had lacked some kind of substance, intellectual or spiritual, to anchor her husband. She let him drift. Why did she not confront him? Wasn't he testing himself that summer in Venice, weighing his desire for that voluptuous teaching assistant against his obligations to his wife and daughter? Or did Edgar find in Sheryl what Malcolm had found in her; had his desire been overwhelming and sweet? And was her father doing what she was doing now — trying to rid himself of tenderness?

Caroline stopped and turned back; she owed it to Malcolm. And she could not surprise Gilbert, corner him into kindness. If he wanted her, it had to be his choice. When she reached the Grand Canal she boarded a *vaporetto* and stood in the stern. That summer, Margaret Edgar had done all she could. She had understood love as not something you won or lost or fought for; it was there — for her it was there — or it was not. There were no explanations.

MALCOLM WAS not yet in the room. She called Gilbert's number; this time she left a message, and she lay on the bed, half dozing, watching the fog and the shifting gray claustrophobic light. When she heard a key in the lock, it was close to one in the afternoon. Through the half-open bedroom door she saw Malcolm put a small package on the desk in the living room. He carried his jacket over his arm. She got up and stood in the doorway. Alert as a predator, Malcolm turned, and she saw his expression: surprise, edged with alarm. "Caroline, you're here!"

"I caught an earlier flight."

"I didn't get the message."

"I didn't leave one."

He tossed his jacket onto the desk, where it just missed concealing the package. She saw that it was a jewelry case.

"I'm glad you came," Malcolm said. "I wasn't sure."

"You should know me better." She crossed to the window. The little square at the back of the hotel was opaque with mist, and the lava paving stones glistened. "It looks like a prison courtyard out there," she said.

"I thought you loved this city."

"It's a reflector of mood, don't you think?"

"I wouldn't know."

"How were your meetings this morning?" She did not turn around; she was not so interested in the truth anymore. The question was whether they could survive on lies.

"Good. I met with Farsetti — Maximo. Structuring the grants. The fund is pretty much set up."

"I thought I saw you this morning."

"Where?"

"Near San Marco. You were with somebody."

Malcolm shrugged; he had lowered the scrim of self-possession over his face. "I'm thinking of opening an office here, the newsletter, to set an example. Would you like that?"

"Does that matter?"

"I don't know, Caroline, does it? That's up to you. What do you want?"

She turned to face him. She knew the answer he wanted. *You.* The necessary lie.

"What is that box?" she asked, reaching for the jewelry case.

He picked it up. "If you want, it's for you. For your birthday."

"My birthday isn't until March."

"Then for Thanksgiving, or Veterans Day."

"Where is it from?"

"A shop on the street that goes under the big clock."

"The Merceria, about a block from San Marco?"

"Probably."

"I did see you."

He handed it to her. His fingers had left marks in the sable suede. "I thought you were worried about money," she said.

"This won't make any difference in the long run."

"Usually you take me with you; usually you make me want something — you make me ask for it — before you'll buy it."

He blinked. "I've changed. Isn't that what you wanted?"

"How? Malcolm, how are we going to live?"

"Open it."

She obeyed. Inside was a necklace, a filigree of golden vines and leaves set with diamond flowers: tiny buds, full blooms. "It's beautiful," she said, feeling a wave of lust and its potential for entrapment.

"Put it on."

"Not now."

"Put it on, please." He lifted the necklace from its case and settled it around her neck. His breath was hot, and she averted her head. "Stand still," he commanded. "Look at yourself." He nudged her toward the mirror over the sofa. "You like it, don't you?"

"It must have cost a fortune. I look exhausted." She was appalled at her weakness.

"It wasn't expensive. The stones are small."

The bell to the suite rang, a high-pitched trill. Malcolm did not move. "Did you order room service?" Caroline asked as she opened the door.

A woman stood there. She was short and slender, with streaked blond hair; her mascara was thick and her sweater was cut low. Her expression changed from expectancy to surprise, to anger, to alarm.

"Can I help you?" Caroline asked, stepping back into the room.

The woman was looking at the necklace.

"*Lei parla italiano?*" Caroline asked.

"*Sì.* And I speak English."

"Speak English," Malcolm said.

Caroline extended her hand. "I'm Caroline Spingold."

"Ada Rivers."

"She's setting up the foundation."

"And you were looking at office space and jewelry this morning."

"Did you bring the papers?" Malcolm asked.

"I had a question," the woman said, with a little edge of irony, and she smiled at Caroline. "But it can wait."

"Please, do what you have to do. I just flew in." She ran the tips of her fingers over the necklace. "Do you like it? Really, I'm not sure it's for me."

She smiled first at Malcolm and then at Ada Rivers. "What do you think?" She turned, headed into the bedroom, and closed the door.

"Caroline," Malcolm said, opening the door.

"You got rid of her quickly."

He took her by the shoulders and pushed her backward onto the bed. She tried to roll away, but he gripped her arms, and his fingers dented her flesh. He tilted her head back and searched for her mouth. She clenched her teeth against him and tried to sit up, but he pinned her beneath him. The necklace bit into the back of her spine.

"Twice in one morning, Malcolm?"

He raised himself onto one elbow, and she shut her eyes. She felt his weight lift from her body, and she lay limp with loss and sadness and ugly knowledge.

"You're better than she is," he said quietly.

She opened her eyes. He was looking at her, and she saw herself reflected in his golden eyes: faithless herself, betrayed and betraying.

MEET ME, *please, if you can, tomorrow morning at the Miracoli.* Gilbert played back Caroline's message when he returned from the State Archives with copies of documents recording deaths by plague in the epidemic of 1630; the death rate in the ghetto was difficult to ascertain, but it was higher than in the other districts of the city.

He was not sure that he could see her. Massimo had told him that Malcolm was in Venice, alone, and Gilbert had been relieved. Actually, not alone, Massimo added, and Gilbert had not known what to feel. The time in New York had been luck, an accident. He had expected to miss her, but he was not prepared for how desolate he had been, for such extremes of feeling. He had not called or written; he did not want to make it worse. If he saw her again — but there was no reason to see her again. It would be better and safer not to.

"I can see into you," she had said.

"Visible Man? My veins and digestive tract?"

"I mean that I can see what you're feeling. You're clear."

"That's dangerous."

"No. I'm not used to it. It's good, it's marvelous."

"No, it isn't. Not for me."

After they had packed up her show, they had driven north in her turquoise station wagon. She was wearing tired jeans and a flannel shirt. He liked her that way more than when she met him sleekly dressed and impermeable, as she had been in Venice with her husband. Then, when she had smiled, Gilbert thought the corners of her lips would crack.

"I'm sorry about the car. Malcolm hates it. It's like driving a mattress."

"It's good for hauling."

"Exactly."

"No radio?"

"Gone, stolen — I keep a tape player behind the seat, under that tarpaulin. Tapes, too. I only listen to music when I'm alone." She drove fast and wove in and out of the lanes. The station wagon swayed dangerously on its suspension.

"Are you in a hurry?" he asked.

"I thought you'd want to get back to — whomever, for your last night."

"No."

She looked at him; he wished she wouldn't. She turned the car in the direction she was looking, then swerved back into the lane, correcting course.

"What happened?" she asked.

"She wanted to know why, but I had no good reasons. Mostly, I listened to her; that was the least I could do. Let her get angry. She told me that Rabbi Leon was obscure and that I was wasting my time. I said that she was probably right."

Caroline looked at him. The car drifted.

"Caro, don't look at me. Or let me drive."

"Sorry. How do you feel?"

"Like a shit. Don't turn your head. You're making me carsick." He watched the horizon, then studied her profile, her sharp chin and long nose, the fullness of her lower lip. "Where's Malcolm today? Is he in the country?"

"He won't be here; he doesn't like the house. He's probably put it on the market."

"I mean the United States."

She pressed down on the gas pedal, and the station wagon lurched and nearly collided with the plumber's van ahead of them. She shot her arm across his chest, protecting him. "Sorry," she said. "Boston, Washington. Probably Boston today, something about the Venice fund — it's a foundation now, or his newsletter; there's an economist in Boston he's got to edit it."

Gilbert watched the horizon until a wave of carsickness subsided. "Why did you make the Daphne?"

"My mother loved the Bernini statue."

"I do, too."

"It used to terrify me. It was what I was afraid of. Being caught, having to lose myself if I resisted, as if his desire mattered more than mine."

When they turned off the highway, Caroline opened the window to the warm wind. Haze diffused the sunlight. The maples lining the driveway were beginning to turn yellow, and the lawn, thriving on cool nights, was a brilliant green. Caroline unlocked the studio door. "It's hot in there. Wait while I air it out."

A pear tree at the edge of the brick terrace hung heavy with fruit. Gilbert breathed the smells of ripeness and cut grass, listened to the slow bees in the asters. Caroline took off her flannel shirt and tied it around her waist over her T-shirt. Gilbert thought that he could encircle her thin arm with his fingers.

"Gilbert," she said, "the figure of the man lying down — do you remember it?"

"Yes. I liked it."

"When I made it this summer, I was thinking about you." She smiled and little lines crinkled at the corners of her eyes.

She untied her shirt and spread it on the grass below the terrace. He was astonished by how badly he wanted her, how he had not permitted himself to admit it. He held her as if she were a confluence of desires roused before waking, a deep joy that would dissipate when he opened his eyes.

"Caroline," he said, "I could not have imagined you."

She touched his shoulder gently. "You can let go."

"I'm sorry," he said.

"For what?"

"For doing this. And I can't even get up and go — it's your car."

"Don't be sorry. I did it, too." Her eyes were light brown in the low afternoon light, her lips swollen, her hair like feathers. "And I'm glad." She laughed, then rolled away from him. Her shoulders were marked with the patterns of blades of grass.

"What is it, Caro?"

When she turned back to him, she pressed her head against him so he couldn't see her face. He held her, and out of the corner of his eye, he saw something bright move at the edge of the woods. A red fox bounded and pounced in quick leaps, hunting voles, upwind and unaware of them. "Look," he told her, "a fox."

She lifted her head. "I thought I saw it this summer," she said. "A fox means a death."

"The little foxes."

She pulled her T-shirt on. "I don't know what to do."

"There's a train, isn't there? Will you drive me to the train?"

"If that's what you want."

THE BANDAGE compressed Malcolm's eyelids. His forehead throbbed; his back ached, and his arm felt like somebody had punched it. Gray light through the window—it could be any time of day in this ghastly fog. The hotel doctor had refused to give him a sedative, but he'd slept anyway; he hoped that wasn't evidence of concussion. The stinging, oily stink of the canal clogged his nostrils. He made out Caroline slumped in an armchair at the foot of the bed. She stretched, and the bedspread covering her slid to the floor; she sat up and coughed violently.

"What time is it?" he asked. "Where's my watch?"

"It's almost eight. Your watch is in the bathroom."

"I slept."

"You did."

"You sat here all night?"

"The doctor was worried about concussion, so I kept you awake for as long as I could. Your pupils weren't dilated, which is a good sign."

"What else did he say?" Caroline and the doctor had spoken Italian, even though the doctor addressed him in English. He had to get back to the States to see his own man.

Caroline said, "He gave you a shot of antibiotics and a typhoid shot; he said you'll be fine. You didn't swallow much water. He gave me a typhoid shot, too. My arm is killing me." She straightened her elbow; she was wearing one of those white hotel bathrobes; Malcolm liked her in them. "I feel like Nurse Caroline—all I do is sit by bedsides."

"You didn't have to stay with Ricky."

"I did, actually."

"What did you talk about?"

"We didn't talk much. Mostly about him, me, you a little bit. Forgiveness. What it was. We didn't agree."

So she wasn't going to tell him what Ricky had told her. Not that Ricky really knew anything. When Ricky started showing up late, claiming illness, Malcolm had assumed that he was planning to quit, not die. The Fondazione Internazionale per la Rinascita di Venezia, FIRV, based in Lugano, was perfectly legal; it might even do some good. That was — was supposed to have been — Caroline's job — helping disburse grants. Ada could run it. She'd put together a good proposal, though Farsetti had complained about cooked data. Of course the numbers were cooked; he wasn't going to waste his time on unpredictable research. Farsetti was arrogant. He shouldn't care; his city would get some money.

If Caroline tried to pursue his money — how he'd lost so much — and if it came to a trial, it would be his word against hers, and her informant was dead. He could have been dead too. He said, "You pulled me out. I could have drowned."

"You hit your head." She sounded unconcerned and detached, clinical, as if he were merely a routine rescue. Maybe she was just tired; she'd been up most of the night.

She said, "I think the blood scared you. Head wounds bleed a lot. And you don't like water. The lagoon isn't very deep, once you get out of the channel. It's just disgusting."

"You jumped overboard after me."

"I didn't see the life ring. I shouldn't have gone in; when you're in the water, it puts you at a disadvantage. You lose leverage."

She sounded like him when he talked about investments. He did not like owing his life to her. He owed that to nobody. If things — if she hadn't changed — if she hadn't grown so selfish, it would have been different; he would have been grateful.

"Anyway," she went on, "it worked out. I ruined my clothes, and I liked that suit. Yours are ruined, too, Mal. That water — it's more like glop — is foul. There was all kinds of gunk in your shoes. I threw them away, too."

"Tell me why," he demanded.

"Tell you why what?" He used to pique her interest with questions; now she seemed annoyed.

"Why didn't you let me drown?"

"You weren't going to drown."

"That's not what I was asking."

"Training, then. Junior lifesaving, senior lifesaving, water safety."

"Not love?"

"It's not water you want anybody to spend a lot of time in. Your head was bleeding. And you panicked."

She had started the fight, in the water taxi going to Torcello for dinner. "So you're consolidating there, too." Malcolm hadn't understood at first, but then he realized she was talking about Ada Rivers. "She's your new Ricky, smart enough to do your math; she can make your money disappear." Caroline should have known he'd never trust his money to a woman he was fucking.

Malcolm wasn't going to bring anything up; what she did was her business, as long as she knew that she didn't have a monopoly on it. He didn't bring up Gilbert Pryce last summer; Ricky's photograph was blurred and the lens was spotted with spray; you couldn't tell anything. Ricky hadn't thought to tell the driver to slow down. But Pryce wasn't her type: too serious, too quiet, no balls.

When Caroline started in on Ada, all he'd said was "What about that boy — that Will Lucas?" He had evidence; he'd seen them himself. He'd gotten to the country early. It was just over a year ago. Caroline was still happy, and they were perfect together, inseparable. Then that afternoon, there he was, innocently looking through the binoculars, and he saw them under those damned lilacs that wrecked his view. It was like in the movies; even the river was sparkling in the background. You could almost hear the violins. "I kissed him. That's all I did. I kissed him goodbye." Bullshit. People didn't kiss each other and stop there anymore; that went out in the sixties.

"Bullshit!" he'd shouted at her. She'd stormed out of the cabin of the water taxi. Malcolm followed; a mistake, but he wanted her. He wanted her back — he still did. He'd had a lot to drink before dinner, and he'd lost his balance.

He touched his forehead; under the bandage, he could feel the heat of the wound. "Did that doctor give me painkillers? How did you know he was any good?"

"Actually, I called Massimo Farsetti. This was his doctor. He was cautious. He disinfected the cut on your head and said he didn't think it needed stitches. He closed it up with little strips of adhesive. If it had been serious, he'd have made you go to the hospital. Do you want aspirin? He said you could have aspirin."

Malcolm nodded and closed his eyes. He heard the slither of the bedspread, her bare feet padding into the bathroom, water running in the sink. "Bottled water?" he called.

"I'll see," she said, and went to check the minibar in the living room. He wished she weren't being so attentive; she used to be like this all the time. He wanted to hurt her. It wasn't what Sam Gruson thought; it wasn't the chance to be a Pygmalion, though he had been. He'd shown her the world. He'd taught her how to dress, how to behave; he'd taught her expectations. Pygmalion and his little statue had lived happily ever after.

But when Caroline had gotten what she wanted out of him, when he wasn't useful anymore, she'd turned on him. He'd spoiled her —she'd had so little. He wouldn't leave her with much.

She brought him the aspirin and a bottle of water. She was dressed now, in jeans and a black sweater. "You look terrific," he said.

"Thank you. The doctor said he would call about nine — in a few minutes — to see how you're doing. Do you want me to order breakfast?"

"Coffee, orange juice, maybe cereal. Special K."

"I'll call it in, and I'll unlock the door, so you won't have to get up when they bring it."

She was wearing red sneakers; he mistrusted them; they seemed outrageous. "Why can't you get the door?"

"I'm going out."

He felt outmaneuvered, abandoned. "You can't do that."

"Why not?"

He hated her. She had rescued him because it made her feel good. He could have been anybody.

"Where are you going? It's too early to go out. Nothing's open. Not even a fucking church."

"I'm going for a walk."

"You haven't had breakfast."

"No."

"You'll be back soon."

"I don't know. You'll be fine, Malcolm. Is it too warm in here? I'll turn on the air conditioning. You can reach the phone. You can get anything you want." She tucked the covers around his shoulders, leaned over him, and kissed him gently on his mouth. Her lips were hot and dry; maybe she was catching something. He touched her soft hair, and she didn't pull away.

She poured more water into his glass. "And the necklace — it's gone. It must have come off when I jumped into the water."

"It's insured."

"So you haven't lost anything?"

"Caroline," he said, "I'll get rid of her."

She turned and looked at him with her dark, glittering eyes. "I know," she said. "Oh, Malcolm, I know you'd do that. But where would we be?"

IN THE Piazza San Marco the stores were shuttered, and Florian's tables were stacked under the loggia. Fog hovered over the great paved space of the trapezoid; it hid the turrets of the basilica and blurred the façade of the Doges' Palace. Waves lapped over the embankment of the Piazzetta and across the pavement. To the east a circle of sky glowed brighter, a pearly gray where the sun was attempting to break through.

Caroline ran, gulping the damp air. A cat stalked a stray pigeon; a priest hurried past, wearing rubber boots under his cassock; at Quadri's an optimistic waiter began setting up a few tables outside. Trestles and planks against the *acqua alta* were stacked beside the loggia.

The cobalt face of the Orologio seemed black in the fog. She stopped, her heart pounding in her chest and in her temples, and watched the procession of the Magi. Nine o'clock.

She hurried through the crowded market in the Campo Santa Maria Formosa. Women in black coats and shawls picked over the produce: blood oranges, porcini, bins of lustrous chestnuts. In the butcher stalls pink, flayed rabbits were strung up by their hind legs; beside them the coffered domes of sea urchins were laid out on ice. A child in his mother's arms reached out and dislodged a bunch of grapes from the pyramids of fruit. Caroline remembered a book her father once showed her — was it in the secondhand shop here? — a heavy book with pictures of paintings.

These were found in an ancient synagogue.

I know what that is! It's the Fox and the Grapes, the Aesop's fable.

No, Caro, it's the Song of Songs, written by Solomon. It's a love poem, and don't let anybody ever tell you that it's about God, because it isn't.

Caroline bought a bunch of red grapes with a dusty sheen, and the old man selling fruit wrapped them in gray paper and tied the bundle with a string.

She crossed the Rio del Paradiso, passing on the bridge a boy and girl, blond curls and brown curls, embracing, oblivious. Anticipation grew in her, and anxiety. She reached the square. She was early; of course Gilbert wasn't there. Santa Maria Sempre Chiusa. The church seemed a marble barge, a pleasure boat, battened down. A black-coated woman shrouded in a shawl, a canvas market bag over her arm, climbed the stairs and entered the church. Caroline sprinted across the square. Inside it was chilly and dim; the geometrically patterned marble walls were dingy, the high windows opaque with dust. The woman genuflected, slid into a chair, and bowed her head while Caroline walked toward the front: the stairway and the choir, a garden wall carved in marble, low relief, a risky subtraction, subtle as a drawing. Delicate tendrils curled in arabesques; putti misbehaved. One pulled the hair of another, providing instruction to centuries of altar boys. Caroline laughed; she couldn't help herself. The woman looked up, offended.

Margaret would have been pleased that the church was open. "Churches should stay open," she'd declared.

"Even in this godless age?" Samuel had asked.

"Especially. Otherwise it's giving up."

"On God?"

"On whatever in us we want to call God."

"And what is that?"

"It's different for everybody. For you, it's art and music, and the mind, and memory. You believe in creation."

"For you?"

Margaret had laughed; Caroline remembered her laugh, light and low. Margaret was provoking her husband, but gently; she glanced at eleven-year-old Caroline.

"Don't you know? I'm more for — evolution, for getting together, for keeping going, changing if you can. A kind of recognition of connection, of something elusive — numinous —"

"Numinous?"

"You know what I mean, Sam. There's something we all possess. I can't exactly call it love — love's been overused and as far as I can tell completely perverted — but love is close."

Caroline touched the teasing putto, the child's convex forehead, fat cheeks, budding nose; the contours of the marble felt like smooth, cool flesh. She shivered with desire, with joy and terror, and curled her hands into fists inside her pockets. It was time to go. She pushed open the door.

Epilogue

London, 29 December 1880

AFTER THE FUNERAL John Cross returned alone to Cheyne Walk. His sisters had urged him to stay with them, to stop either at Weybridge or at Sevenoaks until the shock of his wife's death had passed; they feared for him. But it seemed to him somehow that her spirit had not left the house, and he could not leave her. They had lived here for only eighteen days. *We were to have been so happy.* That statement ran through his mind, a summation of loss and disruption.

He had no time to prepare for death — for her momentous death. The infection overwhelmed her, and she succumbed after only three days. There had been no opportunity to define and diminish the opposition to burying her in Westminster Abbey; even though she was dead there were still those who refused to receive her.

A woman whose life and opinions were antagonistic to Christian practice: Thomas Huxley had objected. Charles Lewes had recalled an old antagonism between his father and Huxley. The refusal had been a blow; Mary Ann died a married woman, married in church, a consecrated union. But Johnnie had managed the right thing.

In the end he had buried her where she would have wanted to be at rest: beside George Lewes in the dissenters' section of Highgate Cemetery. And Highgate was almost as distinguished as the Abbey;

it was fitting that she rest for eternity beside Lewes. In the two years since Lewes's death, that portion of the cemetery had grown unduly crowded. Johnnie had ordered a new, high wrought-iron fence erected around the two graves, and he had had the dying ivy pulled up, to be replanted in the spring.

Everyone had attended: Spencer, of course, and Robert Browning, Lionel Tennyson, Sir Alfred's son. Even Thomas Huxley: it had been difficult to be civil. And Johnnie had recognized, standing in the back in the beastly fog, a tall, slightly bent man; his features were so like hers. Isaac Evans had come to pay his respects to his sister; Johnnie had shaken his hand.

Marian's papers — here was her old unfinished translation of Spinoza, some unfinished letters, the last a letter of condolence, and her journals. She had kept them in plain copybooks, and they lay on the rosewood table in the library.

"Spencer is planning to write his autobiography," Marian had said not a fortnight ago. He heard her voice, still, her wise and measured voice; it was her voice he had loved first.

He had buried with her the packets of her correspondence with George Lewes, as she had stipulated. But she had said nothing about her journals; she had not had time. These records of her thoughts were precious documents.

John Cross opened one of the notebooks and read, pained and appalled. This was not his wife, not the woman he adored. She would not have wanted this writing preserved and made public; he had not suspected — he could not have imagined — what she confided in these pages. She had intended to destroy these passages, these youthful, overwrought outpourings; she had been editing.

What had she written about their marriage? Where was the beautiful little volume he had given her — what had she written in that? He found it in the back of a drawer. *Mrs. John Walter Cross, Mrs. John Walter Cross:* her name — his — again and again. That was all. He bowed his head and blinked back tears.

Perhaps she had jotted something in the last notebook. When he opened it, a piece of thick paper slipped out from between the pages. Whistler's sketch — that presumptuous man. But it was a likeness, and Johnnie was tempted to keep it. Had it been only six months ago that they were in Venice? He considered the drawing: his wife bowing in wonder, worshiping a fossil snail. There was something offhand and crude in its execution, something intimate and distasteful. He crumpled it and tossed it into the grate.

He sat for an hour until he saw his duty. He determined to take up her unfinished task, to compose her life using her letters and journals, to reveal to the world her great soul. The servant came in to draw the curtains.

The paper in the notebooks was flimsy, easy to cut from its binding; it burned quickly and gave off little heat. Shorter passages could be obliterated with heavy pencil lines, and the side of Johnnie's palm grew black. He was weary; he had made a beginning. He must remember to keep up his strength; he had nothing but time.

Northampton, Massachusetts, June 1999

CAROLINE WALKED along the road that passed her mother's farmhouse. The twins came along, and the dog. The field sprouted new, brilliant green grass; the slow river at the edge of the field had subsided from its spring high. Caroline turned onto a trail, an abandoned road, that followed the little river that had once powered a sawmill. Sam and Alice ran ahead, through overgrown pastures, past a swamp that had once been a pond.

Collapsing stone walls bordered the road, and there was the mill's cellar hole, which summer after summer the twins with ropes and planks and tarpaulins had transformed into a fort. But today they had peered in at the splintered wood and frayed rope and kept running; they had turned thirteen. Alice was already as tall as Caroline; Sam lagged, but he'd be tall, too. A wooden bridge crossed the river where it pooled, then splashed over boulders. A rising breeze rippled the water. Caroline did not hold back tears. *Ruach*, wind.

Margaret had died in February, six months after Jack. They had had eight years together after they were married in the garden with the twins in attendance. Margaret had left the house to Caroline. "If you want it," she said. "Otherwise sell it."

"Mom, please don't talk like that. Don't be so practical. Please. You'll be here for a long time."

"Do you want it?"

"The children love it here."

"They're not going to be around forever," said Margaret.

"I can't imagine that; they take up so much of me."

Margaret said, "Of course, for now."

Caroline saw her husband's eyes in her son and her own mother's fragile stubbornness in her daughter; she saw her children at once old and young, generations condensed, recapitulated. One day she would model them; one day she might have time.

"You could have a studio in the barn," Margaret suggested. "Now."

"And work?"

"You do work, don't you?"

"Not enough. But who knows?" Caroline answered. "And it would be a chance to be with you."

In the forest on this bright day the contrasts were sharp, and her eyes were not as good as they used to be. They played tricks on her. She caught her breath in dismay at the carcass of a raccoon stretched across the path until it turned into a protruding stump.

The man stood off to the side, on the bank of the river beside the bridge. He was tall and slender; he leaned on a long walking stick, and a broad-brimmed hat with a round crown, like a pilgrim's hat in a Renaissance painting, concealed his face. Caroline called the twins, who did not hear. She was frightened, and she stood alone.

She recognized him then, at the edge of illusion. As she approached, his walking stick became a broken branch, his hat a sheaf of sere oak leaves left over from autumn. His body was the tilted trunk of a sapling growing too close to water. He was old wishes, rooted sadness, the clay of her imagination.

The dog pricked up her ears, and Caroline turned and saw Gilbert walking toward her. He caught her up in his arms, spun her around, and they headed on their way.

IN 1885, JOHN CROSS did publish his biography of George Eliot; he portrayed the proper and conservative Victorian lady he wished that he had married, and his view of her prevailed for decades. Gordon Haight's compilation of Eliot's letters and his *George Eliot, A Biography*, published in 1968, revised this image and set the standard for subsequent scholarship. Other twentieth-century biographers include Kathryn Hughes, Frederick R. Karl, and Rosemary Ashton, who also wrote a life of George Henry Lewes. Phyllis Rose discussed Eliot and Lewes in her study of Victorian marriage, *Parallel Lives*. Ruby V. Redinger, Rosemarie Bodenheimer, and Nancy Paxton have written important critical studies.

I have, for the most part, relied on primary sources: letters and journals, especially *The Journals of George Eliot*, edited by Margaret Harris and Judith Johnston. Like Courtney and Perry, I profited from the practical information in an old Baedeker.

The novel hinges on pivotal episodes in Marian Evans's life: her refusal to attend church with her father, her complicated relations with John Chapman and Herbert Spencer, her enduring marriage to George Lewes, her short marriage to John Cross, his breakdown on their honeymoon, and their return to England and her last weeks at Cheyne Walk.

But much about the real Marian Evans cannot be ascertained. She was wary of biographers and asked at least one old friend to burn their correspondence. Her novels draw their material from the people and places of her childhood, and her heroines share her ardor — but of course the novels cannot be read as fact.

Her letters to George Lewes are gone; other letters, including some to Herbert Spencer, were sealed for a nearly a century, and for a long time scholars were unaware of the seriousness of that relationship. In many of George Eliot's surviving letters her voice is measured, but in others she is funny and acerbic. Some — especially one to Herbert Spencer after his visit to Broadstairs and another to John Cross during their secret engagement — overflow with intensity of feeling: sorrow in the first case and joy in the second. Sections of her journals have been destroyed; what remains is often laconic. Her brief entries note places and activities, visitors, bills paid, what she was reading, a description of the landscape and the weather, quick and sometimes touching notations of her states of mind. The journal entry for 28 September 1854 reads in its entirety: "Musical party at Liszt's at 2 o'clock. Clara Schumann — a melancholy, interesting looking creature. Her husband went mad a year ago, and she has to support 8 children!"

A scene in *The World Before Her* — the musical party at Liszt's house in Weimar — grew from that brief entry; more precisely, Marian's state of mind emerged from the discrepancies between her description and the reality of Clara Schumann's situation. Schumann had been a beauty; she was a celebrated pianist, and her mad husband, Robert, was not only a brilliant composer but an important critic. Moreover, she was Marian's age. When I wrote the scene, I decided what Liszt and Schumann might have played — and what I wanted to hear them play.

The Crosses did walk through Venice on the tenth of June, 1880; they may or may not have bought jewelry. Later that week, they went to the Accademia, and they visited Mr. and Mrs. Bunney. Mr. Bunney did sell his drawings and watercolors, but perhaps not to Johnnie Cross. Herbert Spencer was one of Marian's last visitors at Cheyne Walk before she fell ill and died.

There is, however, absolutely no evidence that Marian Evans and James McNeill Whistler ever encountered each other in Venice, though they were there at the same time. Whistler's London show, in January 1881, a month after Marian's death, was a triumph; it redeemed his reputation. He did, of course, leave Maud Franklin, though he saw to it that she was supported. Eventually Maud married one of Whistler's friends. Whistler married, too.

Marriage was the happy ending. But George Eliot asked a great deal of the institution. She understood sexual and intellectual happiness; she knew, from her own experience, that it was possible to have both. Her heroines had a sexual nature — and a moral one.

Eliot published *Middlemarch* in 1871–72 but set the story a generation earlier, which gave her distance from a turbulent time. By placing Caroline's story in the near past, in 1980, I followed George Eliot's example, and for similar reasons. Since the 1960s, women's choices have evolved while their dilemmas have remained constant. I gave my twentieth-century heroine a story — and an ending — that George Eliot could not give her nineteenth-century women.

I have taken some liberties in Caroline's story as well. As far as I know, there is no little bronze David/Apollo/St. Sebastian by Giuseppe de Levis, a sculptor who worked in Verona at the beginning of the seventeenth century. Traditionally he has been considered Jewish, and his subject matter ambivalent, but the most recent edition of *Grove's Dictionary of Art* states that the name de Levis refers to Giuseppe's native town. Some scholars, however, disagree. I prefer to think that de Levis was Jewish.

Rabbi Leon Modena's moving and vivid autobiography, his *Life of Judah*, has been beautifully translated and edited by Mark R. Cohen; that translation, accompanied by critical essays, was published in 1985. Rabbi Leon himself published, and thereby preserved, the Jewish liturgical music of Salamone Rossi, the chief musician at the court of the duke of Mantua; Rossi was probably killed in a massacre of the Jews in that city. Incidentally, my father, the composer Hugo Weisgall, edited an edition of Rossi's *Songs of Solomon* that was published in the 1960s. I have imagined that somewhere across the fact-fiction border my Gilbert Pryce might have been one of Professor Cohen's scholarly collaborators.

I have been blessed with generous and wise real-life collaborators. First there is Jill Kneerim, my friend and agent. Her enthusiasm and good sense sustain me, and her wisdom informs every page.

I could not have written this book without Susan Heath; her deep knowledge, insight, and rigor set a high standard, and her friendship made the work a pleasure. With brilliant skill and great kindness, Jane Rosenman has nurtured the book, shaped it gently and firmly, and guided it to completion. When my daughter, Charlotte Wilder, was small, she went with me in a Boston Whaler to see the Dolomites rising behind Venice. Now that she has grown up, her instinct for character and story has enriched this novel.

Cara S. Krenn has been a constant and enthusiastic friend. Benjamin Steinberg has helped in every way while making sure that I watch what's important, and Susanna Brougham's eagle eye and subtle suggestions have improved this book enormously. From the beginning Heidi Pitlor has been generous with her insights — into fiction and reality. The romantic swing Liszt and Schumann give the last movement of Schubert's *Divertissement à l'hongroise* sounds very much like the way Ya-Fei Chuang and Robert Levin play that piece; Bob also discussed nineteenth-century performance practice with me. Alexandra Johnson spoke to me about the connection between George Eliot's journals and her novels; Marcia Folsom directed me to scholarly material on Eliot. Katrinka Wilder tirelessly tracked down information about fauna, flora, and the English gardens of more than a century ago in which they flourished. Not so long ago — not long ago in geological time — Ellen Hume and I learned about the earth's molten core; her friendship means the world to me. Lawrence Buell, Ted Cohen, Ivan Gaskell, Stephen Harder, Anne Hawley, Lisa Herschbach, Erica Hirshler, Christine Kondoleon, Michael Putnam, Anne St. Goar, Patricia Wengraf: these are among the generous friends who took the time to answer my many questions.

My husband, Throop Wilder, provides abundant love and keeps me laughing. Finally, the book is dedicated to my mother, Nathalie Weisgall, who, when I was small, understood that the galleries of the Uffizi in Florence, which at that time were almost always empty of visitors, were a perfect place for my brother and me to play.